CLOSER THAN SHE THINKS

"What are you trying to tell me, Jake?"

His eyes swung back to her, even more intense than they had been. "We routinely use a private investigator to vet every employee. Rueben Sanchez looked into the disappearance of the Duvalls' baby. He questioned the nurse, and later she contacted him and wanted to meet him in private to discuss the case again. Before she could see him, Gracie Harper was shot."

Alyssa huddled in her chair, offering no response. Could the nurse have had information that would have cleared her name? She'd had her hopes raised only to be dashed too many times to count since the baby vanished. Someone *must* know something, but no one had talked. Now the nurse was dead.

"Do the police have—"

"They don't have a single solid lead. We don't even know if it has anything to do with the case."

Alyssa thought a moment. "Why now? Why kill her after all this time? It's almost twelve years now. A long time. Witnesses move, forget—"

"Die." His voice became even more serious. "I want you to be extra cautious, Alyssa. We don't know what we're up against or who they might target next."

"You think my life is in danger?"

"I don't know," Jake said. "Anything's possible . . ."

BOOK YOUR PLACE ON OUR WEBSITE
AND MAKE THE
READING CONNECTION!

We've created a customized website just for our very special readers, where you can get the inside scoop on everything that's going on with Zebra, Pinnacle and Kensington books.

When you come online, you'll have the exciting opportunity to:

- View covers of upcoming books
- Read sample chapters
- Learn about our future publishing schedule (listed by publication month *and author*)
- Find out when your favorite authors will be visiting a city near you
- Search for and order backlist books from our online catalog
- Check out author bios and background information
- Send e-mail to your favorite authors
- Meet the Kensington staff online
- Join us in weekly chats with authors, readers and other guests
- Get writing guidelines
- AND MUCH MORE!

Visit our website at
http://www.zebrabooks.com

CLOSER
THAN
SHE
THINKS

MERYL
SAWYER

ZEBRA BOOKS
KENSINGTON PUBLISHING CORP.
http://www.zebrabooks.com

This book is dedicated to all my special friends in my Hoag group. With heartfelt thanks to our fearless leaders, Patricia and Gary, and our alter ego, Mike. Remember "keep coming back."

The best way to love anything is as if it might be lost.

—G. K. Chesterton

PROLOGUE

The French Quarter, New Orleans

Pale shafts of moonlight filtered through the banana trees and towering elephant ears in the courtyard concealed behind tall plank gates that went unnoticed by most people who passed along Conti Street. The low-slung branches of a crepe myrtle partially concealed a wrought iron bench beside a flowerbed profuse with primroses. The soulful wail of a trumpet drifted in from one of the jazz clubs around the corner.

A man strode across the ancient bricks, passed the splashing lion's head fountain built into the wall, and mounted the sweeping staircase to the second floor. Upstairs, he inserted his brass key into the door's old-fashioned lock. The tumbler opened with a click that echoed across the courtyard of the Creole town house.

"Hello, Clay."

The low throaty voice greeted Clay Duvall with its usual sultry allure, but the sensual impact on him was fleeting. His mind was on a woman. Not this woman, but another woman living an ocean away from the French Quarter.

"Champagne?" Maree asked even though she knew

he would want Johnnie Walker Blue Label. Expensive
Cristal champagne was her favorite, not his. Offering it
was Maree's way of chastising him for arriving after
midnight and not calling.

"Champagne? You *know* what I want."

"You want me, darling?" she asked, her voice even
huskier than normal.

The honeyed syllables revealed a youth spent in a
small bayou town within a shout of New Orleans, but it
might as well have been another planet compared to
Clay's background. Not that it mattered to him. He'd
learned to look beyond New Orleans' inbred society for
his opportunities.

Maree slowly lifted her shapely body from the velvet
chaise and moved toward him. A whisper of silk filled
the candlelit room as the sheer negligee caressed her
smooth skin. She repeated, "You want me?"

"M-m-mm," he muttered, unable to force a lie. What
he wanted, the woman who obsessed him, was well
beyond his reach.

For now.

He didn't know what to say, but he had to terminate
this relationship. Staying with Maree would hurt her
more in the long run.

"You desire me, no?"

Before he could answer, her slender arms wrapped
around his neck and her full breasts nudged his chest.
Pouty lips met his, then parted as her dainty tongue
flicked against his mouth.

"Maree," he half-whispered, half-sighed before he
could stop himself.

Maree was good, he had to admit. She was even better
now than the night he'd met her at a political reception
at the Windsor Court Hotel. Maree had stood off to
one side, clothed in a black linen dress that only suggested the luscious body beneath the dark fabric. There
had been a hint of shyness in her half-smile and gaze
partially concealed by thick alluring lashes.

Across the crowded room he'd detected an undertone of reserve in Maree's manner, a bashful reticence in her refusal to fully return his smile. Even though Maree was a brunette, not a blonde, her attitude had struck a chord, reminding him of the only woman to have captured his heart. He hadn't been able to resist walking over and introducing himself.

It wasn't until after he'd begun his affair with her that Clay realized Maree was obsessed with money and social position. She was nothing like his first love. Instead, Maree was disgustingly similar to his wife—Phoebe LeCroix Duvall.

Maree guided Clay toward the bedroom, where more candles trimmed the fireplace mantel and lined the bookshelves while flickering votives adorned the dressing table. The soft light cast an amber glow across the black satin sheets on the bed she had turned back, obviously anticipating his arrival.

Beep-beep! The chirp of Clay's cell phone reminded him that he'd come to give Maree a bracelet as a parting gift. He reached into the pocket of his sports coat and pulled out the tiny telephone. He had to tilt it toward the nearest bank of candles to read the digital display.

He shrugged out of Maree's embrace. "I have to take this. Business."

Clay walked back into the living room of the apartment he'd leased for Maree a little over a year ago. Her perfume hung in the air like a noxious vapor, then he realized the cloying scent was coming from what Maree called aromatic sandalwood candles. With a sigh of regret for the good times, he hardened his resolve to end their affair.

"Everything is in place," Burt Anders told him the moment Clay came on the line. "Just say the word."

"I want her . . . company," Clay said. "Make the offer, and remember what I told you earlier. Be sure to keep my involvement secret. I don't want Alyssa to know I'm behind this."

He snapped the cell phone shut, then tucked it back in his pocket. *Alyssa Rossi*. The name alone made him smile as he anticipated seeing her again after being apart for almost a dozen years. A lifetime.

"Darling." Maree had come up behind him and was touching his shoulder.

He slipped the small box out of his pocket. Knowing how she adored antique jewelry, he was positive this Edwardian bracelet encrusted with diamonds and sapphires would ease their parting. He regretted what he was about to do, but assured himself that it wouldn't be long before she found another wealthy man. With luck, the new guy would love and marry her the way she deserved.

"I went to see Dante this afternoon," she told him.

Her psychic had moved from the Bahamas to New Orleans to practice voodoo. He'd given it up when his so-called visions had lured him to the more lucrative realm of psychic readings. Maree's obsession with having her future predicted had made her one of Dante's best customers.

"What did he have to say?" he asked, wanting to let her down gently and hoping he could manipulate the flaky psychic's message into a way out of this entanglement.

"Something exciting is about to happen."

"Dante's right. I have a present for you."

"For me?"

"I think you'll like it."

"Just a minute." Maree accepted the small package, then dashed into the bedroom and returned with an envelope. "Dante sent this to you."

"What?" Clay took the envelope from her, noticing the back flap had been secured with a dollop of burgundy-colored sealing wax. "You know I don't believe—"

"I didn't ask Dante to predict your future. This was his idea."

Clay edged away from her, a shadow of alarm troubling him. He put it down to conscience. Dropping Maree was more difficult than he'd anticipated.

He recalled another night long ago. Another woman. The woman he still loved. Leaving a woman was never easy. Not then, not now.

"It's been fun, but—" He charged toward the door, embarrassed and rushing the speech he'd silently rehearsed. "I—I don't know what to say."

She stared at him and the unopened present slipped from her manicured fingers and hit the Oriental carpet with a dull *thunk*.

"The rent is paid through the end of the month." He twisted the brass knob and yanked the door open. "Take care of yourself. Ah . . . Good-bye."

Behind him, she gasped, but Clay shut the door, blocking the sound. He descended the stairs two at a time, crossed the courtyard, and was out on the street in a matter of seconds. He didn't stop until he reached the corner, where a trash can stood outside an espresso bar that was closed until morning.

Clay almost tossed Dante's note on top of a heap of Styrofoam cups, but a surge of curiosity stopped him. He ripped open the envelope, shattering the seal, and chips of burgundy wax plinked onto the sidewalk. Removing the single sheet of paper, he held it up to the streetlight, where palmetto bugs were chasing each other in circles, their wings clicking like tiny castanets. The script on the paper appeared too fine to have come from Dante's blunt fingers.

> *Ashes to ashes,*
> *Dust to dust,*
> *If God won't have you,*
> *the Devil must.*

CHAPTER 1

The air along the narrow cobbled streets was fragrant with the scents of spring in the city. The smell of blossoms tumbling from window boxes combined with the aroma of fresh-baked bread while a trace of mildew seeped out of the cracked stone of the ancient buildings. A cat's paw of a wind delivered a moist whiff of the dank Arno River. The setting sun darkened the mazelike streets and cast the thick plank doorways in shadows that appeared ominous to those who did not realize the forbidding entrances concealed elegant palazzos with formal courtyards.

Ghosts from centuries ago when Florence had given birth to the Renaissance now kept watch on their beloved city from behind the cloistered walls. Dante. Michelangelo. The Medicis. Their spirits had long departed, but they had marked Florence for all time, bestowing on it a priceless treasure of art and architecture.

Along with this legacy came an aura of mystery and intrigue.

This mysterious quality had captivated Alyssa Rossi

from the moment she'd first come to live with her aunt over a decade ago. Like her hometown of New Orleans, Florence was a unique place with history, charm ... dark secrets.

But today Alyssa's mind wasn't on either city. She was too preoccupied with a business proposition to even notice the colorful skiffs drifting down the Arno or the throngs of scooters zipping by her in the gathering dusk.

Harry's Bar was more crowded than usual when Alyssa angled her way inside. Being taller than average gave her an advantage, and she caught Mario's eye immediately. The bartender smiled, his insider's smile, not the vapid grin reserved for the tourists who made the bar one of their stops just as they did the Pitti Palace or the Uffuzi Museum.

The bartender winked and inclined his head toward the sidewalk terrace overlooking the river. Alyssa had called ahead to request Aunt Thee's favorite table. No matter how packed the bar and adjacent café was, Mario always reserved this special table for his old friend, Theodora Rossi Canali.

"Ciao. Come stai?" the waiter greeted Alyssa, recognizing her as a regular.

Alyssa smiled, replied she was well, and sat down, taking care not to rumple her clothes. She had to meet Burt Anders in less than two hours. She didn't want to look as frazzled as she felt when she joined the American businessman for dinner. Adjusting the vibrant rose and lime green scarf around her shoulders, she sensed someone watching her, trying to get her attention.

An Italian man, she decided without looking up. Harry's Bar was a tourists' haunt, but a number of local men stopped by for a drink after work, hoping to get lucky. To Italian men, flirting wasn't just a means of picking up women, it was a way of life. They did it with charm and a sense of humor that Alyssa usually enjoyed, but not this evening.

Mario sent over two glasses of Campari in the crystal

goblets he kept under the counter for special customers. Alyssa sipped hers, watching the entrance for her aunt. It wasn't like Aunt Thee to be late, but Alyssa had to admit her aunt was slowing down. Her seventy-fifth birthday was less than a week away. Of course, Aunt Thee didn't have the energy she did years ago when Alyssa had left New Orleans in disgrace with the only person on earth who believed her.

"Signorina," the waiter spoke to her in Italian, his voice low. "The gentleman at the bar would like to buy your drink."

"No, grazie."

Alyssa answered without looking toward the bar that had been a gathering place for American travelers since Hemingway had made it famous. She realized her shoulder-length blond hair and hazel eyes complemented her tall, slim figure. Most women would envy her, but Alyssa wasn't impressed. The world was full of women who were truly beautiful.

It was her talent that had Alyssa worried, not her looks. Was she ready to take the gamble? Was she ready for the big time?

"Sorry, I'm late."

Alyssa jumped up and gave her aunt a hug. "Is everything all right?" she asked as the older woman sank into the chair opposite her.

The glow of the setting sun burnished Aunt Thee's pewter hair, softening the steel-gray color and bringing amber light to her dark brown eyes. A skein of fine lines netted the corners of Aunt Thee's eyes, saying she'd smiled often. Deep brackets on either side of her full mouth confirmed her good nature.

Despite her congenial manner, Theodora Canali could be serious when necessary. She had a head for business, and had proven it by investing in talented designers in Milan years ago on the eve of its becoming a fashion mecca. Alyssa was counting on her aunt's business acumen to help her make this decision about her own company.

Alyssa tried not to be impatient as she waited for her aunt to drink her Campari, but the years she'd spent in Italy hadn't tempered her enough. She was still an American at heart and found it difficult to adjust her attitude. She was driven, and it was hard for her to live in the moment and enjoy life the relaxed way Italians did.

"Well," she finally asked. "Tell me what you think of TriTech's offer."

Aunt Thee set down her glass, saying, "Take it."

"Take it?" Alyssa repeated, stunned. In the years she'd been with Thee, the older woman had always played the devil's advocate, debating each decision with Alyssa, yet allowing Alyssa to reach her own conclusion.

"Yes. Accept TriTech's offer. Isn't this what you want? Are you going to allow know-nothings to knock off your designs forever?"

Alyssa shrugged, then signaled Mario for more Campari. Rossi Designs, her costume jewelry line, was the most innovative in Italy. Her special creations were being copied ruthlessly. The second she sketched a design, someone was duplicating it.

"Of course I want credit for my jewelry, but I'm concerned about becoming part of a big corporation. TriTech sounds like a software company or something techie. Will they understand the fashion world?"

"I read the documents you sent to me. This appears to be a fabulous offer. Before you accept, find out more about the owners of the company. Then, well, you know what I always say."

" 'Get it in writing.' " Alyssa smiled at her aunt, but knew enough to ask, "What's the real reason you want me to accept this deal?"

Aunt Thee drained her glass. "It's time for you to go home."

"Home? This is my home. I'm happy here."

Aunt Thee's dark brown eyes were steady. "It's time for us both to return to New Orleans."

Alyssa didn't know if she had the mental fortitude to go back to the city she left after nearly being arrested. It would mean facing her past. It would mean she would be confronted by Phoebe Duvall.

It would also mean she would have to avoid the man she once had loved—Clay Duvall.

"Why go back there?" she asked her aunt. "I'm happy here."

"Are you really happy, or are you merely existing?"

Alyssa rushed down the winding side street toward the Piazza della Repubblica, where the Savoy Hotel was located. Her aunt's question still drifted through her mind. Alyssa believed she was happy, but just the thought of Clay Duvall brought a hollow ache deep in her chest. After what he'd done, how could she still miss him?

She forced her thoughts to the acquisition offer. Was Aunt Thee correct? Did TriTech expect Alyssa to move Rossi Designs to New Orleans, where the corporation had its headquarters?

Nothing in TriTech's offer suggested this was the case, but Alyssa had too much respect for her aunt's shrewd business sense to doubt her. Aunt Thee always said: Read between the lines.

It *was* possible TriTech would want her to relocate, Alyssa conceded. Their offer was simply too good not to have a down side, and returning to the city where she'd been raised was a major downer.

She rounded the corner and hurried by the shuttered stalls of the Mercato Nouvo, where vendors sold leather goods, scarves, and souvenirs during the day. A group of Japanese tourists with garlands of cameras around their necks were clustered around the Porcellino Foun-

tain. Rubbing the bronze nose of the wild boar's statue
was supposed to bring good luck.

Alyssa was half tempted to give it a try, but long ago
Lady Luck had turned her back on Alyssa. She'd learned
to rely on herself.

The bustling cafés lining the piazza opposite the Savoy
filled the soft night air with music and the aroma of meat
being grilled Tuscan style. Pausing for just a moment
outside Gilli's, she admired the artful boxes of chocolate. The window display featured egg-shaped containers covered with sequins to look like priceless Fabergé
eggs. Inside each was a selection of handmade choco-
lates.

She admired creativity, prized it for its uniqueness in a
mass market world. But even the most innovative design
could be duplicated, Alyssa reminded herself as she
turned and walked across the narrow street to the Savoy.

"Buono sera," the doorman greeted her.

She stepped through the double-wide glass doors into
the ultramodern lobby. To her right was the Art Deco
bar opening onto the piazza. She spotted the American
businessman already seated at a small table near the
windows.

Burt Anders had noticed Alyssa coming across the
square. Although Florence's streets were filled with elegantly dressed, beautiful women, Alyssa Rossi stood out.
Not only was she taller than most, but she was strikingly
blond in a country known for its attractive brunettes.

Adding to Alyssa's appeal was an air of remoteness,
Burt decided as she walked toward him. It seemed as if
she was always preoccupied, her mind on more
important things.

He rose, realizing how Clay Duvall could be so taken
with Alyssa. But why had Duvall insisted his name be
kept secret?

Smiling at her, Burt couldn't help thinking something

about Alyssa bothered him and had from the first moment he'd met the designer. What was it? He wasn't sure, and he found that even more troubling.

They don't pay you the big bucks to ask questions, Burt reminded himself. He worked as a consultant, putting together small deals like this one for corporations whose executives were too busy with larger, more complicated acquisitions. It was easy money—most of the time—but this one had a slight hook with the secrecy angle. Don't look for trouble, he cautioned himself.

Burt greeted Alyssa as he pulled out her chair. He couldn't help smiling inwardly at the envious looks from the other men in the room. What was an old man with flyaway tufts of gray hair doing with such a beautiful woman? Trying to conclude his last deal, one that would let him retire to his place in Florida and devote himself to his only true love—golf.

"You look nice this evening," he said without going overboard and telling her she was a knockout.

Alyssa Rossi wasn't susceptible to flattery. If she had a weak point, he'd yet to discover it. She often seemed almost shy, yet at other times she was boldly assertive.

"This scarf is one of my designs," she told him, acting as if he'd been complimenting her clothing, not the woman in them. "I plan to add scarves and pashimas to my accessory collection."

"Pashimas?" He signaled the waiter to bring the bottle of Pinot Grigio he'd ordered earlier.

"A cross between a stole and a scarf," she informed him. "They're very in right now."

The waiter arrived with two wineglasses and a silver urn filled with crushed ice. With a deft twist of his hand, he uncorked the bottle, and poured a bit of the vintage *Pinot Grigio Ascoli* into Burt's glass. *"Signore."*

Burt swirled the white wine, then took a small sip. He nodded, indicating he approved. The obsequious waiter bowed before filling their glasses.

"Are we celebrating?" Alyssa asked, her tone measured, and he wondered if she was being sarcastic.

"I assumed having your aunt read the proposal was only a formality. You're the sole owner of Rossi Designs, aren't you?"

"Yes, but I always confer with my aunt. She gave me the start-up money for my firm."

"Did your aunt have any"—he didn't want to say problems—"concerns?"

"Not concerns . . . questions. I want to know more about Jackson Williams, CEO of TriTech. Since this is a private company, I assume he's the one with the power."

Burt had never met the man, but Clay Duvall had given him enough information to make it sound as if he knew Williams personally. "Jake's in his early thirties, tall, athletically built. His education was a bit unusual. He never attended college. He—"

"If I sell to TriTech, will I be allowed to continue running my own company, or is Mr. Williams one of those hands-on executives who constantly meddles?"

Burt listened, striving to appear attentive as Alyssa outlined her concerns. He managed a smile, then said, "Be assured. Jake Williams wants Rossi Designs to expand and grow. By selling it to TriTech, you'll have the infusion of capital you need, but the day-to-day running of the company will continue to be your responsibility. TriTech executives won't bother you, believe me."

"I want it in writing."

Burt sipped his wine before saying, "There may be a slight problem. Jake's hiking in Patagonia right now. That's in a remote part of Argentina. No cell phones or faxes. Jake likes to get away from it all when he can. He's trekked in the Himalayas, run the—"

"I can wait until he comes home."

For the first time, Burt sensed the deal slipping through his fingers. He knew Williams had already returned from Patagonia. Clay Duvall wanted this deal completed before his partner realized what was happening.

"That won't be necessary," Burt said, his tone reassuring. "I'm certain someone in New Orleans is authorized to sign the necessary document."

The waiter topped off their wine. Burt raised his glass, set to seal the agreement with a toast. Mentally, he pictured himself out on the fairway, the stressful world of negotiating deals behind him forever.

"There's one other thing."

Burt lowered his glass and tried for a smile. "Yes?"

"Does TriTech expect me to relocate to New Orleans?"

"Good question," he responded with as much enthusiasm as possible. Clay had warned him to avoid this topic. "All the great Italian designers have bases in the United States. Gucci, Armani, Missoni. Versace put Miami on the map. In New Orleans you'll be global, but you'll have access to the technical and marketing expertise you'll need to ward off counterfeiters."

Her cool, measured look told Burt this was the deal breaker. He had to convince her or postpone a life of golf for another year.

"The minute you post your designs on RossiDesigns .com, they knock off every piece, right? But with a base in the States and the resources of TriTech behind you, those designs will be in the stores nationwide just as they go onto your website. With the market saturated, it won't be lucrative enough for counterfeiters to copy your designs, will it?"

It took her a moment to concede, "I guess not."

Again he raised his glass. "We have a deal?"

She reluctantly clinked the rim of her glass against his. "Yes. Here's to a new start with Jackson Williams in New Orleans. *Buona Fortuna.*"

"Yes. Good luck." Here's to Clay Duvall, Burt silently toasted.

She graced him with a half-smile. Suddenly, it hit him. The picture in Clay's office of his wife, Phoebe. That's what had been knocking around in the back of his mind.

How could you miss it? he asked under his breath. *What was Clay Duvall up to?*

CHAPTER 2

Jake Williams attempted to concentrate on the reports stacked on the Louis XIV desk. There wasn't enough room on the wimpy desk to spread out, Jake decided, riffling through the papers as he searched for the report he'd seen earlier. Which one was it? He racked his brain, but nothing registered.

"Aw, hell. That's jet lag for you."

Unable to locate the troubling document, he glanced around the room, taking in the gilt furniture and drawn brocade drapes. Beams of light from the crystal chandelier played across the highly buffed parquet floors.

"It's a long way from the Redneck Riviera to the French Riviera," he said out loud.

He leaned back in the chair and closed his eyes for a moment, blocking out the company's opulent town house in Monte Carlo. It *was* a stretch from Mobile, Alabama, and the sweeping, picturesque bay Southerners fondly called the Redneck Riviera. Jake had grown up in a trailer park across the street from Mobile's commercial fishing docks.

He lived for boats and the sea the way most young boys lived for sports. Before he was eight, Jake was earning money shucking oysters in a steamy shed behind the wharf where no one would see him and report the situation to Social Services. By the time he was a teen-ager, he was skippering sport fishing boats for the rich men from the North who spent a fortune on yachts and fancy tackle just to catch "the big one."

Jake's life was totally different now, but the lure of the catch, the challenge of the sea, was in his blood.

Exhausted, Jake kept his eyes shut and let his mind drift back to the warm summer days on Mobile Bay. He could almost hear the workers on the wharf as the fishermen returned, flying special flags to announce their catch. A black fish on a small white flag hoisted from a boat brought the loudest cheers.

"Must be black grouper," Jake said to himself as the noise grew louder.

He opened his eyes and shook his head, realizing where he was and mumbling, "Jet lag."

Two days ago he'd flown back from Patagonia through Ecuador to New Orleans, where he'd stopped long enough to pick up clean clothes and collect his papers before flying on to Monte Carlo. His body must not have adjusted, and he was imagining things. It was past midnight in Monte Carlo. For damn sure, he couldn't hear shouting from Mobile's wharf. He'd left there over eight years ago and seldom looked back—except in his dreams.

Eyes gritty from lack of sleep, he reminded himself the meeting tomorrow morning was too important not to be in top form. Rising to go to bed, he stopped. He wasn't imagining the noise. It was very real and getting much louder. Not shouts, he decided, but chanting.

"What the—"

"Saturday night fever," answered a voice from across the room.

He turned and saw his assistant, Troy Chevalier, emerging from another section of the town house. Troy swung back the drapes and opened the French doors onto the balcony. Strange noise, a cross between Rap and a Gregorian chant, burst into the room. Jake walked over to the balcony, curiosity getting the better of fatigue.

The narrow street two floors below was dark, lit only by antique gas lamps that cast dim amber shadows across the uneven cobblestones. It was enough light to see a long, serpentine chain of skaters racing down the street, singing in French.

"A Conga line?" Jake asked. "Of Rollerbladers?"

"No, nothing old-fashioned like a Conga line. It's the latest craze. It started in Paris, where else?"

Jake nodded slowly, watching the seemingly endless chain of people—young and old—skate by single file, their hands on the hips of the person in front of them. Troy Chevalier was a Frenchman who had been raised in Paris and spoke several languages fluently. From his point of view, the world centered around the French capital.

Jake and Troy had stayed with Troy's wealthy parents in Paris. They'd had a blast. Parties. Another seven-course meal every time you turned around. Jake pre-ferred the outdoors for his vacations, but he had to admit the Chevaliers' lifestyle was seductive.

French women were knockouts, but as far as Jake was concerned, French men were prissy wimps who resented anything that wasn't French. Let Troy kiss up to the frogs. Jake would put his money on a good old boy any day.

Despite his fondness for the French, Troy was a stand-up guy in Jake's book. TriTech was a complex company, its deals so friggin' complicated that it took a team of attorneys and accountants to sort them out. Jake had been through the school of hard knocks while Troy had graduated from the London School of Economics. His advice had made it possible for Jake to successfully run TriTech.

"In Paris," Troy continued, his voice low, "they call this Saturday Night Fever. Some radio announcer tells everyone where to assemble at eleven o'clock each Saturday night. The meeting place changes so the police can't shut it down, but the routine is the same. Put on your rollerblades and skate your way through the city, singing at the top of your lungs. I guess the craze has spread to Monte Carlo."

"What next?" Jake turned away, the surge of adrenaline leaving his body. "I'm going to hit the sack."

From his room, Jake could see the boats in the harbor, swaying on the rising tide. He walked into the bathroom. "Rich people have yachts. Poor people have boats."

Gleaming in the moonlight, yachts, moored by the dozens, stood for megabucks. Money was only a way of keeping score in a rich man's game, he reminded himself. In the end, it didn't mean squat. Still, he enjoyed playing the game. It was a challenge—even more of a rush than catching "the big one."

Toothbrush in hand, he swiped at his teeth and gazed into the mirror. Were those puffy slits his dark brown eyes? When was the last time he'd shaved? A jaw grizzled with an emerging beard made his dark hair appear even more unruly. He looked as wild as he had been once—before his father reappeared in his life.

If he didn't get some sleep, Jake was going to be worthless when he went out to the Swiss venture capitalist's yacht to pitch his new project. Suddenly, he remembered he needed to ask Troy an important question.

Christ! Was he losing it? At thirty-three it was too early for his mind to be slipping, but who knew? His life was proof positive *anything* could happen.

He walked back into the living area of the town house, where chanting filled the room. The noise seemed to be tapering off. Troy was still out on the balcony, gazing down at the revelers.

"I need to ask you about an acquisition Clay Duvall made while I was in Patagonia."

Troy turned slowly, seemingly reluctant to take his eyes off the chain of skaters. Jake saw the end was in sight now. A few stranglers were madly lurching over the uneven pavement to grab the last person in line.

"Is there a problem? You authorized Duvall to purchase small companies that fit TriTech's criteria."

"Right." Jake didn't have to add he'd given Clay Duvall this latitude, in effect making him a minor partner, to gain control of Duvall Enterprises. Troy knew as much about TriTech as anyone, even its founder, Jake's father, Max Williams. Troy understood how uncomfortable Jake was with an outsider like Clay Duvall.

Troy continued, "Duvall didn't exceed his limit. It was a cheap acquisition compared to what TriTech usually does."

"Just what is Rossi Designs?"

Troy turned, his thin face appearing even narrower in the dusky light. His receding blond hair made his dark eyes seem larger. "Rossi Designs manufactures costume jewelry."

"Costume jewelry?" Jake echoed, dead certain jet lag was making him wacko. "Earrings and bracelets and . . . stuff?"

"Also pins and necklaces and—"

"Aw, crap! Tell me you're kidding!"

"Don't you wish."

There weren't many men who dared joke with Jake. He took life and the role that had been so unexpectedly thrust upon him with total seriousness, but he had a wry sense of humor that people often misunderstood. Troy had been set to leave the company eight years ago when Max Williams unexpectedly produced his long-lost son and gradually began to turn the company over to his heir.

Jake had tripled Troy's salary and convinced him to stay. He'd never regretted his decision. Jake was unseasoned, but he'd learned quickly and had taken the company into the new millennium in ways that Troy found challenging and exciting.

"Why? Costume jewelry doesn't fit our profile." Jake dropped into an antique chair that hadn't been made to handle his six-foot-plus frame. "What was Duvall thinking?"

"You said to give Duvall some latitude, to make him feel part of TriTech, so I didn't question his reason for buying Rossi Designs." Troy took the chair opposite his boss. "Alyssa Rossi, the founder of the company, has quite a track record for innovative jewelry."

"I don't give a sh—" Jake stopped himself. There was no sense cursing at Troy. It had been Max's idea to bring Clay Duvall into the company. It remained to be seen if this was one of his father's better plans. "A jewelry manufacturer doesn't fit our mix."

"You wanted a diversified group of companies, not just tech businesses."

"True." Jake threw his head back and stared up at the domed ceiling where a bunch of bare-assed angels were laughing down at him from behind banks of fluffy pink clouds. "I want solid companies with good management."

"Alyssa Rossi built her company from nothing."

"It's still a fashion business." He lowered his gaze and looked at his right-hand man. "You know women. They can never make up their minds what they want. One day it's one thing. The next day something else is in style. Rossi may be hot now, but for how long?"

"Long enough to make our investment profitable."

Something clicked in the back of Jake's mind, and he mentally switched gears. The report he'd been trying to find, the reason he'd gotten out of bed. "Did I see a report about the reallocation of space at corporate headquarters?"

"Probably. It was among the papers we brought from New Orleans for you to check over."

"Why is the Bridwell Group's space being downsized? What are we doing with the empty offices?"

Troy hesitated a second as if he already knew Jake

wasn't going to like the answer. "We sold off more than half of Bridwell's unprofitable ventures, remember? Rossi Designs is moving into the empty space."

"Why can't they stay in Italy where they are now?"

"It was your idea to consolidate all of TriTech's companies in one location," Troy reminded him. "It makes good business sense. Rossi is using the capital from the acquisition to expand into the American market. It's better if they're in the States."

"Was the move Duvall's idea?"

"Yes. He ran it by me and I agreed."

Jake stood up and walked over to the open doors to the balcony. The night air was cool with a slight tang of salt drifting in from the sea, and it was quiet now. Taking a deep, calming breath, he thought about Clay Duvall.

Sandy hair, a square jaw. Better looking than most male models. Women found Clay charming. To Jake it meant Duvall smiled more than necessary and had a subtly bored nonchalance as if he had somewhere more important to be. Why women flipped for Clay was a mystery to Jake. But then, a guy could go crazy trying to figure out women.

Clay Duvall looked like a million dollars because that was his yearly clothing budget. Okay, okay, maybe a mil was high, but Jake believed Duvall spent way too much time looking in the mirror. And entertaining in his mansion on Audubon Street, the ritziest part of New Orleans. The pretty boy had coasted through life on money his ancestors had earned.

Watch yourself. It's not a bright idea to underestimate a man who acts and looks like just another hunk from the pages of *Gentlemen's Quarterly*. Especially when he's after your job.

Not that Duvall had ever mentioned one thing about taking over TriTech. But sometimes Jake had a feeling the boys on the dock in Mobile would have called "hinky." Not right.

Max had convinced Jake that they needed the Duvall family's connections as well as their lucrative importing firm. Jake had listened to his father because Max had started the company in a warehouse and built it into a multimillion-dollar corporation.

Still, Jake didn't like this acquisition one damn bit.

"What do we know about the Rossi woman?" Jake asked, already angling to figure out a way of dumping her design company.

"Not much," Troy responded. "Do you want Sanchez to check her out?"

Jake had planned to call the investigator TriTech often used himself. Delegate. His father's words echoed in his mind. Delegating is the only way to run a big company like TriTech. You can't be everywhere all the time.

"Yes. I want to know everything there is to know about Alyssa Rossi. Everything."

Three days later, Jake left Monte Carlo and flew to Florence. He'd accepted the venture capitalist's invitation to spend the weekend at his villa in Tuscany. The villa wasn't far from Florence, where Rossi Designs had their headquarters. Jake stopped in Florence first to check out the operation personally.

Duvall's acquisition was barely a decimal point in TriTech's bottom line. It shouldn't bother Jake, but every time he thought about it, a fist-like knot clenched in his gut. He suspected Duvall had deliberately made the deal while Jake was out of the country so he wouldn't have to discuss it with him.

Why?

Jake didn't have an answer, so he forced himself to think more positively. He had to admit he was pleased with himself. TriTech was moving to another plane. Centered in the South, he'd continually broadened the company's base of operations. No question about it, the world was going global, and he refused to be left behind.

One of the benefits of the technological age was that TriTech's headquarters could be anywhere, not just New York or Silicon Valley. Max Williams wanted to keep TriTech in New Orleans where he "belonged."

Now there was a joke. Jake's father had been an Okie. Nothing—not even millions of dollars and a fancy home near Tulane—was going to make him a New Orleans blue blood.

Jake didn't give a rat's ass about society, but he was crazy about the business world. Making deals gave him a high like nothing else except being at sea during a hurricane. Even now, almost nine years since his father had suddenly reappeared in his life, Jake couldn't believe how his world had changed—thanks to Max. If his father wanted to keep TriTech in New Orleans, Jake wasn't going to complain.

Beep-beep! Beep-beep! The shrill horn of one of thousands of noisy motor scooters clogging Florence's streets warned him not to step off the curb. Jake's death wish days were over. He stayed on the sidewalk and checked the address he'd been given for Rossi Designs. He must have walked by it while he'd been absorbed in thought.

Via Cimatori was yet another narrow street twisting through the old part of Florence. He doubled back, looking for numbers, which were nonexistent or hard to find. Number twenty-one must be up the narrow passageway between the two ancient buildings across the street. He looked both ways, then stepped off the curb and into the path of a car barreling around the corner.

"Vaffanculo!" Screw yourself! he yelled to the taxi driver, who seemed to think he was on a Le Mans course instead of a busy street that would have been a back alley anywhere in America.

The walkway between the buildings was dark and barely wide enough for two people to pass. This couldn't be it, he assured himself. Ferragamo, Ermenegildo Zegna, Armani, and other fashion names he recognized had shops nearby. Nothing out-of-the-way or hard-to-find.

He was turning around, when the sound of excited women's voices stopped him. It was coming from the far end of the passageway. He kept walking, rounding a turn in the walkway, where he came upon a small courtyard.

"Just like the French Quarter," he mumbled to himself.

When he'd moved to New Orleans, Jake had become acquainted with the hidden courtyards concealed from the street by high walls or nearly inaccessible passageways. This fan-shaped courtyard was shaded by a gnarled olive tree whose branches strained upward, seeking sunlight from the swatch of sky between the tall buildings. On a square of grass sat a marble bench flanked by immaculately clipped topiary trees.

Three arched doorways opened onto the courtyard. Two were closed while the third was wide open and women's voices were drifting out into the courtyard. The sign above the door said: ROSSI DISEGNOS. Rossi Designs.

"How did Duvall find this freaking company?" Jake whispered to himself.

He walked inside, planning on how he could dump this loser without alienating Clay Duvall. Not that he cared, but his father was obsessed with the Duvalls and was counting on their connections to bolster his plan to run for the Senate. In preparation, Max intended to adopt New Orleans' genteel life. What a crock! But okay, that's what his old man wanted. Let Max have his fun.

Inside, the shop was much larger than it had appeared. Apparently Rossi Designs had expanded into the shops on either side. The doors facing the courtyard were permanently shut, and display cases had been constructed in front of them. At least a dozen women were pawing through jewelry in trays built into the glass cases.

A quick glance around the place assured him most of the jewelry was funky stuff, nothing like the precious gems found in Italian shops like Bulgari. The women didn't care. They were grabbing bracelets and necklaces and earrings and heaping them on the counter for the clerks to tally. That was his first clue he was in La-La Land. The next sidled up to him, all smiles.

"Isn't this just fab?" A petite brunette sporting a chunky amber necklace and matching earrings flitted her eyelashes at him.

What she was really showing him was a set of breasts too big to be original equipment. "They have your name on them," he agreed, moving away.

He was accustomed to women flirting with him now. He wasn't handsome, far from it. But the years with his father had given him confidence and the money to buy clothes to make him look like a former pro ball player instead of the boat captain he'd been in the days before Max had careened back into his life.

He surveyed the shop once more, wondering if it was even worth his time to ask to speak to Alyssa Rossi. The clerks were swamped and she probably wasn't even here.

Through the partially open door to the back room, a movement caught his attention. He twisted his way between a trio of New Yorkers who were trying on clusters of starburst beads in bubble gum pink. Women would buy anything, he decided as he peered into the back room.

A tall blonde in jeans and a pale blue shirt with cuffs rolled up to the elbow had her back to him. She was pulling files from a cabinet and packing them in a cardboard moving box. She turned, her profile coming into view.

Man, oh, man. He'd know that drop-dead gorgeous face anywhere.

Phoebe Duvall.

So that's why Clay had bought this company. For his wife. The jerk had his nerve! It pissed off Jake big-time. Let Clay buy his wife expensive toys with his own money.

The blonde turned and looked at him with an unwavering stare. There wasn't any indication she recognized him even though he'd met her numerous times when he'd been negotiating to purchase Duvall Enterprises. They'd been out to dinner, and she'd come on to him more than once.

Phoebe wasn't his type—not at all. He had an aversion to snobby women even if they were knock-outs. Give him a woman in cutoffs who would be happy to sit on the dock and eat shrimp with her fingers.

The blonde turned back to the file cabinet and continued packing. Jake angled his shoulders to the side so he could wend his way through the women trying on jewelry. Closer now, he looked again at the blonde.

Suddenly it struck him that the woman wasn't Phoebe Duvall, but she looked amazingly like her. Jake recalled what Phoebe had told him about her family. She had an older brother—no sister.

"Who's that?" Jake asked the nearest clerk, tilting his head toward the office.

"Signorina Rossi."

Alyssa Rossi. No way! The woman was a dead ringer for Clay Duvall's wife, Phoebe. Duvall must be crazy. No, Jake assured himself, his street-smarts kicking in big-time Clay Duvall was about as calculating as they came, but he wasn't pulling a fast one on Jake.

CHAPTER 3

Alyssa looked up from her packing as the manager of her shop walked in, saying, "There's a man here to see you."

"I'm really busy," she responded in Italian. "Ask if someone else can help him."

Her manager left, and Alyssa continued placing files in the box. She assumed the intense, dark-haired man she'd noticed a moment ago wanted to see her. Few men came into her shop unless they were with a woman. He probably wanted to sell her something.

She was going to have to find new suppliers, she thought with an inward smile. Not only was she moving to America, but now she could afford to purchase some of the more expensive beads made from semiprecious stones. There was so much to be excited about, yet a prickle of unease kept niggling at her. Sooner or later, she'd run into Clay Duvall again. New Orleans was too small to avoid him—and Phoebe—indefinitely.

"Alyssa, excuse me."

She turned as her manager handed her a business card. "He insists it's important."

Alyssa read the bold, almost aggressive type on the card:

TriTech
Jackson Williams
Chief Executive Officer

Her breath stalled in her throat, and she stared at the card. "Oh, my God!"

"What's wrong?"

"Nothing," she replied. "Tell him to come in."

What was he doing here so soon after the deal had been signed? Couldn't the man have waited until she moved to New Orleans before descending on her? She wondered if a promise in writing was worth a thing.

Alyssa began shoving more files into the box as she tried to decide how to handle the situation. Arriving unannounced in the middle of the move was an obvious attempt to catch her off-guard. She'd dealt with enough powerful businessmen to know many of them enjoyed intimidating women who had the nerve to believe they, too, could be successful. She didn't want to appear weak, but she'd signed the deal, and she'd received the money. She was committed to this new venture. There was nothing to be gained by alienating the CEO, but anger simmered beneath what she hoped was a calm exterior as he walked into her office.

She'd seen him at a distance, but that glimpse hadn't prepared her to absorb his full impact. She was tall, taller than most Italian men, but he towered over her. A head of unruly dark-brown hair waved across his forehead emphasizing arresting eyes that were almost black and a defiant chin with a deep cleft.

"You must be Jackson Williams."

"Must be."

His deep voice was level but there was an undercurrent in it. Alyssa thought she detected a note of hostility. How could she be in trouble already?

She mustered a smile that usually worked magic on men. "I'm just packing. I couldn't let anyone else do it because I need to make certain I find the files I need the minute I move into my new offices, Mr. Williams."

"Call me Jake," he told her, extending his hand. "Everyone does."

His handshake was firm, yet surprisingly brief, as if her palm was wet or sticky even though it wasn't. Although not handsome, Jake had a certain presence that commanded a greater measure of respect than she was prepared to give him. Long ago, she'd learned how deceiving a man's appearance could be.

After a moment of silence, he asked, "Do your friends call you Allie?"

"No," she snapped before she could stop herself. She attempted another smile, realizing they were getting off to a bad start. "My friends call me Alyssa." She waited a moment for him to respond. When he didn't, she added, "How can I help you?"

"I was curious to see what we'd bought."

Jake's words—had they been spoken by an Italian man—might have sounded like a double entendre, but he was gazing directly at her with a physician's cool detachment. Jake hadn't given her the once-over the way most men did. He was all business, she decided, and no matter what she had in writing, Jake was going to be looking over her shoulder.

"This is my flagship store," she told him in her most professional tone. "I also have shops in Milan, Rome, and Venice. "Of course, I'm represented in the States by—"

"Where do you do your designing?" he asked, cutting her off and looking around at the cramped area that served as an office.

"In a studio nearby where it's quieter." She didn't add that she lived there as well. Interior designers and architects in Italy often had design studios in their homes, but there was more than a touch of the South in his voice. No doubt, Jake had American sensibilities and a CEO's ego to boot. He probably expected an elaborate design studio.

"Where's the manufacturing done?"

Heavens! What had she gotten herself into? If she told him where her designs were produced—no telling what he might say. Without responding, she swung around, grabbed her purse off the desk, and headed for the back door. "It's warm in here. Let's go over to Benito's for coffee. We can talk there."

He was built like a professional athlete, but he moved so quietly that she had to turn around when she was outside in the alley to see if he'd followed her. She nearly collided with him. The impression of rock-solid immovability momentarily unnerved her. This was a man who would not be easy to manipulate.

In silence, they walked shoulder to shoulder, their strides surprisingly well matched. She stopped outside Benito's back door. Before she could open it, Jake reached around and held the door for her.

"Ciao," she greeted the chef. She led Jake through the narrow passageway between the kitchen and the front of the small café.

"Alyssa, mi amore." Benito, the owner greeted her, kissing her on both cheeks.

"Benito, this is Jake Williams."

"Aaah," Benito said with a knowing smile and a wink at Jake.

Alyssa stifled a groan. Benito believed any woman over twenty who didn't have a steady boyfriend needed his help. He'd been trying to fix her up with every single man he knew.

"Jake owns the company that bought Rossi Designs. We're business associates." She motioned to the front of the café where several tables were on the sidewalk under the elms. "Is there a table out there? We have business to discuss."

Alyssa waited while they shook hands and Jake complimented Benito on the quaint café in broken Italian.

The men chatted about soccer, the national pastime and Benito's obsession, as he led them to a table under a shady elm.

"Did you play soccer in college?" she asked after they were seated.

"I didn't attend college," he replied, his tone cool, challenging.

I knew that, she thought, recalling her conversation with Burt Anders. "I don't know what I was thinking. It would have been football, not soccer. I guess I've been in Italy too long." She attempted a smile, praying her growing distrust of this man wasn't reflected in her voice.

He stared directly into her eyes, his no-nonsense expression making her aware of how small the table was. They were barely more than a foot apart, and she sensed he knew how much she resented his sudden appearance.

They ordered lattes and Benito's ginger-glazed biscotti, then Jake said, "You were telling me where you manufactured your jewelry."

Like a heat-seeking missile, his mind locked on to business. The trip up the alley and the exchange with Benito hadn't distracted him. Once again she regretted selling her company. She sat back in her chair to put as much distance between them as possible.

"I don't actually manufacture anything. I purchase beads made in India or South Africa. Sometimes I get them from Japan or China."

"After you buy the beads, where do you assemble them? What kind of equipment does it take?"

"I don't have any machinery."

"You contract out the assembly process?"

There might have been a hint of disapproval in his voice, or maybe that was the way Jake sounded when he was concentrating. She couldn't be certain.

"Yes. I have a talented, low-cost workforce. They string the beads for me."

"Really? Where?"

She hedged, "Right here in Italy."

"Where?"

"I have them assembled in Rome at the *Istituto Religiose Orsoline.*" Alyssa sipped the foam on the top of her latte as he gazed at her with narrowed eyes. She let him hang there.

"Nuns?" he said finally. "Nuns assemble your jewelry?"

"Yes. The Ursuline Sisters were famous for making intricate lace by hand."

"In this century?"

"Well . . . no. Their work was famous in the eighteen hundreds, but they have the attention to detail needed for lace work and knotting the beads I use. I don't string my beads on plastic thread the way most costume jewelers do. I use silk and insist there be a knot between each bead. That way if there's a break, you don't have beads all over the place. The knots have to be minuscule or they'll show."

"I see," he replied, but it was clear that he didn't.

If she hadn't been positive they were going to butt heads, she knew it with absolute certainty now. Why had she been so determined to expand? If she'd been content to remain among the ranks of the small costume jewelers, she wouldn't have to contend with this man.

"So, you work with inexpensive beads," he commented. "Like . . . Mexican Onyx."

"Mexican Onyx is really alabaster. Often less valuable stones are renamed to sound more valuable than they are. I prefer to use antique beads when I can get them."

"Are you trying to say you buy *old* jewelry as well as new beads?"

"Estate jewelry," she corrected. "Henry Dunay recently discovered antique emerald beads that had belonged to a maharaja. They're worth half a million—easily."

If the man was impressed by the name of one of

America's foremost jewelry designers, he didn't show it. Instead, he asked, "How long have you been making jewelry?"

"Since I came to Florence twelve years ago."

"Before that what did you do?"

The question set her teeth on edge. Before that she'd been living in New Orleans—her life set on a much different course. She wondered if he knew anything about her past. He wore a gambler's neutral expression. He could have been holding a winning or a losing hand, and no one would have been able to tell which.

"Before I came here, I was in school in the States."

He dipped his biscotti in the latte he hadn't touched and gazed at her with assessing eyes that missed little. She stared right back, barely suppressing a fresh current of irritation. The silence seemed to echo between them as if he *expected* her to say something more. The underlying tension that had been there since he'd appeared kicked up a notch.

Jake waited for her to continue, thinking he should have ordered an espresso. He needed a major hit of caffeine to handle this woman. Actually, two fingers of sour mash would be even better.

How in hell had he mistaken Alyssa for Phoebe? Alyssa was taller with wickedly long legs and hazel, not blue, eyes. She had a shuttered, distant attitude. Phoebe was the opposite. She would openly and unabashedly flirt with any man even when her husband was nearby.

Of the two, most men would have said Phoebe was prettier, and she probably was if you judged by looks alone. There seemed to be so much *more* to Alyssa. She had an edge to her or maybe she was just driven to succeed.

He had the unmistakable impression she'd despised him on sight. There must be something about him that brought out the worst in women. They either crawled all over him like minks in heat or took one look and told him to take a hike.

He should get up and make tracks for the limo waiting to transport him to the villa in Tuscany, where he was sure to find a woman who went for him big-time, but TriTech had purchased Rossi Designs. He was going to have to learn to deal with this woman.

"Where were you born, Alyssa?"

She gazed at him as if he were nuts for asking. He couldn't deny having a few loose screws. But he'd asked for a specific reason. He wanted to know her connection to the Duvalls, and he wanted her to tell him.

"Slidell, Louisiana," was all she said.

"Across Lake Ponchatrain from New Orleans."

"You sure know your lakes."

He gazed at her for a moment and spotted the glimmer in her eyes. He got it. She was teasing him. He chuckled a couple of seconds too late.

"Do you have relatives in New Orleans?"

"Just cousins."

Christ! This sucked. She had to be related to Phoebe. Why hide it? "Really?"

She smiled with feline inscrutability and dipped the stub of her biscotti into her cup. "You know how New Orleans is."

Indeed he did. Everyone in the city seemed to be related some way or another to everyone else. That explained her resemblance to Phoebe. For all he knew, Clay Duvall's wife had a hundred cousins who could be mistaken for his wife's twin. But he doubted it.

Almost twins. Jewelry-stringing nuns. A business that appeared to be little more than a storefront. What else could go wrong?

Don't ask.

He would have to thoroughly investigate Rossi Designs. He suspected this might be some sort of a scam to bilk TriTech out of money. Was Clay Duvall in on it?

* * *

It was two in the morning before Jake could gracefully leave his host and return to the guest suite he'd been given when he'd been chauffeured to the villa from Florence. He hadn't gotten a damn thing more out of Alyssa Rossi and had given up trying. He knew he should go to sleep, but he couldn't resist calling Troy Chevalier in New Orleans to see if their investigator had a report on Alyssa. Troy answered Jake's private line on the first ring.

"Anything going on?" Jake reminded himself that he had a huge company to run. Rossi Designs wasn't his biggest problem.

"Nothing important. The guys are bouncing off the walls about the deal you negotiated in Monte Carlo."

Jake had been excited, too—until he'd met Alyssa. Now he was royally pissed. Something was wrong, and he wasn't going to rest until he knew the whole truth.

"Did Sanchez file a report?"

"Yes, it's here. Want me to read it to you?"

He knew Troy must have looked at the private investigator's report, but as always, he played his hand close to his chest. "Just give me the highlights."

"Maybe I'd better tell you the whole story."

Uuh-ooh. "I'm listening."

"Alyssa Rossi is Phoebe Duvall's first cousin."

"Bingo! I'd have bet the farm on it."

"What are you talking about?" Troy asked, and Jake told him about his visit to Rossi Designs. Jake knew the women had to be related.

"Weird," was all Troy said. A team player to the end, Troy wouldn't make any negative remarks about Clay Duvall. Instead, he continued telling Jake what was in the report. "Alyssa's parents were killed in a small plane crash. She went to live with Phoebe's family."

"You're saying they were raised together?"

"Not together exactly. Phoebe went to an exclusive

private school while Wyatt, her brother, attended a military academy. Alyssa went to public schools and seems to have been raised by the housekeeper. From what Sanchez found out, the family treated her like a poor relative, barely tolerating her presence.''

Jake's impression of Alyssa softened a bit as he imagined her growing up in Phoebe's shadow. A Cinderella story—only Phoebe got the Prince—if your idea of a prince was Clay Duvall. Okay, okay. Duvall probably was an American prince.

Jake realized Troy was waiting for him to respond and asked, "Where does Clay Duvall fit in?"

"That's the interesting part."

"Define interesting."

Troy laughed, then continued, "Alyssa and Clay were college sweethearts."

"What? You're kidding." Duvall had bought his old girlfriend's company. Maybe they still had a relationship.

"I'm not joking. I'm reading this from the report, and it gets better."

Yeah, right.

"Alyssa and Clay were hot and heavy when Phoebe became pregnant with Clay's baby. They had to get married."

Something in his chest cinched tight as he imagined Phoebe stealing Alyssa's boyfriend. Phoebe was rich and beautiful. She had it all, but she wasn't satisfied. She coveted Alyssa's boyfriend, too.

"The shotgun wedding didn't bother the two families since they were old friends. Phoebe's mother, Hattie LeCroix, had wanted her to marry Clay since they were children."

But he fell for the poor cousin. Interesting. Jake wondered what Alyssa had been like back then. He tried to picture her as a young girl, but kept seeing the attractive woman who had sat across the small table from him, seeming to answer his questions, yet evading any real discussion.

"Their parents threw Clay and Phoebe a big New Orleans-style wedding with everything but the parade."

Jake couldn't help chuckling. Troy hadn't been in New Orleans long, but he was a quick study. Just about anything was an excuse for a parade.

"Five months later, Phoebe delivered a little boy."

"What happened to him? The Duvalls don't have any children now."

"*This* is the weird part. The baby was in the nursery at St. Jude's and Alyssa came to visit. Minutes later, when the night nurse checked the cribs, little Patrick was gone."

"Are you saying—"

"It's a strange case. Everyone thought Alyssa took the baby since she was the last one seen near the infant."

"What happened to it?"

"The police turned the town inside out, but couldn't find a trace of the baby."

"Helpless newborns don't vanish into thin air."

"Phoebe insisted Alyssa was jealous and had taken the baby and tossed it in the bayou, where it would be eaten by alligators."

"Son of a bitch!" Jake had been put off by Alyssa. There was something too reserved, too remote about her, but he couldn't imagine Alyssa killing a child. "What did Clay think?"

"I don't know. The report doesn't say."

Why in hell would Clay buy Rossi Designs? It didn't make any sense at all. The minute he returned, Jake was going to demand an explanation from Duvall.

"Alyssa was arrested, but they had to let her go for lack of evidence," Troy added. "Everyone in town turned their back on her. Theodora Rossi Canali, her aunt, flew in from Florence and took Alyssa away."

"And now she's walking back into the lion's den. Why?"

CHAPTER 4

New Orleans

"You wanted to see me?" Clay Duvall asked without turning to face his wife.

"It's important," Phoebe replied in a voice that was slightly breathless as usual. He knew it was a calculated ploy to enhance her sex appeal, a trick that worked on most men. It had fooled him once, but now it merely annoyed him.

Clay stood at the office window and stared down at the wide, yellowish brown expanse of the Mississippi River many stories below the office tower. The clanging of the streetcars disoriented him for a moment. He had to remind himself that he was in his new office near the waterfront in the Central Business District.

"Why didn't you catch me before I left home?" he asked, knowing full well Phoebe never lifted her beautiful blond head off the satin pillow in her suite until after eleven. He was on the jogging track at Tulane each morning at six.

"I was curious to see your new office."

Phoebe stopped beside him, but he didn't glance at

her. A flash of warm apricot color told him she was dressed in a vibrant peach outfit with a designer label.

"This isn't anything like the genteel suite of offices overlooking Lafayette Square, is it?"

"No, TriTech is too big for that stodgy old building."

The Duvall family had conducted business on Lafayette Square since 1805 when Adam Rollins had flatboated down the river, among the first Americans to arrive after the Louisiana Purchase. Back then, the French Quarter *had been* New Orleans. The clannish Creoles who lived in "the quarter" had created Faubourg Sainte-Marie for the upstart Americans. Rollins had been enterprising enough to open an exporting company and marry his only daughter to Claude Duvall, a wealthy man in the highest echelons of Creole society.

"You sold the family business to a hick," Phoebe said out loud, echoing what his parents kept saying.

Of course, Marie-Claire and Nelson Duvall hadn't been too proud to accept their share of the money. Undoubtedly, Phoebe was spending his portion as fast as she could. She'd just come back from a trip to Paris. He could hardly wait to get his American Express bill.

"Selling to TriTech was a brilliant move," he replied, the words low, yet emphatic. "This is a new century, a new economy. We can't rest on past glory."

"I know you did what you *thought* best . . . ," she said as he faced her for the first time.

He refused to let her widening blue eyes move him. He knew all her tricks. This time he was the one with an ace up his sleeve. "You didn't come here to see my new office. What do you really want?"

He strolled around the Picasso-inspired furniture he'd just ordered. Its stark lines were echoed in charcoal Berber and black suede with sloping touches of stainless steel, the opposite of the antiques he'd inherited from the succession of Duvalls who'd inhabited his old office on Lafayette Square.

"It's about Maxmilian," she told him, her voice off a note.

He glanced across his glass-topped desk at her. As usual, Phoebe was strikingly lovely in a peach-colored suit and the string of priceless pearls her daddy had given her when she'd been chosen to be the Orion krewe's Mardi Gras queen. She was classy, yet sexy, an alluring mix, but she didn't appeal to Clay the way she did to most men.

His heart belonged to another woman who looked remarkably like Phoebe except Alyssa's eyes appeared gray in some lights and green in others.

"What about Max?" Clay refused to add to Max Williams's larger-than-life persona by calling him Maxmilian, as if he had been born to some Roman emperor instead of Okies with prairie dirt under their nails. Williams was plain old Max to Clay, a warehouse owner with a knack for making millions.

"I understand Max's name is going to be put into the hopper at the Orion krewe meeting tonight."

U-u-um," he muttered, his mind on Alyssa Rossi, not on the activities at his Mardi Gras parade club known locally as a krewe. Alyssa was finally home where she belonged. She'd arrived yesterday and was sharing an elegant town house in the French Quarter with her aunt.

"I told you that if you sponsored that lowlife into the Mayfair Club, Max would angle his way to the top of its krewe."

"The captain has the most power in the krewe, and you know it."

The krewe's captain assigned jobs, decided who rode on their float, and in general, greatly influenced every decision the krewe made. Perhaps the captain's most important job was announcing the krewe's king. The vote was taken well in advance, but the king's name wasn't formally announced until the day before Mardi Gras.

"What do you care if Max is lobbying to become

king?" Clay turned away from the face he dreamed about at night. That Alyssa looked so much like Phoebe disgusted him. How could anyone confuse the two women? "Max has been in Mayfair Club for less than five years. It takes years of social service to build up a base of support."

The Mayfair Club along with its rivals the Pickwick and Boston Clubs sponsored krewes or chapters of their clubs whose responsibility it was to finance and design their Mardi Gras floats for the annual parade. The Mayfair Club owned a historical building with a private restaurant where members gathered for lunch and backrooms devoted to their krewe's Mardi Gras activities.

"Max didn't think twice about spending fifty thousand dollars to be on the royal court last year, did he?" Phoebe adjusted the pearl necklace at her throat, angling it to one side so the diamond and ruby clasp, which was almost as valuable as the entire set of pearls, could be seen and admired.

"True," Clay reluctantly admitted.

Designing and building a float and costuming the krewe members cost more and more each year. To offset the expense krewes encouraged their members to donate money. Often those donors were named to the royal court. Last year, Max Williams had given so much money that the krewe had no choice but to make him a duke.

"For as much money as he donated last year, Max should have been chosen king."

"Is there a point to this?" Clay asked, cutting his gaze in the other direction so he wouldn't have to meet her eyes and be reminded of Alyssa. "If it had been anyone else but Max, everyone in the Mayfair Club would have been thrilled to appoint him duke."

"Max has doubled his donation this year because he wants to be king."

"You're joking." Clay didn't bother to ask Phoebe

how she knew this. Like her mother, Hattie LeCroix, his wife thrived on Mardi Gras intrigue. At eighteen, Phoebe had been selected queen of the Orion krewe. She had been a freshman at Old Miss, one of the youngest queens ever chosen, bucking the tradition of crowning debutantes in their junior year of college. No doubt, Hattie LeCroix's scheming had led to Phoebe's crown. Since that time, Phoebe lived on her past glory, scheming and manipulating Mayfield Club members and its Orion krewe like Lucretia Borgia.

She'd played him for a fool once. He'd learned his lesson.

"With enough white marbles in the hopper, Max will be elected king, right?"

"The result of the vote is kept secret for months. We won't know until then."

She sidled closer, a provocative two-step movement intended to be sexy. It merely reminded him of Alyssa's precise, almost athletic way of moving. "Slip in a black marble."

"Blackball Max Williams? Why?"

"Who would ever know?"

True, he silently conceded. The krewe had been created over one hundred years ago in the social upheaval after the Civil War. Under a facade of philanthropy and social consciousness, Orion was elitist to the core—and political. No one got anywhere in city politics without the backing of the Mayfair Club and its Orion krewe.

At the krewe's meeting tonight when the members voted, Clay would be given a packet of black and white marbles. As each name was presented, members dropped a marble in the voting box that had been handhewn by a slave in the final days of the Civil War. No one could see how anyone voted, but with the appearance of a single black marble—you were blackballed. One, anonymous vote could keep a man from being king.

"Why would I?" Clay asked. "I sold the family business to Max. I don't want to embarrass myself."

Phoebe dropped her eyes, but not before Clay caught a glimpse of something he couldn't quite name. "Max has political ambitions."

"He doesn't bother to hide it." Anyone who'd suffered through dinner with Max knew this much. The man was currently serving on several local committees—just for political exposure—gearing up for the race for senator. The less time Max spent at TriTech, the better Clay liked it.

Clay had plans for himself at TriTech. It was a conglomeration of entrepreneurial businesses like Hydra, the multiheaded snake. The deadly viper would bite you, if you didn't outsmart it. Max was a natural. Even without education or connections he managed to have a feel for winners.

Jackson "Jake" Williams was a different story.

Max had dredged his son out of some fishing boat along the Redneck Riviera. For reasons no one understood, Max took in Jake even though they hadn't seen each other in years. Over the next—what was it now?—eight or so years, Max had taught Jake the business.

Or so the old man thought.

TriTech was too complex with so much happening at once that even a top-notch hired gun like Troy Chevalier couldn't properly guide Jake. Clay was counting on the loose management style at TriTech to get what he wanted. Having Max involved in local politics and working hard to be named king suited Clay's plans.

"Level with me, Phoebe. Everyone knows Max has political aspirations. So what? He's nearly sixty. He may become senator, but that's as far as he'll get. Why are you upset?"

"Let him run for president for all I care. I just think . . . well, he isn't our kind."

Clay couldn't really believe that's what was really bothering his manipulative wife. She'd been acting strange since her return from Paris. She probably had a new lover who wanted a place on the royal court and saw Max as an obstacle.

"If you don't like Max, stay away from him."

"It's not that easy!" Phoebe spun toward him, her long blond hair whirling around her cheeks and something akin to fear wavering in her blue eyes. "He's *after* me all the time."

Clay bit back a laugh. Phoebe Duvall was *after* any man who would have her. The minute she ensnared a man, she grew bored and stalked fresh prey.

Max Duvall was *after* Phoebe? And he, Clay, the loving husband, was supposed to care? Who did she think she was kidding?

"I want Max out of my life. It's important to me."

Clay didn't bother to ask why. Phoebe was obsessed by the rituals, the rivalry, and the backstage scheming that was the dark side of Mardi Gras. He didn't know— or care—what Phoebe had against Max Williams.

Beep, beep. Clay glanced down at the telephone console. His private line rang discreetly, its red light blinking. It might be his investigator with news about Alyssa.

"Blackball him, promise?" she asked, in a voice that expected to be obeyed. "You *have* to do this for me."

"I'll see what I can do," he replied to get rid of her.

As she left, Clay made a mental note to call several close friends. The last thing he wanted was Max to have time on his hands and start poking around TriTech. With enough money and Clay's behind-the-scenes support, Max might defy the odds and become king without devoting years of service to the Mayfair Club and the community.

Jake slammed down the receiver. No one was answering Clay's private line. Where was the guy? His secretary had said he was in, but he hadn't answered.

Jake rushed out the back door and took the stairs two at a time until he reached the floor below, where Clay had insisted on a corner office overlooking the Mississippi. Jake couldn't imagine why. The river was nothing more that a swath of brackish water—never blue, always brown.

He barged past the blond secretary, whose only skill seemed to be answering the telephone. "Is Duvall in there?"

"Y-yes. Let me announce—"

Jake swung open the door to the office that was so ultramodern it reminded him of a maximum security institution. Duvall's decorator probably told him it was high-tech. Wonder what happened to all the antiques in his old office?

"Were you trying to phone me?" Clay asked from across a lake of a desk. The glass was at least two inches thick and supported by a reed-thin tube of stainless steel that became a shining puddle on the floor. A lily pad or something.

"I got tired of waiting." He walked around to the side of the desk and hitched his leg up on the glass. Half sitting, half standing, he didn't waste any time on corporate bonding—chitchat. "Why in hell did you buy Rossi Designs?"

Clay didn't appear fazed by the question. "It's a small acquisition. A drop in the bucket."

"Why didn't you wait until I came back?"

Clay smiled, the easy, confident smile that won over so many people. "Others were sniffing around. I didn't want them to cut TriTech out of the deal."

Jake didn't have any indication anyone was interested in Rossi Designs unless they were after Alyssa herself, but he bit back the comment. He wanted to hear what Clay had to say about the knockout blonde.

"Rossi Designs is showing a profit?" Jake asked even though he knew the answer.

"Yes, and their sales have more than doubled every year. With this infusion of cash, it'll go off the charts."

"Solid management?"

"Rossi is top flight. Like Armani or Gucci, it'll be a winner."

Was Clay a piece of work, or what? He'd omitted Alyssa's name, making Rossi Designs sound like a male enterprise. "Rossi's a designer then, a creative type, not a businessman."

Something registered in Clay's too blue eyes. Jake knew the man wanted to strangle him, then decided it wouldn't be his best career move. Instead Clay fell back on his trademark smile, saying, "Alyssa Rossi founded the business. She's both creative and business oriented."

You betcha'. Jewelry stringing nuns. Off-beat shops. Used beads.

"Alyssa's a unique person," Clay added when Jake didn't respond.

Jake drew his line in tighter, waiting to hear how Clay was going to explain his relationship with Alyssa. "You know her?"

"I had her checked out thoroughly," Clay hedged. "I was too busy here with Christmas to go to Florence. And then we were in the midst of Mardi Gras. You know how it is."

"Yeah, I know. That's why I went to Patagonia and let Max have all the fun he could have at the carnival."

"Now, it's over and the krewe's planning next year's float." Clay responded just a little too quickly. "You ought to think about joining the Mayfair Club. The money we raise goes to local charities."

Get real. Much of what they raised lined the pockets of local politicians or went into political coffers. Only a small portion went to fund the Mardi Gras floats. "I leave the club stuff to Max."

Clay nodded as if he understood but didn't quite agree. "Anytime you change your mind . . ."

Jake wasn't letting him off the hook. "So, you've never met Alyssa Rossi."

As Jake had bet, Clay wasn't going to out-and-out lie

about something that would eventually come to light. "We met years ago."

What a guy! Clay made it sound as if they'd been introduced at some damn cotillion ball that led up to Mardi Gras. The parties were part of the ritual to decide which of those white-gowned debutantes would reign as Queen of Mardi Gras. Just another deb waltzing through his charmed life. Tough to remember them all.

Jake vaulted to his feet. "Cut the bullshit! Met her doesn't quite cover it, right?"

The color beneath Clay's golf course tan faded slightly, but he kept his gaze level. "What do you mean?"

"I talked with Alyssa when I was in Florence last week."

Clay shifted in his chair, a slight, almost imperceptible movement. Like a bomb set to explode, silence hung between them. Clay finally asked, "Did you tell Alyssa about me?"

What in hell was going on here? Was he saying Alyssa Rossi didn't *know* Clay was part of TriTech?

"I acquired the company on its merits, I swear. My previous relationship with Alyssa didn't have anything to do with it. I kept my name out of the transaction."

"Why?"

"I didn't want anyone to overbid us."

"For Rossi Designs? No one's ever heard of the company."

"It happens every day in the fashion business."

"Don't give me that crap! TriTech has lots of diverse companies, but we're not in the fashion sector."

"We should be." For the first time, Clay raised his voice. "As long as there are women on this planet, designers will rake in money."

"Okay, we agree on something." The beeper at Jake's hip vibrated, and he glanced down. Priority 17. Troy wanted to speak to him ASAP. "I need to use your phone," he told Clay.

Troy came on the line immediately. "Sanchez is up here. He wants to see you immediately. It's about Alyssa Rossi."

"I'll be right there." His eyes shifted to Clay, who was rearranging papers on the enormous desk.

Jake hung up, conscious of Clay watching him.

"Problems?" Clay asked.

"Not really. Heading TriTech means putting out fires half the time." Jake resisted the urged to tell Clay about the deal he'd concluded with the Swiss. His gut instinct told him to keep Clay at a distance. He asked, "Of all the fashion enterprises you could have acquired, why did you wait until I was out of the country to purchase a business from the woman accused of abducting your son?"

Clay stood up, coming to his feet with an effortless grace that emphasized his well-toned body and designer clothes. It was an unconscious movement, but one that never failed to remind Jake that Clay possessed what Max would have called "real class." Jake's mother— God rest her soul—would have called it breeding.

Jake called it money. Clayton Duvall had been born with the proverbial silver spoon. He'd always gotten what he wanted—before—he even knew *what* he wanted. Add to that good looks and intelligence, and Clay went through life getting anything his heart desired.

Expecting it.

"I never for one moment believed Alyssa was capable of stealing little Patrick," Clay told Jake. "She was framed, then driven out of town. Alyssa deserves another chance."

Clay had to be a few bricks shy of a full load. There was much more emotion in his voice when he said Alyssa's name than when he said his son's.

"Don't you care what happened to your baby?"

"Of course, I care," Clay shot back, his voice unexpectedly loud. "We spent a fortune on private detectives."

"What did they find out?" As if he didn't know.

"Not much more than the police. Their theory was that someone on the inside helped abduct Patrick."

"Alyssa Rossi wasn't involved?"

"They couldn't prove or disprove her involvement. Little Patrick simply"—Clay shrugged his shoulders—"vanished. The private detectives believed a ring of black marketers paid a fortune for a white baby with good genes."

Good genes? Who thought of his son in those terms?

CHAPTER 5

Jake left Clay's office and took the stairs to the top floor, where he had his office. His aversion to elevators kept him fit, he told himself, replaying the conversation with Clay Duvall in his mind.

"Does he take me for a dumb shit?" Jake muttered to himself. No friggin' way did Clay buy Rossi Designs because it was a good investment.

Jake entered his suite of offices and walked by Spencer, the male secretary Troy had hired on Jake's instructions. Why have a pretty woman around to distract everyone?

"Is Mr. Sanchez in my office?" Jake asked Spencer.

"Yes, sir. Mr. Chevalier's in there with him."

The door to his private office was closed, a sure sign Troy thought this was important enough not to have anyone overhear them. Jake opened the door and greeted Rueben Sanchez. The former FBI agent stood up to shake hands, his grip as firm as the rest of his body despite being over fifty.

"What's going on?" Jake pulled up a wing chair beside Sanchez and Troy. The massive oak desk that had been his father's put too much distance between himself and visitors.

"Gracie Harper was murdered last night," Sanchez told him.

It took a moment for the name to register. "The nurse who was on duty the night the Duvall baby was abducted?"

Sanchez's dark eyes narrowed. "Yes. I believe my asking so many questions about the case made somebody nervous."

"Come on. Nervous enough to kill?"

Jake had met Rueben Sanchez the last year he'd been living in Mobile. He'd recently retired from the FBI and had opened a private investigation firm in New Orleans. He'd been working for one of the rich guys who had the bucks to purchase a million-dollar sports fishing boat but knew nothing about fishing or sailing it. Sanchez and Jake had hit it off immediately.

When Max had appeared out of nowhere over eight years ago and persuaded Jake to join TriTech, Jake had moved to New Orleans. He'd seen a lot more of Rueben Sanchez, who preferred to be called by his last name, and began to use his firm. Sanchez vetted prospective employees as well as businesses TriTech considered purchasing.

Like Jake and Troy, the investigator had been against buying Duvall Imports without hiring a forensic accountant to inspect the books. Jake had agreed but Max had insisted on going ahead with the deal. It would solidify TriTech's connections, Max had explained, meaning it would further his political ambitions by being linked to one of the city's elite families.

Sanchez ran one hand through thick dark hair that had yet to show a trace of gray. "I think I caused her death by asking too many questions about the case."

"You didn't keep your investigation secret?" Troy asked.

"No. I didn't broadcast what I was doing, but I did call on an old buddy in the police department to check their files. Then I interviewed hospital employees who were on duty the night the baby disappeared. Gracie seemed upset when I questioned her."

"What did she say about the night the baby vanished?" asked Jake.

"It was after midnight when she showed Alyssa Rossi into the nursery. She assumed Alyssa was Phoebe's sister since they looked so much alike. Gracie left Alyssa on the visitor's side of the glass partition and went to answer a call button from one of the patients. When she returned, Alyssa was gone."

"How much later was it before she missed the baby?"

Sanchez shrugged. "Gracie couldn't be sure. Her first statement to the police said a few minutes. She later changed it to ten minutes, saying she'd responded to a patient's call, then had gone into the lunchroom to smoke a cigarette."

"Leaving the infants alone?" asked Troy.

"They were asleep. None of them was in the incubator. She wasn't violating any rules. But she did admit to me that she might have taken longer than she'd originally told the police."

"How much time do you think the nursery was left unstaffed?"

"The police report says less than five minutes. From what Gracie confessed to me, it could have been as long as half an hour."

"Plenty of time for Alyssa to have left and someone else to have slipped in and taken the child." Jake had that hinky feeling again. "How was the nurse killed?"

"She was shot in the back of the head. It looked like a robbery, but nothing was taken."

"It could be a coincidence," Troy commented.

"That's what I'd say except she'd called my office that morning and said she wanted to see me. Gracie insisted on meeting at Starbucks near Jackson Square where no one would notice us. When she didn't show up, I drove by her house. The police were already there. A neighbor had heard a gunshot."

"Did the neighbor see anyone?"

"No, and the police don't have much to go on."

"Go home, it's late," Alyssa told her assistant. "Get some rest and we'll tackle this again tomorrow."

"Tackle?" Olivia's exhausted expression perked a bit at the unfamiliar word. The younger woman had readily agreed to transfer to Rossi Designs' new headquarters in New Orleans. Although Olivia's English was excellent, she was always interested in picking up American slang.

"Tackle. That's an American football term. It means to knock down. Take it out of the way."

Olivia nodded slowly as she pulled her purse out of the drawer in her desk. "Tackling" the boxes they'd shipped from Italy seemed endless. They'd been at it all day, but as soon as they cleared space, more boxes were brought up from TriTech's basement mailroom.

"I'll see you tomorrow." Olivia slipped out the door.

"Ciao," Alyssa responded, pulling files out of yet another box and turning her back to the door to put them in the cabinet drawer marked *Resources*.

She thumbed through musty files. Some of them dated back to the first year she'd begun designing jewelry. This was her wish list of sources she'd like to use—if she ever had the money. Now she had the money, but time was tight. She had to keep Rossi Designs from being too disrupted by the move.

Still, she couldn't help mentally designing with antique the emerald beads she'd discovered in a flea market in Tuscany last summer. They dated back to the late nineteenth century. She'd been saving them until she could afford to string them with etched platinum beads. Platinum was more expensive than gold, and much more rare.

Platinum had been the metal most jewelers used when the antique beads had been new. It was the standard of excellence up until World War II when the U.S. govern-

ment declared it a precious metal and limited its use
to military applications. By the time the ban was lifted,
many jewelers had switched to gold, but platinum
remained the metal of choice for important firms like
Tiffany and Cartier.

It was only fitting, she thought, staring at the boxes
on her desk, to use hand-etched platinum beads with
the string of antique emerald beads she'd discovered
in a bargain bin at the flea market. Now she could afford
platinum, but she needed to come up with a unique
design worthy of platinum and emeralds.

"The great thing about computer disks is how few
are needed to keep track of information."

The deep voice came from behind her, but she didn't
have to turn around to know it was Jake Williams. What
was he doing here so late? It was well past nine o'clock.
Today was her first day at TriTech's headquarters. After
their unpleasant conversation in Florence, she'd hoped
to avoid Jake.

Common sense told her to keep her mouth shut, but
she couldn't very well stand there with her back toward
him. She turned, mustering what she hoped was a pleasant look. "The accounts receivable and payable as well
as the current data are all on computer. This is just stuff
I may need one day."

He was standing in the door, one strong shoulder
braced against the jamb, his tie pulled down and the
top two buttons of his shirt undone. The jacket to his
suit was tossed over one shoulder. His pose was casual,
as if he welcomed the end of a long tiring day, but the
intense gaze in his eyes told her otherwise.

"It's late. Let's go grab a bite around the corner at
Zubie's."

Alyssa realized it wasn't a social invitation; it was a
command. Without moving, he waited, watching her
while she retrieved her bag from the heap of things on
her desk. Her first impulse was to mutter some excuse.

What good would it do? Sooner or later she was going to have to learn to deal with this man.

They were halfway down the hall to the elevator before she thought of anything to say. "Do you always work this late?"

"Late? It's still early. I'm hungry and I need to talk to you."

Instead of riding the elevator, Jake took the two short flights of stairs to the lobby, and she followed, his words seeming more ominous with each step. What did they have to talk about?

"Tony," Jake greeted the security guard as he opened the door to the lobby for her.

The man posted at the desk turned their way, smiling more broadly than necessary. Obviously, he knew Jake well. Why not? TriTech owned the entire building.

"This is Alyssa Rossi," Jake told the guard. "Sometimes she'll be working late. If she does, keep an eye on her."

"Sure thing." He opened the door for her.

She stepped into a street that glistened with humidity, causing halos around the street lights. The spring air was cool, but the moisture level was high, a harbinger of the sweltering summer days she remembered from her youth.

"This way." Jake took her arm and guided her around the corner.

ZUBIE'S HOT MUFFULETTAS DRESSED TO KILL blared a neon sign above a café wedged between two office towers. Despite the late hour, the place was crowded.

"I've been dying for a muffuletta," Alyssa confessed, her stomach rumbling at the thought of the Italian cold cuts and cheese stuffed into round Italian bread and slathered with olive salad dressing. "I guess I've been gone too long. Muffulettas weren't served warm when I left." Her eye caught the misspelled handwritten *EXPRESSO* sign taped to the window. "And you wouldn't dream of ordering an espresso with your muffuletta."

Jake might have smiled slightly as he held the saloon-style door for her. "Things change. The city with the best coffee in the country now has a Starbucks on every corner. The world changes. Heated muffulettas are the latest."

The mouth-watering aroma of homemade bread and spices whirled through the café, driven by a bamboo ceiling fan hanging above the bar. A vintage stereo system was blasting Cajun music. Alyssa remembered it sounding more like a hybrid of blue grass and country music played on accordions and raspy fiddles, but this had a faster beat, featuring a strong drummer. She recognized the hipper Zydeco version of Cajun music.

Jake nudged her toward a table in the corner where a couple was rising. Several other people were converging on the same table, but one look at the determined set of Jake's jaw kept them at bay. Jake pulled out a chair for her as the table was being cleared.

"Abita's on draught," he informed her, dropping into the chair opposite her.

"Perfect," she said. "Things haven't changed too much if they're still serving beer with muffulettas."

A waitress in leather shorts and a midriff-baring bustier handed them menus while Jake ordered the beer. Zubie's had other things on the menu, but it was clear that hot muffulettas were their specialty. Over the top of the tattered menu, Alyssa watched Jake, wondering what he wanted this time. Once again, they were face-to-face across a table no bigger than her pocketbook.

"Two muffulettas dressed to kill, right?"

Alyssa nodded to the waitress, knowing "dressed to kill" meant they'd put everything on the muffuletta. "Yes. Everything on mine."

"Me, too. The works."

The waitress snatched up their menus and left. Alyssa gazed into Jake's dark eyes, once again feeling the way she had in Florence. He seemed to expect her to say something. What? She was so exhausted from the move that she couldn't guess.

His dark eyes assessed her face, never wavering, never inspecting the buttons on her blouse that she'd unfastened while sifting through dozens of boxes and becoming hot. There was a subtly dangerous glint to his eyes, a slightly feral cast—or maybe it was just her imagination. Since their first meeting, she'd been dreading seeing him again.

"You wanted to talk to me," she said finally in an upbeat tone to disguise how much he unnerved her.

Before he could answer, the waitress appeared with two mugs of dark amber beer. He took a swig, then nodded his approval with a slow smile she found disarming.

"There's nothing like draught beer."

"True." She sipped her Abita, chatting companionably. "Italians are masters of a lot of things, but making beer isn't one of them."

Jake yanked off the tie that was hanging noose-like around his neck and stuffed it in his pocket. His cuffs were already rolled back to the elbow, exposing forearms dusted with dark hair. He made a show of taking a long look at the titanium watch on his strong wrist.

"Eleven minutes and twenty-two seconds," he said with a husky chuckle some women might have found sexy.

"It hasn't been that long since we ordered, has it?"

Another low chuckle revealed a set of even, white teeth. "No. We've been together that long, and you haven't gotten huffy yet."

"Huffy? What do you mean?"

"Okay, bitchy." This time his chuckle became a deep-throated laugh. "I just said huffy to be polite. Last time we were together, you got real huffy before I had a chance to introduce myself."

"I did?" she mumbled, knowing she had, but reluctant to admit it. She thought she'd kept her inner feelings concealed, but Jake was far too perceptive.

"Damn right, you did." He flashed her another wicked grin. "We're on the same team, you know."

She wasn't sure how to take what he was saying. He seemed to be joking but there was a definite undercurrent to his words. "Meaning we work for the same company?"

"Right. Do you have a problem with that?"

"Well, no. It's just that I was expecting . . ."

He leaned toward her. "What were you expecting?"

"Burt told me I would be independent. Next thing I know, you're breathing down my neck."

"Who in hell is Burt?"

The waitress chose that moment to plop two enormous platters with muffuletta sandwiches in front of them.

"Burton Anders. He negotiated the sale of my company to TriTech."

"Yeah, right, right. I was out of the country—"

"You were hiking in Patagonia and couldn't be reached."

That got him. Jake laughed; this time he seemed to be laughing at himself. "Just what did Burt promise you?"

"He said I would continue to run the company the way I had without corporate interference."

"You thought we'd hand you a bunch of cash and walk away?"

"Of course not, but I expected to be given some time before . . . before I had to account for everything I do."

He held up his hand. "You're getting huffy again."

Did she really sound bitchy? She was merely sticking up for herself, she thought, taking a bite. The olive salad dressing was oozing out of her muffuletta, and she put it down long enough to wipe her fingers with the red checkered napkin. Eating a muffuletta after all these years was a religious experience but a messy one. She had to resist the impulse to lick the sticky dressing off her fingers. When she looked up, Jake was staring at her.

"Burt gave me an addendum to the sales agreement. I'm to operate independently and file quarterly earnings reports."

"Did you happen to notice who signed the addendum?" he asked.

She kept chewing, thinking about the signature scrawled across the document. It was a scribbled name resembling something a physician jots across a prescription. She washed down the sandwich with a sip of beer. "I couldn't read it. The typewritten name beneath started with a C, I think."

"Could the signature have been Clay Duvall's?"

The name detonated on impact, tearing at something deep inside her, a wound that still ached even after all this time. Clay Duvall. What did he have to do with this? She tried to swallow, her throat working up and down.

"Wh-what?" Her stomach rose, then fell with a sickening lurch. Her voice was so tight it was all she could do to croak out the question. "Why would Clay Duvall's name be on a TriTech contract?"

Something flashed in his dark eyes, and she drew a deep hitching breath, her mind suddenly clearing. "No. I remember now. The name was Chevalier. Troy Chevalier."

He didn't respond immediately, and the name was drummed out by the Afro-Caribbean beat of the Zydeco music blaring from the stereo.

"Ah, Troy. That explains it," Jake replied, apparently not noticing her panicked response. "My executive assistant."

Alyssa dropped the sandwich, her eyes locked on Jake's. Something was going on; she could sense it in that mysterious way a wild animal senses danger. She forced herself to ask, "Do you know Clay Duvall?"

"Of course, he's a minor partner in TriTech. He negotiated the deal to purchase your company."

She heard his answer, but for a moment the words didn't quite register, the pulsing beat of the Zydeco drums becoming one with the hammering at her temples. Her usual black belt in verbal self-defense vanished, replaced by a juggernaut of panic that curdled her blood. She shoved back her chair, vaulted to her feet, and bolted out of the café, elbowing people aside.

Jake called her name, but she didn't stop. All she could think was her worst nightmare was now reality. If she'd hoped to avoid Clay Duvall, it would now be impossible.

Why had she sold her company? Her sixth sense had warned her, but she hadn't listened. Now she would have to pay the price.

CHAPTER 6

"Aw, hell!" Jake threw a couple of bills on the table, then grabbed the pocketbook that Alyssa had forgotten when she'd stormed out of Zubie's. He was through the small café and on the street in less than a minute, but she wasn't in sight.

Taking his time, thinking, Jake walked back to TriTech. Since his discussion with Clay that morning, Jake had been convinced the acquisition of Rossi Designs wasn't a conspiracy between Clay and his former girlfriend. Alyssa's reaction confirmed it.

"This is my lucky day,"

First Duvall had stonewalled him about his reasons for purchasing Rossi Designs. Then Sanchez had told him about the nurse's murder. Next, the inconsistencies in Duvall Imports' books that he'd discovered needed to be sent to forensic auditors. It was probably nothing more than an accounting glitch, but he wanted to be certain. Now, Alyssa had gone ballistic. What next?

He knew better than to get involved with women. The only time Jake had luck with them was in the sack. The image of Alyssa between the sheets almost—almost—made him smile. She'd probably claw his eyes out if she even suspected it had crossed his mind.

Alyssa wasn't his type, not at all. He preferred petite brunettes with ready smiles. Besides he knew better than to mix business and his private life. Okay, so what was he going to do about her?

He had no choice but to convince her to remain at TriTech. The last thing he needed was a time-consuming lawsuit over a minor acquisition. Enough storm clouds were gathering on TriTech's horizon. He didn't want to add to any problems the company might be developing.

"Alyssa went upstairs," the security guard told Jake the second he walked into the lobby. "Boy, was she in a hurry."

Rather than take an elevator, which he avoided whenever possible, Jake trudged up the two flights of stairs to Alyssa's office. He spotted her inside, cramming files into boxes. Not a promising sign.

"You forgot your purse." He dropped the leather bag on a stack of papers that covered a nearby desk.

She didn't look up.

"Listen, I realize you had no idea Clay Duvall was part of TriTech. How could you? It's a privately owned company. We're not subject to all the disclosure rules publicly held companies are. His name wouldn't have appeared on the purchase agreement you signed."

Alyssa didn't spare him a glance.

"Can't we discuss this rationally?"

"Talk to my lawyer."

"I would never have thought of that. You're so-o-o clever."

She stopped, clutched a stack of files to her partially unbuttoned blouse and zapped him with a what's-your-problem look that would have sent the devil to his knees.

"Jake, you're a real jerk."

"You're not the first to bring it to my attention."

The corners of her mouth tilted upward. Could she be fighting a smile?

"Is this what it's like to work for you?"

"No, babe. I act strange at times."

She actually cracked a smile, but she still looked roy-ally pissed. What was it about him that made women lose it?

"You know, Jake, this isn't the least bit funny. I would never, ever have sold to TriTech had I even *suspected* Clay Duvall had anything to do with the company."

"Really? I wouldn't have guessed."

"Quit it!" she cried. "This is *not* a joke. I don't know what I'm going to do now. I am halfway across the world, having sold my company, and all you can do is make wisecracks. You must be nuts."

He lifted a stack of papers off a chair, then dropped into it. Putting his feet up on the nearby desk, he said, "Poor people are nuts. Rich people are eccentric. I'm just eccentric. Know what your problem is?"

"Dare I ask?"

She ventured a step closer, and he thought he had her, but with women it was hard to tell. He waited a moment, letting curiosity get the better of her.

"Alyssa, you'll never make it in business because you can't think like a man."

An astonished gasp escaped her lips, then in a light-ning-fast move, she hurled a file folder at him. He grabbed her, swinging her sideways and anchoring her to his lap before she could throw anything else. Arms pinned to her sides, she wiggled, attempting to stand up, but he was too strong for her.

Fury smoldered in the depths of her eyes as she sat, her lips within a scant inch of his. He tried not to feel how soft her butt was or how sexy it felt to have her on his lap wiggling with her skirt hiked up exposing most of her thighs. He couldn't help noticing her lips the way he had the first time they'd had coffee in Florence. Again, he wondered what would it be like to have Alyssa smiling up at him, her hair flung wildly across a pillow.

She must have read his mind. "Don't you dare kiss me."

He didn't have the good sense to let go of her. Instead, he traced one thumb down the curve of her jaw. "Are you kidding? Then you'd have your lawyer add sexual harassment to your lawsuit."

"Can't you be serious?"

He released her. She could have jumped up, if she'd wanted, but she remained on his lap. At least she'd stopped wiggling, or he would have really been embarrassed.

"Did you mean what you said about not making it in business because I'm not enough like a man? Or was that just one of your weird remarks that you come up with to confuse the issue?"

"Pul-eeze! Clay insists he purchased Rossi Designs because it's such a great investment. You go ballistic because Clay's involved. Who's confusing the issue? Not me."

As he spoke, letting her have it with both barrels, she seemed to realize she was still on his lap and rose. With a little shake of her hips, the skirt dropped into place, and she buttoned her blouse.

"You meant every word, didn't you? A man would have handled this differently."

Jake stood up to take advantage of being slightly taller than she was. Okay, he didn't know what to do next. He was making this up as he went.

"You're right," she conceded, running her hand through her tousled hair. "I went a little crazy. It just came as such a surprise. I had absolutely no idea Clay had any involvement with your company."

"How would a man have responded to the news?"

She cocked her head to one side, looking at him, her eyes wide. Clueless.

"Don't get mad. Get even."

"Don't get mad," she repeated, a spark appearing in her eyes. "Get even."

"That's right. Get even."

"How? I don't know what he's up to."

He wasn't going for it. "Come on. You must have some idea."

"No. I haven't spoken to him in years."

"Think about it while we head back to Zubie's. I'm starving."

Alyssa let Jake pull out a chair for her at a table by the window. Zubie's was almost deserted now. An elderly man in gangsta jeans was mopping the floor and the bartender was wiping down the wooden counter. Zubie himself was in the back fixing fresh muffulettas for them.

"If I were a man, how would I find out what Clay Duvall is up to?" she asked.

He stared at her, then rolled his eyes toward the ceiling.

"What's wrong now?"

"Comparing you to a man." He flashed her a devilish grin. "It's not working."

"Come on. You may think this is a hoot, but it's my career, my business that's at stake."

He nodded, the teasing light going out of his eyes. "If you'd known from the get-go, it would be different. You would have refused to sell, but you're here now. If you back out of the deal, you'll make a pack of lawyers rich, and you'll lose business, right?"

"True, so . . ."

"Trick Clay into tipping his hand. Once his cards are on the table, you'll deal with it."

Zubie delivered the muffulettas and made small talk with Jake about the Saints' upcoming season. Alyssa took a small bite, but she was too upset to eat.

"I don't want anything to do with Clay Duvall," she told him when Zubie walked away. "You must know what happened last time."

"Tell me about it."

From his tone, she realized Jake knew all about the missing baby. It was old news, but an unsolved mystery involving a prestigious family like the Duvalls was never forgotten. She stalled, taking another bite of her sandwich and wondering how little she could get away with telling him.

What would a man do in this situation, she asked herself. Keep emotions out of it. Stick to the facts.

"There's not much to tell. It happened long ago when Clay and I were freshmen at Tulane while Phoebe was enrolled at Old Miss."

"University of Mississippi, the training ground for Mardi Gras queens." He smiled slightly as he spoke. No doubt, he took the quest to be chosen Mardi Gras queen as another joke, but she knew it was deadly serious.

"True, a number of queens have been debutantes in their junior year at Old Miss." She lifted one shoulder in a halfhearted shrug. "Other Southern schools have had their fair share of Mardi Gras queens. Since each krewe has a queen, there are plenty of opportunities."

"Max tells me only one krewe counts, Orion."

"It's for social climbers." She couldn't resist saying, "You should join the Barkus krewe, assuming you like dogs."

"I have a golden retriever. Name's Benson." His eyes narrowed, suggesting he thought she was putting him on. "There's a krewe for dogs?"

"You bet. They have a motto: 'Cats, while welcome, will not be provided with security.' Benson would love it, but you'd have to get him a special costume. Like the people in Mardi Gras parades, the dogs go all out for their Mardi Paws parade."

He chuckled. "I take it you weren't after the crown."

Alyssa put down her muffuletta and wiped the olive dressing off her fingers, saying, "Are you kidding? I wasn't in their league."

She didn't add that this had been drummed into her head from the time she'd come to live with the LeCroix family. Phoebe's mother, Hattie, kept telling Alyssa that she wasn't debutante material. She wasn't as pretty as

Phoebe, and she didn't have Phoebe's social connections, Hattie had claimed.

"It takes lots of money and time to be a debutante. I had neither. My parents were killed when I was seven. My aunt and uncle took me in, but I made my own way without much help from Hattie or Gordon LeCroix."

The expression on his face never changed, but he seemed to be gazing at her more intently. Stick to the facts. "I worked after school and studied hard. I was awarded an academic scholarship to Tulane. That's where I got to know Clay."

"You must have known him before. The families are old friends."

"Of course, I'd seen him over the years, but the LeCroixs' parties were always large." She didn't add that the family treated her more like a servant than a relative. She was usually in the kitchen during their parties or conveniently away at church camp. "Clay knew Phoebe much better because they went to the same private school while I attended the public school near the house. We didn't become friendly until we began taking prep courses the summer before we entered Tulane."

She carefully modulated her voice, keeping it level, disguising any of the latent anguish she still harbored. Clay was a man you had to release by degrees. It didn't happen overnight. His grip had been too tight to throw off easily. Even now, she felt . . . something—and hated herself for it.

"You got to know Clay better," Jake prompted, and she realized it had been several seconds since she'd spoken.

"Yes. We started dating that summer. Everything was great," she said, then wondered if it had ever been as marvelous as her foolish heart had believed. "By Thanksgiving, Clay was talking about marriage, but we had to wait until we finished school."

"Why wait if you both were so much in love?" There

was an undercurrent to his voice, and she suspected Jake found it hard to believe Clay had planned to marry her.

"He knew his parents wouldn't approve. We wanted to wait until we could support ourselves," she replied, and he gazed at her as if he expected to hear more.

"Where was Phoebe?"

"She was in town a lot that fall, which wasn't surprising. The girls on the deb circuit are often chosen to be part of the queen's court, so they come to the city frequently for parties. What stunned everyone was Phoebe's finding the gold bean in her slice of cake."

"Sounds like some dentist planned to get rich."

"It's tradition. The Orion krewe has a very formal party. The deb who finds a golden bean in her slice of cake is the krewe's queen. What surprised everyone was that Phoebe was so young, a college freshman. Most queens are juniors in college and seasoned on the Mardi Gras circuit. Many have been on the court and really know the ropes."

"Why was Phoebe chosen in her freshman year?"

Alyssa shrugged. "I have no idea. I guess, Hattie— that's Phoebe's mother—persuaded her husband to use his influence as captain of the krewe." She hesitated before making any derogatory remarks about krewes or the men's clubs. Most businessmen in the city belonged to one. "Are you in a club?"

"Nah. I'm a lone wolf. My father belongs to the Mayfair Club. I could join, but I'm not interested."

She considered what he'd said and had a difficult time imagining Jake with a father in the elitist Mayfair Club. Clay was a different story. He came from a long line of New Orleans aristocrats who had founded such clubs. Jake seemed to be his own man unlike Clay, whose life had been dictated by his family and their place in society.

"Clay's father forced him to escort Phoebe to most of the functions after she was chosen queen."

Jake asked, "What about the king?"

"He's an older man who's usually married. He's selected for his service to the community." She could see that Jake hadn't paid much attention to Mardi Gras, despite having lived in New Orleans for years. Alyssa doubted that she would have either, if she hadn't been raised with Hattie grooming Phoebe to become queen and constantly reminiscing about her own reign as Mardi Gras queen.

"The king and queen ride the float together and make public appearances, but there are lots of times when the queen needs a younger escort."

"I get the idea."

"Mardi Gras fell early in March that year. A month after it was over, Clay and Phoebe announced their engagement. They had a May wedding."

"That's fast for a society wedding. Do you think they fooled anyone?"

Only me. I was a fool for ever thinking Clay loved me. "If you have enough money, everyone pretends you're not pregnant when you go down the aisle."

"What did you do?"

She could have told him about the nights she'd walked along the levee, gazing at the muddy Mississippi and longing for Clay, but she kept to the facts. "I worked two jobs and attended classes."

"Didn't Clay ever explain or apologize?"

She dodged the question. There wasn't any reason to discuss the ridiculous excuse Clay had given her for marrying Phoebe. "I was living on campus then. I minded my own business and stayed away from them."

He considered what she'd told him for a moment, then asked, "What happened the night the baby disappeared?"

"My roommate gave me a message from Clay late on the night the baby was born. He asked me to come to the hospital. I almost didn't but . . . I went."

"Did Clay meet you there?"

"No. It was after midnight. There wasn't anyone around except the babies in the nursery. I waited a few minutes, thinking Clay would come."

"You didn't see anyone?"

"Just the nurse who showed me to the nursery."

"How long were you there?"

"Five minutes, maybe less. I decided someone was playing a cruel joke on me. I realized Clay wouldn't have made the call." She didn't tell him how she'd stared at the small infant, wishing he were her baby. She'd run out of the hospital, holding back tears. By the time she reached the parking lot, the unshed tears blinded her. Deep sobs racked her insides, and she allowed herself to cry.

"What did you do?"

"The worst thing I could have done. I had my roommate's car. I drove out to Le Petit Bayou and sat there, watching the fireflies until dawn."

"That's a pretty desolate area of the bayou. I take it no one saw you there."

"Right. It left me without an alibi." She looked directly into his dark, assessing eyes. "It also gave credence to Phoebe's accusation that I'd tossed the infant to the alligators."

"That's pretty far-fetched."

"You'd be surprised how many people believe that's what happened. Ravelle fanned the flames every day in her "Around Town" column. Of course, she's a close friend of Hattie LeCroix." A prickle of unease made her ask, "Is she still writing for the *Sun?*"

"Ravelle's moved to Channel Seven."

"Great." Alyssa was prepared to face the past, but she hadn't counted on the gossip columnist still being around. "Back then, Ravelle badgered everyone in the press until the police dragged the bayou. The Duvalls hired a slew of private investigators, but the baby had vanished without a trace."

She pushed her unfinished sandwich aside. "Many

people believed alligators had eaten the child. As soon as I arrived in Italy, I borrowed the money from Aunt Thee to hire my own investigator. He didn't uncover anything new."

"A baby just can't disappear like that and not leave a single clue."

"That's what happened. It's heartbreaking to think about where little Patrick might be now. Is he happy?" Despite her best effort, her voice betrayed her inner emotions. "Is he healthy? Have people loved him the way every child deserves to be loved?"

A beat of silence. "You're assuming the baby survived."

"Why would anyone want to kill a helpless baby?"

His eyes were intense and troubled. "Remember the nurse on duty that night?"

"You mean Gracie Harper. What about her?"

"She was murdered earlier today."

"Really?" She tried to think clearly but couldn't. Her mind kept replaying a television interview with a very young nurse. The memory was a decade old, but the nurse saying Alyssa had been the last one seen with the infant still sent her stomach into a backflip. "That's terrible."

Despite the horrible memories, Alyssa had never blamed Gracie Harper. The woman had told the truth— as she'd seen it. She wondered about the nurse's family, imagining their shock, their grief. She knew firsthand how devastating it was to suddenly find yourself without a mother. "Did she have children?"

"No. She was divorced." His gaze cut away instead of remaining linked with hers.

"What are you trying to tell me, Jake?"

His eyes swung back to her, even more intense than they had been. "We routinely use a private investigator to vet every employee. Rueben Sanchez looked into the disappearance of the Duvalls' baby. He questioned the nurse, and later she contacted him and wanted to meet him in private to discuss the case again. Before she could see him, Gracie Harper was shot."

Alyssa huddled in her chair, offering no response. Could the nurse have had information that would have cleared her name? She'd had her hopes raised only to be dashed too many times to count since the baby vanished. Someone *must* know something, but no one had talked. Now the nurse was dead.

"Do the police have—"

"They don't have a single solid lead. We don't even know if it has anything to do with the case."

Alyssa thought a moment. "Why now? Why kill her after all this time?"

"Sanchez thinks it's because he's asking questions. He used to be a top FBI agent. He's not afraid to dig for answers."

A warning voice whispered in her head. "You know, I love New Orleans, but it's a city with more than its share of corruption. I've long suspected that the authorities didn't properly investigate the case."

He nodded slowly. "Sanchez will find out the truth, I'm sure."

"It's almost twelve years now. A long time. Witnesses move, forget—"

"Die." His voice became even more serious. "I want you to be extra cautious. We don't know what we're up against or who they might target next."

"You think my life is in danger?"

"I don't know. Anything's possible. Be very careful."

CHAPTER 7

It was nearly midnight before Alyssa finished talking with Jake and drove to the parking garage near the town house Aunt Thee had leased. She locked the rental car and hurried down the narrow passageway between buildings. A dank smell like a musty cellar filled the walkway, which was dimly lit by brass sconces at either end.

Luckily, the town house had come with two parking spaces, a luxury in the French Quarter, which had been built almost two centuries earlier.

Luckily.

The word took on an ominous note.

"Maybe, I'm overreacting," she whispered to herself.

Still, she wondered how Aunt Thee had managed to do the impossible—find a vacant town house with a two-car garage nearby. Was it truly luck or had Clay Duvall covertly managed to arrange for accommodations?

Not only was the area a tourist mecca, but rentals, from small converted slave quarters to large town houses complete with courtyards and fountains, were impossible to find. Many apartment buildings had waiting lists, and it often took years for an opening to become available.

"What is Clay up to?" she asked herself once again.

Alyssa hadn't been totally honest with Jake. Clay had telephoned her when she had been living in Italy, insisting he still loved her, but it had been several years since she'd heard from him. She'd refused to take his calls, and finally he stopped. What kind of man claimed to love you, then got your cousin pregnant?

She came to the end of the passageway and looked around before crossing the narrow street, the key to the town house gate in one hand. The French Quarter was beloved by tourists and residents—and thieves. The deeply shadowed street in the quieter end of the district was deserted except for a stray alley cat foraging for a late-night snack.

Be very careful. Jake's warning echoed in her ears. Tomorrow she was going to buy one of those tiny cans of pepper spray designed to be attached to a key ring. She should get a cell phone, too. She unlocked the massive wooden doors and slipped into the cobbled carriageway that led into a spacious courtyard.

A magnolia tree graced the center of the area near a marble fountain of Venus. During the day, potted palms provided shade for the groupings of wrought iron furniture. The fountain had shut off, signaling it was now past midnight, but the low voltage lighting was on a photoelectric cell. It was light sensitive and stayed on until dawn, casting a soft glow on the bisque-colored walls.

Still spooked, Alyssa checked the deep shadows, but saw nothing. Someone would have to scale the nine foot walls to get into the courtyard. Not likely, she assured herself. Even if they made it, the doors to the main house were locked.

Above the deserted courtyard lace-like wrought iron enclosed a gallery supported from below by pillars of matching ironwork. Lush ferns grew in enormous baskets hanging from the eaves. More flowers cascaded from clay pots attached to the grillwork.

Using the antique skeleton key, she opened the

French doors into the house, then took the stairs to the second floor, where the bedrooms were located. Seeing light filtering down the hallway, she walked toward the south wing where Aunt Thee had her rooms. As usual, Aunt Thee was having trouble sleeping and was in bed reading.

"I'm home," Alyssa called softly. "May I come in?"

"Of course," Aunt Thee replied, and Alyssa rounded the corner. "You're working too hard," scolded her aunt, the minute she saw her.

"Me? You've been working nonstop." Alyssa bent down to kiss her aunt's cheek. "Everything's unpacked and put away."

"The team from Merry Maids did it all. You may want to rearrange your things, but at least they're out of boxes."

"Thanks. I'm sure it's fine." Alyssa sat on the edge of the bed and thought again how frail Aunt Thee appeared. They'd celebrated her seventy-fifth birthday with friends in the dining room of the Savoy Hotel in Florence, and she'd seemed a little tired then. Obviously, the move had taken its toll. Alyssa had planned on telling her about the nurse's death, but decided it could wait.

"Is something the matter?" Aunt Thee asked.

They had always been honest with each other from the moment Alyssa had placed a very desperate call to her father's older sister right after she'd been arrested for abducting the baby. Even though Aunt Thee had visited Alyssa only a few times since her parents had died, Thee had flown immediately to New Orleans and hired the best attorney to represent Alyssa. As it turned out, the police didn't have enough evidence to hold Alyssa, but Aunt Thee's presence and her unwavering support had helped her through the crisis.

"Clay Duvall is a minor partner in TriTech," she replied.

"No! You're joking!"

"Worse, he engineered the deal to buy my company."

"Why?" Aunt Thee's brow knit into tight furrows.

"I don't know. I haven't heard from him in years."

Aunt Thee's mouth formed a thin-lipped smile. "He's still in love with you."

Alyssa shook her head. "He never loved me. I was just . . . convenient."

Aunt Thee covered Alyssa's hand with her own. "Phoebe trapped him into marrying her. He loved you then, he loves you now."

A slight quaver in Thee's voice seemed to reflect her exhaustion. Alyssa didn't want to upset her by resurrecting the difference of agreement that they'd had for years. The older woman stubbornly insisted on accepting Clay's explanation that he'd made love to Phoebe, believing he was with Alyssa. No matter how much she *had* wanted to believe it—at the time—Alyssa wasn't stupid. Nor did she believe Phoebe had become pregnant after just *one* encounter.

"Why now?" Alyssa asked. "It doesn't make any sense."

"Of course, it does. Clay knew contacting you directly wouldn't work. You've become successful, less approachable, but if you're here, you'll meet face-to-face. Then he'll have a chance."

"You're forgetting he's married. Not that I'd want him even if he were free."

"Are you sure?"

Alyssa hesitated.

"That's what I thought. You won't be positive until you see him again and talk to him."

There was a kernel of truth in what Aunt Thee said. Alyssa wondered how she'd feel when she ran into Clay. She couldn't honestly say that she wouldn't feel something. She'd loved him once with all her heart, and as years passed, she'd met other men, but had never allowed herself to fall in love.

"Aunt Thee," she said, deliberately changing the subject, "who owns this house?"

"I do. I've had it leased for years, but several months ago the lease was up and I put the tenants on a month-to-month agreement."

"You own this town house?" Somehow Alyssa wasn't surprised. Aunt Thee rarely discussed her financial holdings. She'd been left a wealthy widow and forced to learn to manage her own affairs. She'd encouraged Alyssa to be just as independent.

"Yes. I've wanted to come back home for some time now."

"You have? Why didn't you say something?"

"I didn't want to leave you." Aunt Thee touched Alyssa's cheek. "I've never forgiven myself for not adopting you when your parents died. If I had, Hattie LeCroix wouldn't have tortured you."

"She didn't mistreat me . . . exactly. I wasn't loved but the LeCroixs provided for me. I turned out all right. Didn't I?"

Aunt Thee's smile was tender. "Yes, but—"

"But nothing. Don't fuss about my childhood. You helped me when I needed it the most." Alyssa leaned over and kissed her aunt's cheek. "I love you. You know that."

"I love you, too."

Alyssa stood up, smiling fondly at her aunt. "It's late. Try to get some sleep."

Aunt Thee held up her hand to stop her. "Have you seen Jake Williams yet?"

"Yes." Alyssa wasn't sure why she hesitated before saying, "I had dinner with him tonight."

"Was he as rude as he was the first time you met?"

"No. Jake. . ." Alyssa was at a loss as to how to describe Jake to Aunt Thee. He was a complex man, and she had no idea what made him tick. He'd been cold and abrupt in Florence, yet tonight he handled a difficult situation with humor and intelligence. Then he'd seemed genuinely concerned about her safety.

"Well?" prompted Aunt Thee.

"He told me about Clay. I explained the situation, and he assured me that I'll report directly to him. Clay may be part of the company, but I won't have to deal with him."

Aunt Thee regarded her with a speculative gaze.

"Jake helped me come up with a plan."

"Really?"

Alyssa explained how they were going to try to force Clay's hand. "By this time tomorrow night, we should know why Clay bought Rossi Designs."

Clay placed his hand on the back of Phoebe's arm and guided her up the sweeping steps of Max Williams's estate on the exclusive guard-gated Audubon Street just down the block from where Phoebe's parents lived. Party lights twinkled in the graceful magnolia trees lining the drive, and chains of red roses laced the marble banister leading into the house. The sound of a band playing Mardi Gras music drifted their way from behind the mansion.

"I refuse to believe Max Williams is going to be king," Phoebe whispered, her tone as frosty as it had been since the Orion krewe's election.

"Sh-h-h!" he cautioned his wife. "No one is supposed to know for months who the next king is. Max will be a good king. He'll throw tons of money at it."

Clay didn't bother to look at his wife as he spoke. She was miffed enough because he'd voted for Max. She'd be furious if she knew how hard he'd lobbied to get Max elected. Now that Max was devoting his time to his Mardi Gras role, he wouldn't be hovering around TriTech.

Clay spotted Max standing in the massive entryway, greeting guests. Tall with broad shoulders and rough-hewn features, Max strongly resembled his son, except Jake's hair was jet-black and Max's full head of wavy hair was burnished with silver. He was over fifty, but he looked much younger because he kept himself in shape and his hairline hadn't receded.

"There's Ravelle." Phoebe waved to Ravelle Renault as the parking valet opened the door to the older woman's Bentley on the driveway at the bottom of the steps. A van marked KTNO pulled up behind Ravelle and a camera crew jumped out, then started to set up for a panoramic shot of the mansion.

Clay smiled at the woman whose human interest show, "About Town," appeared every night on television. It was nothing more than a gossip session about the lives of wealthy local residents. It was hard for him to believe so many people tuned in every night, unable to get enough of what others called "bayou backbiting" because Ravelle had been born in a small Cajun backwater village.

He nudged Phoebe forward in the receiving line, prepared to leave her to chat with Ravelle. He made it a point not to cross Ravelle, but he didn't care for the woman. He'd never forgiven her for the way she'd attacked Alyssa years ago.

"Clay, how'z it goin'?" Max greeted them in his deeptimbered voice.

"Great. Just great."

Max offered Clay a firm but quick handshake as he turned to Phoebe. "Well, I'll be jiggered. You're more beautiful every time I see you, Phoebe."

"Oh, Max, go on." Phoebe blessed him with a brilliant smile, and even Phoebe's own mother would never have guessed that Phoebe had wanted Max blackballed.

"I'm serious," insisted Max. "You're the best lookin' gal here."

Clay noted how taken Max was with Phoebe. She managed to wrap any man around her finger, he thought, then corrected himself. Jake Williams hadn't fallen for his wife. He might be a country boy from the Redneck Riviera, but Jake had street smarts. Clay wondered if Jake would even bother to show up for his father's party. He avoided the social scene and kept to himself.

The crush of people behind them forced Max to urge them to go inside for a drink, and they walked into the antique-filled mansion. Clay ignored Phoebe and glanced around for the bar. It had been a tough day and he needed a double shot of Johnny Walker Gold in the worst way.

"He's in love with me, you know."

Clay spotted a bar set up in the corner of the massive dining room off the entry, and knew there was a wood-paneled taproom down the hall, but he was certain with this big of a crowd the caterers would have set up another bar on the back terrace.

"Are you listening?" Phoebe tugged on his arm.

"Yes. Max is in love with you." He kept walking toward the French doors that were open onto the terrace, hoping Phoebe would stay behind to catch Ravelle.

"He's been crazy about me since I was Mardi Gras queen."

There was something in his wife's tone that made Clay glance at her. Phoebe smiled up at him with an expression he couldn't quite decipher. It had been years since Phoebe had been queen. Max had been in New Orleans back then, his business just beginning to take off, but he hadn't traveled in their social circles.

"How did you meet Max?" he asked, thinking the question underscored how distant they'd become. He'd assumed they'd met at some charity function several years ago when Max had hit the big time and had exploded onto the social scene, buying his way in by donating money to a variety of charities. God knows, Phoebe sat on every committee imaginable.

"We met at a photo shoot after I became Mardi Gras queen. Max came right up and introduced himself."

"You've known him since before we were married?"

"Well, duh! I guess you were too busy chasing Alyssa to notice."

It was true, he had been spending as much time as possible with Alyssa back then, but he was dead certain he would have remembered had he met Max. The man had a brash, go-for-it style that reminded him of Jake.

Alyssa, thought Clay, smiling inwardly. She was a taboo subject between them. Phoebe hadn't mentioned her name in years. How would she react when she found out Alyssa was back in town? First thing Monday morning, Clay planned to go into Alyssa's office and welcome her home.

"He's *still* after you?" Clay asked, remembering what Phoebe had said when she'd dropped by his office to convince him to blackball Max.

"He's never given up." Phoebe's long-suffering sigh nearly made him gag.

Clay greeted friends, but kept moving toward the terrace bar. Phoebe stuck to his side instead of scurrying out to greet Ravelle to be certain she was featured on the television coverage of the party.

"Max frightens me," Phoebe told him.

"Why? You claim he's crazy about you." Personally, Clay thought Max was crazy about politics and only slightly taken with his wife as were too many men around town to count.

"He's never stopped loving me."

"That scares you?" Clay kept his voice low. They were close to a number of other people now, and he didn't want any of them to misinterpret this ridiculous conversation.

"He wants to marry me."

Phoebe's version of reality was suspect at best, but this was a new twist. He called her bluff. "I'll give you a divorce anytime you want."

Not only was Max old enough to be her father, but Phoebe was the epitome of snobbery. Being married to a Duvall was the pinnacle of society. She'd connived her way into the marriage, and she didn't intend to let him go—unless she could move up.

"Don't tempt me," she hissed.

We're stuck with each other, Clay thought as he ordered drinks from the bartender, having to settle for Johnny Walker Black Label. Trust a hick like Max not to make certain Johnny Walker Blue and Gold were available for his guests.

Clay had no intention of divorcing Phoebe and being forced to split the family fortune. He was set to make even more money—not give it away to a woman whose crowning achievement was riding the krewe's float as Mardi Gras queen.

"Phoebe, darling." Ravelle Renault joined them at the bar. "Your dress is divine. As soon as my crew catches up, we'll get a few shots."

"It's a Badgley Mishka." Phoebe did a slow pirouette while Ravelle gushed over the silver beaded gown. Clay was positive it had set him back a bundle.

Ravelle's black hair was piled on top of her head in the updo she'd worn for years. She dyed it black to look good on television, but in person it was much too dark for her pallid skin. She was whippet thin now, but before Ravelle had convinced the owner of a local television station to give her a spot on the news, she'd been overweight.

Clay took a sip of his second Johnny Walker, not paying any attention to the women's chatter until Ravelle began to whisper.

"Darling, who's that stunning woman with Neville Berringer?"

Clay scanned the crowd for the most eligible bachelor in New Orleans. Neville had been in Clay's class at Tulane law school. He'd joined his family's legal firm while Clay had gone into his family's importing business. Neville's wife had died two years ago of cancer. He rarely had ventured out to a party since.

"I have no idea who she is," responded Phoebe, "but she's wearing last season's Armani. I saw it on sale at Neiman Marcus."

Clay spotted Neville and almost choked on the whiskey. Maree Winston was clinging to Neville's arm and smiling up at him. Stay cool, Clay told himself. Maree had stopped calling weeks ago. Now he knew why. He'd wanted her to find someone else, but he couldn't help resenting how easily she'd linked up with one of his friends or how much she seemed to be enjoying it.

"I guess there's a story here," Phoebe said to Ravelle. "Neville's donated a new building at Tulane in his wife's name. You'll want to get his comments on that."

Ravelle waggled her finger at Phoebe. "Darling, you've been naughty—very naughty. You've been holding out on me."

"I have?" Phoebe's tone was coy. "About what?"

"Darling, you know the *really* big story isn't Neville." Ravelle inclined her head toward the terrace.

Clay tore his eyes away from Maree and spotted Max standing on the terrace with Jake. Between them stood Alyssa Rossi.

"That bitch is back!" cried Phoebe.

"Why didn't you tell me?" Ravelle asked.

"I didn't know." Phoebe's reply was barely audible.

"Where's my crew?" Ravelle waved frantically to her cameraman, who was still filming near the gazebo. "I must interview Alyssa."

Clay downed the rest of his Johnny Walker in a single gulp, his angry gaze sweeping over Alyssa. She wore a strapless red gown that showed off her knockout figure and an unusual blue beaded necklace she must have designed. Every man around was gaping at her—but it was Jake Williams who had her on his arm.

Christ. This wasn't going the way he'd planned.

CHAPTER 8

Alyssa stood next to Jake half-listening to him talk to his father. She hated to admit it, but the butterflies in her stomach were as big as bats. She made herself look up at the men, but she'd already spotted Clay Duvall over near the bar. He hadn't noticed her because he'd been gawking at a drop-dead gorgeous brunette in a black gown.

She would have recognized Clay anywhere, Alyssa thought, her breath catching. He was heavier through the chest and shoulders than she'd remembered, having shed any remnants of the boyish Clay Duvall she'd loved. He was mature now; they both were. Time did that to you, she reflected, knowing she'd changed as well.

Smoothing the midriff of the red silk sheath, Alyssa reminded herself that she was no longer the shy, insecure girl Clay had so easily charmed. Not only was she older, but the years in Italy working in the fashion industry had given her confidence and her own unique style. Every woman here would be wearing a designer gown while she'd designed her own gown. True, she'd given the sketch to a dress manufacturer and he'd produced it in exchange for jewelry for his girlfriend, but the idea had been hers and hers alone.

Phoebe appeared only slightly older than when Alyssa had last seen her, but the air of sophistication she'd worn like her own skin had taken on a hard edge. She was glamorous and poised and sure of herself, the way she'd been since Alyssa could remember.

Blond and blue-eyed and statuesque, Phoebe and Clay were a striking couple, she decided. Like a pair of matched Thoroughbreds, they belonged together. They always had. Their backgrounds, their breeding, their view of the world had been preordained long before they had been conceived.

Alyssa had been shackled with an appearance that was disarmingly similar to Phoebe's, but they'd shared little else. Hattie had always pitted them against each other, telling Alyssa she wasn't pretty enough, then taunting Phoebe, saying she wasn't smart enough. Alyssa was positive that time and distance hadn't changed this fact. Was confronting them a good idea? she asked herself yet again.

It had seemed like it when Jake suggested attending his father's party and taking everyone by surprise. "The best defense is a good offense," he'd told her. Now she wasn't so certain.

The fine hair across the back of her neck prickled as she recognized the woman standing next to Phoebe. Ravelle Renault had crucified Alyssa when little Patrick Duvall had been kidnapped, insinuating she was responsible. Her vicious columns had led to Alyssa's arrest.

At the far end of the gardens, Alyssa noticed a gazebo where a band was playing. A camera crew was filming the dancers who were gyrating on the parquet dance floor that had been brought in for the party. She recalled what Jake had told her about Ravelle's television program and realized this must be Ravelle's camera crew. Inwardly, she braced herself.

"I can't get over it," Max Williams was saying to her, and she forced herself to pay attention to him. "You look exactly like Phoebe. Almost twins."

"We've often been mistaken for twins, but we're only second cousins."

"Phoebe's a fine-lookin' gal. Mighty fine. I see my son has great taste in women, too. You're just as beautiful."

Alyssa kept her eyes trained on Max and Jake, aware that conversation on the terrace had become hushed whispers. Jake smiled reassuringly, his hand now on the back of her waist.

"Alyssa's a very talented designer, Max. That's why we acquired her company."

"What do you design?"

Alyssa gazed at Max, thinking this was exactly what Jake would look like when he was older. He'd be athletic and good-looking in a rugged way—not that he wasn't attractive now.

"I design costume jewelry, specializing in beads. Some are semi-precious stones but most are crystal. Like this." She touched the frothy collar of aquamarine briolette beads encircling her neck. "I like to think of it as wearable art."

Max nodded, approval in his dark eyes. "Do you have a shop here?"

"She has representatives in New York the way most jewelry designers do," explained Jake, his hand pressing hard on her back. "Her stores are in Italy, but she's opening a shop here in the Warehouse District."

This was news to Alyssa. They hadn't discussed it, but she assumed the pressure of his hand meant he wanted her to agree. She nodded, thinking it was a good idea. "The French Quarter's too touristy. The Warehouse District with all the art galleries and boutiques would be perfect."

"Isn't there a vacancy on the ground floor of your building?" asked Max.

"Yes. It's a small shop but all she needs is display space. The business division already has relocated its headquarters to TriTech."

"That so?"

Alyssa could tell Max knew nothing about this. From what Jake had told her, his father had retired, but still kept abreast of the inner workings at TriTech. She tried to concentrate on the idea of opening a new shop, but it was difficult with people staring at them. And with Clay so close after so many years apart.

She'd imagined this moment, dreamed about it more than she cared to admit even to herself. But nothing prepared her for the reality of seeing Clay with Phoebe at his side, and with Ravelle Renault coiled like a venomous snake ready to strike. She tamped down her misgivings, reminding herself that she had done nothing wrong. She had every right to be here.

"Seem's like everyone is comparing you to Phoebe," said Max. "They're all looking this way."

Alyssa knew that wasn't what was happening. People couldn't believe she had the nerve to come home let alone brazenly appear at a high society party.

"Let's get a drink," suggested Jake as he nudged her forward.

"Good idea." Max moved with them. "I haven't had a chance to get anything myself."

Ahead, Alyssa saw Ravelle frantically waving to her camera crew, signaling for them to come to her side. Alyssa tried to pretend she didn't notice Phoebe and Clay, but it was impossible. They were directly in front of them only several paces ahead now. She mustered a smile and looked directly at Phoebe.

It was almost like having her own face staring at her except Phoebe's hairstyle was different. She was wearing more makeup than necessary, considering her flawless skin and naturally long eyelashes. Her dress was too low-cut, revealing more cleavage than appropriate. All in all, Phoebe seemed to be waving a red flag that said "Notice me!"

"Phoebe, did you see who's here?" Max said as if he'd discovered a long-lost friend of Phoebe's.

Before Phoebe could respond, Gustavus "Bubba"

Pettibone, Mayor of New Orleans, rushed up. Never one to miss a photo opportunity, the veteran politician extended his hand to Max, but his eyes were on Ravelle and her camera crew. They had pulled off to the side where Ravelle was being filmed in what had to be the introductory segment of her nightly report. They were too far away to hear what was being said, but Alyssa could well imagine the gossip monger reminding New Orleans about the kidnapping of the Duvalls' baby.

"Max," said Bubba. "You've done wonders for this community. What a great party."

"Thanks, Bubba. There's no other city like New Orleans."

They were directly in front of the Duvalls, and Alyssa forced herself to say, "Hello, Phoebe."

Phoebe was a true steel magnolia, too well-bred to be rude in front of so many people. "Hello." The single word could have frozen lava.

Alyssa turned her head slightly and met Clay's blue eyes. "Hello, Clay."

"It's been a long time, Alyssa. You're looking well."

" 'Well' doesn't cover it," Max effused, obviously missing Phoebe's frosty response and the inquisitive stares of those around them. "Alyssa's a knockout just like Phoebe. They could be twins. Right, Bubba?"

Bubba's florid complexion darkened to the color of an eggplant. The smarmy politician had been around long enough to remember the scandal and had the smarts to spot political quicksand before he stepped into it.

"Prettiest da—darn women around," Max added. "Don't you agree, Bubba?"

Alyssa forced herself to pry her gaze away from Clay and smile at Jake. His expression was impossible to read but the warmth of his hand on the back of her waist helped Alyssa play along. Out of the corner of her eye, she saw Clay studying her.

Clay was an extraordinarily handsome man, she

thought, a certified heartbreaker. Suddenly the years she'd been away disappeared, and Alyssa was an awkward teenager again sitting beside Clay in the prep class for Tulane. She'd remembered Clay from family parties, but now he was right next to her, talking to her, his smile for her alone. She'd told herself not to fall for him, but she hadn't been able to stop herself.

She kept her thoughts locked inside, realizing Jake had said something about New Orleans being full of beautiful women. Obviously, he was trying to cover the uncomfortable moment.

"You've got that right," Clay agreed.

Ravelle Renault barged up to them, a microphone in her hand. It was hard to see her face for the glare of the klieg light the crewman held. Another man stood beside him, a bulky video camera balanced on his shoulder.

"We're live," Ravelle warned everyone as she shoved the mike in Alyssa's face. "Alyssa Rossi, what brings you back to New Orleans—after all this time?"

She tried to appear excited, enthusiastic. "I've come home to live. I've sold my company, Rossi Designs, to TriTech."

"R-really?" Ravelle was unprepared for this revelation as was Phoebe. Despite the blinding lights, Alyssa noticed the hostile expression on her cousin's face. She didn't dare look at Clay, but she could feel his eyes on her.

"Yes, TriTech wants to broaden its holdings," Jake interjected. "Alyssa is one of the foremost jewelry designers in the world." He pointed to her necklace. "This is one of her creations."

The camera zoomed in on Alyssa's neck.

"Oh, my. It's lovely." Ravelle recovered her wits, asking, "Alyssa, aren't you concerned about the scandal that forced you to leave New Orleans will hurt your business?"

Bubba jumped in, obviously anxious to get his face

on the evening news and stay on the side of Max, one of his biggest campaign contributors. "That was a long time ago. The city is always happy when its talented residents return."

"That's right," Max chimed in. "TriTech is proud to have Rossi Designs."

"Alyssa was never charged with any crime," added Jake.

"The kidnapper is still at large," Alyssa said directly into the camera. "Someone out there must have information that could help. If you do, please contact the police."

"Alyssa," Ravelle said, and she knew the woman wasn't going to let her off this easily. "What about the Duvalls?" She signaled for the camera to spotlight Phoebe and Clay. "You were suspected of kidnapping their baby."

"Nonsense." The cameraman swung back to her, and Alyssa had to keep her eyes wide open against the blaring lights. "The Duvalls know I had nothing to do with it. That's why Clay Duvall handled TriTech's acquisition of my company."

"Really?" Ravelle gasped, clearly caught off guard by this revelation.

The camera whirled back to the Duvalls. Phoebe's expression became a mask of sorrow as if the baby just had been snatched from her arms, but Alyssa had grown up with her and realized her cousin had been blindsided by this news. Clay appeared cool and slightly aloof.

"Is that correct?" Ravelle poked the mike in Clay's face.

"As you know, TriTech purchased my company, Duvall Imports. I'm on the board of TriTech now. We're committed to acquiring a variety of successful companies."

Alyssa noticed Clay had skillfully dodged the question, probably for Phoebe's benefit, not saying he had actually been the one to seek out and negotiate the purchase of her company.

For a second Ravelle appeared flustered, then she motioned for the camera to focus on her. "There you have it, folks. The latest from 'Around Town.' This is Ravelle Renault for Channel Seven News."

The blinding light clicked off and Ravelle turned toward Phoebe. Before Ravelle could utter a single word, Bubba spotted Governor Culbertson walking through the French doors with an entourage, including more television crews.

"The governor needs me," announced Bubba and he was gone.

Max followed the mayor, and Ravelle scuttled off, her crew in tow. Jake and Alyssa were left alone with Phoebe and Clay.

"There's my brother," announced Phoebe and she marched away.

Wyatt LeCroix was smoking a cigar near the gazebo area, where the band had taken a break. A sexy redhead was at his side. His sister appeared to be the last thing on his mind.

"You certainly know how to make an entrance."

"It was unintentional," Alyssa responded to Clay, her voice shakier than normal.

"What would you like to drink?" Jake asked.

She thought she said Merlot but a second later she couldn't be sure. She felt light-headed now that the worst was over. The harsh, uneven rhythm of her breathing had more to do with Clay than with the television interview. She knew Jake had deliberately left her alone with Clay. Jake was in line at the bar, too far away to hear what they were saying, but he could see them.

In the flickering light of the torchiers illuminating the yard, Clay's eyes were midnight blue. They caught hers and held.

"Welcome home, Alyssa. It's been way too long."

She didn't respond to the hint of intimacy in his tone. It irritated her for him to think he could charm her with those blue eyes and easy smile. Did he seriously expect her to drop at his feet?

"Why did you deliberately conceal your involvement in purchasing my company?"

Her terse question seemed to amuse him. "Would you have sold to TriTech if you'd known?"

"No way!"

"Then you have your answer. Is there anything else you want to know?" His silky voice held a challenge as well as an annoying touch of humor.

She deliberately looked away and noticed Jake watching them. He gave her a strange smile, one impossible to interpret. It flickered so briefly Alyssa had no chance to return it.

"Why purchase a costume jewelry company? It hardly fits TriTech's profile."

"I know a winner when I see one."

Movement to their right distracted them. It was Neville Berringer and the beautiful brunette Clay had been staring at when Alyssa had walked onto the terrace.

"Clay, Alyssa. Hey, it's good to see you."

Neville greeted them, and Alyssa couldn't help smiling. He'd been a classmate at Tulane and one of the few people who'd called to offer her support when she'd been accused of kidnapping the baby. Aunt Thee had hired an attorney in Neville's father's law firm.

"This is Maree Winston." Neville introduced the stunning brunette at his side, then gave Maree a short rundown on Alyssa and Clay, including their time at Tulane together.

"That's a fabulous necklace," Maree told Alyssa, but as she spoke, her eyes drifted toward Clay.

Alyssa opened her mouth to say she designed it, but Clay had Maree's attention. Her luminous eyes reflected raw passion. Alyssa knew that expression, knew she'd looked at Clay with the same heartfelt emotion. She ventured a glance at Clay and instantly realized this wasn't the first time he'd met Maree. They were lovers.

CHAPTER 9

Jake took both drinks from the bartender and turned. Alyssa was standing at his elbow. A few seconds ago she'd been with Clay. She had a phony smile on her face, and he decided something Clay had said upset her. He handed her the glass of merlot. "Did you ask Clay why he hid his part in buying your company?"

"Yes. He just said it was a good buy, and he knew I wouldn't sell if I knew he was part of TriTech."

"You believe him?"

"I don't know what to think. He seemed sincere."

"He has a talent for that."

Jake figured Alyssa would be the first to know why Clay had acquired Rossi Designs. He wasn't a betting man—never having had a spare cent to wager until recently—but he'd bet everything he had that the reason was personal.

"Who's the brunette in the—ah—black dress?" Jake had almost slipped and said "killer" dress. The woman was a looker, but Alyssa had them all beat.

"Her name is Maree Winston. She's involved with Clay."

"Involved? As in sexually?"

"Is there any other way?"

He moved closer, stealing a peak at her cleavage, unable to resist teasing her. "We're involved, right?"

"That's not what I meant." She shook her head at him, sending a ripple of blond hair across her bare shoulders. "And stop looking at my breasts."

"If women don't want men looking, then why do they make dresses like that?"

"You're never serious."

"Wrong. I'm dead serious. Why buy a dress like that—then tell men not to look? Hey, we're only guys."

She rolled her eyes heavenward. He was pretty sure she wasn't praying.

"Okay, so what makes you think they're involved?"

"Women know these things." She sipped her wine, her gaze casually drifting to where Clay stood talking to Maree and the man with her. "Don't you see it in her eyes?"

"No, I don't, but thank you for sharing."

Her gaze reluctantly swung back to him. "Even if Clay didn't tell me the truth, coming here was a good idea. Thanks for suggesting it."

Compliments always made him uncomfortable. "Running into Ravelle was a stroke of luck. I can't take credit for that."

"The worst is over, and I feel better. Now I won't go around dreading seeing the Duvalls."

She smiled at him again, a tentative smile reflecting how nervous she'd been. He wouldn't have guessed. She'd seemed cool and had worn a red dress that was bound to call attention to her. He gave her credit for brazening it out. She had more depth to her than he'd first thought.

"Here come Gordon and Hattie LeCroix," Jake said.

Alyssa looked up and saw the couple walking out of the house. She'd lived with them ten long, miserable years. She hadn't heard from them since Gordon had called to explain to her that Phoebe would be uncomfortable with Alyssa at her wedding. It was the reason she wasn't being invited.

If she hadn't been so hurt, Alyssa would have laughed. Did any of them seriously believe she would have attended? Why torture herself by watching the man she loved marry another woman?

Hattie hadn't changed much, Alyssa noticed. She still had auburn hair and wore it in a chignon at the nape of her neck. A tall woman who carried herself the way she had when she wore the Mardi Gras queen's crown, Hattie wrote the book on elitist attitudes.

Gordon, with his blond hair now feathered with silver, and periwinkle blue eyes looked more like Phoebe and Wyatt than Hattie did. A weak man, Gordon allowed Hattie to bully him. Alyssa knew Hattie had forced Gordon into telling her that she wasn't being invited to Phoebe's wedding. When Alyssa had been living with them, Gordon had tried to be friendly to her, but when Hattie caught him, Gordon would give up.

"I think she's spotted you," Jake murmured.

Hattie stared at Alyssa with hooded, hawk-like eyes that flashed with outrage. She jerked on her husband's arm and said something to him. Alyssa refused to allow them to intimidate her.

Gordon looked at her as if he'd seen the proverbial ghost. He blinked, then smiled, and Alyssa couldn't help returning his smile. He actually appeared to be happy to see her.

"One out of two ain't bad," Jake said.

"Gordon's all right," she said. "But Hattie's . . ."

"A bitch. I had dinner with them a couple of times while we were negotiating to purchase Clay's company. I think my father wanted to impress them. Why, I'll never understand."

"It's a New Orleans society thing."

Gordon walked toward them, Hattie at his side, her eyes cast downward. A few people turned to watch but most were enthralled with the governor.

"Hello, Alyssa," Gordon said. "It's been a long time. Are you here for a visit or—"

"Jake Williams, remember?" Jake extended his hand. "Mrs. LeCroix you look stunning in that dress."

Hattie was forced to look up. "Thank you."

"I'm back to stay," Alyssa informed them.

"Good. Glad to hear it," Gordon said.

Hattie's lips parted in surprise, and Alyssa had to admit she was stunned as well. Some things had changed around here if Gordon dared to cross Hattie.

"Gordon," Hattie barked his name. "Have you forgotten this slut is the reason we don't have our grandson?" Hattie towed him away.

Jake said, "Now, *that* was fun."

He had no idea how much "fun" it had been living under the same roof with Hattie. Could pain be transformed into a positive experience, preparing you for the other tragedies in store for you? Perhaps. Confronting all these hostile people hadn't been nearly as difficult as she would have thought.

"Just when we thought we'd had all the fun we could have," Jake remarked wryly and she saw Phoebe and her brother, Wyatt, approaching.

"How'd you get along with Wyatt?"

"Better than I did with Phoebe. Hattie insisted on sending him off to military school, not because he was troublesome, but because he was a normal boy who made noise and got into things. At least he'd talk to me when he was around."

Phoebe and Wyatt walked closer. "Uh-oh. Looks like they're on the war path. Hold your ground."

Alyssa looked right at them, and he put his hand on the back of her waist for moral support, not just because he liked having an excuse to touch her.

He saw Wyatt whisper something to his sister. He'd met Wyatt a few times when they'd been negotiating for Duvall Imports. Wyatt LeCroix owned the accounting firm that handled the books for several local businesses including Duvall Imports. He'd seemed to be an okay guy, but then, Jake hadn't really paid too much attention to him.

"Hello, Alyssa, it's been a long time," Wyatt greeted her.

Alyssa replied politely, and Jake couldn't help stepping in, "You three look so much alike. It's amazing. Blond hair, blue eyes, tall."

"Her eyes aren't blue." Phoebe hissed out the words. "They're—"

"You're right," Jake cut her off. "They're an unusual shade that's hard to describe, not ordinary blue."

"I'm taller." Wyatt's eyes were on Alyssa, and at his side, Phoebe's mouth was crimped into a tight line.

"All three of you are tall," Jake pointed out, attempting to infuse a note of humor into what had the potential of becoming an ugly confrontation. "Wyatt, if we put makeup and a blond wig on you, then—hell— you'd look like Phoebe in drag."

Wyatt chuckled, but Phoebe appeared to be sucking on a lemon. Alyssa laughed but he wouldn't bet the farm she was laughing at his joke.

Phoebe stabbed the air in front of Alyssa with her finger. "I know what you're trying to do, but you're not getting away with it."

"Just *what* am I trying to do?"

"You came home because you're in love with Clay. You think you can get him back. You won't—"

"Hold it." Jake pulled Alyssa flush against his side. "She's in love with me."

That got them. Wyatt chuckled again, but Phoebe stepped back, confused.

"Jake's right. I couldn't care less about Clay. He's all yours. Unless someone else has already . . ." Alyssa's voice trailed off as she pointedly looked at Clay and Maree.

"Who's that woman?" Phoebe asked her brother.

"I have no idea."

"Come on, darling." Alyssa gave Jake a manufactured smile. "Let's dance."

His arm still around her, they walked away from Phoebe and Wyatt. "Man, oh, man. I've never been in the middle of a cat fight before now."

"You didn't have to protect me. I can take care of myself."

Jake stopped a few feet from the dance floor, where the band was getting ready to play a new song. "Hey! I'm on your side. Don't get pissy."

"I know, I know. It's just that . . . you wouldn't understand."

He set their glasses on a passing waiter's tray, then led her out onto the dance floor and pulled her into his arms. "Try me. What won't I understand?"

Alyssa looked directly into his eyes. "Call it women's intuition, but I think Phoebe knows what happened to her baby."

"Why?"

"I haven't seen her since before the baby was born. When she and Wyatt were walking up to me, I expected Phoebe to demand to know what happened to her child. That's what I would have asked. That's what most women would have done if they truly believed I had stolen their child. Instead, Phoebe warns me to stay away from her husband."

"I see your point."

"Do you? Be serious now. What if Patrick had been your son?"

Jake looked across the backyard to where his father was standing with the governor. Max Williams had married Jake's mother and they'd had him. For reasons no one ever had explained fully to Jake, they'd divorced before Jake had any memory of his father. Max hadn't bothered with his son until about nine years ago when he'd suffered a mild heart attack and decided he needed an heir.

"If he'd been my baby, I'd still be searching for him."

She regarded him with a speculative gaze, and he knew there had been a little more emotion in his voice than he'd intended. He attempted to buffer it with a one-shouldered shrug, then changed his mind. Having a soft spot for children in danger didn't necessarily reflect on his own life.

"I'm going to hire a private investigator. I—"

Jake cut her off. "Been there; done that. What makes you think this time will be different?"

The song ended, and they stopped dancing, but he didn't let her go.

"The dance is over." She started to step out of his arms.

"Don't move. I'm thinking. You'll ruin my train of thought." He held her a little closer. "I know just the man to help you out. Rueben Sanchez used to be with the FBI."

She pulled out of his arms, and he had no choice but to let her go. He ventured another look at her chest.

"Quit that."

"What?" He winked at her, pretending not to understand. "Oh, that. Did I tell you that you look great?"

She gave him the first genuinely enthusiastic smile he'd ever gotten from her. "Thanks." Her smile widened. "For everything. Well, *almost* everything."

"Uh-oh. What's wrong?"

"Why did you tell them I'm in love with you?"

"You're not?"

"Think again."

"Give it some time. You'll be crazy about me."

"Why do I have a*nything* to do with you?"

"You're into sadomasochism big time."

This time she laughed, really laughed. Maybe there was hope for him yet.

"Darling, has anything bad happened?" Maree asked Clay.

"What do you mean?"

Neville had wandered off to the bar to get drinks, leaving Clay alone with Maree.

"Remember? Dante told me he had warned you. 'Ashes to ashes. Dust to dust. If God won't have you, the devil must.' Something terrible—"

"Come on, Maree. You can't believe such nonsense." But he could see that she did, and he remembered only too well her fondness for psychics. He kept his eyes on her, but over Maree's shoulder he'd been watching Alyssa dancing with Jake. Was something going on between them?

"I miss you, Clay." She reached into the small handbag she clutched in one hand, then slipped a card into the pocket of his jacket. "I've leased a carriage house on Julia Street. Here's my address and telephone number."

Out of the corner of his eye, Clay saw Phoebe and her brother watching them. They both saw Maree put the card in his pocket. Great. Now he had even more explaining to do—not that it mattered.

"How did you meet Neville?" he asked.

"I ran into him at a political fund raiser. He's nice but . . ."

Clay let her words hang there. She didn't interest him and hadn't for a long time. He had no intention of encouraging her. She was better off with Neville.

And he wanted Alyssa.

The last thing he'd expected was for Alyssa to show up tonight and take on her enemies. She was braver now than she'd been when he'd first fallen in love with her. She'd idolized him then. He sensed he might have to win her back, and he was prepared to do it.

"How well do you know that woman?" Maree asked.

Clay realized he'd been quiet for a second too long. Always intuitive, Maree had followed his gaze and read his mind.

"TriTech bought her company." He didn't elaborate, wishing Neville would hurry up with those drinks.

"She's beautiful."

Clay knew Maree was fishing for a compliment, but he wasn't in the mood.

"She must be related to your wife."

"Alyssa Rossi is Phoebe's second cousin."

Neville arrived with their drinks, and Clay grabbed his, muttered some excuse, then walked away. He greeted several friends as he made his way through the crowd. Alyssa was still with Jake, and Clay experienced an unwelcome surge of what had to be jealousy when she laughed at something Jake had said.

"Clay, wait a minute." He turned and saw Phoebe and Hattie bearing down on him with Wyatt in tow.

"Why didn't you tell me about Alyssa?" Phoebe's voice was low but charged with emotion.

"I had no idea she was here." This was half true. If it weren't for his investigator, he wouldn't know Alyssa had arrived in New Orleans.

"Did you handle the negotiations?" demanded Hattie.

"TriTech hired a consultant to handle the purchase. I was too busy and Jake was in Patagonia." He resented having to explain himself, but he knew it would happen sooner or later. It was better to do it here than at home, where Phoebe would really pitch a fit.

"You could have stopped it," hissed Phoebe.

"Stop Jake Williams. Are you serious?"

He'd intentionally made it sound as if acquiring the company had been Jake's idea. He pointedly looked at Jake and Alyssa.

"Don't blame Clay," Wyatt told Phoebe. "They're in love. Jake said so, remember? That's why he bought Alyssa's company."

In love? Since when? Clay asked himself. Jake wasn't her type—not at all.

"What are we going to do about her?" Hattie asked Phoebe.

"Nothing," Clay responded. "Leave her alone."

"I don't expect we'll see too much of her," Wyatt said. "Jake isn't the most social guy around."

"True," Clay reluctantly admitted. "He's nothing like his father."

"I need to talk to Ravelle," announced Hattie in the self-important tone his mother-in-law often used.

"I'll see you at home," Phoebe told him.

Clay planned on spending the night at the Mayfair Club to give Phoebe time to cool off, but he didn't mention it. Instead he watched the trio walk away. Out of the corner of his eye, he saw Alyssa with Jake.

He couldn't believe they'd gotten together so fast. Something must have happened in Florence that he hadn't counted on. His temper flared as he imagined Alyssa and Jake in bed. Clay knew he was better looking than Jake, but he had to admit Jake had a certain something that was hard to define. Masculine virility, he decided. He had a presence about him that women would find appealing.

Clay decided he had to act—fast—before he lost the opportunity he'd waited so many years to get.

CHAPTER 10

"Good night," Alyssa said to Jake as she opened the gate to Aunt Thee's town house.

"I'll walk you to the door."

"This is the same as the door."

"Check again. It's a gate." He held the gate open for her.

She wasn't going to argue with him, but she had the sneaking suspicion he planned to kiss her good night. He had a disturbingly sensual way of looking at her, or maybe it was just her imagination.

She found him appealing in a way that was difficult to define. She hadn't thought about it until tonight when she'd taken the chance to compare Clay to Jake. Clay seemed too polished, too sophisticated, she thought. Too much of a stereotype, which made her suspect he had a dark side and kept it concealed.

Jake had a compelling quality, Alyssa decided, a hint of aggressiveness and determination. His stance, legs slightly apart, suggested the readiness of a fighter. His head canted slightly to one side and his eyes were alert, missing nothing.

No matter how intriguing she found Jake, she was

interested in him only as a friend. She had no intention of encouraging him to think otherwise.

"Great place," Jake said when they stepped inside. "That's what I like about the French Quarter. You never know what's behind the walls."

She crossed the courtyard and unlocked the French doors to the main house, then turned to Jake. His head dipped toward her.

"Stop!" she cried, but it was too late.

His mouth overpowered hers as he pulled her against him. The mounds of her breasts flattened, his chest meshing against hers. His tongue traced the soft fullness of her lower lip, then edged inside to caress the tip of her tongue. Alyssa's pulse skittered alarmingly, a fluid warmth seeping through her body.

"Let me go," she said, pushing him away and telling herself that her knees were *not* weak.

"No."

"Why not?"

"Because I'm going to kiss you again."

"No, you're not." She tried to free herself, but he was too strong for her.

"Go on. Admit it. You like kissing me."

She refused to give him the satisfaction of saying he was right, but she had to admit—to herself—she did like it. Actually, she more than liked it.

This time when he lowered his head, she couldn't force herself to turn away. Their lips met, and her arms reflexively circled his neck. In a scorching kiss, his tongue aggressively mated with hers, and her breasts swelled with pleasure.

She wanted him to stop kissing her. She honestly did, but her long dormant sex drive had kicked into high gear. It couldn't help thinking what a great body Jake had. She'd noticed the first moment she set eyes on him, but nothing could compare with having the muscular length of him pressed against her. Nothing.

He had a devastating effect on her that she hadn't

anticipated. True, she'd been kissed many times but not like this. The way Jake kissed triggered a core meltdown that baffled her. No denying it. She was returning the kiss, enjoying every second of it.

He inched away, saying, "There's something I've been dying to do all night."

She wanted to come up with a sarcastic remark, but it was all she could do to breathe somewhat normally.

He lowered his head and kissed the bare skin where the top of the sheath exposed the slope of her breasts. With soft, moist kisses he sampled the smooth skin. His tongue edged into the hollow between her breasts, caressing first one side, then the other. Desire, pure and elemental, shafted through her. A low moan erupted from her throat before she could stop it.

He lifted his head and flashed her the wicked grin she'd come to expect. "You taste every bit as good as you look."

"I—I—"

Suddenly, Aunt Thee swung open the door. "Alyssa? Is that you?"

"Y—yes. I'm just saying good night to—"

"Jake Williams. I saw you two on television." She cinched her lavender bathrobe more tightly around her thin body. "Come in. I've just made herbal tea."

Alyssa said, "Jake's leav—"

"Tea sounds great."

Alyssa had no choice but to go inside with Jake. The aftershock from kissing him still had her rattled, but he didn't seem the least bit bothered. He was chatting with Aunt Thee as if he'd known her all his life, asking her questions about the town house's history.

In the kitchen, her aunt hovered over Jake, helping him select an herbal tea—blackberry—while she brewed Sleepy Time tea for herself. Alyssa wondered what Jake was up to. He was not the kind of man to drink blackberry tea and chitchat with an old lady.

"What did you see on television?" asked Alyssa as soon as her breathing became more normal.

"I couldn't sleep," explained Aunt Thee as she sat down at the oak kitchen table next to Jake. "So I turned on the eleven o'clock news. That dreadful woman Ravelle came on interviewing people at the party." She looked over to Alyssa, who was leaning against the counter sipping her tea. "I was surprised to see you with the Duvalls."

"What did you think of the interview?" asked Jake.

"Ravelle reminded viewers about the missing baby just before she spoke to you. Letting everyone know Clay had purchased Rossi Designs certainly made it seem as if they no longer blame you for the baby's disappearance."

"I hope you're right. I don't want it hanging over my head forever."

"I'm having an investigator I use look into the case," Jake told Aunt Thee. "He's a former FBI agent. I'm sure he'll get results."

"That's wonderful." Her aunt beamed at Jake, and unexpectedly she appeared less frail, less tired.

Oh, great, thought Alyssa. Just what I need. Jake's managed to charm the socks off Aunt Thee.

"I see why you've fallen for him," Aunt Thee told her.

"What?" Alyssa set her coffee mug down on the counter with a thunk.

"Ravelle said you two were—now, how did she put it?—an item. Yes, that's it. An item. She claimed you two were telling everyone you were in love."

"She announced it on the news?"

"That's what Thee just said," Jake told her.

"I wish I'd known—"

"Aunt Thee, there's nothing to know. Phoebe accused me of still being in love with Clay. Jake said I was in love with him just to get rid of Phoebe. It was a joke."

"Was it?" Jake asked.

She permitted herself a withering glare. "Stop. The joke is getting old."

Aunt Thee's amber eyes twinkled with delight. She was really getting a big kick out of this.

Jake put down his cup. "Seriously, there's something I want to talk to you both about. After the nurse's murder—"

"What nurse?" her aunt wanted to know.

Jake gave her the details of Gracie Harper's death, including the investigator's suspicion that his questions might have led to the killing. Alyssa had put off telling Aunt Thee, but now she knew. The furrows in her brow deepened as she listened to Jake.

"I think you should have a security camera at the street and another inside the courtyard," he advised. "In other words, a state-of-the-art security system."

"I suppose it's a good idea considering," Aunt Thee responded. "Do you really think Alyssa's in danger?"

"I don't know what to think, but it doesn't hurt to take precautions."

"I'll make arrangements tomorrow." Aunt Thee studied Jake a moment, then asked, "Why did you look into the baby's abduction?"

"I wanted to know why Clay bought Rossi Designs. It didn't fit into our profile."

"He's still in love with Alyssa. That's why."

"That's not what he said tonight," Alyssa told her. "He claims Rossi Designs was a good buy."

"I doubt if he would have told you the truth with all those people around," said Jake.

Aunt Thee rose, a bit unsteady on her feet. Alyssa took her cup from her. "I'm going up to bed. I think I can sleep now."

Jake stood up and gallantly escorted her aunt out of the kitchen, saying, "Don't worry. I'll take care of Alyssa."

Aunt Thee looked over her shoulder and winked at

Alyssa. Criminy. The guy was bent on causing problems for her.

Jake helped her aunt up the stairs to the second floor, where the bedrooms were. When he returned, Alyssa was waiting for him, holding the front door open.

"I swear, Jake. I'm going to kill you."

"I live in fear."

"Stop telling everyone I love you."

He walked through the door into the courtyard. "Why?"

"Because it isn't true. You're causing trouble."

"Trouble is my middle name."

"I'll go with you to the gate. I want to make sure it's locked." Walking beside him, she added, "Don't get any funny ideas about kissing me again."

"I wouldn't dream of it."

Just saying the word "kiss" reminded her of how marvelously he did kiss. It hadn't been just any erotic kiss. It had been a soul kiss most definitely. A prickle of anticipation tiptoed down her spine. They were almost at the gate.

He stopped, his hand on the wrought iron latch. His eyes scaled her body from the toes of her vampy red pumps to her lips.

"Don't even *think* about it."

His wicked grin would have tested a nun's vows. "What are you doing for birth control?"

For a second she was too astonished to speak. "It's none of your business."

"Sure, it is. I'm not kissing you again until we work out the birth control. Because next time I kiss you, we're going to end up in bed."

"You're hopeless."

"Considering the source, that's high praise." He opened the gate. "Think about the birth control. We're going to need it."

Without another word, she locked the gate behind him. She stood there a moment, leaning against the gate. Good heavens, what had she gotten herself into?

She slowly walked back into the house and went into the kitchen to clean up. She'd been taking birth control pills for several years to help with her irregular periods, but she had no intention of sharing this information with Jake. He was right about one thing, she silently conceded. If he kissed her again, they probably would end up in bed.

It had been over a year since her last relationship. Her biological clock was ticking well on its way to becoming a time bomb. She'd like to find the right man, and it wasn't Jake. He was too. . . Too what?

The buzzer on the front gate sounded. She hurried to the front door, not wanting Jake to ring the bell again in case Aunt Thee had been able to fall asleep. She didn't know what she was going to tell him, she thought, crossing the shadowy courtyard, but he wasn't starting anything tonight.

She unlatched the gate and swung it open. "You—"

"I know it's late, but—"

"Clay. What are you doing here?"

He stepped into the courtyard before she could stop him. "I've been in my car down the street, waiting for Jake to leave."

"What do you want?"

"I've waited years to talk to you. I need you to listen to me, then I'll leave, if that's what you decide."

"All right." She led him across the courtyard, asking herself how she felt about him. With all that had happened tonight, she hadn't taken the time to examine her emotions.

Initially, she'd reverted and become the awestruck young girl she'd been when they'd gotten together at Tulane. Realizing he'd been intimate with Maree Winston had reminded Alyssa of something she'd known, but hadn't been able to face when she was in love with him. Clay was an astonishingly handsome man, so much so that women threw themselves at him, and he wasn't strong enough to resist temptation.

She took him into the antique-filled living room, saying, "We'll need to be quiet. Aunt Thee is upstairs sleeping. I don't want to wake her." She turned on every light; she wanted to look directly into his eyes when he talked to her. "Have a seat."

She waited until he settled into the love seat then sat down in a wingback chair opposite him. A small coffee table with books on Italian art and an orchid plant in one of Aunt Thee's porcelain vases separated them.

"I know you're angry," he began. "I don't blame you. I'm responsible for what happened with Phoebe. You know my parents forced me to escort her to the Mardi Gras parties. I usually arranged to meet you afterward, right?"

She let him hang there, not saying a word.

"You would come over to my apartment, and we'd spend the night together. One night when I came home, I'd had more to drink than I should have. My roommate, Alan, said you were waiting for me in my room. I should have realized that was unusual. You'd never come over unless I called."

Because I was insecure and needed to know you wanted to see me, she silently conceded. She'd grown up with Hattie LeCroix telling her how inferior she was to Phoebe. Back then, she'd believed it. Aunt Thee's love and support had helped overcome her insecurities.

"It wasn't until later that I found out Phoebe and Alan had cooked up the plan. They'd bet that I couldn't tell you two apart. It was dark in the bedroom, music was playing, and Phoebe was in bed naked. Before I knew it, we were . . . well, you know. When I woke up the next morning, Phoebe was sleeping beside me."

He'd explained this before, but it had been over the telephone when she'd fled to Italy. Hearing this and seeing him face-to-face caught her by surprise. An almost imperceptible note of pleading mingled with guilt infused his voice. She thought he sounded sincere and almost felt sorry for him.

"I should have explained to you when it happened, but I was embarrassed. I didn't think anything would come of it. Then Phoebe announced she was pregnant."

"After one night together? That's hard to believe."

He leaned forward, his blue eyes looking directly into hers. "Just once. I swear. I could hardly stand to be with Phoebe after that."

"You married her." She marveled at the way his expression changed at the cold edge of irony in her voice. She wasn't the same young woman he could easily manipulate, and it surprised him.

He rose, crossed the room, and stared out the window at the landscape lights in the courtyard. She wondered what he was thinking, but didn't ask.

He returned to his seat and leaned forward, his elbows resting on his knees, his eyes on her. "You're right. I did marry Phoebe. I'm not proud of the way I allowed my father to manipulate me. I was young with no money of my own. I had no choice but to marry Phoebe. I was the only one upset about it—except for you, of course— my parents, the LeCroixs, and Phoebe were thrilled."

She had to admit this much was true. The LeCroixs were close friends with Clay's family, and more important, Hattie LeCroix envied the Duvalls because the family had more money and a lineage that could be traced back to the earliest Creole families.

"Please believe me, Alyssa. I'm ashamed of what happened, of not being strong enough to tell them all to drop dead and marry you."

He sounded so contrite that she had to remind herself Clay had a knack for getting what he wanted. "I believe you," she told him. "But what difference does it make?"

"Things have changed. I sold Duvall Imports to TriTech. I'm my own man now. My career—"

"You're still married."

His eyes narrowing, he sighed heavily. "Not for long. We can be together now."

"Stop. Do not even *think* about divorcing Phoebe on account of me."

"Don't tell me you're involved with Jake. He's not your type. He—"

"You don't know me, Clay. I'm not the naïve young girl I was when I left here. Jake Williams is exactly the kind of man I like. He has something you never had."

"Oh, really. Just what is that?"

"Integrity. He would have immediately told me had he mistakenly made love to my cousin." She could see the anger simmering in his eyes and the rigid set of his jaw. "He would never rest until he found out what had happened to his son."

He glared at her, frowning. "You're assuming the baby was my son."

"If he wasn't, why did you marry Phoebe?"

"The LeCroixs ambushed me. I was having dinner with my parents, and they came over. I didn't have a chance to get my father aside to tell him I had my doubts. When they left, it was too late. Our mothers were planning the wedding, and my father wouldn't hear of trying to get out of the marriage."

Alyssa didn't know what to say. She'd never considered the possibility the baby wasn't Clay's. Phoebe always had been an outrageous flirt, but Alyssa wasn't sure how far she'd carried these encounters. She was extremely careful not to upset her parents, and many times, her brother, Wyatt, covered up when she'd come in very late at night. Alyssa didn't know how she'd behaved at Old Miss when she'd been unsupervised.

"I believe Phoebe was having an affair with an older married man. He couldn't marry her—even if he wanted to—without causing a major scandal. That's why she pinned it on me."

"DNA tests weren't as common years ago, but a blood test could have determined—"

"I told Phoebe I wanted tests as soon as the baby was born."

"Did you explain all this to the police?" she asked, wondering if his threat could have led to the disappearance of the child.

"Yes, but they didn't think it mattered."

She gazed at him and unexpectedly thought of Jake. What would he have done in the same situation? She doubted his father could have manipulated him into marriage. Jake would not have such a callous attitude concerning an innocent baby.

"Did you know Gracie Harper was murdered?"

"Who's she?"

"The nurse on duty the night the baby disappeared."

"Now I remember her." He didn't sound particularly interested. "What does this have to do with us?"

"Jake hired an investigator to do a background check on me. This raised questions about the disappearance. It might have made someone nervous about what Gracie might say."

"What would make her change her story after all this time?"

Alyssa didn't want to tell Clay the nurse had called the investigator and had arranged to meet him. She wasn't sure it had been made public. "I have no idea what the nurse was thinking."

"Let's talk about us." There was an edge to his voice now. "I want you to give me another chance."

She didn't hesitate. "I don't want to have anything to do with you, Clay. That's final. I've arranged to deal directly with Jake in business matters."

"You're in love with him." It was clear he'd expected her to take him back, and since she hadn't, she *must* be in love with someone else.

"I'm not sure how I feel, but I know there isn't anything between us." She was sure she knew the answer, but she asked, "Why did you buy Rossi Designs?"

Clay stood up; anger etched his patrician features. "You know why."

CHAPTER 11

Jake glanced up from his video conference call monitor and saw his father walking into his office unannounced. Max usually stopped by once a week for lunch and to ask what was happening, but he always called first.

"I'll be off in a minute," Jake mouthed.

Max paced the length of the bank of windows facing the Mississippi, clenching and unclenching his right hand. From the set of his jaw and the agitated movements with his fist, Jake knew something was wrong. Just what he didn't need, thought Jake.

The conference call finally ended, and Jake hung up asking, "I wasn't expecting you. Is something the matter?"

Max turned and faced him, Not for the first time, Jake thought he'd look like Max when he was older.

"I need to talk to you. Let's go to lunch."

Jake really couldn't spare the time, not if he wanted to finish the pile of work on his desk and show Alyssa the shop he thought she should take, but he followed Max out the door. He paused long enough to tell Spencer to reschedule his appointments.

"I want to talk to you about Rossi Designs," Max said while they waited for the elevator.

"What about it?"

"I think you should get rid of it."

Once Jake would have agreed, but not now. They stepped into the elevator, and Jake had to remind himself this was a state-of-the-art elevator. It wasn't likely to get stuck.

"Don't you agree?" asked Max.

"No, I don't. It's profitable with the potential to be even more profitable."

"Well, I don't like the company."

The high-speed elevator reached the lobby and the doors slid open. As they walked out of the building, it occurred to Jake that his father hadn't asked to see the file on Rossi Designs.

"What don't you like about the company?" asked Jake, more than a little irritated. This was the second time his father had interfered in the company since retiring. He'd promised to step aside and allow Jake to run the show. Then Max had unexpectedly reappeared, insisting TriTech purchase Duvall Imports.

Max's dark eyes were exactly like the ones that greeted Jake each morning in the mirror. Right now those eyes were astonishingly troubled. "I don't like that Rossi woman."

Jake took a quick breath, surprised. He'd been prepared to hear his father say a jewelry company wasn't a good fit for TriTech. "Last night you seemed to like her. What changed your mind?"

"I've been talking to people. Alyssa Rossi is trouble."

"Why in hell would you listen to gossip? You told me people gossiped about you and called you a Redneck. They snubbed you until you had so much money they couldn't."

"Yeah, well, this is different."

Jake heard the stubborn tone in his father's voice,

but he was just as obstinate. "Doesn't seem any different to me."

They were outside now walking along the boulevard toward the nearby Windsor Court Hotel. His father liked to have lunch upstairs in the pricey Grill Room. Moss-green streetcars crowded with tourists clanged by, and vendors strolled along, hawking souvenir voodoo dolls and Mardi Gras beads along with T-shirts. The spring air was warm and laden with moisture. Jake loosened his tie and waited for his father to say more.

"I hear you're in love with her."

"Great. Ravelle strikes again."

"Is it true?"

"No, I'm not in love with Alyssa Rossi." True, he silently told himself. He wasn't falling in love or anything so stupid, but he was interested. Okay, okay, more than just interested, but not in love.

"Glad to hear it. She's nothin' but trouble."

Jake was stunned at how his father had let gossip persuade him to hate Alyssa, but then, did he really know his father? He'd appeared out of nowhere and wanted to make up for lost time. Jake had told him to drop dead. Where had Max been when he was growing up?

Against his better judgment, Jake had gone to New Orleans for a trial visit. He found he liked TriTech and stayed. The business world fascinated and challenged him. He'd worked from the crack of dawn until well after midnight, playing catch up. He didn't have the education most men did when they headed a company as large as TriTech.

"Clay Duvall handled the acquisition. You told me to delegate, and I have. I wouldn't want to undermine Duvall."

Max didn't respond, and they entered the lobby of the posh Windsor Court Hotel. As usual they took the stairs to the second floor where the Grill Room was located. On the way up, Jake decided this was bound to happen sooner or later. TriTech was his father's business, and no matter what he'd said, Max had been unable to resist meddling.

"Right this way," said the maitre d' when they walked into the Grill Room.

A knot like a cement fist formed in Jake's stomach. How was he going to handle this? In the years they'd been together, they'd had a few disagreements, but never a fight. They got along, but they weren't close.

Max had tried to be friends with Jake, but they soon discovered they shared few interests. Jake figured he looked like his father, but his personality was more like his mother's. She'd been a loner and so was he.

Jake sensed this would prove to be more than a simple disagreement. Max had built TriTech from nothing into a powerhouse. He hadn't done it by being petty. This seemed to be very important to him. Why?

As they approached the window table they were always given, Jake spotted Phoebe Duval sitting at it, sipping a martini. What in hell?

The sexy blonde was wearing a dress that matched her blue eyes. It was cut low enough to reveal an impressive cleavage. She knew how to make the most out of what she had. Jake would give her that.

"Phoebe's joining us for lunch," announced Max.

"You're lookin' great. Just great." Max bent over and kissed Phoebe on the cheek.

Max sat down beside Phoebe, and Jake had no choice but to sit looking directly at Phoebe. Aw, shit. How stupid could he be? Phoebe—not gossips—had turned his father against Alyssa.

"Aren't you going to say hello to Phoebe?"

Jake raised his eyebrows and went into his joking mode. "Hello, Your Majesty."

"She was the best lookin' Mardi Gras queen New Orleans has ever had."

Jake tried for another joke, but his brain refused to cooperate. His father had courted the Duvalls for years.

Their social status, their connections, impressed him. He'd insisted TriTech acquire Duvall Imports to get closer to the family, but Jake noticed the Duvalls hadn't bothered to show up at the party last night. They were at their condo in Sarasota.

"I know you don't like me," Phoebe said to Jake, "but—"

"What gave you the first clue?"

Max's voice boomed. "I won't have you talking to her like that!"

Several heads turned to look at their table. Jake didn't give a rat's ass. He had a suspicion he knew where this was going, and he didn't want to go there.

"Why don't you like me?" Phoebe's sultry voice threatened tears.

She's missed her calling. Phoebe should have gone to Hollywood instead of hanging around New Orleans living on past glory.

"Let's just say I'm old-fashioned," Jake responded. "I like women who are faithful to their husbands."

"I am faithful to Clay." Phoebe directed her response to Max. "You know that."

"Could have fooled me. You come on to every man who crosses your path."

Max smiled reassuringly at Phoebe. "It's just harmless flirting."

"Yeah, right."

The waiter came by, gave them menus, and took their drink order.

"I'm not staying for lunch," Jake told them. "I assume you two want to talk to me about something. Let's talk."

Phoebe hesitated, looking imploringly at Max as if she was too timid to say what was on her mind. Damn, she was good. His father was buying it big-time. Just goes to show you even the toughest self-made man had an Achilles' heel.

"It's about Alyssa Rossi," Max said for Phoebe.

"Why am I not surprised?"

Max shook his finger in front of Jake. "Don't be such a wiseass."

"The apple never falls very far from the tree." Jake knew he should handle this differently. Okay, more maturely. But he was too royally pissed. How could his father allow Phoebe to manipulate him?

Their drinks arrived and the waiter rattled off the day's specials oblivious to the tense silence. Jake drank his coffee and waited for them to make the next move.

"Act your age," his father said. "Just listen to Phoebe."

"I'm all ears."

Phoebe cast a look at Max as if she was afraid of Jake. Cute. Real cute.

"Go on. Tell him," prompted Max.

Phoebe faced Jake, artfully lowering her lashes, then gazing at him wide-eyed. Man, oh, man, Phoebe was a piece of work.

"Alyssa Rossi is trying to ruin my marriage."

"Suppose she is. What do you expect me to do about it?" He already knew what the answer was going to be, but he wanted to hear her justify it.

"We could give Alyssa a cash settlement," Max suggested. "She could move back to Italy or go to New York, where most jewelry designers have headquarters."

Phoebe nodded and blessed Max with a megawatt smile. Jake could tell they'd discussed this at length. He hadn't realized they were so close.

"Even if I gave her the money, what makes you think Alyssa would leave? What's to keep her from staying here?"

"I'd arrange for her to receive an offer she couldn't refuse." The look on Max's face said he had it all planned out.

"Do you honestly believe getting rid of Alyssa would save your marriage?" Jake asked Phoebe.

"You don't know Alyssa," Phoebe said.

No, he didn't, but he planned to.

"Ever since she came to live with my family, she's been jealous of me."

"Why?"

"Alyssa's pretty but she doesn't have ..." Phoebe paused, searching for the right word.

"Class," Max said.

"Didn't she move in with you when she was a young child? How much class could you have had back then?"

"At first she was just mean," Phoebe continued, ignoring his comment. "As time went on, it got worse. She'd do anything to spite me."

He wasn't buying a word of this, but he kept quiet to see where it would go.

"Clay dated her once or twice and Alyssa got the idea he was in love with her. When he and I became serious, she couldn't handle it. She sulked and refused to attend our wedding."

"Maybe I should get Clay's version of this," Jake said.

"He'll tell you the same thing," Phoebe replied.

Jake thought Phoebe was banking on the typical male aversion to discussing their personal relationships and was counting on Jake not talking to Clay, but she certainly sounded as if she believed Clay would back her up.

"Alyssa tried everything she could to mess up their wedding," Max told him. "She canceled the invitations, spread gossip, and made a pain-in-the-ass of herself because she was jealous."

"She's still after Clay."

Jake smiled at Phoebe, or maybe he just showed her his pearly whites. "Can't you hold on to your husband?"

"We're going through a rough time right now." A faint tremor altered the pitch of her voice. "I don't need Alyssa tempting Clay the way she did last night."

"Last night?"

A swift shadow of anger swept across her face. "Right after you left Alyssa, Clay went in. He didn't come home last night."

"How do you know?"

"I'm having him followed."

"A marriage made in heaven," he joked while he wondered if Phoebe was telling the truth. When it came to relationships with women, he didn't have the experience necessary to deal with a complicated mess like this. He told himself what he was feeling wasn't jealousy.

"Son," Max said, reaching across the table, but stopping short of touching Jake's hand. His father never called him son, and he never called Max father. Jake braced himself. "Alyssa fooled you into thinking she's in love with you, didn't she?"

"No, she didn't."

"Last night you said—"

"Phoebe, I was joking. You came up, ready to claw Alyssa's eyes out. I didn't want a scene at Max's party. That's all."

"You know about Phoebe's baby, don't you?" asked his father.

Jake nodded, watching Phoebe. She dropped her eyes before his steady gaze, and he hadn't a clue what she was thinking.

"It hurts Phoebe too much to talk about little Patrick."

Jake picked up a quaver in his father's voice and noticed the expression of sadness on his face. He wanted to tell him to get a grip and not let Phoebe fool him, but considering a baby had been abducted, even he couldn't make a joke.

"Having Alyssa around only reminds me . . ." Phoebe's voice trailed off, her lower lip trembling.

"Now, Phoebe, don't you cry." Max put his arm around her.

Gimme a break.

"Get rid of that woman," Max demanded.

The waiter hovered, ready to take their order, but Phoebe and Max hadn't touched their menus. Jake finished his coffee and shoved the cup aside.

"Enjoy your lunch." Jake stood up. "Max, come by my office when you're finished."

He didn't wait to hear his father's response. He strode across the restaurant and hurried down the stairs. He was so preoccupied he would have passed Wyatt LeCroix without saying hello.

"Jake, where are you going?" asked Wyatt.

"Back to the office."

"I thought you were joining us for lunch."

Son of a bitch. They'd all planned to gang up on him. Wyatt took off his shades and tucked them into the inside pocket of his sports coat. Jake decided he didn't like him. He wasn't sure why and put it down to gut instinct.

"Wyatt, I need to ask you something."

"Yes?" There was a note of caution in his voice.

"What really happened to Phoebe's baby?"

"How should I know?"

"You were at the hospital that night."

"Yes, Clay called me as soon as the baby was born. I brought Phoebe two dozen red roses. They're her favorite. I looked at the baby and left."

"Do you think Alyssa took him?"

"Who else would have?"

Wyatt hadn't sounded as convincing as his sister, Jake decided after he'd said good-bye and was walking down the street. How in hell had he gotten himself in the middle of this mess, Jake asked himself. The answer came in a single word: Alyssa.

He wouldn't know what to do about this until he'd spoken to her. He made a mental bet with himself that she'd immediately tell him about Clay. If she didn't, then she had something to hide, and she wouldn't be worth taking on his father over getting rid of Rossi Designs.

CHAPTER 12

Alyssa picked up her telephone, but kept her eyes on the computer screen.

"Mr. Williams is here to see you," Olivia told her.

"Send him in." She hung up, a warm glow of excitement making her smile. Despite her best efforts, she hadn't been able to stop thinking about Jake.

"Am I interrupting?" he asked as he came through the door.

"No. I'm just running a few designs." She tried not to sound too eager to see him. "Are you interested in seeing how jewelry is designed on a computer?"

"Sure."

He came around behind her, leaned over her shoulder, and looked at the computer screen. She couldn't help noticing a faint trace of citrus aftershave. She told herself to keep her mind on business, but she couldn't help remembering the way he'd kissed her.

"Wow. That's a necklace, right?"

"Yes." She clicked the mouse and several colors in the necklace changed. "I can experiment with color and designs without touching a stone."

"Saves time and money."

"Yes." She pointed to the large square designer's tray

next to the computer terminal. On the black velvet were about two dozen beads ranging from small morsels of aquamarines to pellets of chalcedony to dollops of citrine to small chunks of sapphires. "I look at the beads I plan to use, then go to the computer to do the actual designing."

"Where did you get the software program?"

"It's mine." She wasn't able to keep the pride out of her voice. "I worked with a couple of techies to get it to run properly, but I designed it. I have it licensed in Europe."

"Everyone using it has to pay you a fee?"

"That's right." She couldn't help being pleased at the admiration she saw in his expression. "I'll need to get it licensed here."

"Call the legal department. That's their job."

She thought a moment. "This is going to sound strange coming from me."

"I doubt it."

She swiveled in her chair so she wasn't talking to him over her shoulder. "Joining TriTech is already giving me much more time to design. I used to spend part of each day invoicing customers and another part of the day working on the accounts receivable and stuff like that. Now someone else will spend time doing the paperwork."

He'd sat down in the chair beside her desk while she'd been talking. "That's the idea behind the company. Certain functions are needed by every business. This way you're free to use your time doing what you do best."

She nodded and struggled not to think about what his shoulders did for a suit. He'd loosened his tie a little, and it gave him an attractively casual look as if he didn't take business clothes all that seriously.

"Did you want to see me about something, Jake?"

His eyes seemed to darken a little as he held her gaze

for a beat before answering. "Have you spoken with Rueben Sanchez?"

"Yes." She checked her watch. "He'll be here in about half an hour."

"I see," he responded and she thought he seemed a little troubled.

"I hope he can solve the mystery."

"If Sanchez can't, no one can."

His voice had a flat tone now almost as if his mind was elsewhere. Why had he come all the way down here from his penthouse office to ask her about the private investigator when he could have used the telephone? She'd like to think he wanted to see her, but that didn't seem to be his purpose. She considered telling him about Clay's visit, but decided now wasn't the time. Jake was too distracted.

"Aunt Thee would like you to come to dinner next Thursday if you're available."

"I'll check my schedule."

The dismissive note in his voice unnerved her. He was a mercurial man, a complex person who was difficult to get to know. Now he seemed more like the Jake Williams she'd met in Florence.

He slowly rose and headed toward the door. "I'm outta here. I'm going up to see Clay."

"Wait!" She jumped up from her chair. "Before you talk to him, I need to tell you something. I think you're going to want to sit down."

He returned to the chair near her desk. She leaned against her desk, half sitting, half standing and faced him.

"Could you. . . I mean, would you mind acting as if something is going on between us when you see Clay?"

"Why?"

She'd expected him to joke the way he usually did but he seemed deadly serious. "After you left last night, Clay came to see me. He explained why he'd married Phoebe."

"Did he have anything new to say?"

"Not really. He wanted to get me back here. That's the reason he bought the company."

"Why am I not surprised?"

"He said he's divorcing Phoebe, and he wants me to give him another chance." She tried not to sound emotional but it was difficult with him looking at her so intently. What was he thinking? "I said no way, and I meant it. Whatever I felt for him is gone, but you know Clay. Women don't tell him no. That's why I led him to believe we're . . . involved."

He came to his feet in one quick motion, and his arms were around her before she could catch her breath. "Darlin', when a couple starts talking about birth control, they're involved."

"I suppose you're trying to be charming." She struggled to throttle the dizzying current racing through her. "I have no intention of sleeping with you."

"Yeah, right, and there could be peace in the Middle East."

She didn't even try to dodge his kiss. There was a controlled strength in his body as his arms held her, but his mouth showed no such restraint. His lips parted hers and his aggressive tongue thrust into her mouth. Longing rose, swift and hot, from someplace deep inside her. She shamelessly returned his kiss, her hands clutching his sturdy shoulders.

"I may not be as handsome as Clay—"

"Of course, you are," she said before she could stop herself.

"Hey, I've got a mirror. I know what I look like."

"You're handsome in a different way. Clay's a pretty boy type. You're more masculine and you've got . . ."

"Go on. I'm dying to hear this."

"Never mind."

"I'm not going to stop kissing you until you tell me."

He reclaimed her lips, crushing her to him. She slid to the side, halfheartedly trying to escape the pressure of his weight, but he had her trapped between his body and the desk. The movement brushed her breasts across the front of his open suit jacket. His heat seeped through his shirt into her clothing, making her nipples acutely sensitive.

"S-stop," she mumbled against his lips.

"You know how to stop me."

"I'll scream and Olivia will call Security."

He mocked her with a shrug. He didn't seem the least bit concerned about TriTech's armed security guards bursting into her office and hauling him out.

"Tell me what I want to know."

"I forgot what I was going to say, honest."

His mouth swooped down and smothered the last word. That couldn't be . . . Oh, my god, she was dealing with a male who was rapidly becoming aroused. Knowing Jake, she wouldn't put it past him to—

She pushed him back, saying. "You win." It took her a second to catch her breath. "I was going to say you have . . . bedroom eyes."

He released her then threw back his head and roared. If Olivia had any brains, hearing this racket, she *would* call Security. When he finally was able to speak, he asked, "Then why aren't we in the bedroom?"

"I'm not some easy piece, you know."

"Coulda' fooled me." He brushed her cheek with the back of his knuckles. "I'm just joking. I respect you. Isn't that what women want? I heard it on a talk show. Okay, so I respect you."

"Isn't your beeper going off?" She pointed to the small black pager attached to his belt. It was vibrating. She couldn't miss the bulge south of the beeper.

"Yeah, but I'm trying to ignore it." He looked down at the digital read out. "Gotta rock and roll." He headed toward the door, adding, "I'll come down here around six. I want to show you the shop I think we should lease for Rossi Designs. Then we'll go to dinner."

The minute the door closed behind him, Alyssa put

her arms around herself, whispering, "What am I going to do about him?"

She was over her head here, and she knew it.

Jake took the stairs to his office to give himself time. He moved slowly. Going up the stairs with a world-class erection was about all the fun he cared to have. In this state, he wouldn't be able to think clearly when he confronted his father. He realized he had a sex drive that wouldn't quit—what red-blooded male didn't?—but he'd never come so close to losing control. In the middle of the day. At the office where he made it a firm policy to have nothing but professional relationships with women. He'd deliberately hired a very competent gay man instead of a woman so he wouldn't be distracted.

"Bedroom eyes," he muttered to himself. No wonder he found Alyssa so fascinating. She came up with the damnedest things, and she took his lame attempts at jokes in stride.

When he'd first talked to her, Jake had thought Alyssa wasn't going to tell him about Clay's visit. He had to admit he'd wondered if there might be some truth in what Phoebe had said. He should have known better. Alyssa hadn't wanted him to find out she'd told Clay that they were involved.

Involved. Only a woman would use that word. Same for bedroom eyes. He chuckled to himself. Then he realized this was the first fun he'd had in years.

Hell, it was the first time since he'd come to New Orleans that he'd really enjoyed himself. He'd worked himself so hard he barely had time to walk his dog. He wondered if Alyssa liked dogs. Who wouldn't like Benson?

He paused, his hand on the door out of the stairwell, wondering about his father. Today he'd seen a side of him that Jake hadn't realized existed.

Max Williams, the entrepreneur with the survival instincts of a cockroach, was basically an insecure man. How else would you explain his need to be accepted by New Orleans society? Why else would he allow Phoebe to manipulate him?

Maybe Max saw acceptance as another challenge like politics. He wanted to be United States senator. When he'd confided this, Jake had been shocked. Politics? Yuck.

No question about it. Jake was like his mother. JoBeth Williams hadn't given two hoots in hell what people thought about her. When she'd found herself alone with a son to raise and no money, she'd taken a job in a bait shop on Mobile's docks. "It's the most money I can make," she'd told him.

She'd worked there up until the day she'd keeled over while hauling fifty pounds of bait-size anchovies onto a sport fishing boat. Jake had few regrets about his life. If he had it to do all over, he'd live it the same way, but he did wish his mother had lived long enough to see him be successful. He could have bought her the house overlooking the bay that she'd always admired.

The most he'd been able to do was erect a magnificent headstone to replace the metal faceplate on his mother's grave. He had a standing order with a florist to always have fresh stargazer lilies—her favorite—in the vase at her grave. It wasn't enough, but it was all he could do.

He pushed open the door, stepped into the hall, and ducked into the executive washroom. He wiped away traces of Alyssa's lipstick. Gazing into the mirror, he said, "Bedroom eyes."

Jake winked and his reflection winked back. He made a few adjustments, then buttoned his suit jacket to cover his trousers.

"Your father's waiting for you," Spencer told him the second Jake stepped into the reception area.

"Thanks." He walked into his office and found his

father standing at the window staring out at the Mississippi. Max was doing the fist thing again.

Max turned and leveled his dark eyes on Jake. "I thought we were going to have to send out the troops to find you."

"Running a company is a full-time job, but I don't have to tell you about it."

"You didn't have to be so rude to Phoebe."

"True, I could let her wrap me around her little finger the way she does the rest of you."

Max shook his head. "I can see there's no reasoning with you. You're as stubborn as—"

"You are."

"I was going to say as stubborn as your mother. When JoBeth set her mind to something, no one could talk her out of it."

"Okay, so I'm double stubborn."

Jake remained standing a few feet from his father. He tried not to feel too defensive, but it was hard. He knew what was coming next.

"Have you decided how to get rid of Alyssa Rossi?"

"I'm not getting rid of her. You said I was in charge of this company. It's my decision, right?"

"See here." Max stabbed the air with his finger. "I built this company. I gave you the opportunity of a lifetime."

"Right, and I've worked my ass off for you. If you want the company back, it's all yours, but I'm not dumping Alyssa Rossi just because Phoebe wants to get rid of her."

"You don't mean it. You wouldn't give up all this—" Max waved his hand at what had once been his own office—"for some woman."

"I wouldn't be giving it up for a woman," Jake replied, shading the truth. "I'd be giving it up because you don't trust my judgment. You said I was ready to run the company. I've made more money each year, right? Now let me run it or take it back yourself."

There was a long moment of astonished silence. They stood facing each other, stances slightly wide like two gunslingers. Jake could almost hear his father thinking how ungrateful he was, but he didn't give a damn.

Jake had already let Max persuade him to buy Duvall Imports against his better judgment. Jake hadn't liked the company, hadn't thought it was worth the money. If he allowed Max to bully him now, Jake never would be the one in charge at TriTech.

"Now, son, don't go off half-cocked. I'm just making a suggestion. You'd save everyone a lot of grief if you took my advice, but I'm not going to force you." Max worked at a smile, then said, "Tell me what else is going on."

I'll be damned, Jake thought. How many times had Max Williams ever backed down?

Rueben Sanchez didn't look anything like Alyssa had expected. He was slightly shorter than average with a full head of dark hair and eyes like chips of obsidian. She'd imagined him as taller and more impressive, but then, she'd never met anyone from the FBI.

Her frame of reference came from too much television in her formative years. Verna, the LeCroixs' housekeeper, was supposed to watch Alyssa. Instead, she planted herself in front of the small television in the servants' quarters, and she ordered Alyssa to stay by her side.

"Is there anything else you can think of to tell me?" he asked.

They'd already been over the case in detail. She couldn't imagine there was anything else to discuss.

"I've told you everything I can remember," she responded. "Do you have any new leads?"

"I'm going over all the information originally collected, and requestioning everyone I can locate. Some leads were never pursued properly."

"Two different private investigators also looked at this case. I hired one of them. They didn't come up with anything."

He regarded her silently for a moment. "You'd be surprised how little experience most private investigators have. They usually handle infidelity investigations, pilferage from small businesses, and that sort of thing. This is a very complex case."

She nodded and silently told herself not to feel too encouraged just because Sanchez—as he wanted to be called—was more competent than previous investigators.

"There might be one new lead."

New lead. All her hopes hung on those two words, then drained away. She'd had her hopes dashed too many times before to put too much stock in this new lead.

"Gracie Harper got married two months after the baby vanished. A year later they divorced. I'm trying to track down Claude Harper to see if Gracie told him anything. So far, I haven't been able to locate him."

Again, Alyssa reminded herself not to become excited. Husbands and wives talked, but Gracie might not have confided in Claude—assuming she knew anything.

"One last question." Sanchez moved closer, bridging the space between them by leaning on her desk. "What's your gut instinct? Who took the baby?"

"Most people think a ring of black market—"

"I'm not interested in what other people think. I want your opinion."

"Phoebe is responsible. That's what I feel, but she had to have had help. She'd had a cesarean section so she wouldn't have been able to get out of bed."

Sanchez watched her, his dark eyes thoughtful, but he didn't comment on her theory.

"You know what I wish—as much or even more—than clearing my name? I'd like you to find Patrick.

Nothing is more tragic than the disappearance of a baby. It's bothered me for years. What happened to him? Is he all right? Is he loved?''

Is he alive?

The unspoken question hung between them. Alyssa longed to find out the baby was alive, but she knew there was a good chance Patrick Duvall was dead.

Her telephone rang, the flashing light indicating it was Olivia. "Excuse me," Alyssa said, slightly annoyed. She'd asked not to be interrupted.

"Mr. Williams is here to see you. He says it's important. Mr. Williams senior."

"I'll be finished in a few minutes." She hung up, wondering what Jake's father could possibly want.

"That's it." Sanchez stood up and extended his hand.

"What about your fee?" she asked as she shook his hand.

"I'm under retainer to TriTech."

"This is a private matter. I can't let—"

"Take it up with Jake."

The second Sanchez was gone, Max stormed through the door. He closed it behind him, and she could see he was upset about something. He stood in front of her desk and she rose so she could look him in the eye.

"What can I do for you?" she asked as pleasantly as possible considering the way he was glowering at her.

"How much money do you want?"

"What are you talking about?"

"I want you out of this company, out of this town."

She was so astonished she couldn't think clearly. "What does Jake have to say about this?"

"Nothin'. This is between you and me. Name your price."

She sighed inwardly. For a fleeting second she'd thought Jake had sent Max to do his dirty work, but when she thought again, she knew Jake would never take the cowardly way out.

"I like this company. It gives me a lot more time to be creative."

"Cut the bullshit. Tell me how much this is going to cost me."

"Why do you want to get rid of me?"

"You're trouble. Always have been. Now you're coming between me and my son."

"How?"

"Never mind. Tell me what it's going to take."

"The only way I'm going to leave is if Jake tells me to go."

The sullen expression on Max's face told her this wasn't likely to happen. Apparently they'd already discussed this and Jake had refused. No wonder she was so attracted to him. Not many people would dare to cross Max Williams.

"I have other ways of getting rid of you." Max spun around and stalked toward the door.

CHAPTER 13

Jake buzzed Spencer again. "Is Troy back yet?"

"He's still at lunch. I'll let you know the minute he comes in."

At lunch this late? Jake settled back in his chair to evaluate yet another report, but his thoughts turned to his father. The old man had been pleasant enough after he'd given in about dumping Rossi Designs, but Jake didn't quite trust him. That's why he was anxious to see his assistant, Troy Chevalier.

Jake had been troubled about the acquisition of Duvall Imports from the very beginning, and Troy had agreed. For a family-owned company, Clay Duvall's importing business was quite complex. They hadn't been able to thoroughly analyze it before Max had pushed for the deal to close. Then Jake had spotted a glitch in Duvall's books. He'd sent them out to a forensic accountant.

Now Jake was even more suspicious. What was going on between his father and the Duvalls? Jake knew Max envied their social connections, which was something Jake found difficult to understand. When he was in a room with a hundred people bent on impressing each other, he reached critical mass and got the hell outta Dodge. Not his father.

Why does Max care so much about Phoebe and Clay? Jake wondered.

Jake picked up the telephone and pressed for Spencer. "Get me Duvall," he said the moment his secretary came on the line. Jake cradled the phone between his head and his shoulder and began to read a troubling earnings projection.

"Mr. Duvall's at lunch," Spencer told him. "I told his secretary to have him call you when he returns."

"Thanks." Jake hung up. What was it with all the late lunches?

A few minutes later, Troy breezed into Jake's office. "You wanted to see me?"

"Did the report come back yet from the forensic accountants going over Duvall Imports' books?"

"No, but we should be getting it soon." His assistant trained his dark eyes directly on Jake while he smoothed back his receding blond hair. It was a familiar gesture, but one he found slightly vain.

"Why's it taking so long?"

"There aren't many companies who understand the importing business. Overton and Overton is the best."

"Okay, I'll have to wait. Here are the preliminary numbers from the Lasko Division." Jake slid the document toward Troy. "Quarterly earnings are going to be down—again."

Troy leaned over and examined the report. Well, I'll be a dog, Jake thought. Is that lipstick on Troy's collar?

"Late lunch?" he asked. It was fast approaching four o'clock.

"Yes. I had to wait to make calls to PanPacific before I could grab a bite." Troy sounded a shade defensive.

"Why don't you take off early," Jake suggested. "You work too hard. Get out and meet some people. Southern women are the greatest."

Troy nodded thoughtfully as if this was new and interesting information. His assistant had been different lately. Maybe Troy was coming around to his wealthy father's point of view. He wanted his son to return to Paris and run one of the family businesses instead of working for someone else.

"I've been thinking. Life's short. We should enjoy it more." He couldn't help smiling, thinking of Alyssa and hoping Troy would get a life. "I don't want to feel guilty about you working late if I'm taking off."

"That's what you pay me the big bucks to do." Troy picked up the Lasko report. "I'll make a copy of this and get it back to you."

Troy walked out of the office, and Jake hoped he hadn't insulted him or something. Troy seemed a little touchy, which was unusual. Maybe because he was covering up the affair he was having. That *was* lipstick on his collar.

Boinking some secretary in the middle of the day? It didn't seem like Troy, but Jake had almost flung Alyssa across her desk. Aw, hell, let Troy do his thing. He made up for it by working as hard as two people. Jake had no idea what he'd do without Troy Chevalier.

Jake had taken night courses and studied business relentlessly. He could hold his own now, and more often than not, he was ahead of everyone in a business meeting. Still, business dealings were complicated and getting more complex all the time. Troy's degree from the London School of Economics made his advice invaluable.

The late afternoon sun slanted through the space between the Mayfair Club and the adjacent building. Clay shielded his eyes with a raised hand, telling himself he shouldn't have spent the afternoon in the bar with old friends from the Orion krewe. He should have gone back to TriTech. Well, it was too late now.

Where was he going to go? He had a room upstairs

at the club, but he didn't want to sit there by himself. Going home was out of the question.

"Clay, Clay."

He recognized Maree Winston's voice. He'd done right by her, hadn't he? What did she want from him now? He wished he hadn't ordered that third Johnny Walker. It had made him a little foggy and not up to dealing with Maree.

"Maree, what are you doing here?"

"Dante and I need to speak to you."

Clay tried not to groan. He'd met Maree's psychic before, a six foot plus Bahamian with a television evangelist's gift for gab and thirst for money. If the South had won the war of Northern Aggression, Clay wouldn't have to deal with the likes of Dante.

Dante stepped forward, blocking Clay's path. "You've had a reversal of fortune, mon."

Clay couldn't believe Dante could master such big words. Clearly, he'd come a long way. "What do you mean?"

"Your wife, mon, she be making big-time trouble for you."

He had no doubt Dante was right, and it didn't take psychic power to know Phoebe was furious with him. She had a sneaky, mean streak that often turned vicious, but she loved him—obsessively—and wouldn't do anything serious to him. She'd content herself with making his life miserable.

"We can help you." Maree grabbed his arm and led him toward a sleek black limousine waiting at the curb.

Clay allowed her to guide him into the limo. "I don't need help. Take me to the office."

"Clay, darling." Maree slid in beside him while Dante sat at the far end of the limo. "I know what you need."

She gazed into his eyes, and all he could think about was Alyssa. What the fuck was she doing with Jake Williams? She belonged to him, and she always had from the moment he'd first seen her at Phoebe's sixteenth birthday party. Alyssa had been living with the LeCroixs before then, but she'd never appeared at family gatherings. That evening she'd been in the kitchen helping fill hors d' ouvre platters.

Clay had been on his way out to the pool house with Wyatt to smoke a joint where their parents wouldn't catch them. Wyatt had introduced him to Alyssa, and they'd spoken briefly before the housekeeper had yelled for her to get to work. He'd called to ask Alyssa out, but Hattie LeCroix had emphatically told him Alyssa wasn't allowed to date because she had to study full-time to be able to stay in school.

Hattie had given Clay the impression that Alyssa had some sort of learning disability. Since Alyssa didn't attend the private school where he and Phoebe went, Clay believed Hattie. Phoebe insisted her cousin was "a bit off" and that was why she wasn't included in family gatherings.

To his surprise, Alyssa had been among the scholarship students at Tulane when he'd enrolled. She wasn't anything like the debutantes he'd dated, girls whose sole aspiration in life was to be Mardi Gras queen. Alyssa had been ambitious, but her goal was to become a jewelry designer, and she'd been putting herself through school.

The only thing "off" about Alyssa was how different she was from the rest of the LeCroix family. The more he saw of her, the more he liked her until he realized he'd fallen in love. Time hadn't changed how he felt about Alyssa Rossi—not a bit.

"I need to go back to work," Clay said to Maree even though he had no intention of staying there. He just wanted to get rid of Maree.

The sultry brunette gazed into his eyes, but her hands were on his belt buckle. "L-let—" he started to say, "Let me out of here," but the idea dissolved as she unzipped his pants.

"It's too, too late to go to work," crooned Maree, stroking the fly of his underwear.

His sex responded shamelessly, surging upward into the experienced palm of her hand. She cradled it, the cotton fabric a barrier to what he really craved. Maree obliged him and slipped her hand inside his briefs. Caressing his bare skin, she teased him, still not giving him what he needed.

"Come on, come on," he coaxed.

She gripped his cock and gave a little tug. He'd been partially erect, and the motion of her hand brought him to a full erection. He sucked in his breath and waited, barely noticing the movement of the limousine or the reggae music coming from the stereo.

Clay sank back against the limo's cushioned leather while Maree positioned herself at his feet. He let her explore the tip of his penis with her deft tongue as if she were eating an ice cream cone.

"She's poison, you know, mon."

It took a moment for Clay to realize Dante meant Phoebe, not Maree. Clay couldn't think clearly thanks to the whiskey and Maree. Her mouth had surrounded his sex and was sucking mercilessly. It was all he could do to remain upright.

"I saw the way you looked at me when I walked into the party last night," Maree whispered, her soft breath swirling across the tip of his turgid erection. "You want me back, don't you, darling?"

No way, Clay told himself. He wanted Alyssa, and he intended to have her. He hadn't spent all these years loving her to give up so easily. If only Alyssa was the woman with her head between his legs.

Maree's mouth closed over him again and the sweet, sweet suction blinded him. A guttural moan escaped his throat. He lifted his hips upward, unable to get enough.

From the back of the limo, Dante began to speak,

and Clay opened his eyes. "We've got a plan. A sure-fire winner."

Clay blinked his eyes. Despite the dim light inside the limo, there was no mistaking the king size erection jutting against Dante's trousers. The psychic was getting off watching them.

"You're gonna thank me, mon. And make me big-time rich."

The Warehouse District had changed since Alyssa had wandered up and down its streets as a freshman at Tulane. Revitalization had transformed the rundown buildings into the go-go center of the art world in New Orleans as well as a trendy residential neighborhood. Art, hip people, interesting upscale shops, she observed.

"The available space is right there." Jake took her to a small, empty store fronting on the busy sidewalk. He unlocked the door and flicked on the lights.

The shop was about the size of her boutique in Milan, and a little smaller than the shop she had in Florence. It would certainly work, she thought, excited.

"What do you think?" he asked.

She strolled around, inspecting the premises. "The lighting will have to be improved to properly show the jewelry. Other than that, it's perfect. What are the terms of the lease like?"

"I own the building."

"You mean TriTech owns it."

"No, I bought it myself. I live in the loft upstairs." He winked. "I'll cut you a special deal."

"I'm positive Eve said the same thing to Adam when she offered him the apple."

He chuckled, then asked, "Do you want to meet Benson?"

"Benson?"

"My golden retriever. He's upstairs."

"Is this like showing me your etchings?"

"Right, except Benson is a lot more fun."

She knew better, but she responded, "I want to meet him."

Jake locked up the shop and led her up the nearby stairs. At the top he slid his key into an industrial door. He unlocked it, then swung it wide.

"Welcome to my place."

She stepped into a single room the size of a cathedral with a fifteen-foot open ceiling that exposed duct work artistically lighted by incandescent bulbs. To the right was a kitchen partially concealed by a magnificent black and red lacquer Chinese screen. A matching screen divided the living area from the bedroom, where she glimpsed a four-poster bed that appeared to be an antique.

"Hey, Benson, I'm home," Jake called. "He's not much of a watchdog. He's probably out on the roof deck sleeping on guard duty."

A honey-blond retriever bounded from around the corner at the far end of the loft. He skidded to a halt near the kitchen area and picked up a stuffed rabbit with long fluffy ears. The dog scampered up to Jake, wagging his tail so enthusiastically that his rear end swung from side to side.

"Benson always brings me a present." Jake accepted the rabbit and gave the dog a pat. "Good boy, good boy. This is my main squeeze, Alyssa."

She leveled him with a drop-dead-you-creep look while Benson slathered her extended hand with kisses. "Benson, you're totally cool even if your owner is a bit weird."

"Trust me, sweet cheeks, you haven't seen weird yet."

The retriever shamelessly collapsed in a heap at her toes. Alyssa bent over and scratched his chest. Benson flayed the air with his paws and grunted with delight.

"What a great dog," she told Jake, thinking how lonely she'd been growing up and how much she'd wanted a dog, but Hattie LeCroix hated pets. She deliberately ignored Jake, who was watching her, a strange smile on his face. Knowing him, Jake could be up to anything.

"Okay, Benson, go get your leash."

The retriever rolled to his feet, sprinted across the entire length of the huge room, and skidded to a stop on the oak plank floor. He stood up on his hind legs and grabbed a leash off a hook on the wall. His tail whipping the air, he charged back to Jake.

Jake snapped the black fabric leash with white paw prints onto the matching collar Benson wore. He dropped his end of the leash onto the floor, and the dog gathered it up in his mouth.

"Let's go," Jake said. "There's a sidewalk café down the street. If we take a table outside, Benson can stay with us."

The dog pranced over to the door, tail wagging, and waited for them. Alyssa followed, asking herself why Jake hadn't tried anything since picking her up. Men, weren't they a trip? Who knew what went through their minds.

Downstairs on the sidewalk, Jake made no attempt to take the leash from Benson. The dog lifted his leg on the fire hydrant in front of the shop Alyssa intended to lease.

"Aren't you going to hold his leash?" she asked.

"Nope. Benson won't leave my side, but there's a leash law. Dogs must be on a leash." He grinned at her and she was instantly reminded of a naughty little boy. "Benson's on a leash."

She couldn't help chuckling. "What if a policeman tickets you?"

"I've fought one ticket already. The law is very clear. Dogs must be on a leash, but it doesn't say the owner has to hold the leash."

"You got away with it?"

"You bet. I'm complying with the letter of the law."

She shook her head and pretended to be outraged, but she thought he was very clever. There was a lot more to him that she'd imagined. When they'd first met, she hadn't liked him much and thought he was cold, controlling. When he came on to her, Alyssa decided he was a poster boy for the single life, but now she wondered.

She intended to get to know him better instead of allowing him to seduce her and then find out what kind of a man he was. Still, she couldn't help being a touch disappointed that he hadn't at least attempted to kiss her when he had her alone in his loft.

"Why did you choose a loft?" she asked.

He walked beside her, then unexpectedly, he took her hand and laced his fingers through hers. A stab of something she couldn't quite name hit her. When was the last time a guy had held her hand?

"Benson, cookie, cookie," called a man from the entrance to Wok on The Wild Side.

The retriever sashayed over, tail in motion. He dropped the leash and took the cookie the waiter offered.

"He's got fans up and down the street," Jake told her after he'd greeted the man who was giving Benson a treat.

"Why a loft?" she repeated her question.

He waited until Benson had downed the cookie in a single gulp and had returned to his side. He searched her face for a moment, considering the question for longer than it seemed to merit.

"When I was a kid," he responded, then stopped.

Alyssa realized something about the question bothered him. She was curious, but she'd just been making conversation.

"In Mobile, right?"

"Yes, I grew up there in a tin trailer the size of a"— he looked around—"a fire hydrant. The outhouse was a few feet away, but in the summer, it might as well have been in the middle of the living room. When I could afford my own place, I wanted something big, spacious."

She sensed it had been difficult for him to tell her this. She wasn't sure why, but knew she was right.

"I know what you mean," she felt obliged to confess. "I spent years in a converted laundry room with a tiny window. I couldn't get enough air, especially in the summer when it was hot and humid."

He stopped, released her hand, and gazed down at her as if seeing her for the first time. "Why would they treat you like that?"

She shrugged. "Who cares? I stopped asking myself why years ago. Gordon LeCroix ignored me—when he was around—but Hattie despised me." And I hated her, she silently admitted.

Br-ring, br-ring. Her brand-new cell phone rang from where she'd dropped it into her purse. Almost no one had the number. She reached into the bag slung from her shoulder and retrieved the phone.

"Hello . . . hello."

"Is this Alyssa Rossi?"

"Yes, who is this?"

"Mercy General Hospital. Your aunt—" She hardly heard the rest. Tears blurred her vision.

Jake grabbed her arm. "What's wrong?"

"Aunt Thee's been taken to the hospital. I have to go." She sprinted down the street.

Jake caught up with her. "Wait. I'll take you. You're in no condition to drive."

CHAPTER 14

Alyssa shifted on the sofa in the waiting room outside the cardiac unit at Mercy General Hospital. Several hours had dragged by since they'd raced to the hospital. Aunt Thee was still in surgery.

"Don't worry, she'll be okay." Jake sat beside her, his arm draped across the back of the sofa just above her shoulders.

"I hope so," she whispered, her throat so tight she could barely speak.

"The nurse said Thee was conscious when the ambulance brought her in. That's a good sign."

"She hasn't been herself for months."

"What do you mean?"

"Aunt Thee has seemed slower . . . more tired. I just thought she was getting older. I should have made her go to a doctor."

"Sometimes it's difficult to tell what's age related and what isn't. It doesn't do any good to beat yourself up. You'll just need to watch her more carefully in the future."

The note of compassion in his voice surprised her. She wasn't sure what she expected from him. He joked a lot, yet he could be alarmingly serious. She'd told him that he didn't have to stay with her, but Jake insisted on waiting, and she was grateful he was keeping her company.

"I had been planning on getting my own place," she said. "Maybe I should stay with Aunt Thee. She's all the family I have. I love her so much."

Until now it hadn't dawned on Alyssa how alone she'd feel without her aunt. When she'd been growing up in the LeCroix household, she'd missed her parents terribly. Then she'd been devastated by the way everyone blamed her for the baby's disappearance. Alyssa had been totally unprepared for the love Aunt Thee offered. At first she'd been shell-shocked and couldn't respond, but as time went on, Alyssa came to think of her aunt as a second mother.

The door to the cardiac unit swung open and a man clad in an operating gown and cap walked into the waiting area. Jake rose, bringing Alyssa up with him, his arm bracing her.

"You're Theodora Canali's daughter?"

Alyssa managed to nod and chose not to explain she was a niece not a daughter. After he introduced himself as Dr. Robinson, Alyssa asked, "How is she?"

"We had to insert a pacemaker, but it went very smoothly. I expect her to make a full recovery."

"When may I see her?"

"It'll be an hour or so that they can bring her out of recovery into ICU. You'll be able to see her then. I'll have the nurse come get you." The surgeon spoke to her for a few minutes, discussing Aunt Thee's condition before leaving.

"Are you all right?" Jake asked, and she realized she was trembling.

"I'm fine. I'm relieved, but—"

"When was the last time you ate?"

She had to think a second. "This morning."

His sturdy arm bracing her, he guided Alyssa out of the waiting area. "Let's go to the cafeteria and grab a bite. By the time we finish, your aunt should be out of recovery.''

The cafeteria was closed, and they had to settle for packaged sandwiches from a vending machine. They took the food up to the waiting room. Alyssa wanted to be there in case the nurse came to find her.

"What about your mother?" she asked, realizing she'd been talking more and more about herself each time she was with Jake. He rarely mentioned anything personal.

"My mother died ten years ago next month." His tone was surprisingly gentle. "I was nearby when it happened. I got to her immediately, but she was gone."

"A heart attack?"

He shook his head, his dark eyes intense. "Aneurysm. At least she didn't suffer."

"Seeing her like that must have been terrible." She couldn't imagine what she would have done had Aunt Thee collapsed and died in front of her. His mother's tragic death was bound to have left an emotional scar. "What happened?"

He hesitated a moment, unspoken pain reflected in his eyes. "My mother was a strong woman. She'd worked for years at Billie Bob's Bait Barge on the commercial dock in Mobile. For a woman with no education, the pay was good. She claimed it kept the bills paid."

"Did your father give her money for child support?"

"He said he tried, but she wouldn't accept it. I believe him. My mother was stubborn. She didn't want a thing to do with Max after the divorce."

"I see," Alyssa replied, but she didn't. Why hadn't Max found a way to help his son?

"Even after I graduated from high school and was on my own, Mother insisted on staying at Billie Bob's. She was lugging a fifty pound bucket of bait anchovies when she keeled over."

"Oh, my God! Why was she carrying such a heavy load?"

"Tips. It's a four-letter word. The rich dudes who sport fish out of Mobile are big tippers—especially if a woman brings them the bait. For years my mother delivered the bait to make extra money."

She didn't have to ask if they'd been close; she could hear it in his voice. But what about Max? Was Jake close to his father now? Should she tell him about Max's visit?

"Your parents were divorced when you were little, right?" she asked. He'd told her this much when he'd taken her to his father's party, but he'd seemed reluctant to reveal anything more.

"They'd married because Mother was pregnant. They were divorced right after I was born. Max didn't show up again until the year after my mother died." He studied her a moment as if weighing whether or not to say more. "Max decided he needed an heir. He'd had a heart attack and was feeling vulnerable."

"You hadn't seen him *once* in all those years?"

"Nope. Max was too busy making money, and he wasn't interested in me. When he reappeared, I didn't know who he was until he told me."

"Are you two close now?"

Jake shrugged. "Not really. Max tries but we don't have much in common except the business."

Don't tell him about Max's visit, she cautioned herself. Don't come between a father and his son. She realized now how much Aunt Thee meant to her even though she'd belatedly appeared in her life. Let Jake and his father work things out. Obviously, they'd discussed getting rid of Rossi Designs, and Jake had refused. Why make matters worse by telling him about Max's threat?

"I suppose you think I'm damn lucky," he said.

"What do you mean?" Actually, she'd thought the opposite. A father who hadn't been interested in his son and a mother who'd died so tragically did not seem to be lucky.

"I've been given a business without having to lift a finger."

"I assumed you earned it by working extra hard for your father." Having seen the ugly side of Max Williams, she was positive this was true. He would be a difficult man to please.

"I've done my best. Max doesn't give compliments, but he officially retired and made me CEO."

"That says a lot."

His dark, earnest eyes sought hers. "I've made a number of very profitable acquisitions since I've been with TriTech."

She tried to joke, but it was difficult knowing Aunt Thee was so ill. "Other than Rossi Designs, tell me about your most interesting acquisition."

"Is this a test?"

"I'm curious, that's all." Knowing more about him made her feel connected to him in a way that was difficult to explain. Here she was in the city where she'd grown up with no one to keep her company in a crisis except a man she hardly knew.

His head dropped back and he gazed up at the ceiling. "Agave. I cornered the agave market."

She racked her brains but couldn't come up with anything. "I give up. What's agave?"

"Cactus. It's a spindly blue plant. When you hack away the leaves you have something that looks like a huge pineapple. It weighs a hundred pounds or more. Chop up the *pina*, roast it in steam ovens and you have the basis of tequila."

"You cornered the tequila market?"

"Damn right. On the yachts I skippered before good old Max decided to reappear in my life, margaritas were the rage. With each drink the guys liked to have a shooter, a shot glass of straight tequila.

"After Max brought me onboard, I started thinking. People were beginning to drink Tequila straight like martinis, and they paid a premium for fine tequila. Where did it come from? How was it produced? The

Kennedys made their fortune from imported Scotch. Why not tequila?''

"Interesting."

"It takes eight years for an agave plant to reach maturity. So what they're harvesting now reflects what was planted when tequila wasn't in demand the way it is now."

"You've made a killing."

He nodded, obviously pleased with himself. "I engineered the deal to purchase the agave fields once owned by José Cuevo and Sauza. To have the word 'tequila' on the label, it must be certified as coming from blue agave plants from the Jalisco region of Mexico. Anything else *cannot* be labeled tequila."

"Like champagne. It has to be called sparkling wine unless it comes from the Champagne region of France, right?"

"Correct."

"Same thing for Chianti and sherry, I think," she said and he nodded, seeming surprised. "See, I'm not just a bimbo who makes jewelry."

"You sure had me fooled."

She socked him in the arm. It felt good to be teasing again, but she wouldn't be able to relax until Aunt Thee was out of the hospital.

"Even my father has been blown away by what tequila nets worldwide. Tequila bars are sprouting up everywhere. People sit down and sample tequila that's been aged for years like Scotch."

"Is it that expensive?"

"Close enough for government work," he said, his tone joking. "Max has to admit I've taken the company in new directions not only with tequila but with other ideas I've had."

"Like what?"

"Like a lot of things." There was an edge to his voice now. "My father was a master of what he did. Times are changing. We need to think globally now. TriTech

started out being a group of Southern companies. Now
we're international.''

She wondered where Rossi Designs fit in. She didn't
view the world in such a big scope. She designed for a
special woman—no matter what country she lived in—
who wanted a unique piece of jewelry.

"Clay, I've been waiting for you."

"Wyatt, what are you doing here so late?" Clay asked.
It was well after midnight and his mind was on overload
from everything Maree and Dante had told him. He
didn't want to deal with his brother-in-law right now.

Wyatt had been waiting for him in the wood-paneled
lobby of the Mayfair Club. Photographs of krewes who
had won awards for their Mardi Gras floats decorated
the walls. Early photographs showed floats that were
laughably primitive when compared with the elaborate
floats of today. From the far end of the lobby came the
faint sound of voices. The bar was still open, but the
lobby was deserted.

"Jake Williams is nothing like his father," Wyatt said.
"He's still digging into Duvall Importing records."

"So?"

Wyatt stabbed the air in front of Clay's face with his
finger. "So, he'll find out about our scheme sooner or
later."

"Don't worry about it." Clay kept walking toward the
bar. "Duvall Importing is part of TriTech now. There's
not much he can do."

"I guess you're right. I still can't help worrying."

Clay walked into the pub-style bar with his brother-
in-law. He waved to the two old-timers leaning on the bar
and chatting. They'd been friends of his grandfather,
important men in their day, but now they didn't have
anything better to do than hang around the club and
drink.

"Two cognacs," he called to the bartender. He didn't

have to say Le Paradis. Joseph had been tending bar at the Mayfair Club for as long as Clay could remember. He knew exactly what each member drank.

"There's another problem," Wyatt said as they sat down in one of the red leather booths. "Phoebe."

Clay almost felt sorry for Wyatt. For years, Wyatt had been in the middle between Clay and Phoebe. Wyatt ran interference for the whole dysfunctional LeCroix family. Hattie LeCroix was a bitch who didn't care about anyone, and her husband, Gordon, survived by working nonstop and spending the rest of his time on the golf course where Hattie couldn't pester him.

Wyatt constantly explained or apologized for one family member to another. It was a family joke that Wyatt should have been a shrink instead of an accountant. He'd changed a lot since he'd been young and Hattie had forced Gordon to send him to military school.

Joseph delivered the cognac in crystal snifters etched with a bold MC for Mayfair Club. Clay took a sip, savoring the ultrasmooth Le Paradis, thinking it was worth every penny and waiting for Wyatt to apologize for Phoebe.

"There's no easy way to say this." Wyatt hadn't touched his drink. "Phoebe wants a divorce."

"What?" Clay said the word so loudly that the men at the bar turned toward them. "It's a joke, right?"

Clay had told Alyssa that he was getting a divorce. It was a ploy to smooth things over between them. Once they were lovers again, Clay was convinced he could persuade Alyssa that his marriage was nothing more than a marriage of convenience. He had absolutely no intention of splitting his fortune with his wife.

"Phoebe isn't kidding." Wyatt knocked back his cognac in a single gulp. "She's in love with someone else."

Clay didn't believe Phoebe was serious, although she'd managed to convince her brother. She'd been in love with Clay since they were in high school. She'd gone to extraordinary lengths to trap him into marriage. Over the years, she'd continually cheated on him—to make him jealous.

"Tell Phoebe to get a lawyer, a good lawyer," Clay replied, determined to call her bluff.

"She's hired Mitchell Petersen."

Clay swore under his breath. His wife had hired the best divorce attorney in the city. What was she up to?

"One more thing, Clay. There's something I need you to do for me."

Clay knew he couldn't refuse. When he'd come to Wyatt, desperate to save his company, his brother-in-law had put him onto the scheme that had saved Duvall Imports. "Sure. What is it?"

"Don't say one word to my parents about this divorce. You know how crazy my mother can get. Hattie adores you. She'll do anything to keep Phoebe from divorcing you."

"I won't mention it," he replied, still trying to come to grips with the possibility Phoebe really did intend to dump him. "Hattie's a little crazy at times."

CHAPTER 15

"How's she doing?" Jake whispered to Alyssa.

It was early evening two days after Aunt Thee had been hospitalized. They'd moved her from the ICU to a private room. Alyssa had hardly left her side, and Jake stopped by each evening to keep her company.

"She's better, and she keeps trying to talk, but her voice is raspy from having the tube down her throat."

"It probably hurts a lot."

Alyssa signaled for him to step into the hall with her. "I have been able to do some work. When Aunt Thee is sleeping, I've been sketching new designs, and going over the proposals for the winter show."

"Don't worry about it."

She couldn't help thinking how understanding Jake could be. He'd been very supportive, something she wouldn't have imagined considering their first meeting in Florence.

A delivery boy walked down the hall, an enormous vase of roses in each arm. He stopped outside Aunt Thee's room.

"Are those for Theodora Canali?" she asked.

"Yes, ma'am."

"She's asleep. If you give them to me, I'll take them inside later."

He put down the two vases and left. She wondered who would be sending such extravagant arrangements. She hadn't phoned her aunt's friends in Italy, so it couldn't be any of them. Jake had already brought a lovely bouquet, and she'd purchased an orchid plant, her aunt's favorite, in the gift shop.

She took the small cards off the spiked card holder in each vase and read them. "They're both from Clay." She spoke with light bitterness. "He doesn't even know my aunt. They've never met."

"They're really for you."

"Then he's wasting his money. Doesn't he understand the meaning of the word 'no'?"

"Do you want my opinion?"

"If you insist."

He chuckled, but there was something unsettling about the way he was looking at her. "Clay Duvall has had everything go his way from the moment he was born. It's hard for him to accept anything else. He has the nothing-can-touch-us confidence of the rich."

"I suppose." She wondered if Clay really was in love with her—not that it would change her mind—or did he see her as a challenge?

"I'd better be going," he said. "I've got a business dinner at Emeril's. If it's not too late, I'll come back when it's over."

"Knock 'em dead," she told him.

He walked away, his jacket hitched over his shoulder, dangling from his thumb, and she watched, thinking of Clay. Men's clothes were designed for bodies like Clay's. Lank, lean. Jake was a shade too tall, a bit too muscular, but infinitely more masculine, sexier.

Aunt Thee didn't know Clay, but she knew what had happened with the baby. Clay hadn't openly accused Alyssa, but he hadn't defended her either. Aunt Thee had just met Jake, but she had taken to him immediately.

The beautiful bouquet he'd brought last night had made her aunt's eyes sparkle. She'd been too ill to talk, but Alyssa knew her well enough to realize how much Aunt Thee liked Jake.

Jake didn't seem to realize he was moving into their lives with amazing ease. Alyssa kept telling herself that becoming close to someone you worked with wasn't a good idea, but she seemed powerless to stop it. In Italy, she would have had many friends to see her through this ordeal, but here she felt alone and vulnerable. It was comforting to have Jake's support.

At the far end of the corridor, just as he was about to disappear from view, Jake turned and waved with a grin. He had a melt-your-heart smile, she thought, waving back. No wonder Aunt Thee couldn't resist him.

She tiptoed into the room, carrying one vase at a time, and placed them where Aunt Thee could see the flowers. Closing the door behind her to keep out the noise in the hall during visiting hours, Alyssa sat down beside her bed. There was just enough light coming from the bank of machines monitoring Aunt Thee's condition for Alyssa to sketch.

Ideas came quickly—for a change—and she had over half a dozen new pieces of jewelry in her sketch pad before she checked her watch and realized two hours had elapsed. No one had come in to check on her aunt. Typical, she thought. The crisis in medical care meant the nurses were overworked. If there had been a critical change in her aunt's condition, the machines would have alerted the nurses at the nurses' station.

But if her aunt had been thirsty or uncomfortable, no one would have known. Alyssa assured herself that staying beside Aunt Thee was the only way to make certain she was taken care of properly. She didn't want her aunt to suffer for one moment, so she'd kept the bedside vigil, sleeping sitting up in the chair and going home only to shower and change.

Alyssa heard her aunt trying to talk and jumped up. "Do you need something? Should I call the nurse?"

Aunt Thee slowly shook her head. "You ... I need ..."

Alyssa bent closer. "Yes?"

"I need ... to tell ... you ... something."

Her aunt had been trying to talk to her for two days now. Alyssa kept putting her off, believing it could wait until her aunt's throat had healed. Now, though, she seemed frantic.

"What is it?"

Aunt Thee motioned for Alyssa to help her sit more upright. She adjusted the pillows behind Aunt Thee's back, taking care not to dislodge the IV attached to her right arm.

"Better?"

Aunt Thee nodded, then took a deep breath. "I—I want you ... to know something."

"Can't it wait? You shouldn't be talking yet."

"No. I've waited too long."

The ominous note in her voice caused Alyssa to brace herself. She had the disturbing thought she would remember this moment forever.

"My brother. . . Robert Rossi ..."

"What about my father?" she asked, amazed to discover the image of her father was nothing more than a blurry, watercolor memory of a dark-haired man with amber eyes like Aunt Thee's.

"My brother, Robert ... Robert Rossi met your mother when she was a sophomore at Newcomb College. He fell for her ... well, what can I say? He was so head over heels in love with her that he asked me how to make Pamela Ardmore love him."

"Why didn't she love him?"

"Who knows? They'd begun dating that spring, but your mother moved out to the Delcambre Resort on Gulf Shores to work during the summer." Her tone implied something terrible had happened there.

"What happened?"

"Your mother met someone else at the resort." She gazed at Alyssa as if she had more to say but couldn't bring herself to say it. Finally, she continued. "Well, you were the result of a summer . . . affair."

"A summer affair? Are you saying . . ." She broke off, searching for words to express herself. Had she heard what she thought she'd heard?

"Robert Rossi was not your father."

Robert Rossi, the man who'd loved her so much, the man she'd called Daddy, was not her father. She was the result of a summer affair. An emotional vise cinched around her chest, causing a sharp pain and bringing her dangerously close to tears.

"I'm so sorry, dear. I should have told you years ago."

"Who is my father?" Alyssa whispered the question, positive if she spoke normally, she'd start to cry.

"A young man from New Orleans who played the drums in a rock band that performed on weekends at the resort. Your father loved your mother so much," Aunt Thee continued, heartfelt emotion in every word. "He didn't confess he was already engaged."

"Why not?"

"Thirty years ago . . . even today, parents manipulate their children. Your father loved your mother, but he didn't have the courage to cross his parents."

A host of conflicting emotions warred inside her. Anger, sadness, and above all, an acute sense of betrayal. Her mother had loved a man enough to conceive a child, but he hadn't had the guts to marry her. "Mother could have . . ."

"Yes, she could have had an abortion, but she didn't. Robert called me to tell me what he was going to do. He knew your mother was pregnant, but he wanted to marry her anyway."

"Why?"

"Robert adored your mother, and she came to love him. They had a happy marriage." She reached for

Alyssa's hand, and she took her aunt's frail hand. "They both loved you very much. Never doubt that."

"Why didn't you tell me sooner?"

"Guilt. Plain and simple. I felt tremendously guilty about not adopting you myself after your parents died, but I was living in Italy and Charles had just been diagnosed with Parkinson's."

"A young child would have been too much. I understand. You called me each month to see how I was, and you never forgot my birthday." Alyssa didn't tell her that no one else remembered. Why make her feel any worse?

"No. A child would not have been too much. I just thought you'd be better off . . ."

"In America."

There was a long, bewildering silence, then Aunt Thee said, "No. I thought you'd be better off with your real father."

The words detonated on impact, siphoning the air from her lungs. The room slammed to an abrupt halt. The dim lights now seemed unnaturally bright. Sound ceased. She saw her aunt's lips moving, but the words didn't register.

Uncle Gordon was her father. Memories rippled through her thoughts, then crystallized on a single memory, the day she came to live with the LeCroix family. They had been strangers to her; she'd never met any of them before the funeral the previous day.

Phoebe looked amazingly like her, but from the first moment, Phoebe had made it clear Alyssa wasn't welcome. Wyatt had been friendlier in a loud, boisterous way. Hattie and Gordon LeCroix had regarded her with tight-lipped silence.

Even though she was young, Alyssa had known something was terribly wrong. She was shown into their house, a home much grander than her parents', and taken to a small bedroom off the kitchen. It wasn't until later that she learned there were two empty bedrooms upstairs where the family lived.

It didn't matter. She'd gotten the unspoken message. She could live in this house, but she would never be part of the family. The world around her had seemed so empty, so threatening—so intent on betraying her. Even though he must have known she was feeling isolated, vulnerable, and desperately needed comfort, Gordon LeCroix had tried to be friendly, but he'd allowed Hattie to drive him away.

"Alyssa, Alyssa." Her aunt's voice seemed to come from a great distance. "Are you all right?"

She mustered the strength to nod. "Gordon LeCroix is my father?" she asked, praying it wasn't true, needing for it not to be the truth.

"Yes, he is."

"But you said he was a drummer in a band."

"He'd played in a band when he was young. He met your mother the summer after he'd finished law school. He was taking time off before he went to work in his father's law firm."

"He never said a word. I never would have guessed. Never." Betrayal whiplashed through her. There were so many times he could have made her young life easier, but he'd never really tried. How could a father do that to a child?

"Gordon loved your mother even after he married Hattie. He tried to see her, but she wouldn't have anything to do with him."

Alyssa battled a wave of dizziness and nausea. "Oh, my God! That's just like what happened to me."

Aunt Thee's smile seemed bleak. "Yes. So I've noticed."

"My mother must have known Hattie and Gordon were engaged. Did she deliberately try to break them up?"

"No. Even though they were cousins, the families weren't close. They rarely saw each other. The Ardmores were the poor cousins who lived in Baton Rouge. Hattie's engagement wasn't going to be formally announced until September when Hattie and her parents came home from spending the summer in the South of France."

"Gordon LeCroix—" she couldn't call him 'father'—"didn't lift a finger to help me when I was accused of abducting little Patrick."

A too familiar ache of despair swept through her as she recalled being taken to the police station for questioning. Some wounds never fully heal and she knew this one never would, especially now that she knew her father had been right there.

"Don't be too hard on Gordon. He's a weak man. He should have broken his engagement and married the woman he really loved, the woman who was carrying his child, but he didn't want to go up against his father. When the baby disappeared, both his daughters were involved. He called me. That was the best he could do."

Alyssa let go of her aunt's hand and slumped back in her chair. She gazed at the bank of machines that were ticking and blinking and burbling, but she didn't see them. In her mind's eye she saw Uncle Gordon over the years. He'd seemed quiet, withdrawn, and interested in nothing but his legal career and golf.

She tried to recall their private conversations. He'd asked her how she was doing, but she had the impression he was just being polite. Each week he'd slipped her a little money. "Our secret," he'd say.

"I wish I'd brought you to Italy. I could have spared you so much pain." Her eyes were awash with unshed tears, pleading for forgiveness. "I never imagined what you were going through. I believed Hattie had forgiven Gordon—"

"You don't know Hattie."

"When I called to check on you, why didn't you say something . . . anything to let me know how they were treating you?"

Alyssa shrugged, feeling emotionally drained and physically exhausted. "I was afraid to complain. If it got back to Hattie, no telling what she would have done."

Hattie had been hard on all three children, but most of all—Alyssa. Gordon hadn't been strong enough to stop her. Now she understood that Hattie had been making Gordon pay for loving another woman. And she'd been punishing an innocent child who knew nothing about it.

Hattie had never physically abused Alyssa. Most of the time she ignored her, but if Alyssa did anger Hattie, she knew how to destroy a child with just a few well-chosen words. Sometimes emotional terrorism was worse than physical abuse. It left scars that couldn't be seen.

"I'm sorry, so sorry." Aunt Thee was crying now.

Alyssa stood up and plucked a Kleenex from the bed-side stand. She dabbed at the tears streaming from her aunt's eyes. "Please, don't cry. You were there when I needed you the most. That's what counts."

Slowly, Aunt Thee's tears subsided, and Alyssa sat down again. Her aunt closed her eyes, and her eyelashes glistened in the dim light.

"Why did you tell me now?" Alyssa asked.

Aunt Thee didn't open her eyes. "In case I die. You have a right to know the truth."

"Oh, Aunt Thee, you're not going to die," Alyssa assured her. "The doctor said it was a very mild heart attack. Lots of people have pacemakers and lead very normal lives."

"I hope you're right." Her voice sounded weak.

Alyssa slumped back in the chair and stared up at the acoustical ceiling. Phoebe was her half-sister. All those years she must have known. It explained so much.

Oh, my God, she thought. Little Patrick was her nephew! She'd always felt an acute sense of anguish about the baby. Now that feeling intensified when she realized how closely they were related. What could have happed to him?

"Go home," Aunt Thee said, her voice a little stronger now. "You need your sleep. I'm better now. I don't want you spending the night in the chair."

Alyssa hesitated. She'd been hoping Jake would come back, but when she glanced at her watch, she saw it was nearly midnight. "All right. I do need a shower, and my own bed sounds great. I'll be back first thing—"

"CODE PINK! CODE PINK!" The voice blared into the room from the hospital's public address system. "CODE PINK! CODE PINK!"

Warning spasms of alarm erupted inside her. Considering all that had happened, the last place Alyssa wanted to be was in a hospital where a baby was missing.

CHAPTER 16

"What's wrong, dear?" asked Aunt Thee.

"Code Pink. It's . . ." She hesitated to use the word "scary," but it was frightening.

"What is Code Pink?"

"A hospital code like Code Blue. Code Pink means a baby is missing."

"Really?"

"They'll lock every possible exit. No one can leave the hospital until Security checks them to make certain they don't have the baby." She thought a moment. "If the code had been used when little Patrick was abducted, the tragedy would have been prevented. Other states were using it but not Louisiana. They adopted it a few months after his disappearance."

"When too much time lapses before the infant is missed, no code procedure can save him."

"You're right." Alyssa tried to imagine losing her own baby. She knew she'd be frantic and her heart went out to the mother whose child was missing.

Two sharp raps sounded on the door, then it swung open. A security guard and a young policeman with a clipboard walked in followed by a nurse. The prickle of uneasiness she'd been feeling intensified.

"We have a situation," said the policeman. "A baby has been taken from the maternity ward on the floor below this one."

"That's terrible," Aunt Thee said, and Alyssa managed to nod her agreement. "What happened?"

"We're not sure, ma'am." His tone implied he knew but wasn't discussing it.

While he was talking, the nurse peeked under Aunt Thee's bed, and the security guard checked the small bathroom. Alyssa told herself not to be intimidated. She hadn't done anything wrong.

"Have you seen anyone or anything suspicious?"

"No. I haven't been out of this room in hours," she answered.

"I'll need your name for the record."

She told him, thinking he was too young to have been on the force when the Duvall baby had vanished. He probably wouldn't recognize her name, but when she told him, his brows drew together. Suddenly, it was impossible to steady her erratic pulse.

"Alyssa Rossi," he repeated. "Why is your name familiar?"

Alyssa smiled—or tried to—and shrugged.

The nurse, the same surly redhead who'd been on duty for the last two nights, stepped forward. "Ravelle did a piece on her recently."

"Oh, yeah?" Clearly, he knew who Ravelle was but he must not have seen the broadcast from the party. Alyssa became increasingly uneasy under his scrutiny but forced herself to keep looking directly into his eyes.

"She was involved in another baby's disappearance. Ask her." The nurse brushed by the officer and stomped out the door with a belittling huff.

"Is she right?" he asked, looking her over as if she might have the baby under her skirt.

"Yes. It happened years ago." The metallic taste of fear made it difficult to talk normally. "My cousin's baby was taken not long after I'd visited the nursery. I had nothing to do with it and no charges were filed."

"I remember the case," said the beefy security guard. "The baby was never found." He moved to block the door, seeming to expect her to make a run for it.

"The police were certain a black market ring took the child," Aunt Thee said.

The cop studied the tips of his shoes for a moment. "Don't go anywhere. I'll need to—"

"CODE PINK CLEAR! CODE PINK CLEAR!"

A wild flash of relief ripped through her. She turned her back on the men and walked over to her aunt. The older woman tried to reassure her with a smile, but didn't succeed. Alyssa clutched her hand like a lifeline.

"Looks like they've found the baby."

"Am I free to go?" Alyssa asked without looking directly at the officer. They'd opened the door and were leaving.

"Of course. Sorry about the mix-up."

The second the door closed, Alyssa collapsed into the chair beside the bed. "For a moment there, I thought I was going to be blamed again."

"I wouldn't let that happen."

"Thank you. It's important to know someone cares."

Even though Aunt Thee was smiling, sadness lingered in her amber-brown eyes. "I couldn't love you more if you had been my own child."

"I love you, too. What you told me tonight doesn't change anything between us. It's shocking. Actually, it's disgusting to know Gordon LeCroix is my father."

"You favor your mother. Not only do you look like her, you have her brains and artistic talent."

"I hope I'm not—well, how can I put it?—emotionally detached like Gordon LeCroix. I want the people I love like you to know I care."

"You've always been a very loving person. You'll make a wonderful wife and mother. Don't worry about it."

Her aunt closed her eyes for a moment, and Alyssa knew she'd overexerted herself.

Aunt Thee opened her eyes saying, "Why don't you go home and get some rest? I'm going to sleep myself."

Alyssa stood up and kissed her aunt's cheek. "I'll be back first thing in the morning."

Out in the hall, she saw a group of policemen at the far end of the corridor. The exit was the other way, and she walked off as quickly as possible without attracting attention.

Why was she so jumpy? They'd found the missing baby. Thank heavens, it was not a repeat of what had happened to Patrick Duvall. The incident had frightened her and had made her feel young and vulnerable, the way she'd been years ago.

She wondered how Phoebe had felt when her baby had been kidnapped. She'd assumed—perhaps mistakenly—that Phoebe had been involved. There was something strange about the whole affair, but it was possible Phoebe had nothing to do with it.

Knowing Phoebe was her half-sister, not her second cousin, made Alyssa more sympathetic. She decided Phoebe had known all along Alyssa was her father's illegitimate daughter. That would account for her contemptible behavior.

Should I try to talk to her?

Alyssa crossed the deserted lobby and walked outside. Going from the air conditioning to the warm, moist air caused pinpricks of moisture to pepper the back of her shoulders, then begin to creep downward.

Should I talk to my father?

It was an even bigger question. Part of her wanted to confront him and make sure he knew she had found out the truth. What good could come of it? If he'd wanted to have a relationship with her, there had been enough opportunities. Maybe she should go on pretending she knew nothing.

It certainly would be easier.

She told herself that she wasn't hurt, and it was true. Long ago, the LeCroixs had lost their power to hurt her. She was grateful she hadn't known the truth when she'd been living with them. She'd been devastated by the loss of her parents. If she'd realized Gordon was her father, the way he acted could only have been interpreted by a child as the worst kind of rejection imaginable.

She didn't know what she felt, what she should do. Entering the nearly empty parking lot, she decided a good night's sleep would help. She'd like to talk to someone about this. Not just anyone. Jake.

He would understand because he'd been rejected by his father. At least Max had finally decided he wanted a relationship with his son. She doubted Gordon would ever feel the same way. He didn't seem connected to anyone in his family. Even though he accompanied his wife to numerous social functions, it was obvious he lived for his career and golf.

"Alyssa," called a male voice from the shadows of the parking lot.

"Jake, is that you?"

"No, it's not Jake." Clay Duvall walked forward.

She was so tired her nerves throbbed. The last thing she wanted to deal with was this man and the reminders of their past.

"Are you all right?" he asked before she could speak. "You look upset."

Something clicked in her weary brain. Clay had been at the hospital on the day his son was born, and he was here tonight when another infant had vanished. Could he, would he have done something so terrible?

She halted a few feet from her car, then moved aside so the light from the overhead fixture illuminated Clay's face. "Tell me the truth. Do you know what happened to your son?"

"I have no idea. None. I've asked myself a thousand

times what could have happened, but I don't have an answer except I know you weren't responsible."

If he was lying, he deserved an Academy Award. His low-pitched voice contained an edge of concern as well as sympathy for her.

"Why?" He put his hand on her shoulder.

"Tonight there was a Code Pink here. They just located the baby."

"No wonder I couldn't get in. There was a policeman guarding the entrance. I assumed some celebrity was visiting—" His hand tightened on her shoulder and the warmth in his voice vanished. "Hey, you don't think I had anything to do with it, do you?"

She was completely honest. "I'm so exhausted. I don't know what to think."

He put his arm around her. "Let me drive you home."

She wanted to tell him to leave her alone, but she was too overwhelmed by all that had happened in the last few hours. She started to refuse, then decided this was an opportunity to ask Clay a few questions.

Clay's arm circled her shoulders, and he guided her to his low-slung Masarati. It was fire engine red, but definitely not built for a woman as tall as Alyssa. Inside, her head almost touched the ceiling.

He drove quietly through the nearly empty streets, and she was conscious of her shoulder brushing against his. Handsome and sophisticated, Clay would appeal to most women, the way he'd appealed to her years ago.

"Clay, what has Phoebe told you about me?"

"Let's get some coffee and talk."

She almost insisted he take her home but changed her mind. There were questions Clay could answer without her having to contact any of the LeCroixs. They were near Frenchmen Street, and he drove the Masarati fast, its engine roaring like a caged tiger.

Bourbon Street in the French Quarter was very much like Times Square in New York, she thought. Frenchmen Street was a smaller version of Greenwich Village with its hip clubs being the heart of the music scene in the city. She hadn't been here since her days at Tulane, and she was too exhausted to appreciate its quaintness now.

They rocketed down the street and screeched to a stop in front of Check Point Charlie, one of the better known clubs. The parking valet rushed out to take his car. Ever the gentleman, Clay quickly came around and opened the door for her. The smile on his face disconcerted her, and she wondered if she'd made a mistake by coming here.

They walked inside the club where the waiter escorted them to a table in the corner at a distance from the stage where a rock band was playing. She marveled at how the club managed to pack the house even though it was midweek. It wasn't a quiet place to talk.

"Why are we at a club? There are lots of great places for coffee."

"Not much is open this late and we were close. The best new talent opens here."

"Clay—"

"Hi, I'm Mindy Jo," interrupted a blond waitress in red leather shorts and a bustier. "What can I get for you?"

They ordered two cappuccinos, then he asked, "Go on, what were you saying?"

She hesitated a moment. What if Phoebe didn't know they shared the same father? Did she want her to find out? Suddenly discussing this with Clay seemed like a terrible idea. She rolled the dice, hoping she wouldn't regret it.

"Phoebe . . . I was wondering if—"

"If I knew she was a nymphomaniac—"

"Are you serious?" Alyssa couldn't quite believe it. Phoebe had always been flirtatious to the point of being obsessed with men, but was her sister addicted to sex?

"Yes. I'm dead serious. Phoebe couldn't resist men— especially older men like her father."

Her father. Alyssa stared at Clay, wondering. Had Phoebe groveled for her father's love only to discover he couldn't care less? Was that why she enjoyed seducing older men? It was twisted, but from what she'd read, women who felt rejected by their fathers, often went for older men. They were subconsciously searching for a father figure to add meaning to their lives.

"Are you implying one of those men was the father of the baby?"

"Possibly. She was seeing Bubba Pettibone on the sly."

"The mayor?"

"Back then he was a councilman, but Bubba was married. There were others, too. Ask Wyatt, he'll tell you it's the truth."

"Phoebe was crazy about you. Everyone knew it."

"True," he responded without a trace of conceit. "We'd dated in high school, but she liked to run on the wild side and meet older men. I'm not denying I had sex with Phoebe. The baby could have been mine."

The anguish in his voice startled Alyssa. At least he was being honest, she thought as the waitress arrived with steaming mugs of cappuccino topped with a mountain of whipped cream and chocolate shavings.

"It's over between us. I'm getting a divorce."

He'd told her this the last time she'd seen him. Alyssa spooned the delicious whipped cream off her drink and didn't comment on his marital problems.

"Has Phoebe ever told you anything about my parents?"

"Your parents?" He said the words tentatively as if testing the idea. When she nodded, he added, "You mean about your father?"

She realized he knew and wondered how long he'd known. "Yes."

"You're Gordon's daughter. Phoebe claimed you didn't have a clue."

"I found out recently. Phoebe's known for a long time, hasn't she?"

"At your parents' funeral, Gordon spoke with your aunt. Since she was your closest relative, people assumed you would go live with her." He drank a little cappuccino before continuing. "Gordon went home and confessed the truth to Hattie."

"Knowing Hattie, there must have been a real blowup."

"No question about it. Gordon stood his ground and insisted on bringing you to live with them. There was so much shouting that Phoebe and Wyatt overheard their parents. They immediately knew you were their half-sister. Hattie swore everyone to secrecy."

"She didn't want to be embarrassed in front of her friends."

"Exactly. She kept you out of sight and out of their lives as much as possible." He shook his head. "I thought there was something wrong with you because you never appeared at family parties. Like I told you, a lot of people thought you might be retarded."

"I know. Even though I went to public school, where most of the children's parents weren't in the same social circle with the LeCroixs, word got around." She masked her inner turmoil with a deceptive calmness. That part of her life was over, thank God. "Clay, why didn't you tell me about Gordon? We were close ... once. You could have told me."

He leaned forward and covered her hand with his. "I cared about you too much to hurt you. After the way the LeCroixs treated you, I thought you'd be crushed if you knew about Gordon."

She withdrew her hand, thinking that young, vulnerable girl might have been devastated to learn the truth. But she wasn't that girl any longer. She could handle the truth now.

"Clay, do you think I ought to talk to Phoebe?"

"About what?"

His incredulous expression was her answer, but she told him anyway. "About being her half-sister."

"There's nothing you can say or do to make Phoebe like you. Trust me."

"She doesn't have to like me. I just think we should talk."

He leaned closer, his handsome face grave. "Look at it from Phoebe's point of view. Hattie always made a big deal about your good grades. When you got into Tulane on a scholarship and Phoebe was rejected, Hattie pitched a fit."

"I had no idea. Phoebe insisted she wanted to go to Old Miss because so many Mardi Gras queens had gone there." She gazed at the last bit of foam floating in the center of her cup. "I always felt inferior because Phoebe was prettier and had fabulous clothes and a convertible."

His gaze was as soft as a caress. "You're just as pretty. More important, you're smart and creative. Phoebe peaked when she was Mardi Gras queen. You've gone on to make something of yourself. I'm proud of you."

She wondered if her father was proud of her. He acknowledged her excellent grades and praised her for winning a scholarship to a first-rate college, but she'd interpreted his compliments as being nothing more than a Southern gentleman's response to the situation. He'd never made her feel he actually cared.

"Aren't you going to ask me why I've stayed with Phoebe all these years?"

"No. It doesn't matter."

"I stayed because Duvall Imports got into financial trouble about a year after we were married." A vein twitched on the side of his throat. "Phoebe's trust fund saved the company."

The band took a break, and she said, "I'd better get home." She knew where this was going but had no intention of encouraging him by discussing his marriage.

He reached across the small table and took her hand. "Give me another chance. I still love you."

She pulled her hand away. "I meant what I said. It's over. Don't divorce Phoebe on my account."

CHAPTER 17

"Here's the report from Overton and Overton." Troy handed Jake the document.

"What does it say?"

"Duvall Imports was on the verge of bankruptcy about eight years ago. The money from Phoebe LeCroix Duvall's trust fund saved the company. Winston Duvall retired and Clay took over. He turned the company around."

"Reassuring." It *was* possible Clay knew what he was doing. Doubtful, but possible. Maybe he'd just gotten lucky.

Jake had been in his office since seven. He hadn't been able to sleep and would have been in earlier except Benson insisted on going for a walk. Jake had given in, knowing rain was predicted and the poor dog wouldn't get any exercise if he didn't take him then.

"What does it say about Wyatt LeCroix's accounting practices?"

"They had one fine from the IRS for understating Duvall Imports earnings, but that's it," Troy added. "Nothing underhanded."

Jake thumbed the report. "Not very many pages, considering it took so long."

"Forensic accounting is mostly research. They go over the numbers and compare them with other companies in the same business." Troy sounded a bit defensive. "Overton and Overton doesn't pad their reports the way some accounting firms do."

"Okay, I'll read it."

Troy left, and Jake stared at the cover sheet on the report. He should read it, but he doubted he could concentrate. He was all kinds of pissed. He'd pulled up to the parking lot last night in time to see Alyssa getting into Clay's Masarati.

He told himself that he didn't give a damn. The real kicker was he'd believed her when she'd told him that Clay was history. Think again.

Alyssa had almost brought him back to life again, making him want to do something besides work. For years now, he'd driven himself hard, playing catch-up. Damn her. She'd made him want so much more.

If he drove himself hard enough again and got back into the groove, he could forget her. When he was putting a deal together, he was excited and edgy. Pulling it off, there was no bigger high. He'd start looking for another deal to distract him.

He skimmed the report on Clay's company and looked for the part mentioning Wyatt LeCroix's accounting firm. He read it too fast and didn't find it. The document did seem a little brief to have taken so long. But what did he know? If Clay Duvall was a turnaround artist, corporate America was in trouble.

Maybe he was just jealous. He hesitated to label the twist in his gut last night as jealousy, but it was possible. He'd watched Clay put his arm around Alyssa and something very ugly mushroomed inside him.

Normally, he made every attempt to set aside personal feelings. He was usually right about people. When he'd met Clay, Jake's sixth sense had kicked in and told him the guy couldn't be trusted.

So what if Clay was sophisticated and had a business

degree from a top-notch university? So what if he drove a Masarati and had a home on Audubon Street? So what if women were bonkers about him?

Jake was still convinced the guy was a scumbag in an Armani suit. If Alyssa still loved him, well, hey, it was her problem. They deserved each other.

He returned some calls and ran a spreadsheet on his computer, one of his favorite activities. Today it was about as exciting as watching flies screw. He stared at the screen but saw Alyssa's smiling face. He could almost hear her laugh. The genuine happiness of her laughter brought her closer to him in a way words could not.

Face it, shmuck, she's never far from your mind.

Spencer buzzed him and said, "Zane Welsh is here . I know he doesn't have an appointment. Do you have time to see him?"

"Welsh. The *Times-Picayune* reporter?"

"Yes. He says it's important."

Welsh was a respected investigative journalist. Jake read his pieces with interest. When he wasn't investigating a homicide, he was exposing corrupt politicians. Since it was common knowledge Max planned to run for the Senate, Jake assumed this was about his father.

He hesitated a moment, wondering if there were skeletons in Max's closet he didn't know about. Probably. New Orleans, the whole state, was full of corrupt politicians and bureaucrats salivating for a bribe. Who knew what his father might have done on his way up the slippery ladder of success?

"Send him in."

The fiftyish reporter was short and built like a fireplug with a barren head peppered with freckles. What remaining hair he had was pulled back into a scraggly gray ponytail.

He was wearing jeans and a denim jacket with the sleeves cut out. The blue plaid shirt he had on underneath was rolled back at the cuffs to reveal a tattoo of a tarantula. He would have been right at home in a biker bar.

"I like your articles." Jake shook his hand, then gestured toward the chair opposite his desk. "Have a seat."

Welsh sat down without acknowledging the compliment. Not a good sign.

"I need to ask you a few questions about Alyssa Rossi."

Aw, crap. If he'd known, Jake wouldn't have seen the man. "What about her?"

"I understand you two are involved."

"Nope. She heads one of our companies. That's all."

"At your father's party I was told you—"

"It was a joke. Okay?"

Welsh's expression remained flat, unreadable, but Jake suspected the jerk knew he wasn't telling the whole truth. He did his damnedest to look sincere, but faking it wasn't his long suit.

"That explains why she was out at Check Point Charlie's with Clay Duvall last night."

He hoped his expression didn't reveal how royally pissed he was. "So?"

"Duvall's married."

"It must be a slow day for news. You don't usually write about extramarital affairs."

The guy didn't take the bait. He kept studying Jake as if he were a rat in the lab, and he was about to dissect him. Welsh was not his idea of a fun guy.

"I'm investigating a kidnapping. Last night a baby was taken from the nursery at Mercy General Hospital."

Shock seeped from every pore, racing through his body with a mind-numbing punch. He wasn't sure how long it took him to recover enough to ask, "Do the police have any leads?"

"They found the baby in a storage room down the hall from Theodora Canali's room."

"Really?" He was going to pretend he had no idea who she was, but that would have been pushing his luck.

"I'm checking into a link between this attempted

kidnapping and the disappearance of the Duvall baby years ago." He shifted in his chair, and gave Jake what was meant to be a smile, but he might have been showing off his capped teeth. "You know what I find interesting?"

"I give up. What?"

"Alyssa Rossi was accused of taking Duvall's baby, yet he purchased her company, and he's obviously seeing her. He was spotted at the hospital last night. I think there's a connection between the two cases."

"You could be on to something."

"What do you think happened?"

"How would I know? I didn't realize a baby was missing at the hospital last night."

"Don't you watch the news?'

"No. I read the paper."

Haar Haar. Was he supposed to be laughing? Definitely not a fun guy, but he undoubtedly had excellent sources and knew Jake had been at the hospital earlier in the evening as well as the two previous nights.

"You might want to interview Clay Duvall about this. He's one floor down."

"He's in Baton Rouge today."

"We're buying a company there." True, but he hadn't known Clay was involved in the acquisition.

"Are you always this way?"

"What way?"

"So irreverent."

"Most people would go ahead and say I'm an asshole."

"You know what I think?"

"I hate to be the bearer of bad news, but I don't give a damn what you—or anyone—thinks about me."

Welsh stood up slowly and flipped his ponytail with his hand in an obviously unconscious habit. "For what it's worth, Alyssa Rossi has been taken to the police station for questioning." He headed toward the door. "You may have two employees in deep Tapioca."

Deep Tapioca? Why didn't he just say deep shit? Jake cursed under his breath as the door closed. Not for one minute did he believe Alyssa had touched either baby. But something was going on.

She got herself into this mess. Let her get herself out of it. Better yet, let lover boy Duvall get her—or them—out of it.

He picked up the telephone and called Troy. "Is Duvall working on the Ab-Cam deal?"

"No. Roth's handling it."

"Do you know why Duvall is in Baton Rouge?"

"I have no idea. His secretary might know."

Of course, Miss Silicone had no idea where he was. She hadn't been able to reach him on his cell phone.

Weird. Friggin' weird.

He went back to his spreadsheet. He could have been reading hieroglyphics for all the sense the numbers were making. Why had he been more obnoxious than usual to Welsh? He wasn't a man who lied and never to himself, but it took him a few minutes to admit the truth. He was crazy about Alyssa Rossi and angry with her for lying about Clay, so he'd taken it out on the reporter.

Very mature.

He swiveled his chair around and stared out at the sky. Clouds laden with moisture sulked over the Mississippi and made the river appear more gray than its usual brown color. He noticed the wind had risen, driving the incoming storm closer and whipping up whitecaps on the water.

Alyssa didn't have any friends here unless you counted the secretary she'd brought with her from Italy. He doubted she would know a criminal lawyer to call. He knew plenty of attorneys from TriTech's business deals but none of them specialized in criminal law.

Forget it, he told himself, but he couldn't. He kept seeing the way she'd looked when her aunt had been in surgery. She might not care about him, but she cared deeply about Aunt Thee. Her aunt was in no position to help her, but he was.

He swung back to his desk and flipped through his Rolodex, then called Sanchez's cell phone. "It's Jake. Do you know a good criminal lawyer?"

"I'm an attorney. I entered the FBI academy after they changed the rule requiring agents to be an attorney first, but I figured passing the bar would come in handy, and it has."

"Are you licensed in Louisiana?"

"Yes. What do you need?"

He explained, and they arranged to meet at the police station.

"She's being questioned, but she hasn't asked for an attorney," the sergeant told them when they informed him Alyssa Rossi's attorney wanted to see her.

"She has a right to an attorney," Sanchez insisted. "You're violating her civil rights."

A home run. The sergeant's lip curled, and any fool could tell he was holding back a choice four-letter word.

"All right," he said grudgingly. "She's down the hall in room seven."

Sanchez walked down the long corridor. Jake stayed at his side and the sergeant didn't challenge him. Civil rights worked wonders. Sanchez knocked on the door and it immediately swung open. Jake looked into the small room and saw Alyssa sitting across the table from a detective.

"Who are you?" asked the second detective, blocking the entrance with his body.

"Rueben Sanchez. I'm Alyssa Rossi's lawyer."

"She hasn't asked for a lawyer."

"Mental telepathy," Jake said and Sanchez elbowed him in the ribs.

"She's being questioned voluntarily," said the detective opposite Alyssa.

"How long have you been questioning her?" Sanchez asked.

"Almost four hours," Alyssa answered, a hitch in her voice.

What a bunch of jerks. Jake clamped down his jaw before he got himself in trouble and blew it for Alyssa.

"That's too long not to have a lawyer with you," Sanchez said. "As your attorney I advise you to allow me to speak with you before you answer another question."

"I want to speak with my attorney," Alyssa said.

The two detectives looked at each other, obviously not happy campers. They gathered some papers off the table and prepared to leave the room. Sanchez walked in and Jake followed him.

"Just a minute," said the detective who'd answered the door. "Who are you?"

"A paralegal specializing in civil rights."

They left without a word.

"What's going on?" Sanchez asked.

Jake wanted to go over to Alyssa and put his arm around her but resisted the urge. She offered him a welcoming smile. He lifted his shoulders. He meant his shrug to say: Who cares if you're happy to see me? But he didn't quite pull it off.

"They've been asking the same questions for hours," she told Sanchez, but her eyes never left Jake's.

He had to admit she was damn good. Most men would be fooled into believing she was glad to see him.

"They kept wanting to know if I'd left Aunt Thee's room and had taken the stairs down to the nursery. I hadn't left the room at all, but it looked suspicious because the linen storage room where they found the baby is close to the stairs and it's right down the hall from my aunt's room."

"Sounds like a setup to me," Jake said. "Someone knew you were at the hospital. They framed you."

"Like before." Her voice was pitched low.

"I'm going to insist they charge you or let you go," Sanchez said.

He left the room, and Jake stood where he was near the door. Alyssa rose and walked over to him. She put her arms around him and rested her head on his shoulder. "I knew you'd come. I knew I could count on you."

He almost told her that he'd come because he'd liked her aunt. She reminded him, in a strange way, of his mother, but he didn't. Alyssa seemed so genuinely thrilled to see him that he couldn't bring himself to hurt her.

Okay, so she had a thing for Clay Duvall. Half the women in town did. It didn't mean she'd taken the baby.

His arms were around her before he knew it, and he allowed himself to breathe in the fresh floral scent coming from her hair. The image of Clay, his arm around these very shoulders, hit Jake like a sucker punch to the gut. His body stiffened and he dropped his arms.

For a minute she didn't notice. Her arms were still around him, the heat of her body seeping into his. Then she seemed to realize what she was doing and released him.

"I'm not the clinging type, honest," she told him. "The one person in the world who loves me is ill. Aunt Thee is probably frantic. I was supposed to be back at the hospital early this morning. I'm frightened, but more than anything, I'm angry. Who's doing this to me? Why?"

CHAPTER 18

"Tell me what happened," Sanchez said.

"The police appeared at my door this morning, asking questions. I volunteered to go down to the station. I don't have anything to hide."

"Four hours is a long time. They were trying to make you break down."

"I know, but I refused to allow them to frighten me. That's why I didn't ask for an attorney. I thought it would make me look guilty."

She didn't sound like herself at all. She'd been intimidated when the hospital sounded the Code Pink, but when the police had rung her bell early this morning, a cold fury crept through her, strengthened the knowledge she was no longer a vulnerable young girl.

They were gathered around the coffee table in Jake's loft, Benson at their feet. The crush of reporters had forced them out the service exit at the police station. She hadn't been able to go home because there were more reporters hovering around her front gate.

Just about the last place she wanted to be right now was at Jake's. He'd driven her while Sanchez had followed in his car. Jake had said almost nothing to her except to suggest she use his car phone to call Aunt

Thee. She'd placed the call and reassured her aunt. Out of the corner of her eye she'd watched Jake. He checked the rearview mirror to keep track of Sanchez, but he didn't pay any attention to her. No doubt, she was bringing unfavorable publicity to TriTech and he resented it.

"This whole thing sounds like a setup to me," said Jake.

Sanchez nodded, thoughtfully. "Looks that way. The question is why?"

"Do you have any idea?" Jake asked her.

"None." She thought about his father's threat, but decided not to mention it. Jake was hostile enough as it was. Anyway, whoever had done this wanted to link her to the abduction of the Duvall baby. It didn't seem to be Max's style.

"It was designed to get you in trouble without actually having enough evidence to warrant your arrest," Sanchez added. "The media would convict you."

"How do you know what evidence they have?" Jake asked Sanchez.

"I don't. By their questions, they don't have her fingerprints in the storage room, and they don't have a single witness who can place Alyssa in the maternity ward."

"Because I was never there."

Sanchez gazed at her with sympathy in his dark eyes, but Jake turned his attention to Benson and was preoccupied with petting the dog. His physical presence tugged at her with a force she hadn't anticipated. She wanted to be sitting next to him on the sofa, his nearness a comfort the way it had been when they'd waited for Aunt Thee to come out of surgery, but he didn't want her close to him. She'd already embarrassed herself enough by throwing herself into his arms when he'd arrived at the police station.

"Is there something—anything—you can think of that might help me?" Sanchez asked.

She hesitated, reluctant to tell them about her real father. It would be humiliating to admit how badly the LeCroixs had treated her while her father had stood by, not caring. What could it have to do with this incident?

"What aren't you telling us?" Jake asked.

He was more perceptive than she would have imagined. He was watching her intently, giving her the feeling she was on trial.

"There is something I just learned, but I don't think it has anything to do with the case."

"You'd be surprised how seemingly unrelated incidents are linked," Sanchez told her. "I can't help you unless I know everything."

"Maybe you'll be more comfortable if I leave." Jake stood up.

"There's nothing I can't say in front of you."

"It's all right. I have to get back to the office anyway." He couldn't have appeared less interested.

She told herself not to let it bother her. She had more important issues to deal with, but she couldn't help being a little hurt. She'd thought they'd become closer these last few days. Considering the way Jake had acted when Aunt Thee had been taken to the hospital, Alyssa had expected Jake to be more supportive now. Instead, he couldn't wait to distance himself.

"What is it you haven't told me?" Sanchez asked when Jake closed the door behind him.

She confessed that Gordon LeCroix was her real father. He didn't seem particularly surprised.

"Stranger things have happened," he finally said, then changed the subject. "I understand Clay Duvall was at the hospital last night."

"He was waiting for me outside. He couldn't get in because the building was in a Code Pink lockdown."

His expression stilled and grew serious, but he didn't verbalize what he was thinking. Benson came over and put his head under her hand, silently demanding she take up petting duty.

"Clay's divorcing Phoebe. That's what he came to tell me. Earlier he'd sent flowers to my aunt. He's trying to persuade me to give him another chance, but I'm not interested."

"I don't like coincidences. Clay has been on the scene twice when babies disappeared."

"The thought occurred to me, too, but why would Clay do such a thing?"

Sanchez arched one eyebrow. "It doesn't make any sense, does it?"

"No. Clay would have a hard time pulling it off. He isn't exactly the type of man who could sneak into a nursery without being noticed. He's too good looking."

"I'd agree but in hospital greens people tend to look alike. There are lots of men trooping in and out of the delivery room these days—all of them in greens. I'll show his picture to the staff and see if anyone recognizes him."

"Maybe I'm being naïve but I don't think Clay would hurt me."

Sanchez's expression said he had his doubts. "When his son disappeared, Clay Duvall didn't have an alibi. He'd been at the hospital earlier. Then he'd gone home to get some sleep, but no one could substantiate his story."

"Why would he kidnap his own son?"

Sanchez didn't have an answer.

"Clay thinks there's a good chance the baby wasn't his. He claims Phoebe was . . . is promiscuous, and she has a thing for older men."

"He's right. There's hardly a well-known man in this town who hasn't been approached by Phoebe. The chase is more fun than the catch, apparently. She dumps them quickly."

"Clay said Bubba Pettibone could have been the baby's father. If the mayor fathered her child, it could ruin his career. There were others, too. Phoebe was supposed to be at Old Miss but she had a flat in the French Quarter. She entertained several older men."

"It's possible one of them took the baby to protect himself. Clay planned to have a DNA test as soon as the child was born." Benson nudged her hand, and she realized she'd stopped petting him. She fondled his ears, saying, "Assuming one of those older men did take the baby, they wouldn't have any reason to take another baby."

"You wouldn't think so, but we could be missing something."

"Did you locate Gracie Harper's husband yet?"

"No. He vanished after the divorce. Usually we can track down people through IRS records, but he hasn't filed a return in years."

"I thought those records were confidential."

Sanchez almost smiled. "They are but some of us have ways of getting the information. I suspect the nurse's husband is working somewhere and getting paid in cash. That way he doesn't have income the feds can tax."

"Then you may never find—what was his name?— Claude." She was glad she hadn't pinned her hopes on this new lead.

"I'll find him, if he's still alive. I'm checking DMV records in nearby states. Most people don't stray too far from where they grew up. When they do, they go to Alaska or California. They always get a driver's license."

"He could have changed his name."

"I don't think he did. By all accounts, he was a good old boy with no criminal record and no child support payments to avoid. That's the reason most men change their name. If he did, the DMV computers will pick up his fingerprints and let me know."

Again, she experienced a flare of hope, but she tamped it down.

"If all else fails, I have my secret weapon," he assured

her with another smile. "There's a central database that registers warranty cards people send in. Most big-ticket items like televisions and computers and stereo equipment get registered. Even if you're doing your best to hide, the temptation to protect your investment is impossible to resist."

"Why not check this database first?"

"It's harder to get into."

"Harder than the IRS files?"

"Sure. Everyone thinks about the IRS files. Checking warranty cards doesn't occur to as many people. You have to pay someone with access to the confidential files."

"I don't want to get my hopes up," she admitted. "Claude Harper may not know anything."

"I disagree. Most people can't keep a secret. They're very likely to tell their spouses or a close friend. Gracie didn't have any close friends. The other nurses at the convalescent hospital where she was working said she kept to herself. My money's on the former husband. He knows something. They had a very fancy wedding a few months after the baby disappeared. All the bills were paid in cash."

"Really? Why didn't any of the investigators discover this?" she asked, angry that this hadn't been unearthed earlier.

"The police investigation was concluded *before* the wedding. According to their reports, no unusual amount of money appeared in her account. There weren't excess funds in Claude's account either. The private investigators hired afterward didn't check closely enough to discover the whole wedding had been paid for in cash."

She stroked Benson's head thoughtfully. "You think someone paid off the nurse."

"It's a definite possibility. The police have no leads in her killing. It couldn't have been robbery. Nothing was taken. I suspect they killed her to shut her up."

"It could be coincidence that she had arranged to meet you."

"Like I said, I don't buy all this coincidence."

"You're probably right. I want to see this solved. It's been a monkey on my back for years now."

He regarded her silently for a moment. "Is there anything else you haven't told me? Even if you don't think it pertains to the case, it might be helpful."

She doubted Max's threat had anything to do with her problems, but it might. "Max Williams wants me out of TriTech."

When she finished explaining how Max had threatened her, Sanchez asked, "Did you tell Jake?"

She shook her head. "No, and I'd rather you don't say anything either. I don't want to come between a father and his son."

"I understand," he said. "Max has underworld connections. He—"

"He does?"

"It's not unusual in New Orleans. It's always been a corrupt city with an active criminal element. Max started with warehouses on the wharves where the wise guys are most active. He had to spread a little money around and establish a few connections to get ahead."

"He has political ambitions. Won't this hurt him?"

Sanchez chuckled, and she realized how naïve she sounded. "It hasn't hurt any of the politicians so far. I'm not saying Max is trafficking drugs or anything, but he knows the right people. If he wanted to take care of you, all he had to do was make a phone call.

"Taking a baby isn't their style. Trust me. I worked in the FBI profiling unit for two years. There are male crimes and female crimes. Women rarely strangle or stab anyone, yet men often do. Women are more likely to shoot or poison their enemies."

"You're saying taking a baby is something a female would do."

"Yes, in this case where it appears the intent was to make you *look* guilty. The Duvall baby may be a different story. It's possible the real father took the baby, or Clay might have taken the baby for his own purposes."

"You don't buy the theory a black market ring stole the baby."

"No. There is an underground network in babies. Sometimes they trade over the Internet, but if they got their babies by stealing them from hospitals, there would be a national outcry." He shook his head, dismissing the idea. "It doesn't mean the baby wasn't handed over to the black market, but they didn't abduct him from the nursery."

She had to admit everything he said made sense. Ghosts of the past no longer rushed at her, promising to bring back the pain, the helplessness. Not only was she older and stronger and better able to protect herself, but she had a true professional working on the case. Her spirits lifted just a little.

The answer to this complex mystery was out there. It hovered in the distance like a mirage, but it was visible. Her enemies were not going to get the best of her. Not this time.

Sanchez rose. "I've got work to do. Stay out of sight. Don't talk to the media. I suggest you spend the night here."

"I can't stay here. In case you haven't noticed, Jake isn't exactly thrilled with me right now. I'm embarrassing him. What would it look like if someone discovered I spent the night with him?"

"I've known Jake for years, and I can tell you the last thing he worries about is what people think."

"But TriTech—"

"Is a private company. A conglomeration of companies. Except for Rossi Designs, what you do won't have any fallout for them."

"He's upset with me about something."

"You spent hours facing down the NOPD. You have more guts than most men under the same circumstances. Don't tell me you're afraid to ask Jake what's wrong."

CHAPTER 19

"This is just so like, embarrassing," said Ami Sue when Clay walked into his office in the middle of the afternoon.

"What?" He couldn't help being irritated. He'd been in a foul mood since Alyssa had turned him down again last night. Who in hell did Alyssa think she was?

"Everyone's been calling. The newspapers. Television. Radio stations. I'm your secretary. I'm supposed to know where you are. I so, like, didn't know what to do. I couldn't get you on your cell phone. It was *sooo* embarrassing."

He'd deliberately turned off his cell phone. Threesomes in the sack were getting to be fun, a way to keep his mind off Alyssa. Why would he want to be disturbed?

"The battery is out on my cell phone." He stopped at the starry-eyed blonde's desk and picked up a stack of messages. He tried to remember why he'd hired Ami Sue. She was nearly thirty but talked like a teenager who hung out at the mall. Oh, yes, he recalled as he glanced at boobs fit for a porn queen. He was saving her for a rainy day.

"What's all the fuss about?"

Didn't she read the papers or watch the news? "Someone tried to take a baby from Mercy General last night."

"Oh, that's, like, so . . . terrible."

"Don't tell anyone I'm in," he said, opening the door to his private office. He planned to let the media dangle. The more they wanted you and had to fight for you, the longer your interview.

"Not even Mr. Williams? He's called three times."

"Jake?" he asked, and she bobbed her head. "I'll call him."

Clay expected Jake to ask why he'd been at the hospital last night, the same question the media was salivating to know. He intended to avoid the media, but Jake was different.

He'd concocted a "special" story to tell Jake, one sure to drive a wedged between Alyssa and Jake. Alyssa had called him would be his explanation, of course. She'd begged him to come. He'd gone to the hospital reluctantly, still believing she hadn't been involved in the kidnapping of his own son. Naturally, he'd been too trusting. She must have been the one involved in this latest babynapping.

He'd known Jake was going to be at Emeril's, having a business dinner last night. It had all played out quite nicely—especially the disappearance of another baby while Alyssa had been at the hospital. He'd say he took Alyssa to Checkpoint Charlie's because she was so stressed over her aunt. Going to the club had been her idea. Of course, he hadn't suspected she really wanted to spend time with him..

After all, not only was he drop-dead handsome, he was a nice guy. A woman like Alyssa Rossi could take advantage of him. Jake would buy the story and it would serve her right. If she wasn't under arrest right now, she was cloistered with some criminal attorney trying to figure out how she'd gotten into this mess.

She'd probably call him and ask for help. He could hardly wait to spell out his terms. Alyssa Rossi wouldn't have any choice. She would be forced to give him another chance.

He thumbed through the stack of messages, but none of them were from Alyssa. One was from Mitchell Petersen, the lawyer Phoebe had hired. He decided to call him back and see what was going on.

Phoebe had been ominously quiet. He'd phoned the house today, and the maid told him she'd gone away. Knowing Phoebe, she had run home to Mommy and Daddy. It took a few minutes, but he finally got through to the lawyer.

"I thought I'd put you on notice, as a fellow krewe member," Mitchell said, and Clay almost laughed. The lawyer was a member of the Orion krewe, but he hardly participated. Still this was a small town where the Duvall family packed a lot of clout. No doubt, Petersen respected this. "I've filed divorce papers on behalf of your wife. You need an attorney. We need to settle the spousal support question ASAP."

Shit! That bitch planned to make him pay royally for bringing Alyssa home. Worse, he didn't have anything to show for it. Alyssa seemed to mean what she said. She didn't want to have anything to do with him. Phoebe was going to drag him through the muck.

"You're right," he replied, injecting a note of humor into his voice. "I need an attorney. Could you recommend someone?"

By the time Clay hung up, he had a name, and he was fried. At Phoebe. At Alyssa. Women were nothing but trouble.

He was in a spiteful mood, and he decided to go up and talk to Jake in person. He wanted to see the look on his face when Clay told him how Alyssa had called and begged him to come to the hospital.

His attitude didn't improve when the fag Jake had hired instead of a looker like Ami Sue kept him waiting for fifteen minutes.

He plastered a smile on his face and sauntered into

Jake's office as if he had the world by the tail, which he did. Dante and Maree had a plan that would make them all rich. Technically, Clay was already wealthy, but why limit himself? On the other hand, what Dante proposed was risky. He needed to consider the proposition carefully.

"You wanted to talk to me?" Clay stood in front of the massive oak desk that had once belonged to Max Williams. Why didn't Jake get his own furniture?

"Yes. I need to—"

The phone rang and cut him off. Clay glanced down at the terminal and saw it was the interoffice line. The fag had deliberately interrupted them, he decided.

"Ask them to wait just a few minutes." Jake hung up and looked at Clay.

He waited, savoring the moment. Jake acted more and more like his father every day. He had an imperious attitude that made Clay want to tear him down. He was nothing more than the captain of a sport fishing fleet who'd gotten lucky because his father had been even luckier and somehow had managed to catapult a warehouse business into TriTech.

"I wanted to talk to you about Duvall Imports' books."

"Books?" Clay responded. Not Alyssa?

"Yes. Specifically the accounting."

"What about it?" Clay recalled Wyatt's warning. How much did Jake know?

"I'm going to have the accounting done here at TriTech, the way the rest of our companies are handled."

Ah, ha! Jake didn't know anything. This was a cost-cutting measure. "Wyatt LeCroix's firm has always done our accounting. Importing isn't like other businesses. It requires special techniques. TriTech has a great accounting department, but no one is familiar—"

"Rossi Designs also imports—"

"Not the way we do. We're bringing in ship after ship with containers. Rossi Design's orders wouldn't fill a tenth of a container." At least they were finally working their way around to Alyssa. Before Clay laid his story on Jake, he had to persuade him that switching the accounting was a terrible idea. Clay couldn't afford to have anyone knowledgeable in the sophisticated area of importing inspect his books too closely.

"TriTech is acquiring another importing company, Pacific Rim Imports. You've heard of it?"

All Clay could do was nod. Pac Rim was the leader in Asian imports and made Duvall Importing look like a third tier company.

"I'm moving their accounting team here. They'll take care of all the import accounts. They've done it for a long time and have a superior track record."

"I'd rather keep Duvall's accounts with Wyatt. He's always handled us and understands our business."

"I know Wyatt's your brother-in-law and this is difficult. Just blame me. Tell him I didn't like that IRS fine and insisted on the change."

"What IRS fine?"

"For understating your earnings."

"Understating?" He scrambled to think what Jake could mean. If anything, Duvall Imports overstated—everything—but Jake couldn't know that.

"Two years ago you were fined for understating earnings."

Jake sounded so sure of himself Clay couldn't respond. He had absolutely no respect for a man who grew up on the Redneck Riviera and never graduated from college, taking night courses instead. But he had to admit Jake didn't blow smoke. He had his facts down and kept numbers in his head like a computer chip despite his lack of a formal education.

"We've never—ever—been fined by the IRS." Clay could feel the heat creeping up his neck and knew his face would be scarlet in a second. It rarely happened, but when he was really angry, he turned red and pinpricks of sweat appeared on his upper lip. "Before my father retired, we were in financial trouble, but that was straightened out. We've never had an IRS fine or any other problem with them."

"You might check with Wyatt," Jake said. "He probably forgot to tell you about the fine."

Clay knew enough to keep his mouth shut.

Jake continued, "Pac Rim won't come onboard for another two months. That'll give Wyatt time to prepare the books for transfer."

Clay's swallowed hard and resisted the urge to wipe away the film of moisture on his upper lip. He wanted to throw Alyssa in Jake's smug face but couldn't think of a way of doing it and still sound professional.

"On your way out," Jake said, picking up the telephone, effectively dismissing him in a rude way, "there are two detectives from the NOPD. They want to talk to you about a missing baby."

Flushed with humiliation and furious, Clay made himself a promise. Jake Williams was going to pay.

Bewildered, Jake watched Clay leave. The man seemed dead sure his company had never been fined by the IRS. Jake's first reaction was to reread the forensic accountant's brief report, then he changed his mind. He was over double-checking himself all the time. He'd made damn few mistakes and this wasn't one of them.

Was Clay lying?

He didn't trust him—not for one second. Clay had mastered the art of being convincing and charming, but this time he seemed really nervous. Clay's face had become flushed and he'd been sweating. Live and learn.

Jake picked up the phone and punched Spencer's line. His secretary answered immediately. "Are those detectives questioning Duvall?"

"They've taken him to the station."

Jake detected an undercurrent of glee in Spencer's voice. Who could blame him? Clay Duvall was about as homophobic as they came. He put down Spencer to Jake every chance he had until Jake told him to mind his own business. A pinup for silicone implants might be what Clay needed in his office, but Jake wanted someone a hellava lot smarter working for him.

"Really? They're interrogating Duvall?"

Jake suspected his voice betrayed some inner sense of satisfaction as well. He told himself it wasn't Clay's fault Alyssa still loved him, but it didn't quite ring true. He could still feel the suffocating sensation of his throat tightening, the way it had last night when he'd seen Clay's arm around Alyssa.

"Yes. They took him away."

Jake couldn't help smiling. He hoped the police had something to go on besides coincidence. Two babies abducted. Clay on the scene both times. Somehow he doubted any man as slick as Clay would be caught this easily, assuming, of course, he'd done it.

"Is Troy around? I need to talk to him."

"Hold on. Let me check with Thelma and Louise."

Jake almost smiled—for the first time today. Thelma and Louise were the nicknames Spencer had given Abigail and Alexis, two middle-aged lesbians who worked as Spencer's assistants. They did all of Jake and Troy's work that wasn't important enough to demand Spencer's personal attention.

Spencer came back on the line. "He's still at lunch."

"Again? It's almost four."

Spencer was strangely silent. "I guess."

"Okay."

Jake hung up. Spencer never guessed. He *knew*. That's why Jake had hired him. He'd known from the moment he'd met Spencer that he was the epitome of efficiency and intelligence. Nothing got past Spencer Farenholt. Nothing.

Jake walked out to Spencer's desk. "What's going on?"

Spencer looked him in the eye, and Jake realized he

was right. There was something Spencer wasn't telling him, and it concerned Troy.

"Tell me. I won't say a thing." Jake knew Spencer had divided loyalties since he reported to both Jake and Troy. "I promise."

"Something . . . is wrong." The words came out slowly as Spencer looked up at Jake. "Troy isn't himself. He's gone most afternoons. He keeps calling Paris."

"Paris?" Troy was returning home to run one of his father's businesses. It shouldn't surprise him. Troy had done nothing to explore New Orleans even though it offered a rich selection of arts and music and women. Troy's heart belonged to Paris.

Jake didn't get it, but then, you either loved Paris or you were intimidated by the Parisians. He had to admit he didn't get it. Maybe a youth spent in Mobile, Alabama, ruined your ability to go bananas over a bunch of frogs who spent hours eating and the rest of their time talking about wine and art. Oh, well.

"He's also contacted a travel agent. I think he's planning to leave . . . with someone."

Two beats of silence while Jake tried to imagine being on his own without Troy. He'd realized it would happen eventually. *Face it. You're on your own.*

Jake expected to feel a second of unease, but he didn't. He'd known this day was coming from the moment he'd persuaded Troy to stay on with TriTech. Jake figured he might not be totally ready, but hey, would he ever be one hundred percent confident? Now was as good a time as any. He needed to get his mind off Alyssa. What better way to do it than to be forced to concentrate on TriTech's business?

"Spencer, don't mention any of this to Troy," said Jake. "I'll take care of everything."

His mind was on Alyssa. How was she doing? he wondered. This had to be an ordeal for her. Even if he blamed her for being involved with Clay, he still didn't believe she had anything to do with either baby's disappearance.

He picked up the telephone and instructed Spencer to connect him with Overton and Overton. The forensic accountants assigned to analyze Duvall Imports were in Chicago. He explained who he was, and they transferred him to Simon Overton.

"I've read your investigation of Duvall Imports' books," he said. "I'm curious about the IRS fine."

"What fine?" Simon asked. "I prepared the report. There wasn't any IRS fine."

"A-a-a-h, perhaps I was mistaken—"

"It was an interesting scam. If you don't straighten it out, you are going to have big-time trouble with the IRS."

Son of a bitch, Jake cursed under his breath. "How long was your report?"

"Don't you have a copy of it?"

"I don't think so."

"It was about two hundred and fifty pages."

"No wonder it took so long."

"Long? I analyzed that company in less than a week."

"Of course, sorry. So much is going on around here." Where in hell had that report been? "Could you have your secretary fax me another copy?"

"We sent four copies. Can't you find any of them?"

Jake didn't give a damn if he sounded incompetent. "No. Have her fax me another copy at this number." He gave Overton his home fax number.

Jake thanked him and hung up. He rocked back in his chair and studied the ceiling. It took some time before his mind adjusted to what could only be a cover-up on Troy's part. Why? What did the report say that he would want to cover up? It was possible, more than possible considering the way Clay had acted today, that he'd paid Troy to keep quiet.

Someone had altered the report. It would be easy enough with the computer scanners to scan Overton and Overton's letterhead. Writing the report, using forensic accounting lingo, would be more difficult. That's why the report was much shorter than the original.

Then it dawned on him. Max was responsible for this, not Clay. Troy wouldn't have risked his professional reputation for someone on a lower level. Even though Max had retired, there were a lot of people who thought of him as the owner of TriTech.

Assuming his analysis was correct, why would Max want a company like Duvall Imports? The answer had to be in the report itself. His split-second decision to send it to his home was dead-on. He didn't want anyone to know he suspected a thing until he knew exactly what was happening.

CHAPTER 20

It had taken Alyssa over an hour to go back to the hospital and sneak into the parking lot to retrieve the car she'd rented when she'd arrived from Italy. She'd wasted another half-hour going to the French Quarter only to find a coven of reporters outside Aunt Thee's house. She hadn't bothered going inside. She called Clay's house from a pay phone and found out Phoebe was spending the next several days at her parent's home.

The guard at the gate of Audubon Street, where she had once lived with the LeCroix family, still remembered her and waved her into the compound of expensive homes. The LeCroix home was at the far end of the street, where Jake's father had bought a mansion. The other night when Alyssa had been there, she'd blotted out memories of her youth, but now they rushed back into her consciousness with a vengeance.

A small child walking up the street alone, not realizing this was among the most exclusive neighborhoods in New Orleans. Nothing was going to bound out from behind the immaculately clipped shrubs to pounce on her. Later, she saw herself as a middle school student trudging her way up the street in the pouring rain, her books in her backpack. In either scenario no one would be there to greet her. Hattie LeCroix was always gone or upstairs resting. Verna, the housekeeper, who was formally in charge of Alyssa, was too swamped with work to be bothered.

Alyssa had been all alone, the way she was today. Now, there was one difference. Someone cared—Aunt Thee.

"They have company," Alyssa mumbled under her breath as she approached the place she'd called home for so many years. Luxury cars lined the drive. No doubt, Hattie was having a tea or a committee meeting for one of the myriad charities she joined in order to show off her home, her clothes, her jewelry.

Alyssa rang the bell and waited, hearing the faint murmur of voices. Finally, a uniformed maid Alyssa didn't know answered the door.

"I'm here to see Phoebe Le—Duvall," she said.

"They're in a meeting, Miss—"

"Tell Phoebe it's an emergency. Alyssa Rossi is here to see her."

The maid backed away, and Alyssa couldn't tell if she'd recognized her name or if her firm tone had persuaded her. She didn't care. What mattered now was talking to Phoebe.

After Sanchez had left her in Jake's loft, Alyssa had paced the rooftop deck with Benson, thinking. Bloated clouds with leaden underbellies had clustered overhead, promising rain soon. Benson had taken his time, but finally left a healthy deposit on the turf that had been planted especially for him.

By then, Alyssa was determined to talk to Phoebe. They'd lived under the same roof—this roof—for all those years, but they hardly knew each other. They looked alike, but had little in common except a father who had rejected them.

And a brother. Wyatt was closer to Phoebe, of course, being her full brother. Still, he was also related to Alyssa. Looking back, she realized Wyatt had been kind to her—in his own way. Hattie had been absorbed with comparing the two girls and ignored Wyatt. She guessed he'd never felt the same level of competition that Phoebe had.

"This way," the maid said a few minutes later.

She led Alyssa into the small library adjacent to the living room. Alyssa rarely had been in this room when she'd lived with the LeCroix family. It had been Gordon's exclusive domain even though he was seldom in the house.

She glanced around, inhaling the sweet scent of the Cuban cigars Gordon smoked in here, indulging his bad habit despite Hattie's disapproval. The shelves were lined with books and golf trophies. She'd forgotten how good a golfer Gordon was. He'd won the club championship several times and had other trophies as well. Among the many photos of his golfing buddies, there wasn't a single photograph of the family.

"Alyssa . . . what are you doing here?"

Phoebe spoke in a hushed voice as if she didn't want the women down the hall to know what was happening. Alyssa faced the person she'd always thought of as her cousin. Her half-sister. Her father's other daughter.

"I need to talk to you." She motioned to the two wing chairs opposite Gordon's desk.

Phoebe took the chair beside Alyssa, like a reigning queen, her back rigid, her chin tilted upward. "Hurry up. The committee is waiting for my report."

For a heartbeat, Alyssa studied the face that was so much like her own. They were sisters. They shouldn't be enemies.

"We're sisters. I just found out."

Phoebe arched one plucked eyebrow. "You should have realized the truth a long time ago."

True. Alyssa silently admitted she had been too intimidated to look beyond what she'd been told. She was stronger now, thanks to Aunt Thee's love.

"Don't you think it's time we acted more like sisters?" she asked.

"What?" The single word echoed through the small room like the brittle crack of a rifle. "Don't you dare come waltzing in here expecting me to welcome you just because you figured out we're half-sisters. Forget it. You want Clay."

"I don't care about Clay. I—"

"Don't lie to me." Phoebe's voice kept getting louder with each word. "You've always loved Clay. You'd do anything to break us up."

Alyssa couldn't believe how stubborn and irrational Phoebe was. "I've lived in Italy for years now. There's nothing between Clay—"

"Really? Then what were you doing last night at Check Point Charlie's?"

Alyssa had known better than to appear at such a public spot. Obviously, someone had seen them and reported it to Phoebe. "I wanted to talk to Clay about you."

Phoebe sat up straighter—if possible—and trained her eyes on Alyssa. "You did. Why?"

"I wanted to ask him if he'd known we were sisters not just cousins." She waited for a response from Phoebe, but received nothing more than a hostile stare. "He said he'd known for years."

"So what?"

"I also asked him if I should try to patch up our differences."

Phoebe leaped to her feet, yelling, "It was just an excuse to be with Clay."

Alyssa motioned for her to calm down and kept her voice low so they didn't disturb the meeting. "This isn't about Clay. It's about us."

"What's going on?" Hattie asked as she burst into the room followed by several other women.

"She's after Clay," Phoebe insisted.

Hattie leveled Alyssa with the censuring glare she'd remembered from her childhood. "Leave now."

Alyssa looked beyond Hattie and saw Ravelle Renault

standing in the hall. Criminy! Clay was right. This had been a terrible idea.

"Get out!" screamed Hattie.

Alyssa rose slowly and left, ignoring the hostile stares of the women gathered in the hall. What had she hoped to accomplish? For years, Phoebe had known the truth. What had made Alyssa think that Phoebe would now be willing to discuss their differences?

She wanted to go home and change clothes, but a bevy of reporters was standing in front of Aunt Thee's town house. Suddenly, heavy plops of rain pummeled the windshield of the car. Within seconds the rain became a torrential downpour, the kind that often flooded New Orleans.

She had no choice but to go back to Jake's. She drove over to the Warehouse District and spotted a parking space a pizza delivery van had just vacated. She pulled in, grateful she was less than a block from Jake's loft.

She slipped out of the subcompact and dashed for the loft. She found the key she'd hidden—just in case—under the fifth pot on the way up the stairs.

"Jake? Jake?"

No one answered when she unlocked the front door. Benson greeted her with an excited bark and a slather of kisses on her extended hand. It was too early to expect Jake to be home. She could take a hot shower while drying her soaked clothes before having to deal with him.

She knew Sanchez was right. Jake didn't give a hoot what people thought. He was giving her the deep freeze for some other reason. She was going to ask him and hope she had more luck than she'd had with Phoebe.

Rain hammered the skylight and filled the huge loft with the racket. She flicked on the lights and walked across the room. Benson trotted behind her as she went into the kitchen to use the telephone.

Alyssa called Aunt Thee's room, but a nurse answered and told her Aunt Thee was sleeping. Her condition had improved and they expected her to be released tomorrow. She hung up, hoping by tomorrow she'd be yesterday's news and she could bring Aunt Thee home without having to run a gauntlet of reporters.

Jake left the office early. He wanted to see what the fax from Overton and Overton revealed. He'd arranged to have Sanchez meet him here instead of the office. He unlocked the front door and expected Benson to greet him. The retriever wasn't anywhere in sight. A female voice coming from the bathroom was singing "Amazing Grace."

Alyssa. Aw, hell. He thought she would have gone home by now. He didn't want to deal with her. Too much was happening, too fast He didn't want to believe Troy, his main man, had done this, but there wasn't any other explanation for the altered report Jake had seen. Disillusionment and a bone-deep sense of betrayal left him tight-lipped, repressing his anger, his hurt.

Worse, he didn't want to find out Max had been behind the scheme. They didn't have much in common, but Jake had become accustomed to having a father. He wanted to believe Max trusted him to run the company on his own.

If the emotion Jake was riding had been simple anger, he might have cooled down by now. But it wasn't. They'd turned on him.

Would he be forced to go back to Mobile's docks? Possibly. Would he give a damn? Yes. . . and no. He'd grown these last few years. Mobile and the sport fishing fleet he still owned seemed like a distant memory, a life that had belonged to someone else. Yet Mobile was a safe harbor. He could go home again, but he'd always ask himself if he'd missed something.

He put down his briefcase and hung up his raincoat

on the hall tree he'd purchased at Aunt Annie's Antique Shoppe down the street. He shrugged out of his sport coat and removed his tie.

What was he going to do about Alyssa? Before he could answer his own question, she came out of the bathroom at the far side of the loft.

Wearing nothing but a towel.

Like a siren, she called to him, urging him to come closer and be destroyed. Fool that he was, Jake had been prepared to do anything for her.

"Oh, my God!" she shrieked, jumping to one side. "What are you doing here?"

"I live here, remember?"

"I know. You frightened me." She clutched the towel around her. "I wasn't expecting you to come home so early. I got caught in the rain, so I put my clothes in the dryer and took a hot shower. I hope you don't mind."

"It's too late if I did." He knew he sounded like a real prick, but he couldn't help himself. Just thinking of Alyssa with Clay sent a rush of scalding fury through his body.

"Is there a robe or something I could put on while my clothes dry?"

Without a word, he walked into his bedroom and took his robe off the hook inside the large armoire he used as a closet. He walked back into the living area where she was waiting for him. Benson, the traitor, was beside Alyssa, gazing up at her with adoring eyes, tail wagging. He handed her the robe and turned to go into the office area to check the fax.

She caught his arm. "I need to talk to you."

"So talk."

She slipped into the robe and belted it without taking off the towel. "Let's sit down."

He sat in the chair to prevent her from sitting beside him on the couch. "I'm in a hurry. I've got work to do."

She sat on the sofa opposite him, her expression concerned. What did she expect from him?

"I can tell you're upset with me. I want to know why."

He wanted to blow off this whole situation. He knew better than to get involved with a woman who worked for him. Trying to think of something to say, he gazed at her. He hated liars and refused to demean himself by not telling the truth.

Still, male pride, or whatever, kept him silent. He did not want to admit he was jealous of Clay Duvall. Doing so would give Alyssa power over him, something he'd never given a woman before now.

"I don't like being in the middle of a mess like this," he said.

"I know what you mean. I've been nothing but trouble. I'm sorry," she replied, sounding genuinely upset. "You've been very understanding. I would never have expected as much from . . . anyone in your position."

He nodded, unsure of what to say.

"Forgive me for embarrassing you—embarrassing TriTech with my problems."

"Embarrassed? I'm not embarrassed. Why would you think I am?"

"I know this is a difficult time, but you keep distancing yourself from me." She leaned across the coffee table as if to close the space between them. "Even though I've thought we had become close."

"Close?" He spit it out as if it were a four-letter word.

She studied his face intently, her eyes narrowing. "Is this about my being with Clay last night at Check Point Charlie's?"

He considered denying it, but knew he'd be pissed with himself if he did. "No. Not exactly," he hedged. "You claim you can't stand Clay. You pitched a fit when you found out he was part of TriTech. Yet every chance you get, you're with him."

"No, I'm not! He came by the hospital last night, and I was very upset over the Code Pink. I had this terrible feeling, and I was right. I would be blamed. Something else happened, and I wanted to talk to you in the worst way."

"What about?"

"It doesn't matter now. You don't want to get involved. I understand." She stood up. "I'm sure my clothes are dry by now. I'll get dressed and go."

He watched her walk away. Getting sex had always been a cinch. He never looked beyond the moment. He'd never wanted a lasting relationship until now. Face it, schmuck, she's got your number.

A bolt of lightning arced across the sky and flooded the loft with searing blue-white light. Half a second later a crack of thunder like an explosion rattled the windows. He couldn't let Alyssa go out in this storm. He lunged to his feet and followed her to the laundry room concealed behind screens at the far side of the loft. The dryer was still running, and he thought her clothes weren't done.

He stepped around the screen and stopped. Alyssa was standing there stark naked. His heart seized, and he couldn't draw a breath. Sweet Jesus.

He'd never seen her without clothes, but he'd imagined it once or twice. Okay, more than once or twice. Too many times to count. His wildest dreams were nothing compared to the real deal.

Time halted, seconds fractured. Neither of them looked away. In the shadowy darkness her eyes seemed greener than usual. She made no attempt to cover up even though his robe and the towel were on top of the washing machine close by.

His eyes roved over her body. Not centerfold material but damn close. High full breasts crowned by dusky nipples. A small waist. Slim tapered hips. A triangle of downy golden hair. Long, showgirl legs.

A jolt of quivery heat spread through his body. Every muscle in his body tightened with primal need. Aw, hell. He was achingly hard.

Inwardly cursing his own weakness, he reached out

and touched her bare shoulder. His fingertips skimmed downward, barely maintaining contact as he traced the soft curve of her breast. The nipple formed a tight bead. He cradled her warm breast in the palm of his hand and brushed his thumb across the taut nipple.

"Jake."

Something about the erotic way she whispered his name, so softly he could barely hear it above the rain pummeling the skylight, extinguished what remained of his willpower. He smothered her lips with his. He didn't want to hear what she might say. He didn't want to think or rationalize or anything. He intended to lose himself in her. Regrets could come later.

CHAPTER 21

Jake grabbed her, his momentum pushing her backward half a foot until she was trapped against the washing machine by his weight, and his lips covered hers, hot, demanding. A sudden, unexpected explosion of warmth streaked through her body and erupted in a rush of desire. Her instinctive response to him overpowered her better judgment. A few minutes ago he'd been angry and she had been ready to leave. Now she was allowing him to kiss her.

She should have grabbed the towel and covered herself, but the expression on his face had been so galvanizing. Raw lust smoldered in his eyes. She'd realized immediately this was her opportunity to break through the protective barrier he kept around himself. She'd never resorted to using her sex appeal, but this wasn't an ordinary situation.

Had she fallen in love with him? No, surely not. She needed his strength, his friendship, to help her weather this crisis. That's all.

His tongue, sleek and agile and swift, mated with hers. Her heart beating lawlessly, she kissed him with shocking passion. The more familiar she became with his body, the more she wanted, the more she sought, moving against him, letting her hands explore his back and shoulders down to the rise of his buttocks. And lower.

She attempted to shift to one side, but he had her pinned against the cold machine. Heat radiated from his body flowing into hers and triggering a rush of dampness. Her taut nipples tingled where they were flattened against his chest. Her breath left her body in a tortured moan.

Her arms were around his neck now, her fingers in his thick hair. She wanted to feel every inch of him—especially the bulging erection jutting against her. She was tall for a woman, but he was taller. She had to stand on tiptoes to position his erection where it would feel even better.

He rhythmically moved his hips, slowly at first, a counterpoint to the stroking motion of his tongue. Picking up the pace, he ground against her, making absolutely clear what was coming next.

Dimly she noticed another bolt of lightning followed by an ominous crack of thunder, then the staccato beat of what had to be hail pinging against the skylight, but the sounds barely registered. Her body was too focused on feeling the rough texture of his whiskers where they brushed her sensitive skin, the solid strength of his body against hers, the iron heat of his sex.

He pulled his head back, his breathing ragged. He went rigid, every muscle tense, his face a grimace.

"Why . . . are you stopping? Come on."

"Listen."

Above the noisy thud of her heart, she head the clatter of hail on the skylight and Benson barking. Then the doorbell rang again. She realized she'd heard it the first time, but her brain hadn't quite comprehended the sound.

"Someone is at the door. In this storm?"

"I'm expecting Sanchez." The words came out from

between clenched teeth, and he backed away, moving slowly, stiffly.

Struggling to control her erratic breathing, she watched him walk out of the laundry area. It took another second for it to dawn on her that the power had gone out. There had been a small light on when she'd come in to check on her clothes.

She fumbled around until she found the latch on the dryer. Her clothes were dry and very warm. She pulled on her panties and hooked her bra. The dress was probably hopelessly wrinkled, but she didn't care. She pulled it over her head with unsteady hands. There had been a moment—no more than a breath—when she could have turned away. Then Jake had touched her.

Cursing under his breath, Jake shifted himself into a more comfortable position, which wasn't possible. His throbbing sex was a stick of dynamite What in hell had he been thinking?

His famous remoteness, his self-control, had deserted him in a heartbeat. He'd wanted her with an intensity that blinded him to everything else. When he should be concentrating on his problems at TriTech, he'd been unable to get his mind off Alyssa. Not a good sign.

"I brought pizza," Sanchez said when he opened the door. "I thought we could eat while we talk." He stepped inside, handed Jake the large box of pizza, then shucked his dripping raincoat and hung it on the hall tree next to Jake's. "What's the problem?"

"The lights are out," answered Jake as if it wasn't perfectly obvious.

Benson whipped the air with his tail, thrilled to see Sanchez, and no doubt, smelling the anchovies he adored.

"It's just this block. Jo'Mama's Pizza had electricity. You must have a flashlight."

"Sure. Let me get them." He was positive Sanchez

detected the huskiness Jake heard in his own voice. As soon as he saw Alyssa, Sanchez would figure out what was going on.

He placed two flashlights on the table, casting long tunnels of light in the darkness. Alyssa emerged from the back of the loft, walking slowly toward the light.

"Hello." She bent down to pet Benson, who was hovering around her knees.

"Hope you like pepperoni pizza with cheese and anchovies." Sanchez acted as if it was perfectly normal to find Alyssa here.

"Anything's fine, really."

"I've got good news," Sanchez told them as he pulled out a chair at the kitchen table for Alyssa. "They've solved the missing baby crime. The police questioned an LVN. She'd been given ten thousand dollars in cash to take a baby—any baby—and put it in the linen room on your aunt's floor."

"Who gave her the money?" Jake used another flashlight to sort through a drawer for the pizza cutter.

"She claims she doesn't know, but it was a man. He contacted her, gave her five thousand up front and another five when she finished."

"Don't they have a description or something?" Alyssa asked, and Jake could hear the relief in her voice.

"No. It was dark when he approached her in the parking structure the staff uses. He arranged to leave the final payment in the trunk of her car after she'd taken the baby."

"She saw him only once?" Jake rolled the cutter through the pizza. It was emitting a mouth-watering aroma that had Benson drooling.

"That's right. I'm positive if she knew his identity, she'd trade the information for a lesser charge."

"Someone deliberately wanted to get me in trouble."

"We figured that out already." Jake realized he sounded curt, but a man about to get lucky is in a world of hurt when interrupted.

"I know but this seems so . . . calculated."

"Clay Duvall was at the hospital that night," Sanchez pointed out. "I did a quick check of his financial accounts. There haven't been any large withdrawals I could find, but I'll keep investigating."

Jake handed each of them a slice of pizza and tossed an anchovy to Benson before taking drink orders, then sitting down. While he'd been getting the sodas, neither of them had said a word.

Finally, Alyssa spoke. "I don't believe Clay is responsible."

Aw, hell. What was it going to take before she figured out what kind of man Duvall was?

They ate in silence for a few minutes. The hail had stopped, and the rain was tapering off, lightly pattering against the skylight now.

"There is some bad news," Sanchez said. "Ravelle was on TV at five o'clock. She claims you threatened Phoebe Duvall's life."

"That's a lie!" Alyssa shook her head and her blond hair caught the back lighting of the flashlights. "I never threatened Phoebe. I went to see her this afternoon, that's all."

"She told you to drop dead?" asked Sanchez.

"She wasn't that polite. She kept insisting I was after Clay. That's what Ravelle overheard."

"She managed to twist it."

"I should sue."

Sanchez helped himself to another slice. "Not a bad idea. Ravelle thrives on tabloid-like sensationalism. Someone should call her on it."

It dawned on Jake that something wasn't right. Sanchez and Alyssa were acting as if visiting Phoebe was perfectly normal. "Why would you go to see Phoebe?"

Two long beats of silence. "I wanted to talk to her about something."

"What?"

Another tense pause, and he realized Sanchez knew

what was going on, but he was waiting for Alyssa to explain.

"Aunt Thee told me Gordon LeCroix is my real father."

Jake stared at her slack-jawed, feeling like a Neanderthal morphed into Times Square, clueless. He managed to say, "You're kidding."

"I wish I were."

It took him a minute to fully recover. The bitter edge in her voice told him all he needed to know. She'd lived with them all those years, and they'd been shitty to her. One of them had been her own father. It was a wonder she was as well adjusted as she was.

"You never had any idea?"

"No, but everyone else knew. That's what Clay told me when we went for coffee at Check Point Charlie's. I wanted to talk to you about it, but you weren't around. I thought Clay could answer some of my questions."

"What questions?"

"I asked if he thought I should talk to Phoebe. He advised me not to, but I couldn't help myself. We share the same father. We shouldn't be enemies."

He wasn't sure he followed her logic, considering the way they'd treated her, but women were softhearted about their family. He asked a few more questions and finally understood what had happened and why Aunt Thee hadn't told her until now.

He was a jerk. Okay, Jake admitted it was much worse. He was proud to a fault. He'd indulged his jealousy over . . . nothing. She didn't care about Clay. He'd almost lost her, lost the chance to be with her because he jumped to the wrong conclusion and was too proud, too stubborn, to ask about it.

"After we finished discussing Phoebe, Clay told me they're getting a divorce." She looked at him with such intensity in her expression that he felt something in his chest tighten. Had she read his mind? "Clay wanted me to give him another chance. Again, I told him no. That's why I don't think he's responsible for the baby's disappearance. If he wants me back, he wouldn't make trouble for me."

"Stranger things have happened," Sanchez replied.

Suddenly the electricity came on, blasting the room with light. She looked sexy as hell was his first reaction when he saw her tousled hair and the smudge of tomato sauce on her upper lip. She gazed at him across the small table with those gray-green eyes. It was too easy to get lost in the way she looked at him, the way she responded to his touch. They kept gazing at each other, neither able to pull away.

"It's stopped raining," Sanchez announced, breaking the silence. "Maybe we should wait until morning to discuss your business."

Jake came to his senses. "It can't wait." He jumped up, realizing he'd neglected to check the fax machine.

Alyssa flipped an anchovy to Benson and he caught it midair. "I'm going to see my aunt, then I'm going home. I need some sleep."

It was all he could do not to beg her to stay, but he knew how worried she was about her aunt. The reporters probably weren't around now that the nurse had been apprehended. She didn't need him, and he had a real mess on his hands.

"Take my raincoat," he told her as he walked her to the door. The fresh scent of soap rose from her skin when he helped her into the trench coat. Even though she was tall, he was much bigger, it fit her like a choir robe.

He opened the door and handed her the umbrella he'd left on the landing. He would have kissed her goodbye, but if he did, he knew he wouldn't be able to let her go.

"Remember what I said, Alyssa. Watch yourself. The nurse was murdered and someone has tried to frame you. Be careful. Your enemies are closer than you think."

"Don't worry. I will," she assured him.

He watched her go down the stairs, his raincoat brushing each stair like a bride's train. He had an uneasy feeling. He couldn't tell if it came from the trouble at TriTech or concerns about Alyssa's safety.

It had to be TriTech, he rationalized. Whoever was after Alyssa wanted her embarrassed and humiliated. They wanted to drive her out of New Orleans. Something in his chest constricted.

Max.

His father had lobbied hard to get rid of Alyssa. He also appeared to be the one behind the phony report. It was sneaky and underhanded, which didn't seem to be Max's style. But who knew?

Back inside, he explained the situation at TriTech to Sanchez, including his suspicion Max had strong-armed Troy into altering the report. The fax had come in and the thick document was piled in the tray. Jake ran it through the copy machine, so they'd each have a report to read.

It took almost an hour to wade through it, since it was so technical. When Jake had finished it, he understood why Clay Duvall had been nervous. His company was next to worthless.

The money Clay had came from what TriTech had paid and his family's real estate holdings—not Duvall Imports. He wasn't a successful businessman the way he had people believe. Far, far from it.

"Your father pressed hard to acquire this company, didn't he? Why?"

"I have no idea except he thinks the Duvalls—and the LeCroixs—hold the keys to his political success. I wanted to check out Duvall Imports more thoroughly, and so did Troy." Jake again experienced a twinge of regret when he thought of how he'd trusted Troy.

"It's a clever scheme. Import a container of goods and get an invoice to show the purchase at an inflated price, sell them here for the real price, then it looks to the IRS like you've sold for a loss. Why hasn't the IRS picked up on it?''

Jake flipped through the pages to make certain he'd understood it correctly. He reread the paragraph, searching for the agency involved. "Here it is. The Port Authority is responsible for checking invoices and verifying market price, not the IRS."

"What page are you on?"

"Twenty-seven. Halfway down. It tracks one container of ballpoint pens from Hong Kong. They're invoiced at over one hundred dollars. Mont Blanc prices, right?"

Sanchez nodded. "Except they later marketed them like Bics. They sold them for seventy-nine cents each."

"They got away with it because the port officials are too swamped to accurately assess every container that comes into New Orleans."

Sanchez barked a laugh. "Maybe. I'd buy it in Seattle or L.A., but in New Orleans? Hell, you know the docks down here are controlled by Venezio and his boys. With mob contacts and the right amount of money—presto your goods come through no questions asked."

"Right." Jake scanned the final page, the forensic auditor's conclusions. "Duvall Imports was actually losing money, selling at a loss most of the time. That way they never owed taxes."

"TriTech shelled out a lot of money for a worthless company."

In a strange way, Jake felt proud of himself. His instincts had told him this was a bad acquisition, and he'd been right.

"They must have cooked the books you checked before making this acquisition," added Sanchez.

"Obviously. Wyatt LeCroix's accounting firm must be in on this. He handles their books, and Clay nearly had a coronary when I mentioned bringing the accounting in-house."

"Okay, so how can I help?"

"I want to find out exactly who's behind this. Any ideas?"

"It's pretty obvious, isn't it? Your father pushed this acquisition through before anyone could take too close a look at Duvall Imports. I think your hunch is correct. Max got to Troy. That's why he compiled a phony report."

"I don't want to guess. I need to know."

CHAPTER 22

Clay looked across the coffee table at Phoebe. He would have bet his life she would run home to her parents. He'd let her stew for a while, but Ravelle's bombshell on the evening news made him curious.

"Did Alyssa really threaten you?" he asked, already having decided it couldn't possibly be true. He wanted to hear what his wife had to say. Obviously, Alyssa hadn't taken his advice. She'd gone to visit Phoebe.

"Aren't you going to ask how I've been or anything?"

Clay stared at Phoebe and attempted to conceal his disgust. She was beautiful and captivating, but she could turn off the charm as quickly as shutting off the lights. Most people never saw her dark side. He'd lived with her, so he knew. Boy, did he ever.

"I can see how you've been. Beautiful as always." He waited for her smile. Years ago, he'd learned to dole out compliments. He refused to fawn over her the way other men did. When he complimented her, Phoebe beamed. Today, his remark didn't earn him a flicker of a smile.

"Did Alyssa say she was going to kill you?"

"Of course not, but you know my mother and Ravelle."

"They blow everything out of proportion."

"Absolutely." There was a grating edge to her voice that he'd never heard before.

"Alyssa just found out you two are sisters."

"Half-sisters."

"She talked to me about it last night at Check Point Charlie's. She was very upset because she hadn't realized . . ." He deliberately let the words hang in the air.

"It's too late now, don't you think?" Scorn etched each syllable.

Clay gazed at her, suddenly exhausted. How many times over the years had they fought about this? Too many to count. Every time he'd gone out of town on business, Phoebe had checked up on him. She'd been positive he was slipping off to see Alyssa.

"When it comes to Alyssa, you're totally irrational," he told her. "Totally. You always have been."

"You would be, too, if your father ignored you, and your mother continually threw your stupid half-sister in your face. I'm sick of her. I want to get as far away from Alyssa as possible."

Clay let it go. For some time now, he'd believed Phoebe needed psychiatric help. He'd mentioned it to her mother, but Hattie went ballistic, saying no LeCroix had ever been "unbalanced."

Not only was Phoebe paranoid about Alyssa, but she had serious issues with sex. What would happen to her when she was older and her looks faded? Without a constant string of men to boost her ego, Phoebe would become . . . become what? He didn't want to be around to find out.

"I hear you've filed for divorce," Clay said casually, having worked his way around to the subject he'd come to discuss.

"That's right." Phoebe's tone was matter-of-fact. "I'm leaving you."

"Unless . . ." He waited for the other shoe to drop.

She would demand something like paying off Alyssa to get out of town.

"Unless nothing. I want a divorce."

A flash of anger invigorated him. The limp, tired feeling vanished, replaced by something he couldn't quite name. Clay pretended to go along with this. After all, it was what he wanted. He just didn't intend to give her half of the money and real estate he owned. "I suggest we hold off for a while. Jake Williams is giving us a hard time right now."

"I don't care. I want out—now. I gave you the money in my trust fund. I want it back plus interest and a fair settlement."

Her vehement insistence knocked the wind out of him for a moment, then fury replaced disbelief. His outrage must have shown on his face. She beamed her megawatt smile at him, evidently thoroughly proud of herself.

If he could stall Phoebe long enough for Jake to discover Duvall Imports was worthless and to hide his other assets and put the real estate in his parents' name, he could divorce her without it costing him so much. Then he'd be a free man, able to go after the woman he really loved.

Alyssa wasn't going to give him the chance he deserved until he was divorced. He should have realized this. Unlike Phoebe, who played around with married men, Alyssa had too much class. She wasn't in love with Jake Williams, but he was available. Soon Clay would be available, too.

These thoughts running through his mind, he caught Phoebe's sly expression. Now, he got it. She wanted him to grovel.

"You're sure, Phoebe?" He forced himself to try for a touch of homespun humility, something he never did. "Our family has a lot of history, and you love me. Admit it. Don't do anything for spite."

She surged to her feet in a movement that he had to

admit was full of feline grace. She crossed the Aubusson carpet in lithe strides. "Get out. If you want to talk to me about anything else, call my attorney. From now on, all communication will be through Mitchell Petersen."

"Phoebe, wait—"

She paused in the doorway. Her blue eyes generated a lethal heat. "If you mention this divorce to my parents, before we agree to the settlement terms, it will cost you double. I swear."

An hour later, Clay walked toward the entrance to The Lion's Den, a mid-city club where he'd never have gone except he was meeting Maree and Dante. It was owned by Irma Thomas the Soul Queen of New Orleans, but it was not a place that Clay would have patronized before now.

Lately, his life had taken a new direction. Everything had been going along well enough, considering his disastrous marriage, until he'd engineered the deal that brought Alyssa home. Then his life had become hell. A rational man wouldn't blame Alyssa, but Clay wasn't sure how rational he was right now.

Two nights in a row; two very different women. They'd told him to get out of their lives. Nothing like this had happened to him and wasn't supposed to happen to him, or so he'd thought.

Now, he had the distinct feeling, he'd lost control. These women were out to get him. Phoebe was going to make him pay for the years he hadn't loved her. Alyssa was going to make him pay for the years they'd spent apart.

Shit! What was he going to do?

It was dark inside the club except for the spotlight beaming down on the small stage where a woman was belting out a song he knew but couldn't name. Maree and Dante were waiting for him at a small table. He dropped into the chair, ordering the waiter to bring him a double Johnny Walker. Of course, a joint like this didn't have Gold Label, so he had to settle for ordinary Johnny Walker.

Maree scooted her chair closer to his, and Clay attempted a smile at Dante, who was on his other side. The Bahamian psychic gave him the willies. Dante lived to watch other people have sex, but that wasn't what bothered Clay. There was something a little off about Dante.

The song ended, the waiter brought his drink, and Maree asked, "How did your meeting with Phoebe go?"

Clay mustered his most assured smile. "Same old; same old. She wants me home where I belong."

Dante regarded him with a skeptical glint in his brown eyes, and Clay wondered if he'd heard the lie in his voice. "Mon, oh, mon. This is—how you say it—way cool? She love you, no?"

No. He'd left the LeCroix home realizing Phoebe had changed. How or when, he didn't know, but she no longer thought he hung the moon. And he hated her for it. He gulped his whiskey.

He'd even begun to worry about Jake and Duvall Imports. What if it wasn't devalued to its proper level and he had to make a huge payoff to Phoebe? It wasn't fair. She'd tricked him into marriage, and now she wanted out—with everything.

"You know Phoebe," he said lightly—as if these two would ever be among his wife's circle of friends—"she's still upset Alyssa is here."

"Sisters, mon. One is the evil twin."

"They're half-sisters, not twins. They had the same father and they were born four months apart."

"Really?" Maree said with a smile.

He was sorry he'd opened his mouth. How Dante knew about them, Clay didn't know, but Maree had no idea. It took him the next few minutes to tell her the story.

"How did you know about Alyssa and Phoebe?" he asked Dante.

The Bahamian flashed him a cunning smile—all teeth. "I be psychic, mon."

Psychic? Of course not, but he had to admit Dante was clever and ruthless. For a moment he was tempted to confess to him the real situation with Phoebe and ask his advice. Clay decided he could handle this himself.

"Have you thought about our plan?" Maree asked.

"Make us big-time rich." Again Dante showed him his teeth, but Clay wasn't sure the man was actually smiling.

Clay was set to stall them for a while longer. Then it hit him. It was a risky proposition, but it could net him the money he needed immediately. He didn't know what game Phoebe was playing—he still couldn't believe she wanted a divorce—but he hadn't lured Alyssa back here to sit around and watch her with Jake.

"We need to work out a few details," Clay told them. "Maybe we should go to Maree's. It's a little noisy here to discuss it."

"No hurry, mon. Relax. Listen to de music. Then we go home and have some real fun."

Clay was getting a little bored with putting on a show for Dante, but he went along with it. He needed them, he realized with a start. He slugged back the rest of his whiskey.

The singer began to croon a song about lost love. Clay closed his eyes for a second and assured himself everything would turn out all right. He was a winner and always had been. This was a hurtle—nothing more.

They sat there, making small talk and listening to the music. Irma Thomas, the Soul Queen of New Orleans came on stage with a blare of music and raucous applause. Although she owned the club, Irma also performed on special nights, Dante informed him.

She began to sing and Clay had to admit she was good, but what did he know? He was no expert, but since he was on his third double whiskey, everything seemed great. He caught Dante eyeing him strangely, and Clay wondered if he was acting drunk or something. He resisted the urge to order another drink.

Clay wished they weren't so scrunched around the small table. He didn't like being so close to Dante. Sometimes he thought the man could read his mind, which was ridiculous.

Dante reached over and touched Clay's forearm. His big, dark fingers had neatly clipped, buffed nails, Clay noticed. Those fingers wrapped around Clay's wrist and in a quick, snake-like movement, Dante had Clay's hand under the table. Before Clay could react or utter a protest, Dante placed Clay's hand over a world-class erection.

Clay could have kicked himself for not catching on sooner. He'd assumed Dante had been watching Maree with Clay. Now he understood. Dante had been watching him.

He tried to jerk away, but Dante's powerful hand held his in place. The scorching heat of Dante's erection shot through Clay's palm. He struggled to free his hand, checking on Maree out of the corner of his eye. She was watching the show, oblivious to what was going on under the table.

It's the Johnny Walker, Clay told himself, but he couldn't resist curling his fingers around Dante's erection. The man was hung like a horse. Clay suddenly had the urge to see him in action. Tonight, he'd insist Dante take his turn with Maree.

Alyssa left the hospital, satisfied Aunt Thee was much better. She'd made arrangements for a private nurse to come home with her tomorrow. The nurse would stay at the house for as long as Aunt Thee needed her.

Remembering Jake's warning, Alyssa looked around the parking lot. It had stopped raining, but puddles dotted the pavement. Humidity haloed the streetlights and hung in the thick, hot air, making it harder to breathe. No one was around except an elderly couple who were walking toward the hospital's entrance.

She drove home, thinking about Jake. He was an insular man, an enigma. He allowed her just so close, then he shut her out. They needed to talk, she thought, then laughed out loud.

"Who are you kidding? Talk? We can't keep our hands off each other."

She parked in the garage near Aunt Thee's town house. The route to the garage had taken her by the front gate. Of course, the reporters were gone. She was yesterday's news.

She parked, grabbed Jake's raincoat, and locked the car. Thinking about Jake again, she hurried into the passageway leading from the garage to the town house. She was several steps into the walkway before she realized the only light was coming from the garage behind her where the automatic light triggered by the garage door opener was still on.

The last time she'd parked here, one of the two passageway lights had been out. Now they both were, which struck her as strange. This was a six-car garage shared by several town houses. Why hadn't someone fixed the lights?

She slowed down, remembering Jake's words of caution. It wasn't very far to the end. If she sprinted, she could make it in no time, but something told her to turn around. It would take longer, but she could go out through the garage door.

She hurried back and pressed the button on the wall to lift the garage door again. It creaked upward just as she sensed movement behind her. She bolted toward the opening door. Before she reached it, someone grabbed her from behind.

"Don't make a sound." The cold blade of a knife against her throat reinforced the man's ominous words.

"Just listen. I could kill you right here. Next time I will . . ."

"W-what do you want?"

"Leave town"—he pricked the tender flesh behind her ear—"or die, bitch."

He released her, bolted out the now open garage door, and disappeared into the darkness, leaving her with nothing more than a fleeting glimpse of a tall, hulking man dressed in black who smelled of menthol cigarettes.

CHAPTER 23

The message light on her telephone was blinking when Alyssa walked into her bedroom. She was still shaken from the incident in the garage. It was only a threat, she kept telling herself. If he'd wanted to kill her, he could have. The opportunity had been there.

Max had to be the one behind it. What had he told her when she refused to be bought off? *I have other ways of getting rid of you.*

It could be Phoebe, she thought, then decided it wasn't likely. Phoebe was a drama queen personified, and she hated Alyssa, but it was doubtful Phoebe would know how to contact a thug like the one who'd jumped her.

She listened to the messages in case the hospital had called about Aunt Thee. They were mostly calls from the previous day when reporters had been hell-bent to interview her. The last message was from Jake.

"Call me when you're home. I'm worried. I should have gone with you."

She clicked off and wished Jake had been with her. If he had, the man wouldn't have accosted her. So what? It would have postponed the inevitable. The creep would have waited until he caught her alone. Someone desperately wanted her out of New Orleans.

Fear and anger knotted inside her chest. She had no doubt he would try to kill her if she didn't leave. Why? What could be so important to Max? She'd barely met him.

Alyssa refused to be frightened away. Aunt Thee was here—she thought a moment—Jake was here. She had no intention of leaving them. She'd just have to be careful.

Should she tell Jake? She considered it as she took off her clothes and prepared for bed. No, she decided. If she did, she would have to tell him about his father's threat. Despite what Jake had said about not being close to his father, she still was reluctant to drive them apart.

The best approach to the problem was to tell Sanchez. He could talk to Max Williams and see if something could be done. She wasn't going anywhere. She would put pepper spray on her key ring, the way she'd planned. She'd purchased the cell phone easily enough, but she had to fill out a form for the pepper spray. She could pick it up tomorrow.

Thinking of security precautions made her realize she hadn't seen her cell phone in her purse when she'd gotten out her house keys. She must be mistaken, she thought, but when she checked, the new cell phone had disappeared.

"Way to go, Alyssa. You're not on a roll here."

It could be inside her car, she decided. Going back to when she'd last seen it, she remembered the lights had gone out at Jake's. It could have fallen out of her bag there.

The telephone beside the bed rang, and she walked slowly over to it. Picking up the receiver, she braced herself for a threatening call or a reporter.

"Hey, you're home." It was Jake. "Why didn't you call me?"

"I just came in."

"Is something wrong? You sound funny. Is Thee all right?"

"Aunt Thee is getting better. She's coming home tomorrow. I've hired a private nurse. That's what kept me at the hospital for so long. The referral desk has a list, but you have to contact the person to see if they are available."

"Sounds encouraging. I have more good news. After you left, Sanchez got a call. Claude Harper's been located."

The murdered nurse's husband. Great, she thought, then cautioned herself that he might not know anything about the baby's disappearance. Her nephew, she thought, troubled even more now that she knew their relationship.

"Harper's in Cabo San Lucas."

"Mexico, right?"

"Yes. Baja California. Sanchez is catching a flight tonight from here to L.A., then down to Baja. He'll get back to me as soon as he speaks to Harper."

"That's great." She climbed into her bed. "With luck this won't be another dead end."

"There's an answer somewhere. It might have a lot to do with what's going on now."

She didn't see the connection, but the whole thing was so strange, she didn't know what to think. She was tempted to tell Jake about the latest threat. Sanchez might be gone several days before she could talk to him. Jake kept talking, sounding tired but upbeat. She decided to wait until she consulted with Sanchez.

"Since Thee's going to have a nurse, do you think you could go to the Vampire Ball with me tomorrow night?"

"What's a Vampire Ball?"

"It's a full costume dinner-dance put on by the Orion krewe. I don't go in for this society stuff, but my father asked me to come. I've bought four tables. What do you say? I don't want to be caught with all those vampires by myself."

"Sure," she responded, a plan in mind. "I'm certain Aunt Thee won't care. She'll probably go to sleep early, and the nurse will be here."

"Great. I'll pick you up at seven."

"What do you wear to a Vampire Ball?"

"Fangs presumably."

She giggled, and turned off the bedside light. "Be serious. I need to know."

"It's one of those fancy costume balls where everyone has custom-made vampire outfits. Don't ask."

She'd never traveled in these circles when she'd lived here. But she was familiar with the local penchant for elaborate costumes, a legacy of a society whose most important event was Mardi Gras and the debutante balls that led up to it. Hattie and Gordon—it was hard to think of him as her father—attended several costume balls given throughout the year to raise money for the krewe.

"I'm wearing the same thing I've worn for the three years I've been going," Jake added.

She listened, the dark room enveloping her, leaving nothing except the erotic sound of his husky voice. It was almost as good as being in his arms—almost—but nothing was quite like the real thing.

"I give up," she said when she realized he'd stopped talking. "Were you Count Dracula—fangs and all?"

Several seconds of silence. "Where are you?"

"At home."

"Hel—lo. Of course, you're at home. Where exactly?"

She hesitated. "In bed."

"I'll be right over."

"No, you won't. I need my sleep. Tomorrow will be the first day in nearly a week that I've been able to work. I have a microbead salesman from Istanbul coming to see me."

"You're right. I need to get up early, too." His voice seemed deeper yet mellow like fine, aged scotch. "Tell me what you're wearing."

"Why?"

"I'm into phone sex."

"No, you're not. You like to joke around."

He heaved an affronted sigh. "If we were together, you wouldn't be wearing anything but a smile. For sure, we wouldn't be sleeping. Not after what went on this evening."

She couldn't agree more, but she didn't want to encourage him.

"I need to tell you something." His voice had shifted gears again. The smooth tone had been replaced by a strained note. "I have this . . . thing about Clay Duvall. It's complicated. A lot of it has to do with business."

When he didn't continue, she prompted him. "Your father admires the Duvalls, and it bothers you."

"In a way, you're right. Max would rather I be Clay, but he didn't bother to appear in my life until it was too late for me to have the advantages and the education it would require. But that's not what bothers me the most about Clay."

She gazed into the darkness, only a ribbon of light wavering through the shutters from the streetlight outside her window. She waited, hearing something strange in his voice, but not knowing what to say.

"It's knowing you loved him, and you might still be in love with him. When I saw you last night, his arm was around you. I couldn't help thinking . . ."

"Is that why you were giving me the deep freeze?"

"Yes. I don't know what got into me. I've never been the jealous type."

She couldn't help smiling inwardly. It was hard to think of Jake being jealous, but the thought pleased her. It meant he cared. This wasn't just about sex.

"Like I told you, I went with him because I was in shock over discovering Gordon LeCroix is my father, and I was shaken when that baby disappeared. I wanted to talk to you in the worst way, but I thought you weren't coming back.'' She took a deep breath. ''I knew you'd understand since Max came back into your life after you'd grown up.''

''You wonder where they were when you really needed them. It has to be rougher on you than it was on me. Gordon was there, but he ignored you, right?''

''He ignored everyone,'' she said, unable to keep the bitterness out of her voice. ''I can understand why Phoebe is so . . .''

''Screwed up.''

''Yes. I lived in their house never expecting anything from them, but Phoebe tried everything to make them love her. Phoebe could never please Hattie. No one could. The woman cares about nothing except her place in society and impressing her friends. Poor Phoebe didn't stand a chance.''

''A tragedy, I'm sure.''

Again Alyssa laughed softly and cradled the phone to her ear while she snuggled against her pillow. Talking to him like this was intimate, yet safe. ''Do you think I should talk to Gordon? He doesn't realize I know the truth.''

''It's a tough call. I knew where Max was, but I never contacted him. Too much pride, I guess.''

''That's how I feel, too. Gordon had plenty of opportunities to get to know me or even just tell me he was my father, but he didn't. I don't want anything from him, and I certainly don't expect anything. After all, I've lived with him. I know what a cold man he is. I just want to look him in the eye and tell him I know.''

''You'll get your chance tomorrow night. The LeCroixs will be at the Vampire Ball with the Duvalls.''

Alyssa inhaled a stabilizing breath. She should have anticipated this. The Orion krewe was the pinnacle of society. Everyone who was anyone in New Orleans would be there.

"Jake, I'd almost forgot. That stupid piece Ravelle did, accusing me of wanting Phoebe dead. Ravelle will be there for sure."

"So? I'll be with you."

"I know. I guess facing everyone says I have nothing to hide, right?"

"You got it."

"One other thing, Jake. Did I drop my cell phone at your place?"

"No. I haven't seen it. You didn't lose it, I hope. I don't like you wandering around without a telephone."

"Don't worry. It's probably in my car."

"If it isn't, let me know. I'll get you another one," he said. "Now let me tell you about our costumes before I change my mind and come over there and slip under those covers to see what you're wearing."

"Are you going to be there tomorrow night?" Maree asked. When Clay raised his eyebrows, showing he didn't know what she was talking about, she added, "The Vampire Ball."

"Shit!" He'd forgotten all about it.

"Neville's taking me."

Was he supposed to care? Let Maree show up with Neville Berringer. Clay wondered how he was going to handle this. He was supposed to be there with Phoebe at a table with both their parents. He couldn't imagine how he was going to explain the situation because he wasn't sure where he stood.

"I'm wearing this slinky black dress made of feathers," Maree said. "The mask is all feathers, too. I'm carrying a leather whip decorated with feathers."

"She's going as a vampire who's into S and M," Dante said.

Clay could believe it. The Vampire Ball was the first big event after Mardi Gras, a season opener for the following Mardi Gras. People let their imaginations descend into the dark side of New Orleans, the days of voodoo and black magic.

They were back at Maree's place now, a cramped house on Julia Street with kitchy rattan walls and rattan shades covering the windows. Maree was talking over her shoulder as she busily lit the candles she always put on every available surface. The last of a pyramid of miniature votives was lit, and Maree flicked off the lamp. The scent of sandalwood and jasmine began to fill the room.

Dante was in the kitchen, partially visible from where Clay was sitting on the sofa, his feet up on the coffee table. The big Bahamian had his back to him as he whipped up his favorite concoction, Cajun Martinis, gin with pepper vodka and a sprinkle of jalapeño peppers on top. He had a tight ass and a weight lifter's shoulders to go along with his hefty cock.

Just remembering how it had felt in his hand turned his own penis rock-hard. Usually, when he'd had this much to drink, he had trouble getting it up, but the little episode in the club had titillated him. He'd been thinking about it ever since and anticipating seeing Dante on top of Maree. Who knew? Maybe Clay would learn a few new tricks.

"Take dis." Dante handed him the Cajun Martini. Not that he needed anything else to drink. He'd been so shaken by his meeting with Phoebe that he'd had too much already.

Maree grabbed her drink from Dante and twitted off toward the bedroom. "Wait until you see this."

Clay sipped his drink. It was a little spicy for his taste, but he drank it anyway. This was the same drill they'd been through before. Cajun Martinis and a lingerie show. Clay and Dante would sit side by side while Maree paraded around in the latest, skimpiest lingerie.

Maree was good, he had to admit, much better than what you saw in the sex clubs. She never failed to arouse him. They'd end up in her bedroom with Dante hovering nearby. Tonight, Clay intended to do the watching.

They waited, the room glowing in the amber candle-light, sandalwood perfuming the close air, drinking the Cajun Martinis and listening to the throbbing beat of reggae music. It made Clay's head ache, a sure sign he'd had too much alcohol, but he kept sipping to avoid talking to Dante. He could feel the big man watching him.

"Well, what do you think?" Maree asked in a breath-less Marilyn Monroe voice, prancing out in a bra that had no straps or bands. It was merely separate cups, which lifted her tits upward like pagan offerings. Below a cherry-colored triangle of fabric formed the largest part of the thong, the color matching the bra.

She sashayed around the coffee table, her drink in one hand, treating them to a close look. Her body was flawless, he had to concede. Not a ripple, not a mark on her except for the dime-sized mole on her ass, clearly visible to the right of the thong's spaghetti strap separat-ing her cheeks.

"It's the latest," she informed them in the same breathy voice. "Self-adhesive cups instead of a dumb old bra."

She bent over and jiggled her tits in Clay's face, and he said, "Not bad, Maree. Not bad."

She gyrated to the music, sipping her drink. Now and then, she'd stop and toss her head from side to side, the way she did when she was having an orgasm. Her hair swished back and forth, up and down with a whooshing sound.

Clay ventured a look at Dante out of the corner of his eye. Nice work, Maree. The solid ridge of Dante's erection pushed against his fly. Dante caught him look-ing and winked.

Maree shimmied to a stop in front of Clay. She thrust her hips forward, saying, "Guess what? Edible undies."

"Cherry?" he heard himself ask.

She wiggled closer until her crotch was two inches from his nose. "Sniff. Then take a bite."

The sickening aroma of imitation cherry hit his nose and dove into his stomach, where it mingled with the whiskey and the Cajun Martini and did a belly flop. He gagged, but managed to recover enough to push her toward Dante, "I hate cherry. You try."

Dante didn't need any encouraging. He grabbed Maree by her bare buns and pulled her up to his mouth. He munched on the cherry-colored triangle and consumed it in two bites. Maree arched backward and let her long hair hang down her shoulders like a dark cape while Dante used his tongue to explore her crotch.

Maree waxed her pussy every week, so it was creamy and soft. Clay could imagine what she smelled like down there. She used sandalwood perfume to compliment the aromatic candles she adored.

Dante tried to hand her off to Clay, but he said, "I'm watching tonight."

Without a word, Dante hefted Maree over his shoulder. The big man had her in the bedroom, on her back across the bed in less time than it took for Clay to toss back the rest of his martini.

Dante stood beside the bed and toed off his loafers. His big, bare feet were dark at the ankles, but brownish-pink around the toes. He didn't bother to unbutton his shirt. He yanked the front panel and the buttons flew off, pinging across the wood floor except for one, which gave way with a rip. He released his belt and dropped his pants in one quick movement.

He wasn't wearing anything underneath. His cock sprang forward at an angle, like a caged beast escaping. Shit. He was better hung than any of the guys Clay had seen when he'd been in school, including Stan the Man, center on the football team. He'd been the envy of all the guys because his dick was like a long-neck beer bottle.

Watching them, anticipating, turned the heat in

Clay's groin into a very painful erection. He put his hand in his pants to make an adjustment.

Dante glanced over his shoulder at him and winked. Then he positioned himself between Maree's spread legs. He licked the insides of her thighs like a cat cleaning itself with long, lazy strokes. Maree writhed under him, moaning softly.

"Come on, Clay," Maree called. "The bra is edible, too."

"Join the party, mon."

What could it hurt? he asked himself. He'd have a better feel for things closer. He put one knee on the king-size bed.

"No clothes!" Dante ordered, then went back to using his tongue on Maree.

Clay's whole body burned, and his penis pressed against his pants, begging to be released. He was a little embarrassed to be compared to Dante, but decided it didn't matter. They were too involved to pay attention to him.

He stripped and climbed on the bed beside them. Dante had his head between her legs, and Maree's eyes were squeezed shut while the tip of her tongue ran across her lower lip. Clay fondled one breast, but she didn't seem to notice.

Dante stopped, raised his head, and grinned at Clay. A shiver of something he had never experienced chilled his body for an instant. Dante reared back on his knees, his erection jutting high and proud from between his dark thighs.

"Your turn," he told Clay in a hoarse whisper.

Clay levered himself upright and straddled Maree. He needed release so badly he couldn't wait around to see them fuck. Her eyes were still closed; she seemed oblivious to what was happening. She was used to threesomes, he decided.

Suddenly, Dante's hand covered Clay's pulsating cock from behind. It wrapped around him like an iron glove, then his thumb brushed the bulbous tip. Clay held his breath to keep from losing it.

"That's not what I meant, mon." Dante nipped the back of Clay's neck and another burst of fire shot through his body.

Clay looked over his shoulder into his liquid brown eyes and knew exactly what Dante wanted. He opened his mouth, but couldn't say no.

"Ashes to ashes. Dust to dust. If God won't have you, de devil must."

CHAPTER 24

It was after lunch the following day when Alyssa finished with the microbead salesman from Istanbul. She was excited about the tiny beads being milled by machine and strung on invisible filament. The finished pieces looked like clusters of star dust. She disliked using machines but there was no other way to produce such tiny beads and string them.

Olivia handed her another cup of coffee, saying, "The people from the advertising agency have been waiting."

"The brochure," she muttered to her secretary. She needed to get out of here in the next two hours to bring Aunt Thee home and pick up her costume for the Vampire Ball. "Send them in."

A man and a woman hardly out of their teens entered. Both of their ears had multiple piercings, and they both had dark maroon hair gelled into chunky spikes. She couldn't believe this was the advertising agency the company used.

"What projects have you done for TriTech?"

They named several, and she told herself to calm down. This was America, not Italy, where being fashionable was a way of life. These weirdos were probably from L.A.

"Let me explain what I want," Alyssa began, "so there's no mistake. I need a small insert that's classy to go inside each box of Rossi Designs jewelry."

They nodded in unison, bobbing their glossy maroon heads like puppets.

"I want it to say something like this." They both scrambled to take notes. "Since ancient times man has polished and strung pebbles into rows of beads to adorn himself. The earliest beads were worn by Neanderthals, but it was the Egyptians who are credited with perfecting the art."

"Art—that's a good word," the girl said to her companion, and he nodded.

"Beads worn as amulets or talismans have been found from ancient China to England. The word *bede* is an Anglo-Saxon term meaning prayer. Among the earliest beads were prayer beads. Other beads like rosary beads—"

Her intraoffice line buzzed, interrupting Alyssa. "Yes?"

"Mr. Williams is here," Olivia said. "He'd like you to step into the reception office for a minute."

"Of course," she said and excused herself, knowing what she'd given them so far sounded too much like a textbook. Could they improvise the way her ad agency in Florence had?

"Jake," she said with a smile as she emerged from her office. "What brings you all the way down here?"

"I heard from Sanchez."

She could tell from his expression it wasn't good news. "What did he say?"

"Harper is out on a boat in the Sea of Cortez photographing the whales. It's calving time. Sanchez has contacted the ship by radio, but he doesn't want to ask sensitive questions over the air."

Alyssa tried not to be disappointed. It was merely another delay among many delays; she could wait. "Thanks for telling me."

"Was your telephone in your car?"

"No. I notified the phone company. I'm going to get a new one."

"Good." He studied her, his eyes level under drawn brows. "I thought the day might have gotten away from you, the way it does when I've been out of the office for a while."

"Has it ever."

"Let me bring Thee and the nurse home. I'll have my secretary pick up your costume and deliver it to the house. Will that help?"

A wave of utter relief rushed over her. "Yes! I could kiss you."

"You'll have to do better than that—later."

She noticed a flush had crept up Olivia's cheeks as her secretary pretended to sort files. Alyssa took his arm, unable to resist pulling him closer and looking flirtatiously into his eyes. "I need to ask you something. I've got the team from Nolan and Bland in my office. You've used them, right?"

His expression stilled and grew serious. "Yes. Trust me. They're from L.A. That's why they seem strange, but they deliver."

"L.A. I knew it," she said as he left, saying he'd see her tonight.

She went back inside her office. "Where was I?"

"Rosary beads."

"Prayer beads."

"Right. Besides having religious significance, beads were currency in the ancient world. Traders used strings of beads to pay for things. They carried them around their necks because it left their hands free, and the beads couldn't be stolen. That's how beads became a symbols of wealth and status. When coins were invented, beads became jewelry." She tried a smile on the duo, but they looked at her with blank expressions. "Do you think you can rephrase this information into a short, yet interesting insert?"

"No problem."

"We're outta here."

They left and she sank into her chair, not knowing if she should laugh or cry. She decided to trust Jake, and let them come up with an insert. She immersed herself in the paperwork she hadn't done, thankful for Jake's help.

She resisted the urge to confront Max Williams by calling him on the telephone or going over to his home to see him, but the vicious threat lingered, and she reminded herself to be careful. She was positive she would see him tonight. Telling him off in person would be much more satisfying.

Jake walked into the Vampire Ball with Alyssa at his side. Despite the mess at TriTech, he couldn't help smiling inwardly. He might be able to endure all this society BS if he had Alyssa with him.

"I wonder whose idea it was to throw a vampire ball?" she asked with a laugh.

"It's given at this time every year. Late spring, after Mardi Gras. During the carnival there are countless masked balls and costumes in the parades. I suppose everything had been done but a vampire theme."

He scanned the ballroom filled with masked people, wearing black vampire outfits with swirling capes. Many of the women had plunging necklines that made them look like Elvira. He'd never seen so many fangs since last year's Vampire Ball, when the costume shops in the city sold out of fangs and fake blood.

"Hold it," he told Alyssa as a waiter passed by. "Grab one of those skewers of pasta. I'll bet they're loaded with garlic."

The waiter stopped and they helped themselves to the skewers of penne pasta drenched in sauce.

"M-m-m," Jake said. "There's enough garlic here to ward off all the vampires on the planet."

Alyssa laughed and held up the antique beaded cross she was wearing on a long chain around her neck. It was one of a number of antique crosses with beads she collected. "The clergy will do the rest."

They chuckled together. He was dressed as a priest, and she was a nun—a damn sexy nun. Both wore crosses to keep them safe from the vampires.

They wandered through the enormous ballroom of the private home in the Garden District where the costume party was being held. Like many homes from the period, the ballroom was on the third floor. The perimeter of the room was draped in black and festooned with skulls and crossbones and satanic symbols.

Groups of potted palms and upright coffins divided the room into several sections. The bar was stationed in one corner, ringed by gargoyles on pillars. Nearby, a chef was serving freshly prepared sushi beneath a mammoth cross with RIP burned into the wood. There were several game booths off to the side, including a Voodoo Parlor.

Tables with black satin tablecloths and blood-red napkins were clustered at the far end of the room. Rows of gleaming silver and crystal glasses promised a five-course dinner. In the center of each table, rising from a miniature coffin of red roses was what appeared to be a human skull with a table number written in blood across the forehead. If you asked him, the whole damn thing was a morbid waste of money.

"Hello, Jake."

He wouldn't have recognized Troy in his vampire getup, but he knew the voice. This was the man he'd trusted to help him run TriTech, the man who had betrayed him. His happy mood evaporated.

"Our table is over there," Troy told them.

Jake had forgotten that he'd invited Troy to be at one of TriTech's tables. He'd tried to greet Troy as if nothing were wrong. "Troy, this is Alyssa Rossi. She's—"

"The head of Rossi Designs. I know all about your company."

What a surprise. Jake bit back a snide remark. Troy adored Paris and its sophisticated nightlife. He probably thought this was beneath him.

"Really?" Alyssa said.

"Beads. An international reputation."

They kept talking, but Jake didn't pay attention to their conversation. It struck him—not for the first time—that Troy knew all sorts of insider information. There wasn't a major deal or minor transaction the man hadn't worked on. He could turn TriTech inside out. Again, Jake kicked himself for allowing this to happen.

"I'm going to experiment with microbeads—" She was cut off as Jake pulled her away, saying they'd see Troy later. "What's wrong? That was very rude."

"Sorry." He'd spotted the LeCroix family coming their way. They were wearing masks but Phoebe's blond hair was unmistakable. She was one of the few women not wearing a long, black wig. The vampire with the gray hair had to be her father. "Over there. Gordon LeCroix with Hattie and Phoebe. Wonder where Clay is."

Alyssa froze, standing where the potted palms concealed her.

"Do you want to talk to your father?" Jake asked.

"Not with Phoebe and Hattie around. Remember, the last time I was with Phoebe, Ravelle accused me of wanting her dead."

"And you didn't kill her? A missed opportunity." He watched them over Alyssa's shoulder. "Phoebe and her mother have stopped to talk to a couple of fat vampires. Not a pretty sight." He grinned at her, but she didn't return his smile. "Looks like Gordon's heading toward the bar alone." He tugged her arm. "We can catch him."

He stepped out from behind the palms, extending his hand, "Gordon, hey. How are you?"

"Fine-ah—"

"Jake Williams." He nudged Alyssa forward. "You know Alyssa Rossi."

"Of course, I know Alyssa," snapped Gordon.

"Hello, Father."

Through the slits in his black mask, Gordon's eyes narrowed just slightly. "Clever costume, Alyssa."

They stood looking at each other, neither saying anything. Jake noticed Phoebe staring at them, and he figured she'd guessed the masked nun was Alyssa.

Finally, Alyssa said, "Nice seeing you . . . again."

They walked away, and over his shoulder Jake noticed Phoebe making a beeline for her father. He didn't mention it to Alyssa.

"Do you think he got the message?" she asked.

"If all you wanted to say to him is: I know. He understood."

Her chin jutted upward. "That's all. I'm on my own. I always have been. I don't need him. I have Aunt Thee."

Jake spotted his father on the far side of the room with the Duvalls. At least, Jake thought the other couple was Clay's parents. Nelson Duvall was a glimpse into Clay's future. Someday his blond hair would be riddled with gray, and he'd have a paunch. While most of the other men wore black wigs or slicked back their hair a la Elvis in order to transform themselves into vampires, Nelson was wearing a black headpiece that made him look like Bat Man.

"There's my father over there dressed as the devil. Now, is that fitting or what?"

"It's perfect."

"We'd better say hello." He knew his father wasn't going to be thrilled to see him with Alyssa, but he didn't give a damn.

"Hey, Max," Jake greeted the masked man. "You remember Alyssa."

His father grunted his hello through the devil's mask he wore. His long tail was slung over his shoulder, and

Jake almost laughed. Max looked so . . . right as the devil.

The band was beginning to play "Proud Mary." Alyssa grabbed his father's hand, saying, "Let's dance."

Max scowled at Jake. He shrugged his shoulders and wondered what possessed Alyssa. With women, you never knew. They seemed to be doing more talking than dancing, he thought, watching them. When the song was over, Alyssa left the old devil standing by himself in the middle of the dance area.

She came over and took his arm. "Come on."

"Hey, what was going on with my father?"

"I just wanted to tell him what a great son he had."

"Why am I not buying this?"

She laughed but it had an odd strangled sound. Women. Go figure.

Clay walked into the party by himself. The vampire's tuxedo his tailor had so painstakingly fitted on him two years ago had gotten a little tight in the waist. Since he'd stopped running at Tulane every morning, it was beginning to show.

He looked at the table number they'd given him in the reception area. His parents would be at the table with Phoebe. He kept telling himself she was bluffing. Why else would she insist he didn't tell her parents?

"Wyatt would know," he mumbled to himself, feeling foolish for trying to say anything with fake fangs in his mouth. He looked around for his brother-in-law, but with so many men in vampire garb, it was impossible to immediately spot Wyatt.

Scanning the crowd for tall men like Wyatt, he noticed the tall priest on the dance floor. A nun who was almost as tall was waltzing with him. Alyssa.

He stood watching and seethed with mounting rage. They were laughing and having fun, oblivious to everyone around them. A bitter jealousy morphed into something much more intense.

Alyssa was his. Hadn't he moved heaven and earth to get her back here? He elbowed his way through the milling vampires to the bar, where he ordered a double Johnny Walker Gold Label straight up.

What was he going to do about Alyssa? Right now he had so much going on, it was impossible to decide how to handle the situation. As if this wasn't enough, he had Dante and Maree to consider.

His pulse quickened when he thought about last night. He popped out his fangs and shoved them in his pocket. A long swig of the whiskey helped, but not enough. Threesomes were more fun than he would have thought. That's what it had been, he assured himself, a threesome.

"Clay, man, is that you?"

"Wyatt. Just the guy I wanted to see."

Wyatt reached around him and handed the bartender his glass for a refill. "What's up?"

"Does Phoebe really want a divorce or is this another game of hers?"

Wyatt waited until he had his drink before responding. "How many times do you have to be told? She's serious."

"That's what I thought," he responded as if he couldn't care less.

"Is that Jake with Alyssa over there at Marie Laveau's Voodoo Parlor?"

"Yes. It is." His words came out from between clenched teeth.

Each year the krewe raised money by invoking the name and the powers of the Voodoo Queen who'd lived in the early 1800s. It was always one of the most popular events at the Vampire Ball.

"This year you have to say 'black bats bleed black blood' five times in fifteen seconds to win the pot of prize money," Wyatt told him. "You try it."

"Forget it. I've never been good at tongue twisters. I'm not wasting ten dollars to have a crowd of people laugh at me when I stumble over the words."

"It's all in good fun." Wyatt nudged him. "Check that woman."

Shit! It was Maree. When she'd described the feathered gown she was going to wear, she failed to mention it looked as if the feathers had been glued on to every sexy curve of her body. As she passed, people turned and gawked.

"It's Neville Berringer and his new girlfriend," Clay said, more than a little disgusted at the display Maree was making of herself. "Her name is Maree Winston."

"Bet she's pretty hot in bed."

For a moment, Clay's breath burned in his throat. What would Wyatt say if he'd seen them last night?

CHAPTER 25

"You totally muffed 'black bats bleed black blood.' Do you want to try 'the city sheriff shoots sharp six-shooters'?" Alyssa asked Jake.

"Are you kidding? I'm no good at this. I kept saying, black blats. You know how the city sheriff would come out—the shitty sheriff."

"Alyssa," someone behind her said her name, and she turned and found Gordon LeCroix. "May I have a word with you?"

She opened her mouth to say no when Jake spoke up. "You two go on. I'll meet you at my table—number twenty three."

"Let's go down stairs where we can talk in private."

Alyssa decided Gordon wanted to discuss being her father. She was angry with him for the years of neglect, but she had to admit she was curious about what he might say. She walked at his side down the sweeping staircase to the first floor. There were a few latecomers arriving at the front door and being directed up the stairs by a ghoul with a bloody spear in his hand.

A narrow hall off the entry went to the back of the house. She saw a tall man in a devil's costume stepping into a room opening off the hall. Max Williams. What was he doing down here? She didn't have time to speculate. Her father took her into a living room elegantly furnished in period pieces.

Gordon LeCroix closed the double doors behind them. He pulled off his mask and gestured toward a sofa. Alyssa sat down and he seated himself beside her. It was impossible to take off her mask without disturbing the nun's whipple covering her head. She slid the mask upward to her forehead in order to look her father right in the eyes as he talked.

Gordon studied her for a moment, and it seemed he expected her to say something. She waited him out. This was his idea; she had nothing more to say to him.

"I should have told you the truth years ago." His words were spoken in a low voice charged with more emotion than she'd ever heard when she'd been living under his roof. "After you went to Italy with Theodora, I assumed she told you then. I never heard from you—"

"You could have contacted me."

"I wouldn't have known what to say."

The tightness in her chest became a cramp. Her own father wouldn't have known what to say to her? She suddenly saw through what she'd always assumed was a veneer of coldness bordering on contempt. He was a weak, ineffectual man who didn't know how to deal with his wife or children and sought refuge in his job and on the golf course.

"What bothers me is having everyone know the truth but me. I lived with your family all those years. I never suspected. Why didn't you tell me? How difficult could that have been?"

His throat worked hard, his Adam's apple sliding up and down. "You'd have to understand what happened with your mother. I met her not long after I'd gotten engaged to Hattie. I thought I loved Hattie. We'd dated for years and our families expected . . ." He gazed across the room at an oil painting of the River Road. "When

I met Pamela, how I felt was so different. I didn't intend to hide the truth from her, but I knew she'd refuse to see me if she knew. The longer I waited, the more I loved her until it became impossible to confess. I didn't tell her I was engaged until we were going back to New Orleans, and I knew she'd find out.''

"What did she say when you told her?"

A shadow of a smile crossed his lips. "I expected her to pitch a fit, the way Hattie would have, but your mother merely asked if, after spending the summer with her, I still intended to marry Hattie. I said I couldn't get out of it."

"You must not have loved her enough—"

"Wait! You didn't know my father. I mentioned to him I would like to postpone the wedding because I wasn't sure. I thought in time he would gradually become accustomed to the idea that I didn't want to marry Hattie. Dad threatened to disown me, cut me out of his will, if the wedding didn't go on as planned."

"Would that have been so bad—if you could have been with the woman you loved?"

He let out a long, audible breath. "No, it wouldn't have been. Believe me, I've spent the rest of my life suffering for my mistake, but back then I was young. I couldn't imagine my family disowning me and trying to survive without a penny." He hesitated a moment, then added, "I might have mustered the courage. . . if your mother had told me she was pregnant."

"You didn't know?" Of all the scenarios she'd imagined between her parents, this wasn't one of them.

He shook his head, saying, "No. When Pamela married so quickly, and you arrived *early*, I guessed. I confronted your mother, and she said she didn't want to force me into marriage." The corner of his mouth twisted to one side in a gesture she'd forgotten until now. "She told me Robert loved her and you. Now she knew the meaning of true love. She didn't want to have anything to do with me. I respected her wishes."

His words had the ring of truth to them. She saw him the way he really was—an older man, disillusioned and lonely. Still, there were things she didn't understand. "Why didn't you tell me the truth when you took me in?"

"Believe me, I wanted to, but, well, you know Hattie." He ran his hand through his thinning hair. "I hadn't told her about you until your mother died and there wasn't anyone to take you in except Theodora, and she was living in Italy with a terminally ill husband. The only way Hattie would allow me to bring you home was if I kept it a secret."

Alyssa could only imagine Hattie's ballistic reaction. It wasn't any wonder Phoebe could be so temperamental. She'd inherited it from her mother.

"I got what I deserved for knuckling under to my father. I've had a miserable marriage."

Just like Clay, she thought, amazed at how her life had been so very much like her mother's. "You could have left—anytime."

A burst of raucous laughter from the entry hall outside the living room interrupted them. They waited in silence until the voices trailed away as the group went up the stairs.

"You may find this hard to believe, but I stayed to protect you three. Hattie is so high strung, she would have taken it out on you children if I'd left. As it was, I had to send Wyatt away to Phillips Military Academy to prevent Hattie from ruining a very normal boy."

"It was a good move," she admitted. "Wyatt seemed much better after he left the house."

Her father stared up at the crown molding for a moment, then gazed into her eyes. "You realize Phoebe has serious adjustment problems, don't you?"

"It's pretty obvious. She's beautiful and intelligent, yet where I'm concerned, she isn't able to accept that I have no interest in her husband."

Gordon rose slowly and walked across the room to

the French doors opening onto the garden. He shoved his hands in his pockets, then turned to face her. "I failed Phoebe somehow. I stayed married to help her, yet Phoebe and I never connected."

"You were never around. She didn't have the chance to really get to know you." Alyssa couldn't believe she was defending Phoebe, but everything she'd said was true. This weak man *thought* he was helping the children when, in reality, he was a big zero.

He slowly crossed the highly buffed parquet floor, his footsteps becoming muffled when he reached the Persian carpet in the center of the room. "I did the best I could under the circumstances. You're right, though, Phoebe suffered the lack of a father. I think that's why she's so . . . taken with older men."

He sat beside her again, his expression conveying his concern. "I didn't want to talk about Phoebe. I just want you to know how very proud I am of you."

She couldn't resist saying, "I'm proud of myself. I went from Cinderella, living with the servants to a successful jewelry designer. I—"

"Look, you were better off with the help, believe me. Had you lived upstairs with Phoebe, you'd be just as disturbed. Hattie destroys everyone around her."

"Then why haven't you left her?"

He shrugged. "At this point, why bother? We've arrived at a place in our lives where we're comfortable."

How tragic, she thought, trying to imagine herself staying with someone she didn't love. She prayed her mother had meant it when she'd told Gordon that Robert's love was the real thing. She didn't want to think of her mother dying without having loved and been loved in the deepest sense.

"There's something I need to say," he told her. "I never believed you took Phoebe's baby."

"Aunt Thee stepped in when *no one* else would."

"I'm sorry I didn't come forward to help you, but I

didn't know what to think. The whole situation was so strange. If there's anything I can do now—"

"Like what?"

"You tell me." The echo of despair in his voice punctured her defenses in a way that she could never have anticipated.

It was a long moment before she could respond. "I'll never be free until I can clear my name. Do you have any idea what happened to Phoebe's baby?"

His brows furrowed with regret. "I wish I could help, but I don't know anything. Patrick is my grandchild. I just hope he's alive somewhere. Safe and happy."

There was no mistaking the heartfelt anguish in his voice. She realized he was telling the truth. What was there left to say? A dull silence full of lost opportunities and heartache filled the room. Alyssa wanted to run home and hug Aunt Thee and thank her for a love that couldn't be replaced.

"Do something for me, please." Her father's words took her by surprise. "Phoebe is down the hall in the study. I told her I was going to talk to you. I'd like the two of you to try to patch up your relationship. You're—"

"I tried just yesterday but Phoebe accused me of being after Clay."

He shrugged apologetically. "You know how overwrought Phoebe gets. Try to talk to her again. Please, she's waiting."

She slowly rose and looked at her father. Did he know what he was asking? Phoebe was never going to accept her.

"Thanks," he said as she opened the door to the hall. "She's down there. The door on the left." He appeared to be struggling for a smile. "I'll see you later."

No one was around except the ghoul positioned at the front door to direct the guests up to the ballroom. He waved at her. Alyssa had to force herself to place one foot in front of the other to get down the hall.

Halfway there she remembered seeing Max go inside. Was he still in there talking to Phoebe? She'd seen the two of them dancing earlier, and they seemed to be very chummy.

No telling what Max might say to Phoebe, Alyssa decided. She'd tricked him into dancing so she could tell him that she knew he'd sent the goon who'd threatened her. Of course, he'd denied it. He'd even managed to seem surprised and outraged, but she wasn't fooled.

She put her hand up and knocked. A rustling noise came through the solid wood door. "It's me, Alyssa."

After a long silence, Phoebe called, "Come in." The words sounded more welcoming than she'd expected.

Phoebe was sitting in an overstuffed chair near a desk where a small lamp provided the only light in the room. French doors opened out from the study onto the garden where a white gazebo gleamed in the moonlight. Alyssa thought she saw a flash of red in the azaleas just outside the doors and decided Max had slipped out into the yard rather than face her.

She edged into the room, a step at a time until she stood before her half-sister. "I've been talking with . . . our father. He thinks we should—"

"Settle our differences."

"Something like that."

Phoebe rose and walked over to the French doors. With her back to Alyssa, she said, "Daddy's right. It's time to forget . . . everything. I'm making a lot of changes in my life."

Alyssa thought about Clay divorcing her but didn't say a word. Just mentioning his name might set off Phoebe again. She wanted to get this over with, to know she'd done her best, then she would distance herself from the whole family.

Phoebe turned to face her, smiling the charming smile she used when she wanted something. "I'm divorcing Clay."

Alyssa nodded, silently letting Phoebe put her own

spin on the story that Clay had already told her. She leaned against the desk, half-sitting, half-standing, and waited to hear more.

"I'm still young. There's time to start over, to have another life."

"With your beauty and brains, you could do anything."

"I have plans, bigger plans than living for Mardi Gras."

Again Alyssa nodded, not knowing what to say, afraid anything she did say would upset Phoebe.

"You may not believe this, but I'm sorry about the way I treated you." Phoebe's voice was soft, almost lost to the sound of the band playing in the ballroom two floors up. "I knew I was prettier, but I was jealous of you. Daddy loved your mother, not mine. I thought he loved you more."

"I didn't even know he was my father. He never did anything to suggest he cared about me."

"I know he's sorry. Daddy doesn't know how to love."

Alyssa nodded her agreement while an inner voice cautioned her not to trust Phoebe's apparent change of heart.

"You're welcome to Clay. I don't want him now."

This was more like what Alyssa had expected. "I don't care about Clay. I'm crazy about Jake Williams." The minute the words were out of her mouth, she knew it was true. She had fallen for Jake. She wouldn't call it love—exactly—but it was close.

"You're smart. Clay's not worth your time." Phoebe's words took her by surprise.

Alyssa decided to quit while she was ahead. "Jake's waiting upstairs." She edged toward the door. "I'm glad we had this talk. I want only the best for you. If you need me, call me."

She walked into the hall, closing the door behind her. Wow! What had Gordon LeCroix said to change Phoebe's mind? Or had something else happened? She thought about Max being in the room before she'd come to talk to Phoebe.

Sounds of voices at the entry interrupted her thoughts. Ravelle Renault was coming through the front door followed by her crew. Great! Just what Alyssa did not want—a confrontation with the conniving gossip.

She ducked back into the study and found Phoebe sitting in the chair again. "I think I'll get some fresh air." It was a lame excuse, she thought, opening the door to the garden.

"Check out the gazebo," Phoebe told her. "It was brought here from England. They say the Prince Regent used to seduce women in it."

"Thanks. I will." She closed the door behind her.

Artistically placed nightscaping lit the manicured gardens. Up-lights bathed the Victorian gazebo in a pale glow. She mounted the steps to the gazebo, thinking about Phoebe's sudden turnaround and wondering. What was going on with Phoebe?

CHAPTER 26

Alyssa dropped onto the circular bench inside the gazebo. The night air was warm and moist, a harbinger of the hot, humid summer that was fast approaching. Music blared from the third-floor ballroom, where they seemed to be performing some voodoo reenactment. A series of loud bangs from the drums were followed by a popping sound like a firecracker.

Despite the noise, Alyssa's mind drifted back to the conversation with her father. Gordon LeCroix—her father. It still didn't seem possible. How could she have lived all those years in the same house and not have suspected the truth?

Even more surprising, her father seemed to care about her and had always worried about her in his own way. She tried to put herself in his place, yet the image wouldn't come. It was doubtful she would ever understand him.

Alyssa decided she was even less likely to fathom what made Phoebe tick. Her half-sister had made it sound as if the divorce was her idea, not Clay's. It would have been easy to believe her except yesterday Phoebe had accused her of wanting Clay. Phoebe's concept of reality and hers were very different.

"Does it matter who wants the divorce?" she whispered to herself.

It wasn't her problem. She'd meant what she said to Phoebe. She had come to care for Jake much more than she wanted to admit. His abrupt change of attitude had upset her—a lot. She'd liked the way he'd supported her when Aunt Thee was hospitalized. She'd wanted to get closer to him, then he'd unexpectedly turned away.

She closed her eyes and smiled in the darkness. He'd been jealous because he'd believed something was going on with Clay. Once they'd straightened out the misunderstanding, Jake seemed to be . . . to be what? Where was their relationship going?

Where do you want it to go?

"Good question," she muttered under her breath. What did she want from him? Foolish as it seemed now, she'd lived so many years with Clay Duvall in the back of her mind, the image of the perfect man. Now, she understood how stupid she'd been. Clay was—well, how would she describe him?—shallow, conceited, self-centered.

He wasn't half the man Jake Williams was, but this didn't mean Jake was *the one* she'd been waiting for, did it? He didn't seem to be the type to commit. He was already dedicated to his career, and she couldn't imagine him taking the time for a family.

She stopped herself, realizing her career meant just as much. She was on overload right now with Aunt Thee ill, and trying to reestablish her business in New Orleans. She looked into the future and decided she wanted a family, but she didn't have the time for one.

"You could make the time," whispered an inner voice.

The thought made her pause; she could find the time for a family. It would mean designing fewer pieces, being less ambitious, but she could still keep her business especially now that she was backed by TriTech's large support staff.

"It's something to consider," cautioned her more practical self. "Your biological clock is ticking very loudly."

She closed her eyes for a moment, resting her head against a support post in the gazebo. Aunt Thee would be an excellent grandmother, she thought with a smile. And her aunt was taken with Jake. She would be thrilled beyond belief to have her marry Jake.

Marry?

They hardly knew each other. She couldn't believe the turn her thoughts had taken. Surely, it was from lack of sleep and worry. A clearer head never would allow her imagination to run wild. She tried to relax and told herself to give it a few more minutes before going upstairs again. With luck Ravelle would have left by then.

"Alyssa? Is that you?"

Her head jerked up and she realized she had dozed off. For how long?

"Jake?"

The shadowy figure mounted the steps into the gazebo. "Yes. What are you doing out here?"

"I—I just came out for a moment to avoid Ravelle."

Jake sat down beside her. Even in the darkness, he radiated a virility that drew her like a magnet. She was grateful he couldn't read her mind and know what she'd been thinking.

"What did your father have to say?"

She permitted herself a sigh, knowing Jake would understand. "He didn't know what to do about me, but he cared. He never believed I stole Phoebe's baby." She pressed her lips together for a moment, then added, "He wanted me to talk to her, so I did."

"Really? Tonight?"

"Yes. Phoebe was surprisingly"—she searched for the word—"understanding. She claims she's divorcing Clay—"

"Didn't Clay tell you he was the one who wanted the divorce?"

"Yes. I don't care whose idea it is. It's not my business."

Jake was sitting beside her, his long legs stretched out from beneath his priest's robe. He studied her for a moment, his expression concealed by the darkness and the mask he was wearing. She realized her mask was still on her forehead. She must look very silly.

"Phoebe told me she's starting over, getting a new life without Clay."

"Who's she involved with?"

"What do you mean?"

Jake leaned closer, and a sliver of light from the spots on the gazebo highlighted his black mask. "Women don't leave their husbands without someone in the wings."

The hair on her neck bristled. "Wait a minute—"

"Ditto for men," he told her. "Spouses stay in relationships unless they have someone they would rather be with—men or women. That's what divorce attorneys will tell you."

Alyssa was silent for a moment, reluctant to admit Jake might be correct. "Phoebe just said she was starting over. It's possible she's doing this on her own."

"Possible, but not likely."

Alyssa had to admit she was having difficulty imagining Phoebe out on her own. She didn't have a career the way Alyssa did. Someone might be encouraging her.

Jake pulled her into his arms, hearing what she didn't say, understanding her frustration, her anxiety. "Let's get out of here."

She mumbled her consent and Jake guided her out of the gazebo and down the path that led around the side of the house.

"Isn't it shorter to go through the house?" she asked.

"The door to the back study is locked." He took her down the used brick path to the porte cochere on the side of the house. The overhang was a vestige of the turn of the century in the Garden District when automobiles pulled up along the side of the house to unload passengers.

"Is Phoebe all your father wanted to talk to you about?" Jake asked as he handed the parking valet his claim ticket.

"He says he's proud of me."

Jake kept a silent curse to himself. It was easy to be proud of Alyssa now that she was a success. Where had Gordon LeCroix been when Alyssa had needed him? The same place Max Williams had been. Absent fathers. Both had decided to reappear in their children's lives.

Jake didn't know what to say. He'd never been good at situations like this. He'd known his mother loved him, but she'd rarely expressed it in so many words. He'd never told her what she meant to him. He'd always believed she knew. Now, he wondered, and cursed himself because it was too late.

"Let's have a quiet dinner somewhere," he said, opening the Porsche's door for her.

"I need to check on Aunt Thee." Alyssa pulled off the headpiece of her nun's habit and mask. Her tousled hair hung in loose waves down to her shoulders.

Twenty minutes later, he was astounded to find a parking place near the French Quarter town house Alyssa shared with her aunt. He parked and locked the car, then took Alyssa's arm to walk her up the street.

"Shawn," Alyssa called softly once they were inside the town house.

The male nurse came down the stairs, his raised finger in front of his lips. "I just checked on her. She's still asleep."

"I'll just go in and give her a kiss."

Jake walked softly into the upstairs bedroom behind Alyssa. Jake stopped just inside the doorway and watched. Alyssa tiptoed toward the bed where the shadowy form of her aunt was barely visible beneath a fluffy comforter.

"I love you, Aunt Thee," she whispered. "Thank you for all you did for me."

"Are we having fun yet?"

She laughed and gazed up at the stars. They were on Jake's roof terrace, having opted for bringing home pizza from Mama Rosa's Slice of Italy rather than wait for a table at a restaurant. Benson sat between them, silently begging for anchovies.

"How many nights a week do you eat pizza?" she asked.

"Hey! Benson makes me do it." He stroked the retriever's back. "Don't you, boy?"

She cocked her head, picking up a sound. "Is that your telephone?"

Jake pushed back from the table and stood up. "Maybe it's Sanchez. He should have reported in by now."

Alyssa cleaned up the table, and tossed the pizza box into the trash chute that went into a bin in the garage. She wandered across the terrace, Benson at her heels, marveling at how the potted trees and containers filled with flowers created an amazing garden in the middle of the Warehouse District. At the edge of the roof, a brick wall as high as her waist kept anyone from falling off. She peered over the side to the lighted street below where people were coming and going from the restaurants and art galleries that stayed open late on Saturday nights.

She'd changed out of the nun's habit into a pale blue gauze dress and sandals. It might be fun to take Benson for a walk and check out some of the galleries. As if sensing she was thinking about him, Benson nuzzled her leg.

"It wasn't Sanchez," Jake said, coming up behind her. He brushed her hair aside and kissed her neck just below her ear.

She gripped the wall with both hands. The touch of his lips, even on her neck, elicited reactions she'd come to expect, even anticipate. Her nipples constricted, her heart beat in uneven lurches, a sensation of heat and fullness built between her thighs.

"What are we doing about birth control?" he asked.

"What do you mean *we?*"

"The mouse in my pocket wants to know."

She felt the thrust of his erection against her buttocks. He spun her around so they were nose-to-nose. He cupped her bottom and hoisted her up against his arousal—just in case she hadn't already gotten the message.

"I'm on the pill," she confessed.

"For how long?"

"A-ah . . . years."

"Years?" His outrage echoed across the rooftops. "Years? You've been holding out on me."

His lips captured hers in a fierce, hot kiss. His tongue invaded her mouth, commanding hers to respond. She couldn't resist melting into him, allowing his strong arms to lock her against him. After the emotional roller coaster she'd been on for the last few days, it felt so right to push it all aside and live in the moment.

She succumbed to the forceful domination of his lips, his body. Arching against him, savoring the heat and hardness of his erection, she kissed him with the kind of passion she'd never known with a man. This was the way it was supposed to be, she told herself as she inhaled his rich, musky scent and allowed herself this night of pleasure.

He lifted her skirt up and had her panties down to her knees in one swift movement. She stepped out of them and kicked off her sandals. He unhooked his belt and let his pants drop. His penis sprang forward, fully erect. He was so masculine, so heart-stoppingly male.

His hand cupped her between the thighs, and he stroked her with expert precision. Oh, my. She was afraid she was going to climax before he was inside her.

He braced her against the wall and nuzzled her with the velvet smooth tip of his penis. She was slick, ready for him. His hot, hard length penetrated her with a single, powerful thrust. Arousal, strong and demanding, throbbed in every nerve ending in her body. Unexpectedly, he froze.

"Why are you stopping?"

"I'm giving you some of your own medicine." His voice was gritty, a shade shy of a whisper. "You've been torturing me for weeks."

She would have laughed except every inch of her body was aching with frustration. "I'll make it up to you."

"Promise?"

"Yes."

"Swear you'll let me make love to you as often as I want."

Uh-oh. This sounded like trouble. His insolent smile made it plain he'd wait until hell froze over—or he got what he wanted—whichever came first.

"All right. I swear it. Come on."

He delved deeper, then pulled back only to thrust forward again, using his body like an exquisite weapon of torture. Picking up the pace, he hammered against her. With each thrust, she lifted her hips to meet his. For the next few minutes, nothing on earth mattered except the relentless pounding of his body against hers.

Unexpectedly something released deep within the very core of her being, reverberating through her with a convulsive shudder. For half a heartbeat, she saw stars. A few seconds later Jake followed, throwing back his head with a moan so deep it almost sounded as if he were in pain.

She rested her head against his shoulder. They were both breathing like racehorses, their skin damp, their hearts slamming against the walls of their chests. It was a full minute before the world returned, and she realized Benson was barking at them, his tail wagging.

"He thinks it's some kind of a game," Jake told her, his voice a little raw. "He's never seen sex up close and personal before."

She had to ask, "What about the other women?"

He pulled back and looked at her with eyes still smoldering with lust. "I didn't care enough about them to bring them home."

CHAPTER 27

"Now, where were we?" Jake asked.

He'd carried her inside, and they were sprawled across his unmade bed. Benson had positioned himself on the bench at the foot of the bed, enjoying the show. The room was dark and much cooler than it had been outside. In the background she heard soft music playing on the stereo.

"We were discussing corporate strategies," she said, all innocence.

"No, we weren't." The weight of his body was on the bed, but his hip and leg had her anchored in place. "Remember your promise."

"Promise?"

"You're welching on me?" He could have convinced the toughest jury he shocked beyond belief.

"Of course, not. Refresh my memory."

They were both naked now, although she couldn't remember how or when they'd taken off the rest of their clothes. The hair on his chest and his emerging beard rasped her tender skin, but she didn't complain. It was a powerfully erotic sensation, and she wiggled a little just to feel the enticing prickle.

"You promised I could make love to you as often as I wanted, and you'd be my sex slave."

"Wait! You never mentioned becoming a sex slave."

"What about the first part?"

"I vaguely recall . . . saying something."

"Okay, so show me."

She reached up and pulled his head down, intending to give him a quick kiss, then come up with some clever remark. She thought she'd given it her all when they'd been out on the terrace, but she was mistaken. In a second, the heat returned, and with it came her obsessive desire to feel him inside her again, to have the erotic experience all over again.

Both hands on his shoulders, she pushed him back. "I get to be on top."

"Hold it. Sex slaves don't call the shots."

"Being a sex slave wasn't part of the deal, and you know it."

He considered it a moment, his dark eyes glittering in the dim light. "It's still my turn. What happened outside was rushed. I'm better than that."

Better? She doubted she would survive any better sex, but refused to feed his ego by telling him so. "No way."

She straddled him, taking care not to touch his erection and smiled inwardly at his startled expression. She bent over just far enough for her breasts to graze the dark whorl of hair feathering across his chest. Her nipples, already hard, tingled, and a low moan escaped her lips. She kept rubbing, a shocking heat invading her body.

Edging forward, she silently encouraged him to taste her breasts. He got the message and took one nipple between his lips. The sweet suction and the rasp of his tongue over her beaded nipple sent a lancing jolt of desire down to her groin.

She tried to reposition herself to take advantage of his fully erect penis, but he wasn't having any of it.

"Don't rush me."

He began to kiss her other breast as his hand stole between her legs. She cautioned herself not to make a sound, but another little moan came out as he began to stroke her. She squeezed her eyes shut, telling herself she couldn't possibly be on the verge of another orgasm.

"Like that, huh?"

She heard the triumphant smile in his voice. Responding was out of the question even if she could have come up with some witty remark. She was close, so close. Her body was trembling, the vibration coming from deep within, the way it had not so long ago.

He guided the tip of his erection into her, then put both hands on her hips and brought her down hard. She gasped, impaled, afraid if she moved she would instantly climax.

"Come, on, baby. Ride me. Ride me hard."

She did what she was told, and found she had more self-control than she had thought. They moved together, in perfect sync, like dancers hearing their own tune. This time he came first with a rough growl and an upward buck of his hips. Within a few seconds, a ripple of unadulterated pleasure became a white-hot upheaval of satisfaction.

She pitched forward, and he caught her in his arms. It was a moment before she realized Benson was standing on all fours on the bench, barking, his tail thumping against the bedpost. She rolled to one side, a little embarrassed at her wanton behavior. She stared up at the loft's ceiling with its open beams and shadowy recesses.

"Where are my clothes?"

"Outside," came the hoarse response. "You don't need them."

"I have to go home."

"No, you don't. Thee's still asleep." He pulled her close and she nestled against his shoulder. "I guess we should talk."

"Talk?" She was so exhausted she could hardly get out the word. Snuggling seemed like a better idea.

"That's what smart men do after sex. I read it in *Cosmo*."

She couldn't help giggling.

"What's so funny?"

"You reading *Cosmo*. It's hard to imagine."

"Hey, I was stranded in a Japanese hotel. The only magazine I could find in English was *Cosmopolitan*. Read it cover to cover." He nuzzled her ear. "Know what it said? Women hate men who roll over and go to sleep after sex. True?"

"M-m-m, I guess." She snuggled closer, closing her eyes. "What do you want to talk about?"

He said something about bringing in another armoire so she could have closet space in his loft. Closet space, she thought as she drifted off. He was thinking in terms of a permanent relationship. She liked the idea, more than liked it actually.

The *br-ring—br-ring* of the telephone awakened them. Jake levered himself into an upright position and picked up the telephone on the stand beside the bed. Alyssa lay flat on her back, trying to muster the strength to get up, find her clothes, and get dressed to go home. Jake listened and muttered a few words before hanging up.

"Sanchez is flying in this morning. He wants to talk to me in person."

It took a minute for the words to register. What couldn't Sanchez say over the telephone?

Jake was waiting outside the Million-Aire terminal when TriTech's Gulfstream landed. From pockmarks in the tarmac minute tendrils of steam rose, a reminder of the predawn rain shower. The private jet taxied to a stop, and the ground crew rolled up a ramp. Sanchez hurried down the steps, his Tumi duffel slung over one shoulder.

It hadn't taken much to convince Alyssa to go home to her aunt. He'd promised to come over later with a full report. The minute Sanchez was within earshot, Jake asked, "What did you find out?"

"I was right. Gracie Harper did talk to her husband. Claude said she accepted twenty thousand dollars—in cash—to hand the baby over to a man."

"Is Harper willing to testify about it?"

Sanchez's dark eyes narrowed. "No. He has IRS problems, so he's living in Mexico. Even if he did return, he wouldn't want to incriminate himself. There's no statute of limitations on kidnapping."

"But if he didn't take the baby—"

"He was an accomplice. Not only did he know about it before the fact, he placed the call to Alyssa's apartment and pretended he was Clay Duvall."

Jake halted, his hand on the detective's arm. "They deliberately framed Alyssa? Shit! Who's the son-of-a-bitch?"

"Phoebe Duvall made the arrangements."

"Why am I not surprised?" Jake had always thought Phoebe was a little off.

"Harper claims his wife would never have taken the baby from its mother unless the mother consented. Apparently, Gracie always felt guilty about what she'd done."

"But not guilty enough to take the money and hand over the baby to the black market." He thought a moment, then added, "Why did Phoebe do it? Because Clay wasn't the father, and she didn't want him to find out. Right?"

"Apparently."

"Even if Claude Harper won't testify, we can try to locate the baby. Finding him will clear Alyssa."

Sanchez didn't reply.

Jake started walking again, verbalizing his thoughts

as he moved. "Phoebe has to know who took little Patrick. I'll make her tell me."

"She arranged for the baby's father to take it. He's the one who put up the money."

"Makes sense. Wait. Wouldn't someone have noticed a family who unexpected turned up with an infant? The case was all over television and the papers."

"The father took the baby to his parents' farm . . . outside Oklahoma City."

"Okay, so it won't be hard to find him."

"Patrick died almost nine years ago." The note of concern in Sanchez's voice disturbed Jake. "The child contracted a rare virus. The doctors couldn't save him."

"Claude Harper knew all this?"

"Yes. He and Gracie remained close. She stayed in contact with the father as well as Phoebe."

"Sounds like she was blackmailing them. Maybe they're the ones who killed her."

"No, not from what Claude said. Gracie never forgave herself for taking the child. She kept in touch with the mother to make sure the baby was all right."

"Can we find the father?"

Sanchez waited a second too long before responding. Something clicked in Jake's head, and he cursed himself for not having guessed sooner.

"It's Max, isn't it? My father had an affair with Phoebe."

"Yes. Your father took the baby."

Clay woke up in Maree's bed, and for once, Dante wasn't around. He lifted his head off the pillow, then let it drop again. It felt as if someone had buried an ax in his skull. He'd stayed at the party too late and had drunk too much. After his talk with Phoebe, who could blame him?

Phoebe wanted a divorce, and she wanted it immediately. She knew all about Duvall Imports' accounting problems, but she didn't care. She wasn't willing to give him any more time.

He kept his eyes shut to block out the shafts of glaring sunlight streaking through the rattan shades in Maree's bedroom. In his mind's eye, he could see Phoebe, the way she'd been last night—sitting regally in the downstairs study—telling him to go to hell.

She'd cost him the woman he loved, made his life miserable for years, and now she was going to ruin him financially. Then it struck him like a bolt out of the blue. She was leaving him for another man. That had to be the reason she wanted a divorce. It was difficult to imagine, given the fact that she'd tricked him into marriage. She'd had numerous affairs over the years—not that he cared. So why would she want to marry this particular man?

Money?

Who had enough money to entice Phoebe to leave him and disappoint her family? He couldn't think of anyone that wealthy except Max Williams. Christ! The man was old enough to be her father. True, she had a thing for older men. But if she wanted Max, why now? He'd been sniffing around for years, always single, and getting richer every day. It didn't make any sense.

"Clay . . . darling."

Great, Maree was awake. She'd come in so late last night, after being with Neville Berringer, that Clay had almost fallen asleep before she'd returned.

"Yes?" Clay opened his eyes and found Maree leaning over him.

"We're good together, aren't we?"

They had their moments, sure, but he wouldn't brag about it. He tried for a smile, but it made his head hurt more.

"We should get married."

"I am married, remember?"

Her dark eyes glittered with something he couldn't name. "But if you were free . . ."

He closed his eyes again and yawned. He didn't want her to guess his thoughts. He hadn't told anyone except Alyssa about the impending divorce.

"What about Neville?" As he said the name, Clay's eyes flew open. Berringer was rich and eligible. Was he the man Phoebe was involved with?

"Neville's nice but he's gay. He gets me into the right parties. That's all."

"He's not gay. He was married for years."

"So?"

Maree never lied, forcing him to believe her. Like Phoebe, Maree Winston lived to move in high society. He understood why Maree would use Neville to gain entrée to places she wouldn't be invited.

"I know it would cost you a lot to divorce your wife."

Clay nodded at the excuse he'd given Maree when he'd first started seeing her. Now, unfortunately, it was the absolute truth.

"Divorces are expensive, and they're hard on families." Clay tried to put as much concern in his voice as possible.

The doorbell rang, and Maree jumped up, saving him from dodging her questions. Maree was determined to become Mrs. Clay Duvall. Of all the damn luck. Neville Berringer was gay. Clay had been hoping Berringer would take care of Maree for him.

Maree shrugged into a diaphanous robe and belted it, saying, "It must be Dante. He said he'd be over this morning with beignets from Croissant D'Or. He wants to finalize the deal."

She rushed out of the room, and Clay forced himself to get up. He staggered into the bathroom, the blood pounding in his temples like a jackhammer. He heard Dante's voice coming from the living room.

Of course, Dante hadn't been around last night. A woman with Maree's looks could finagle her way into a society party on Neville's arm, but Dante would never be welcome. Clay smiled despite the haggard face he saw in the mirror.

He liked having something on Dante. The Bahamian thought he could own anyone just by discovering their weaknesses. Once this deal was over, Clay intended to cut his losses and get rid of both Maree and Dante.

CHAPTER 28

Clay put on his trousers and found one of his polo shirts hanging in Maree's closet. By keeping some clothes here and having sex, he was encouraging Maree to believe they had a future together. He'd be smart to move back home, especially with Phoebe staying with her parents.

"We saved you a few beignets, mon," Dante told Clay the second he walked out of the bedroom.

The aroma of the bits of dough deep-fried, then tossed in powdered sugar, a favorite of Maree's, usually made Clay's mouth water. Not this morning. His stomach was queasy and the handful of aspirin he'd downed hadn't improved his headache.

He sat down opposite Maree and Dante who were side by side on the couch drinking coffee and sprinkling even more powdered sugar on their beignets.

"I've made de arrangements," Dante said. "The heroin will be loaded on your boat in Singapore."

"They've hidden it in containers filled with children's toys." Excitement punctuated every syllable Maree spoke.

"Wait a minute! I haven't contacted my people here.

Asking them to sign off on invoices is one thing. Heroin smuggling is another."

"Look, mon. For de right price, anyone will turn his back."

"True, but the Port Authority is using drug-sniffing dogs now."

"Dante's thought of everything," Maree informed him. "The packages are wrapped in cloth doused with formaldehyde. It throws off the dog's scent."

"I see," he responded.

What he really saw was the need to talk to Phoebe again. It was her connection who originally put him in touch with the men on the dock who were willing to sign off the invoices—for a price. He'd never asked who she knew or how she knew them. Back then, when they first started their little scam, his only concern had been saving Duvall Imports.

Phoebe had a thing not only for older men but also for the lowlifes who inhabited the dark underbelly of New Orleans. Drugs and crime of all sorts were rampant in the city. This was going to take someone more influential than the guys who checked cargo containers' invoices.

"Clay, Clay, are you listening?" Maree asked.

"Yes. I was just thinking when to make arrangements at the dock."

"Don't you be worrin'. I take care of it."

Dante was studying him with a strange expression on his face, one that made Clay edgy. A sickening thought hit him and make his queasy stomach lurch. Had Phoebe found out about Dante?

It was possible, he decided, upset that he hadn't thought of it sooner. That might account for Phoebe's decision. He didn't know anyone more prejudiced than Phoebe. She hid it well, of course. She sat on too many committees where it would have been unthinkable to voice her true feelings. She would never understand about Dante.

* * *

Jake sat across from his father in the sunroom, over-looking the garden in the mansion where Max had recently thrown the party. After hearing what Sanchez had to say, Jake had come directly here. He'd found his father reading the paper and having coffee.

"Something wrong?" Max asked.

"You were Patrick Duvall's father, weren't you?"

"Yes," Max replied, his tone flat. "How did you find out?"

"It doesn't matter." Considering Gracie Harper had been murdered, Jake wasn't sure he should trust his father. "Did you try to frame Alyssa for what you'd done?"

Max shoved his chair back and stood up. He walked over to the French doors that opened out onto the garden. "I didn't know a thing about it until it was over." His back was to Jake, but his shoulders were hunched forward, and he suddenly seemed much older. Max slowly turned and looked directly at him with the same brown eyes Jake saw whenever he bothered to look in the mirror. "Phoebe did it to protect me. She thought if there was another suspect, the police would be thrown off."

"I'm not buying it. Phoebe was jealous of Alyssa. She still is."

"You're in love with her."

"Yes. I do love her." He saw no point in denying it. For some time, he'd suspected he'd fallen for her. Last night had cinched it.

Without commenting, Max returned to his seat. "Then you'll understand how I felt—still feel—about Phoebe."

"The woman is a nutcase. She's shallow and self-centered. Alyssa is talented and intelligent and—" He stopped. This was getting him nowhere.

"Phoebe's a little troubled."

Troubled? Yeah, right, and he was as pious as the Pope.

"If you were willing to take the baby, why didn't you marry Phoebe?"

"I wanted to, believe me. The minute she found out she was pregnant, I told her I'd marry her. Hell, I'd asked her to marry me way before that."

Jake thought he knew what was coming next, but he let his father say it.

"Phoebe felt she had to marry someone from her own circle of friends."

"In other words, you weren't good enough for her." Jake could just imagine how upset Hattie LeCroix would have been about Max. Not only was he not part of their circle of friends, Max's parents were "stone" Okies. Dirt farmers with no education at all. Jake had met them a few times and liked them, but Hattie would have died before she would have introduced them to her friends.

Max gazed at Jake with a bland half-smile. "When Phoebe became pregnant, I was on my way, but I hadn't made the kind of money I have now."

Jake wondered if things had changed. He'd told Alyssa that Phoebe wouldn't divorce Clay without some other sucker in the wings. It had never occurred to him the sucker might be his own father. "Are you two getting together now?"

"Lord, no. We've stayed friends over the years, but Phoebe will never leave Clay. I'd do anything for her, but I've given up on convincing her to marry me."

Jake decided the divorce bit might be a ploy to get at Alyssa somehow. Phoebe was more than just a little nutty. In his opinion, she was dangerous.

"Alyssa's life was nearly ruined."

"I'm sorry. I truly am. I took Patrick to my parents' farm and stayed until he was settled. I didn't know what was happening back here. When I returned and found out, Alyssa had left for Italy."

"You could have cleared her name."

"I could have," he admitted, "but I didn't. They would have taken my son away from me."

The impact of the emotion in his words immobilized Jake. His father hadn't just taken the child out of duty. He'd loved the little boy.

Something else Sanchez told him unexpectedly took on new meaning. Patrick had died almost nine years ago. That was about the time Max had suddenly appeared in his life.

"You didn't have a heart attack, did you, Max? Patrick was going to be your heir, then he died. That's why you came to me."

With a sweeping gesture, Max waved his arm. "Yes, but I had my reasons for not having been part of your life sooner. Your mother didn't want me around you. She sent back every support check. She refused to let me see you."

"The courts could have forced her." Jake detected the bitter edge of cynicism in his own voice. "But you didn't think of that, did you?"

"I considered it, but I didn't follow through. I was focused on my business, and you were living far away."

Jake told himself he was too old to be hurt, but he refused to lie to himself. He'd spent almost nine years doing his damnedest for a man who'd been too busy to make an effort to be a father. Well, what did he expect of a man who could fall in love with a woman like Phoebe?

Jake had been an accident. His mother never hid that fact. It was the reason he was so cautious when he had sex. No child of his was going without a father.

Jake started to get up. He wanted to get as far away from Max as he possibly could.

"Son, wait."

Jake was tempted to hit him. What right did he have to call him son?

"I know you think I'm a lousy father. I can't deny it. I came for you because I'd worked a lifetime building TriTech. I wanted someone to carry on after me. I thought it was going to be Patrick. I didn't expect you to be as bright and savvy as you are."

Once Jake would have taken this as a compliment, but it didn't matter to him now. He'd take the next plane out of New Orleans if it weren't for Alyssa.

"I'm proud of you. That's why I bowed out of the business. I wanted TriTech to be yours. You've earned it."

"You can take it back." He stood up and walked away. "I don't want it."

Max followed him across the room. "I've tried to make it up to you, to be friends with you, but you insist on keeping a wall between us no matter how hard I try."

Jake spun around to face his father, and Max nearly collided with him. "I guess my sixth sense told me that I was second choice."

"You wouldn't have been if your mother had allowed me to get to know you."

There was no denying the sincerity in his voice. They were the words of a desperate man. Suddenly, Jake saw Max for what he was—an old man who'd wasted his life pursuing money and loving the wrong woman for her beauty and social connections.

"Did you have Gracie Harper killed?"

"No," Max said without hesitation. "I read about it in the paper. It was probably a botched robbery attempt. The nurse's death sent Phoebe into a tailspin. She thought the case would be reopened, and the truth would come out."

"It wouldn't have done your political career a helluva lot of good either."

Max studied him with wary eyes. "True. It's something

I've always known. The past has a way of coming back to haunt you."

What was there left to say? Jake started toward the front door again.

"You're not walking out on TriTech, the opportunity of a lifetime, are you?"

"Damn right, I am."

"You're just like your mother—stubborn like an Arkansas mule."

Jake could have reminded Max—yet again—he was just as stubborn but didn't bother. He wasn't certain how he felt about his father, but he refused to be drawn into an argument over the mother who'd loved him.

Max caught up with Jake in the two-story entry hall where a massive Baccarat chandelier hung from the domed ceiling. Sunlight streamed in through the beveled glass windows and bounced off the prisms of crystal like a rainbow.

"Look, I'm sorry. I didn't mean to attack your mother." Max put his hand on Jake's shoulder. "JoBeth was a wonderful woman in many ways, but when she made up her mind about something, there was no changing it."

It was the truth, and Jake couldn't deny it, but he couldn't bring himself to say it. His mother had her faults, but she loved him with all her heart.

"Jake, what can I do to make it right between us?" The expression in his father's dark eyes seemed to plead with him.

Go to hell, was on the tip of Jake's tongue, but he stopped himself. *Get over it!* There was more at stake here than Jake's ego.

"You could tell the truth and clear Alyssa's name."

The corner of Max's mouth twisted with exasperation. "She means that much to you? Enough to see me go to prison?"

"You won't go to prison. I doubt if they'd even bring charges considering you were the father." He studied

Max for a moment, attempting to measure his father's sincerity. Did he really want to salvage their relationship? "The truth might be a death knell for your political ambitions."

"It's not that important to me. It was something to do after building TriTech." He lowered his voice, adding, "I don't know what this will do to Phoebe."

"Why do you care? It's crazy. Phoebe wouldn't marry you. She's used you for years." Jake told himself to calm down. He was yelling now. "What kind of a woman gives her baby away—even to its father?"

Max shrugged, but didn't say one word in Phoebe's defense.

"Was Phoebe the one who arranged to have the second baby stolen to implicate Alyssa?"

"I don't know anything about it," Max responded. "And I don't know anything about the man who attacked Alyssa either."

"What man?"

"I don't know. Last night, she made me dance with her. I'm telling you, Alyssa is one tough broad. She threatened to cut my heart out if I sent anyone else to hurt her. I said I didn't know a thing about it, but she didn't believe me."

Someone had threatened Alyssa, and she hadn't told him? Why not? The answer came as soon as he'd asked himself the question. She thought his father was responsible, and she didn't want to cause trouble.

"There's something else I need to ask you," Jake said. "You insisted on buying Duvall Imports because of Phoebe, right?" When Max nodded, he continued. "You knew it was defrauding the government."

"No. It's shaky financially. I figured you could turn it around."

Max sounded sincere. If anything, he seemed beaten down, his eyes world-weary and his shoulders stooped.

"Then why did you have Troy Conway falsify the forensic accountant's report?"

"What report? I didn't have Troy do anything. I don't know what you're talking about."

His father was so genuinely shocked that Jake had no choice but to believe him. Suddenly, he felt as old and as tired as his father looked. This whole mess was a can of worms. It was impossible to tell what was going on.

CHAPTER 29

Alyssa sat with Aunt Thee in the courtyard of the town house. Her aunt was weak, but she'd insisted on having lunch outside where she could enjoy the spring air. Soon it would be too hot to eat outdoors.

"Gordon took me aside last night and talked to me," Alyssa said, still unable to call him "father."

"Really? What did he have to say for himself?"

"He claims he's proud of me."

"Well, he should be." Aunt Thee took a small bite of the ham sandwich Alyssa had made. "You're a wonderful person, not to mention being an international star on the jewelry scene."

"Costume jewelry. A few people know me, true—"

"Give yourself credit. You're a name in those circles. With Jake's backing, you'll become a household word."

When Aunt Thee was on a roll, there was no arguing with her. She had absolute faith in Alyssa's talent, and to her credit, she always had. From the moment Aunt Thee had whisked Alyssa away from New Orleans, and Alyssa had shown her the few pieces of jewelry she'd made for herself, Aunt Thee had encouraged her.

"Is that all dear Gordon had to say?"

"No. He wanted me to talk to Phoebe. He really wants us to be friends."

Aunt Thee put down her sandwich. "Do you seriously believe that's possible?"

"Maybe I'm being naïve, but I'd like to think so. We're half-sisters. Why should we be enemies?"

Aunt Thee shook her head as if baffled by her niece's stupidity. "Don't trust her. Not for one minute. She convinced everyone you'd kidnapped her baby and threw it into the bayou. I'm in the hospital and another baby vanishes in much the same way—casting more blame on you. Phoebe's responsible. She's jealous of you. She'll stop at nothing."

"You may be right. I did talk to her last night after Gordon insisted. She seemed to have come to terms with our situation. She says she's divorcing Clay and starting over. I think . . . I hope, she wants to put the past behind us."

"That'll be the day."

Alyssa respected Aunt Thee's business acumen, but her aunt had met Phoebe only a few times. She didn't know her and had no idea how difficult life in the LeCroix house had been. Hattie emotionally abused everyone—especially Phoebe.

"I'm going to give Phoebe a chance."

Aunt Thee's expression said: You'll regret it.

Alyssa changed the subject to one she knew would have her aunt's approval. "Jake's coming to dinner tonight. Actually, he's bringing dinner from Emeril's."

Emeril Lagasse was New Orleans' premier chef who had his own nationally syndicated television show. His restaurant, Emeril's, was the toast of the city, but Alyssa knew this wouldn't impress her aunt. Thee was more taken with Jake.

"I can hardly wait," Aunt Thee told her. "Considering you didn't come home last night, I suspect this is a serious relationship."

She couldn't lie to the one person who truly loved her. "I'm very interested in Jake. I can't speak for him."

"I can. I'm an excellent judge of character. Jake is going to be the father of your children. I'm going to be a grandmother before I go to my great reward."

Alyssa felt the heat creeping up her neck. She couldn't be blushing; she never blushed. Yet the way she'd made love to Jake last night made her want to blush.

She managed to say, "It's a little early to be planning on grandchildren. We hardly know each other. This could turn out to be nothing."

The buzzer to the front gate sounded and Alyssa stood up, saved from having to answer another personal question. She opened the gate and found two policemen standing there.

"Alyssa Rossi?"

"Yes," she responded with a dizzying awareness something terrible was about to happen.

"You're under arrest for murder."

Jake had left his father's home, shaken, yet determined. This was a mess worthy of a soap opera, but he thought he knew how to fix it. Well, maybe. It all depended on how much Max really cared about him.

It was difficult to find a parking place in Faubourg Marigny where Troy Chevalier had rented a restored Creole cottage. The hip area was adjacent to the French Quarter and not far from Thee's town house. As soon as Jake had spoken to Troy, he could go talk to Alyssa. He'd left a message earlier saying he'd spoken with Sanchez and was coming over to tell her about it. He needed to fit together a few more pieces of the puzzle before he attempted to explain this predicament.

Jake decided Troy had chosen this area because of its bohemian atmosphere and its French name. The man idolized all things French. With his wealthy family living in Paris, Jake was surprised Troy had stayed at TriTech for as long as he had.

What he hadn't expected was Troy's betrayal. It seemed totally out of character for someone so proud of his family, his education. Go figure. Jake was a piss-poor judge of people. Even though he and Troy had worked together closely for years, Jake realized he knew little about the man's personal life.

If Max hadn't persuaded Troy to alter the report, who had? Clay Duvall? Possibly. He had the most to lose, and he certainly hadn't been happy to learn Duvall Imports' accounting was being moved in-house.

He finally shoehorned his Porsche into a parking place near one of the nightclubs that drew people to the area after dark. He walked toward the river where Troy lived and spotted a Lucky Dog on the corner. Just seeing the giant hot dog-shaped cart made his stomach rumble. He stopped for a hot dog and ate it while he continued down the block to Troy's cottage.

"Let's hope he's home," Jake muttered to himself.

Jake rang the bell, and the door immediately swung open. Troy had the widest, most enthusiastic smile Jake had ever seen. His face crumbled as if someone had punched him in the gut when he saw Jake.

"I was expecting someone else," Troy said.

"Go on. You can't mean it."

"Come in." Troy gestured toward the inside of the cottage. "Is something wrong?"

"What would be wrong?" Jake walked inside and was not surprised to see the living room was furnished with French antiques.

"Last night you left the party early." He motioned toward a love seat and a pair of chairs. "You've never come over, so I assume this is very important."

Jake sat in one of the chairs and waited until Troy took a seat before speaking. He wanted to look him right in the eye when he questioned him. Troy sat on the love seat opposite Jake and smoothed back his receding blond hair. If he was nervous, it didn't show.

Jake came right to the point. "I want to know why you falsified the Overton and Overton report."

A shadow of alarm touched Troy's face, and his dark eyes darted around the room as if looking for a way to escape. "You know."

"Answer the damn question. Why? How much were you paid?"

"Paid? I wouldn't take money." Two deep lines of worry appeared between his brows. "I've never done anything like this in my life."

Jake cursed himself for believing him. "Then why did you do it?"

"A . . . friend needed help. I planned to tell you about it soon."

"Before or after you left for Paris?"

"Paris?" Troy responded as if Jake was speaking in tongues.

"You reserved two first-class tickets to Paris."

"Oh . . . yes . . . well. I haven't had a vacation in several years. I—"

"Cut the bullshit. Who persuaded you to doctor the report?"

Troy rose slowly and walked across the cottage to a set of windows looking out onto a small courtyard. "I did it to help Phoebe Duvall."

Jake sucked in a quick breath of utter astonishment. He heard himself gasp, "Phoebe?"

Troy shuffled back to the love seat and plopped down, his eyes on Jake. "Yes. She's been having terrible problems with Clay. She's going to divorce him, but if the value of Duvall Imports falls, she won't get the settlement she deserves. You see, she put all the money from her trust fund into Clay's company."

"Phoebe's leaving Clay for *you?*"

"Yes. Obviously, you find it hard to believe."

This sucked. Troy actually sounded insulted when

Jake was the one who had the right to be royally pissed off. Jake cautioned himself not to lose his temper. "No. You're worth ten of Clay Duvall. I just didn't realize you knew Phoebe so well."

"We met during the negotiations to buy Duvall Imports."

Is this great, or what? Troy had attended all the meetings and several dinners. Of course, he'd met Phoebe. She'd come on to every man. Why not Troy?

"Phoebe visited my parents when she was in Paris."

Now Jake got it. Phoebe had fallen—not for Troy—but for his wealthy parents' lifestyle.

"She'd like to live there, and I'd like to go home." Troy spread his hands wide as if this explained everything. "As soon as Phoebe's divorce is final, we'll get married."

It took a leap of faith to envision Troy and Phoebe and a lifetime of wedded bliss, but there you go. Life was proving to be a helluva lot stranger than he would ever have imagined.

"Congratulations." He fought the urge to kick his sorry butt around the room. How could a man with so much talent fall for Phoebe? "Explain what you see in her."

"She needs me." Troy gazed at Jake, his expression earnest. "You see, women that beautiful are never . . . approachable. Phoebe's different. Without help, she's lost."

Puh-leeze. Was Phoebe good, or what? She'd managed to convince two intelligent men—Troy and Max—to do her dirty work. Who knew how many others there had been?

She must be dynamite in bed—or something. She'd always struck Jake as being a little off. Why didn't they see it?

Then he got it. Live and learn. Troy and Max were basically insecure men, and Phoebe played to their low self-esteem. She made them feel powerful and protective.

With Max it was more obvious. His craving for social acceptance had bothered Jake from the very first. He hadn't understood why his father would care. Troy had been less noticeable. His wealthy family and superior education appeared to have given him all the self-confidence in the world, but beneath the thin veneer was an insecure man.

What had attracted Jake to Alyssa was her independent nature. From their first meeting, he'd noticed she had a power and depth to her that other women lacked. She hadn't played the beautiful woman card on him— far from it. She'd all but told him to kiss off.

He'd always been drawn to confident, self-reliant women. Like his mother. Aw, hell. The psychobabble bullshit couldn't be right, could it? Did everything start and end with your parents?

Troy interrupted his thoughts. "I knew there was a good chance you'd catch me. You're a lot smarter than you think. You don't need me. Phoebe does."

"Don't start."

"I mean it. You're just like Max. You have a natural gift for business."

"And here I was just telling myself that I'm like my mother."

"You're going to find this hard to believe—"

Jake shook his head, saying, "No, I'm not. I've heard just about everything in the last twenty-four hours."

"Phoebe's life has been hell."

"Could have fooled me."

Troy jumped to his feet. "Know what your problem is? You've got a wiseass remark about everything. The more serious something is, the more likely you are to come up with some outrageous remark."

"You've got a point," Jake conceded.

Troy blinked a few times as if he couldn't quite believe what Jake had said. He sat down again, adding, "Clay has made Phoebe miserable. He's had a mistress for the last few years. You saw her last night. She was wearing feathers.''

"I noticed her." He'd met the bombshell at Max's party but couldn't recall her name.

"Not only has Clay been seeing her, but Clay's been having sex with her and some Bahamian psychic."

Sounds like a party. Not that he went in for a ménage à trois, but many people must. They were featured on soft porn movies available in most hotel rooms. Okay, so he'd watched a few, but he'd never been tempted to try it himself.

"Phoebe's afraid she'll get some dreadful disease."

"You can't say enough for safe sex."

The words had slipped out. Troy shot him a disgusted looked, then sagged back against the sofa. "What are you going to do to me?"

Jake resisted the urge to warn him that living with Phoebe would be punishment enough. Now was the time to press for the truth.

"Did Phoebe arrange to have the second baby taken?"

"Of course not," snapped Troy. "Why would she?"

"Revenge."

"No way. Phoebe is leaving all this behind. Alyssa doesn't bother her anymore."

Don't bet on it.

"Are you going to file charges against me?" Troy asked.

"No. You've worked harder than I've had any right to expect. Brief Spencer on your projects, then let's go our separate ways."

Jake rose to go, but a knock on the front door stopped him.

Troy jumped up. "It's Phoebe."

Can you believe it? This was his lucky day. He waited for Troy to answer the door, prepared to escape and leave the lovebirds alone. Two men were on the porch, not Phoebe. One of them flipped open his wallet to show them a New Orleans police badge.

"Mind if we come in and ask you a few questions?"

"No, of course not. Come in." Troy looked at Jake with stony brown eyes.

"I don't know anything about this," Jake whispered.

The detectives asked him to identify himself. When he did, they merely nodded, apparently recognizing his name.

"When was the last time you saw Phoebe Duvall?"

In a heartbeat the remaining color leached from Troy's already pale face. "Why? Is something wrong?"

"I'm afraid Mrs. Duvall is dead."

"Dead? How?" Troy swayed toward Jake, and Jake put his hand on his shoulder.

"She was murdered."

Troy staggered to the couch and dropped down. "No! No! That's impossible. She's coming here in a few minutes."

The detectives looked at each other. Jake motioned for them to sit down. They all found seats while Troy stared, unseeing, at the ceiling fan.

"What happened?" Jake asked.

"This morning the Carreres' maid discovered Mrs. Duvall's body in the downstairs study. We haven't established an exact time of death, but it appears she was killed during the Vampire Ball last night."

"We're trying to find out who saw her and when," added the second detective.

The bottom dropped out of Jake's stomach. Alyssa had been in the study with Phoebe last night. Not that he thought Alyssa had killed her, but considering their past troubles, Alyssa would be high on the list of suspects.

"Why wasn't the body discovered earlier?" Jake asked.

"The family went to bed upstairs after the party. It wasn't until the maid began cleaning up this morning that she discovered the study was locked from the inside. She thought one of the guests must have locked it and gone out the French doors to the garden. She came around to unlock the door and discovered the body."

Jake remembered trying the door when he was searching for Alyssa, and it had been locked. He decided to keep this to himself for the time being.

"The last time I saw Phoebe was before dinner was served." Troy's voice was husky as if he were holding back tears. "She was on her way downstairs to talk to Clay. He wouldn't accept the fact she wanted a divorce. When she didn't return, I assumed she was upset and went back to her parents' house."

"They thought she'd gone to her own home. That's why she wasn't missed." The detective made a note on is pad. "Why didn't you contact her there?"

"I tried her cell phone, but didn't get an answer. I assumed the battery had died. Her parents don't know about our relationship, so I didn't want to chance calling the house. Since we'd already made arrangements to spend today here, I didn't do anything else."

"Did you see Mrs. Duvall after dinner last night?" one of the detectives asked Jake.

"No. I just saw her briefly when I first arrived." He saw no reason to tell them about Alyssa's talk with Phoebe until he'd had time to warn her.

"Would either of you have any idea where we could find Clay Duvall?"

"I do." Troy perked up. "He probably spent the night at Maree Winston's apartment."

CHAPTER 30

"Thank God," Aunt Thee said the instant Jake walked into the town house. "I've been trying to find you."

Jake didn't have to ask why. From the moment the police had told them Phoebe had been murdered, he'd known Alyssa would be a prime suspect. "I left my pager at home. I just heard about Phoebe."

"They've arrested Alyssa." Aunt Thee's lined face conveyed frantic desperation. She was on the chaise in the living room propped up by pillows.

Shawn was at her side, appearing very anxious. Small wonder. The elegant home looked more like a frat house after a trashing by a rival fraternity.

"It happened just a little over two hours ago," the nurse said. "The police had a search warrant. They turned the house inside out."

"They took Alyssa's laptop with all her designs on it," her aunt said.

"I overheard one of the detectives saying they'd found the gun," Shawn told him.

"What gun? You didn't tell me," Aunt Thee said.

"I didn't want to upset you," Shawn explained. "It's the same caliber as the murder weapon—a .22."

A suffocating sensation made it difficult to think.

Jake's throat, parched with fear, worked hard to get out the words. "Did Alyssa have a gun?"

"Absolutely not! She hates guns." Aunt Thee stopped abruptly, staring at Shawn. "How could they find a gun? I don't own a gun. You must have misunderstood them."

"I'm sure I didn't."

A rivulet of cold sweat slithered down between Jake's shoulder blades. He felt powerless, trapped by something he couldn't control, the way he had when he'd been a kid and had been stuck overnight in an old freight elevator. He'd sworn nothing—no one—would put him in this position again.

"I didn't have time to have a security system installed. Someone must have slipped in and planted the gun." Aunt Thee attempted to rise to a sitting position, but fell back, her chest heaving.

"Take it easy," Shawn said as he adjusted the pillows supporting her. "Being sent back to the hospital won't help your niece."

"I warned her," Aunt Thee cried. "Alyssa should never have gone near Phoebe. She only wanted to hurt Alyssa."

"Phoebe is the one who's dead, not Alyssa," Shawn reminded Aunt Thee.

A deadweight in his chest, Jake rushed over to the telephone. "She'll need a top-flight criminal attorney. Let me see what I can do." He dialed Sanchez and asked the detective to meet Jake at police headquarters with the best criminal defense attorney in the city.

"Your attorney is going through Security. He'll be in to see you soon," the detective informed Alyssa in a terse voice.

Alyssa was sitting alone at the central police station in an interrogation room no bigger than her closet, choking on her fear, a sob trapped deep inside her. How could it have come to this?

Phoebe had been shot to death in the study during the Vampire Ball. Why? Why? Why? The tightness in her chest became a cramp, and she almost doubled over.

No matter what their differences, there always had been a bond between them. They looked so much alike, and they shared the same father. Last night Phoebe had seemed willing to accept Alyssa, and her sister appeared to be looking forward to making changes in her own life.

The weight of the loss, knowing she'd never have a chance to really get to know Phoebe, surprised Alyssa. It took her a moment to realize what she was experiencing was partly guilt. All these years she'd believed Phoebe knew more about her baby's disappearance than she was telling. Now, Alyssa wondered if she'd been wrong. Perhaps Phoebe had lived all these years with the horrendous loss of her baby, and it was the cause of her sometimes strange behavior.

Alyssa couldn't imagine it. Just having Aunt Thee in the hospital had traumatized her. What if she'd carried a child only to have it abducted? Then just as you were on the verge of getting your life together, you were brutally murdered?

Something inside her longed for what could have been . . . but would never be. They would never be able to share anything now. The pain reverberated through her, a keening cry she had to struggle to suppress.

Once again, she was standing at the edge of an unforeseen precipice in her life—just like last time. The memory of being accused of kidnapping little Patrick had cast a dark, painful shadow. It had almost ruined her life.

When she thought about the past, she burned with humiliation that had been transformed over time into anger. Now, anger morphed into white-hot fury. Someone had diabolically set out to murder Phoebe and frame her for it.

The door swung open unexpectedly. An older man with close-cropped gun-metal gray hair and a stocky build walked past the detective into the room.

"I'm Vincent Crowe." He lowered his Mark Cross briefcase onto the small table and sat down as the door to the room shut. "Jackson Williams hired me to represent you."

Jake. Just thinking about him sent a powerful surge of relief through her entire body. He believed in her.

The lawyer said without missing a beat, "They can only hold you forty-eight hours without charging you. If they have enough evidence, you'll be arraigned tomorrow."

He was a lawyer far above emotional involvement, Alyssa decided. She struggled to control her pent-up feelings. Bolstering her courage, very aware of the seriousness of the situation, she couldn't allow herself to break down.

"They keep asking about my gun. I don't own a gun."

"They're not telling me anything yet, but unofficially I understand they found a .22 caliber handgun in your home. The murder weapon was a .22."

"That's impossible! I don't own a gun and neither does my aunt." Be businesslike, she told herself. You sound hysterical.

"I'm told your fingerprints were on the desk in the study where Phoebe Duvall was shot."

"I can explain. I leaned against the desk when we were talking."

"What else have you told the police?"

"Just what I've said. I did mention I went out to the gazebo not far from the study after Phoebe and I talked. I heard a popping sound like a firecracker. Looking back, it might have been a shot."

He nodded slowly. "A .22 is a small gun that's easily concealed. It doesn't make a loud noise. People often mistake a gunshot for a car backfiring or a firecracker."

"The band was playing loud music at the same time."

"Did you see or hear anything else I should know about? I'll have to relay the information to Rueben Sanchez and have him work on it. You're not going to be allowed to see anyone until after you're arraigned."

She wasn't going to be able to see Jake. Nothing on earth was lonelier, more isolating, than being arrested. Keep your mind on helping the attorney, she warned herself.

"I didn't tell the police, but before I talked with Phoebe, I went into the living room with Gordon LeCroix. I saw a man in a devil's costume walking down the hall and going into the study. Later, when I went into the study, I saw a flash of red outside. I thought someone went out the French doors."

"I'll see if Sanchez can find out which men were dressed as the devil."

"I only saw one—Max Williams."

Vincent Crowe's expression didn't change, but she had the impression he had mastered the poker face long ago, and it served him well in his profession. She suspected, though, he was shocked, considering who had hired him, to discover Jake's father might be a suspect.

She couldn't help wondering herself what Jake would do. Would he turn his back on her in order to protect his father? She didn't think so, but her experience with Clay all those years ago warned her not to be too trusting. Prepare for the worst. Aunt Thee would help her, but she was ill and didn't have a former FBI agent on the payroll.

"Don't talk to anyone about your case," Vincent warned her as he stood up to leave. "Be especially careful of the other prisoners. Some of them will sell out their own mother in return for a reduced sentence. They'll make up anything. If you talk to them and they have enough facts about your case, they'll be able to fabricate a credible story."

He left and a guard appeared seconds later and

escorted her to a cell where three other women were stretched out on bunks. None of them so much as glanced at Alyssa when she was shoved into the cell.

She slowly lowered herself onto the only vacant cot. A paper pillow lay at the head of the space while an institutional blanket was folded at her feet. She instinctively tried to become invisible as she lay down on the bunk.

Desperation metastasized into a mind-numbing bitterness and anger so raw it felt like a physical wound. How could she help herself when she was locked in here?

"It's possible," Jake conceded when Sanchez told him about his conversation with Vincent Crowe about the man dressed as the devil. They were sitting in the living room area of Jake's loft. Benson lay at his feet, his head on his paws, a bewildered look in his eyes as if he understood something was terribly wrong.

"My father was the only one at the party dressed as a devil—at least while we were there. Alyssa and I left early. Someone could have arrived later, but Alyssa wouldn't have seen him."

"Your father didn't have any reason to kill Phoebe."

Man, oh, man, don't you wish? Who knew what went on in Max Williams's head? He'd abducted his own son and was obsessed by Phoebe Duvall.

It wasn't that his father didn't mean anything to Jake. In his own way, Max had tried very hard to make up for lost time. He'd willingly handed over his business to him . . . yet the financial angle meant nothing to Jake.

When he'd told his father that he didn't want TriTech, Jake meant it. He'd never been emotionally threatened like this, but then, he'd never been so . . . taken with a woman. When had he begun to long for more? His need had escalated, disguised by sexual interest until the full-blown intensity of his feelings had caught him off-guard.

Now he knew with absolute certainty that losing Alyssa would be worse than anything that could possibly happen with TriTech. He had to level with Sanchez. It was the only way to help Alyssa.

"My father and Phoebe go way, way back," Jake began. It took him another few minutes to fill in the private detective. "So, it's possible that my father might have had a reason to kill Phoebe if he knew she intended to divorce Clay and marry Troy."

"Troy Chevalier, hmmm," Sanchez responded and Jake could almost hear him trying to put Jake's assistant together with Phoebe Duvall. Sanchez knew Troy fairly well, having reported to him several times during various company investigations.

"Troy's family is very wealthy. They live in Paris and have a home in the south of France and another in Marrakesh."

"Marrakesh?"

"A lot of rich Parisians have places there. It's a very seductive lifestyle. I could see it appealing to a woman like Phoebe."

Sanchez nodded thoughtfully. "What if Phoebe was only leading Troy on to get back at her husband or some other man? Troy was at the Vampire Ball. He had the big two—motive and opportunity."

"Nah, I was with him when the detectives told him about her murder, Troy seemed genuinely shocked." Jake caught the slight furrow between Sanchez's eyes. "Gotcha! I know what you're thinking. Troy had me fooled into accepting that phony report. He could be a world-class liar. Hell, I don't know."

"What about Clay? He would have every reason to want Phoebe dead, wouldn't he? If she divorced him, Clay would have to fork over a chunk of money."

"Yes, and Clay was trying to get Alyssa back. So he

had more than one reason to want his wife out of the way."

"From what I gather, Phoebe had been involved with a number of men. Any of them or their wives could have murdered her. The Vampire Ball was the perfect setting with everyone in masks and costumes. Anyone could have slipped into the party, killed Phoebe, and left. It didn't have to be a guest."

"Someone had to know she was downstairs in the study alone."

"True, but she could have been lured there by the killer who was in disguise and pretending to be someone else."

"Troy mentioned Clay was having an affair with Maree Winston," Jake said. "He indicated something . . . kinky was going on with a third person, a Bahamian psychic."

"Maybe we should start with a list of people who are not suspects. It'll be easier."

"You might also want to take a look at Wyatt LeCroix, Phoebe's brother."

"Any particular reason why?"

"Not really, but he was helping Clay with the Port Authority scam. Maybe Phoebe knew about it and was planning on turning them in. I know it sounds far-fetched, but with this family, you never know."

Sanchez rose. "I'd better get on this. If anything else comes up, call me on my cell phone."

Clay walked into the small living room of Maree's apartment, where his former mistress and Dante were watching television. Dante clicked off the newscast the moment the door opened. Clay had just spent the last two hours at the police station answering questions.

"Did the police call to verify my alibi?" Clay asked Maree. He plopped onto the sofa next to her. "Good thing I was with you last night."

"No," Maree said. "They haven't called."

"I conveniently forgot to tell them how late you came home from Neville's," he said.

"What if they ask Neville?" Dante wanted to know.

Clay eyed Maree; she claimed to love him. Now was the time to prove it. The half-smile curving her lips assured him that she was crazy about him.

"Their questions seemed to have more to do with my relationship with Alyssa Rossi," he observed. "I think asking for my alibi was just routine. I spent the night here and you can verify it."

"We jus' saw Ravelle on television, mon. She says your wife may have been shot during the party."

"I was with people the whole time. I gave them names. They can check if they want." Clay wasn't admitting he'd been in the study with Phoebe. Why should he? It had only been for a few minutes. No one had seen him.

"Ravelle said Alyssa Rossi is in custody," Maree said. She seemed to be studying him for his reaction. "They expect to charge her with the murder."

Clay shrugged as if to say: Who cares?

"I'd better go home," Clay said to deflect Maree's unwavering stare. "The LeCroixs will be looking for me. We have a funeral to plan."

"Oh, Clay. I almost forgot. Some lawyer called. He said to get in touch with him right away."

Clay did not like the sound of it. "How would he know to contact me here?"

Dante laughed, a dark laugh that made Clay's skin prickle. He ignored him and went over to the telephone. He didn't recognize the attorney's name, but he could imagine what this lawyer was billing to work on a Sunday.

He dialed the number, and a man answered. When Clay identified himself, the attorney immediately launched into his reason for calling. Clay listened, blinding panic crawling through his veins, mounting with each word the attorney uttered. What in hell was going on?

He hung up, and slowly turned around. "You're not

going to believe this. Max Williams has given me what
amounts to a quit claim on Duvall Imports.''

"What does that mean?" Maree asked.

"He gave my company back to me."

"Why would he, mon? Doesn't make sense."

Clay thought a minute. "Maybe the IRS is on to me,
but I don't think so. They always notify you before anyone else."

"I don't like it, mon."

"Well, if you're psychic, tell me what he's up to."

Dante chuckled, then winked.

"I think it's good news," Maree said. "Phoebe's gone.
You have your company back. We'll wait a respectable
amount of time before getting married."

CHAPTER 31

At dusk, Jake was in his loft, sitting where he'd been when Sanchez had left. He was staring up at the skylight, looking for answers that weren't there. Benson had remained at his feet, his soulful eyes still troubled. Above the skylight, bloated clouds laden with moisture huddled over the city, promising another downpour. The sullen sky reflected his mood.

He'd been waiting, hoping his father would do what was right and go to the police. His information might not free Alyssa, but it would give the authorities less reason to think of her as a criminal who'd gotten away with a crime once already.

It wasn't going to happen. Jake should have known. His father was a complex man with a lot of money. No doubt, he didn't believe Jake would walk away from a fortune by turning him in.

Okey dokey. Two could play this game. No way in hell was he going to let Alyssa go to prison for something she didn't do. He'd have to go to the police himself. So be it.

He rose, his legs stiff from sitting for so long. "Come on, Benson. Din-din. As soon as you eat, I want you to go outside. I won't be back until late."

Benson surged up onto all fours, tail wagging for the first time in hours. He'd picked up one of his favorite words, din-din. He trotted at Jake's heels into the kitchen, where Jake pulled out a sliding bin containing Benson's kibble.

A sharp knock on the door startled him. He gave Benson a quick pat and went to answer it. Max stood there, appearing exhausted, subdued.

"I've told the police everything I know." Max's voice seemed dry and matter-of-fact, the way people sounded when they'd explained something over and over to different groups of people. "Phoebe's been murdered."

"I know."

Tears flashed in Max's dark eyes. "I can't believe it."

"I'm sorry. I know how much you cared about her."

He'd written off his father, and he'd been wrong. An ache of relief nearly overcame him. It was a second before he found his voice. "Come in. Let's talk."

Max walked slowly into the loft, and Jake realized this was only the second time his father had been here. The first time, he'd proudly shown his father the place he'd bought to renovate. Max had freaked. Why would anyone want to live in a huge room divided by screens when they could buy the nicest place in town?

This time Max didn't make any comment on the way Jake had remodeled the loft. He collapsed into a leather chair, asking, "Do you have any Wild Turkey?"

"You've got it."

Strangely enough Jake had bought his father's favorite years ago in case Max came over again. Jake walked over to the bar housed in a breakfront. He cranked open the cap of the sealed bottle, then poured a generous portion into a cut crystal glass. He fixed himself two fingers of his favorite single malt Scotch, Springbank.

"Here you go." He handed his father the Wild Turkey and waited for him to take a drink before asking, "What happened?"

"I told the police everything." The words were spoken in a tone Jake barely recognized. Gone was the commanding voice Max usually had. "All about Patrick. All about my relationship with Phoebe through the years."

A wave of concern for his father swept over Jake. "Did you have your lawyer with you?"

"Yes. Since you'd hired Vincent Crowe, I had to go with second best, Amory Binochette."

Jake waited until his father took another long pull on his drink, leaning down to pet Benson, who'd given up on din-din and had again settled at his feet. "How did they react?"

"They were shocked about Patrick, but it's yesterday's news. They have a murder to solve." His expression telegraphed the pain he still felt for his young son. "They kept asking if I'd gone into the study to talk to Phoebe. Apparently they have a witness who claims a person dressed as the devil joined her in the study."

Jesus H. Christ, I ask you, who would so diabolically come up with a plan like this? He'd never believed his father had killed Phoebe—although it was in the realm of possibility—but he had thought his father had gone into the study.

"You don't know how much I want them to find Phoebe's killer."

Now there was an undercurrent of sadness in his father's voice. Jake reminded himself Max had lost the woman he loved. Jake might have found Phoebe shallow and conniving, but his father had cared deeply for her.

Not only had Max suffered an irreplaceable loss, he'd sacrificed any chance he had of a political career. Just as bad, when the truth about the baby was public, Max would become a social pariah. He'd never be the Orion krewe's king of Mardi Gras.

Max might even be kicked out of the Mayfair Club, although Jake didn't think this was as likely. *Sin cojones* as the guys at the dock used to say. No balls. The members of the Mayfair Club were more likely to snub his

father than risk a direct confrontation. Still, the damage
would be the same because Max *cared*. He'd spent the
last decade trying to win social acceptance in a city
where your ancestors were the bottom line.

He did it for me, Jake thought, an unwelcome tightening in his throat. Okay, okay, this is no time to be
overly sentimental. His father also had gone to the
police because he genuinely wanted the murderer
caught.

Still, Jake felt compelled to say, "How can I tell you
how much this means to me?"

"Men don't talk enough about how they feel," his
father's voice deepened, putting him on alert. "You
love Alyssa. I understand what you're going through. I
loved Phoebe. I can't believe s-she's . . ." Max's voice
broke and he self-consciously averted his head.

Jake tried to put himself in his father's place. What
if he'd loved Alyssa for all those years, then she'd been
murdered in cold blood?

"I'm sorry, I—" He broke off, searching for the right
words to express his feelings. He realized when he was
emotionally threatened, he withdrew behind the shield
of a joke or silence.

He leaned across the coffee table, attempting to get
closer to his father. "I've never been the son you've
wanted me to be. I'm sorry."

Max sank back against the plush cushions. "What
can I say? I fathered you at a time in my life when I was
young and didn't think about what it meant to have
children. Then Phoebe announced she was pregnant,
and I discovered I was ready—more than ready—to be
a father."

He stared at Jake as if he had more to say, but hadn't
a clue how to say it. "When Patrick died, I-I missed him
so much. He was young. He never had the chance to
live. I couldn't have Phoebe, and no other woman
appealed to me. I had more money than I could ever
have imagined, but I was miserable." His world-weary

eyes reflected his sorrow. "I decided to look you up, not knowing what to expect."

Jake tried to keep his expression neutral. Why tell Max he had ignored a son who had spent years praying for his father to remember him?

"Right from the start, you were perfect. You reminded me of how I'd been at the same age. You were stubborn, full of pride. You didn't want a damn thing to do with me, and I couldn't blame you." His dry, self-deprecating chuckle cracked and woke up the snoozing Benson. The dog cocked his head and trained his eyes on Max. "I had to lure you to New Orleans, but once you were here, the challenge excited you."

Jake couldn't deny it, but some wounds never completely heal. He resented those years he'd gone without the benefit of a father. Sure, his mother had loved him, and she'd done her best, but knowing he had a father living not too far away in New Orleans, a man who never bothered to see him, or even call—hurt.

"I couldn't have had a better son. You mean the world to me. When you asked me to come forward, I was happy to do it—for you. I know how much pride you have, how you hate to ask for anything, but loving someone changes us. You wanted to help Alyssa, and I wanted to help you." He dredged up something that might have been a smile. "I arranged to talk to the police *before* I discovered Phoebe had been murdered."

"You did?" Jake's voice was low, disbelieving.

"You bet. I knew you weren't making idle threats. I lost you once. I have no intention of losing you again."

Max's confession released something deep inside Jake. His father cared, he truly cared. The bitterness Jake had harbored for so long evaporated, thrust aside by the revelation. Now they were united against a common enemy.

"Oh, yeah, and I cut Clay Duvall loose. I had my attorney prepare something like a quit claim, which gives Clay back his company."

"You took a loss?" Jake had to admit he was totally amazed. It was not in character for his father to leave money on the table in any business deal.

Max didn't respond. The silence in the loft thickened, and Jake realized it was now totally dark. He leaned over and turned on a lamp. The sudden glare threw his father's features into stark relief, his own face years from now. Jake prayed he would be happier.

"I mean what I said," Max told him. "I'd rather lose money than lose you."

"Thanks," Jake managed to whisper. "I mean it. I appreciate all you've done."

There was a knock on the door, and it saved him from sinking in a quicksand of emotions. His father was right, he thought, heading to the door with Benson dogging every step. Jake had little experience in expressing his feelings.

"Yo, I've got news," Sanchez said the second Jake opened the door.

"Come in. My father's here. He's told the police everything he knows." Jake led Sanchez into the living area and turned on another light. Sanchez refused a drink, saying he still had more work to do tonight.

"What did you find out?" Jake asked as he took the chair next to his father rather than putting distance between them the way he usually did by sitting across from him on the sofa.

Sanchez plopped down, saying, "Phoebe told her attorney to prepare the divorce papers and send them to her in France. The address she gave—"

"Belongs to Troy Chevalier's parents," Jake said.

"You're kidding." Max's voice was disheartened.

"I wish." It took Jake a few minutes to explain to Max all about Troy.

"Why would Phoebe leave Clay now?" Max asked. "I never thought she'd leave him."

Jake shrugged. "Money. Social position. A new, glamorous life in one of the most sophisticated cities in the world."

"It sounds like Phoebe," Max admitted.

"There might be something else." Sanchez put in. "No one saw Wyatt LeCroix after the cocktail hour, although it's hard to be positive with so many vampires on the scene."

"Why would he kill his sister?" Max asked Sanchez.

"The divorce would force Clay to buy out her portion of Duvall Imports. The little scam Wyatt had been running with the Port Authority might be exposed," Jake guessed. "Wyatt would face jail time."

"That's right," Sanchez said. "It would give Clay an even better reason for killing her than Wyatt. But Clay has convinced the police he has an alibi for every minute of the party as well as the entire night. I have a contact on the force, and I suggested they give him a lie detector test."

"Where was he all night?" Max wanted to know.

"He claims he was with Maree Winston."

Max nodded, a flicker of interest in his eyes. Jake gave his father credit. The old goat still appreciated a killer bod. "The feathered vampire outfit."

"That's the woman. She came with Neville Berringer, but according to Clay, he dropped Maree off at her carriage house where Clay was waiting."

"Have the police confirmed this?" Jake asked.

"The authorities have tried to locate Berringer, but he's fishing in Cancun for a week."

"It probably doesn't matter," Jake said. "I'm betting Phoebe was killed during the party, not later that night. Why would she still be in the study after everyone had left?"

Sanchez's dark eyes roved from father to son. "Alyssa had told the police she believes she heard a shot just before dinner was served. That was nine o'clock."

"You sure have a pipeline to the police," Jake said. "What else has she told them?"

"About the devil going into the study."

"I was the only one at the party in a devil's costume," Max said.

Sanchez nodded thoughtfully. "Someone could have been attempting to frame you, Max. Then Alyssa made herself an easier target."

The fine hair across the back of his neck prickled to life. Alyssa. His father. Why was the killer getting so close to the people he cared about? Was it coincidence? Was it his imagination?

"Do you know what else the police have on Alyssa?" Jake asked.

"They're checking her nun's costume for residue from the gun."

"They won't find anything." Jake gave this a second thought. "Unless there's a way of tampering with clothing after the fact."

Sanchez shook his head. "Highly unlikely. It's not as easy as slipping in, planting a murder weapon, and slipping out. The killer may not be half as clever as he thinks. A .22 isn't very powerful—"

"But it's small, easy to conceal," Jake said. "Everyone there—except for the feathered vampire—could hide it on them."

"Maree Winston was carrying a feathery purse. It could have been in there," Max told them.

"Possibly," Sanchez agreed. "Back to the bullet. A .22's bullet isn't very powerful. Actually, many victims recover."

Jake remembered the locked door. "I went downstairs, looking for Alyssa. The door to the study was locked. I'll bet the killer shot once and was afraid to shoot again because someone might recognize the sound. If Phoebe wasn't dead, locking the door would ensure no one found her in time to save her."

A choking sound came from Max. "Oh, my God. Who could be that cruel?"

His father's dark eyes met his, and Jake leaned over

and put his hand on his father's shoulder. "An autopsy should show if the shot killed her or she bled to death, right, Sanchez?"

"Correct." Sanchez waited a minute before adding, "When the killer planted the gun, he must have thought it could be matched to the bullet."

"I thought that was a no-brainer," Jake said.

"With other caliber guns, it is, but a .22 usually distorts on impact. That makes a ballistics match impossible."

Usually. Jake wanted to be encouraged but it was difficult. Someone had tried seven ways to hell to frame Alyssa. Could they get lucky for a change?

"Anything else?" asked Max.

"They're checking her laptop for incriminating e-mails or whatever they can find. The doorman at the party is one of their witnesses. He saw Alyssa going into the study. He didn't see her come out, which is at odds with the story she told police about coming into the hall again and seeing Ravelle."

"With a television celebrity and her crew at the door, doesn't it seem logical that the doorman wouldn't have noticed Alyssa?"

"True, but he is a witness who can put her at the murder scene."

CHAPTER 32

Alyssa put the pillow on her face to block out the lights. It had to be after midnight, but the lights in the cell block hadn't dimmed, much less gone off. One of her cellmates had made a comment that led Alyssa to believe the lights in the jail block were always on so the guards could check on the prisoners.

The metal bars clanged, bringing Alyssa out of what must have been a few minutes of sleep.

"Rossi. Get your ass outta the sack. Your attorney is here."

At this hour? Alyssa sprang to her feet, dazed. She slipped through the barely opened cell door into the corridor. The lights blazed, but the women in the cells huddled under blankets, under pillows, under their arms to avoid the invasive light.

The matron marched her down a long, brightly lit hallway to the room where prisoners met their attorneys. She saw Gordon LeCroix seated at a station, the only person in the room. Her mind formed one word. Why?

She sank down onto the metal chair. Over her shoulder, she saw the guard leave the room but knew they would be watched through the window in the door. "You came to see me?"

"Yes. Are you all right?" Gordon LeCroix asked.

"Never better." She couldn't help the sarcasm. "How did you get in here? They told me I couldn't have visitors."

"I'm an attorney, remember? I don't take criminal cases, but I have friends—"

"In high places."

He lowered his head, then gazed back up at her. "Yes. That's right. I called in all my favors. Unlike last time, I don't care what anyone thinks—least of all my family. I want to help you."

Did he seriously expect her to believe he cared one iota about her? What happened to all those years when she had been relegated to the first floor, nothing more than a servant?

Alyssa took a deep breath, then asked, "Have you told the police all you know?"

"The authorities haven't questioned me yet but—"

"But nothing. You claim you want to help me. The truth, no matter how ugly, is the only way to help me."

"I'll contact them. I'll tell them you're my daughter."

"It would be helpful if they knew you asked me to go into the study and talk to Phoebe."

"Of course." He hesitated a second. "I heard on the news the murder weapon was found at your house."

"Someone planted it." She couldn't tell if he believed her, and she didn't care. All she wanted from this man was to have him tell the truth.

"Do you have a lawyer?"

"Jake hired Vincent Crowe."

"He's the best. Unquestionably." He smiled a little, then added, "Is there anything I can do for you? Anything you need?"

She shook her head. "Do you have any idea who killed Phoebe?"

"No. We were never close. Over the years, I heard rumors. Older men. Underworld characters." He spoke with light bitterness, and she wondered if he blamed himself for not being a better father. "Phoebe never seemed to be happy."

Alyssa had to agree. Even as a young girl, Phoebe had a petulant streak. It became worse over time.

"Her death has nearly destroyed Hattie."

"She believes I killed Phoebe."

He lifted his shoulders in a weary shrug. "Well, you know Hattie."

Did she ever. The thought of how Hattie treated her tore at something in a distant part of her psyche. It hurt. God, how it still hurt.

"I'd better go before they discover I'm not your attorney." Gordon rose. "I'll be at the arraignment."

Why had her father come to see her? she wondered as she was being led back to her cell. He said he wanted to help, yet he hadn't bothered to go to the police. Would he now? If the truth came out, it would be damaging to his reputation, his career. No telling what Hattie would do.

Did he feel guilty for the times he'd let her down? Was that why he'd come? Did he want to be part of her life? My, that would be something.

"Alyssa Rossi," trumpeted a very loud voice.

Alyssa nosed her head out from under the pillow. She saw light coming through the high windows near the ceiling. It was the morning of the second day of her incarceration. The shift had changed and a new matron was unlocking her cell.

She jumped up. "Is it time for the arraignment?"

Without answering, the woman motioned for her to leave the cell. They could only hold her forty-eight hours without charging her. According to Alyssa's calculations, there were about five hours to go.

Outside the cell block, the matron spoke. "You're being released."

A cry of relief broke from her lips. "Released. Yes!

There is a God!" A sense of strength surged through her, lifting the despair that had burdened her like a physical weight.

"Have they caught the killer?" she asked.

"Dunno. They don't tell me squat."

Changing out of the Day-glo orange jumpsuit she'd been given, putting on her own clothes, and getting her purse from the property department passed in a blur. All she could think about was being free. She wanted to go home, see Jake, and check on her aunt. She was excited yet anxious for some reason she couldn't quite define.

Vincent Crowe was waiting for her outside the detention area. Jake and Max were with him. Jake smiled and a charge of sexual chemistry arced between them. It was all she could do not to hurl herself into Jake's arms, but the sight of his father stopped her from doing anything more than saying hello. She would never forget Max threatening her.

"Why are they releasing me?" she asked. "Have they found the killer?"

She could tell by Jake's expression something was wrong. A frission of uneasiness skittered through her. Suddenly her palms were damp, and she wiped them on her dress.

"The ballistics test on the .22 is inconclusive," Vincent told her.

"What does that mean?"

"The bullet twisted when it entered the body, which isn't unusual for a .22. It isn't as distorted as most, which are impossible to test, but this bullet is difficult. Without the test, the DA doesn't have enough evidence to charge you yet."

"Yet?" With a sense of doom, her brain scrambled to make sense of this. She drew in a hitching breath and reminded herself to be brave.

"They're going to rerun the ballistics test. If it's the murder weapon, they'll arrest you again."

* * *

Jake wasn't sure what he expected from Alyssa. She'd taken the news better than he'd expected, he thought as he watched her talking to Thee.

"It's time for her nap," Shawn informed them.

Alyssa kissed her aunt and allowed the nurse to wheel Thee out of the living room. She slowly turned to Jake and Max. Vincent Crowe had left them at the station, and they'd brought her home.

"I guess I'm on borrowed time."

"Not necessarily," Jake responded. "We're making progress. With luck, we'll find the killer before the police arrest you again because there's zero chance that .22 isn't the murder weapon or it wouldn't have been planted here."

"Do you know how many times I've been to the police station? It's getting to be a joke." She tried for a laugh but it sounded brittle.

"Max." He nudged his father toward Alyssa. "Explain why you threatened her."

Max smiled—or tried to—and crossed the room to stand close to Alyssa. "Phoebe and I go way, way back."

Alyssa's puzzled expression made Jake say, "Explain everything."

Max launched into an explanation of his relationship with Phoebe, and her pregnancy with his son, Patrick.

"Patrick?" The word was barely a gasp. "*Your* son?"

"You were right," Jake told her. "Phoebe knew what happened to her baby. She was afraid Clay would have him tested and discover he wasn't the father."

Alyssa slowly sank into a chair. "Where is he now?"

Jake sat on the sofa near Alyssa and motioned for his father to join him. "He died almost nine years ago of a viral infection."

"Oh, my God. That's terrible."

Max went on to explain the details in a low-pitched voice that revealed an undercurrent of emotion. Alyssa scrutinized his face, taking in every word. Jake knew how worried she'd been about the baby. Now she knew he'd been loved.

"I would never have allowed you to be arrested for what I'd done," Max said. "I was in Oklahoma with the baby. When I returned, you'd gone to Italy."

"Have you told this to the police?" she asked

Max nodded. "I told them. I know it's a lot to ask, but please forgive me. I never meant you any harm." The sincerity in his father's voice was unmistakable.

"I forgive you, but I can't say I understand. You're so successful, so intelligent ... What did you see in Phoebe?"

Max looked at Jake and smiled. "My son asked me the same thing. She needed me in a way that no one else has ever needed me. I would have done anything for her. That's why I got ugly with you. Phoebe thought if you stayed in New Orleans, the truth would come out about the baby."

"Why didn't you tell me Max threatened you?" Jake asked.

"I didn't want to come between a father and son."

Why was he not surprised? She'd missed having a father in her own life, and she didn't want to deprive him of any chance he might have in building a relationship with Max.

He had to admit she was right even though he cursed himself for not knowing she was in danger. Had she told him the threat, he would have confronted his father. Undoubtedly, he would have lost his temper. If that had happened, Max might have been too alienated to go to the police when it counted.

Alyssa gazed at Max. "Did you hire the man with the knife?"

Jake jumped up. "What knife?"

"When you accused me of threatening you, you didn't mention a knife," Max added.

He stood by the side of Alyssa's chair while she told

them all about the man waiting for her in the parking garage. Holding raw emotion in check, he tried to remain calm. She could have been killed, and she hadn't told him because she thought Max was responsible.

"I wanted to scare you," Max said, "but I never followed up."

"The man could have killed me if he'd wanted," she told them. "He planned to frighten me into leaving. That's all."

"Don't be too sure," Jake countered.

She thought for a moment, then spoke to Max. "You said Phoebe wanted to get rid of me. Could she have hired the man to threaten me?"

"I don't think so. She didn't tell me about it." Max's dark eyes reflected the tortured dullness of disbelief. "But then, she didn't tell me she was divorcing Clay to marry Troy Chevalier until the night she died."

"What?" Alyssa cried. "She was leaving Clay for Troy?"

Jake resisted the urge to pace the room. He explained about Troy's wealthy family and the lure of Paris. "You see, while you were under arrest, we've all been working hard to untangle this mess."

"It's complicated, real complicated," Max added.

Jake told her about the scheme Duvall Imports was running at the wharves, aided by Wyatt LeCroix. "That's how I discovered Troy and Phoebe had this thing going."

"It's hard for me to imagine Phoebe leaving New Orleans. Her whole life revolved around Mardi Gras and krewe functions," Alyssa said. "But she did tell me she was starting over, getting a new life."

"I think we can assume it's true," Jake said. "While we were waiting for you to be released, Sanchez called. He'd spoken with Wyatt. He verified that his sister did plan to move to Paris with Troy."

"Does Wyatt have an alibi?" Alyssa wanted to know.

"Not really. He claims he was at the party but left before dinner. No one can verify his story."

"Why would he want to kill his sister?" she asked.

"It's doubtful he would." Jake hesitated before adding, "Sanchez thinks Wyatt isn't telling all he knows. I want to put a little pressure on him. I could turn him in to the authorities for his scam with Duvall Imports, if he doesn't tell me the whole truth."

"Good idea," Max responded.

"The night Phoebe was killed, I thought I saw you going into the study," Alyssa said to Max.

His father shook his head.

"How tall was the person?" Jake asked.

"As tall as you two. His back was to me. I didn't get a really good look, but later when I went to talk to Phoebe, I thought someone had gone out the French doors. I saw a flash of red outside."

"So, it had to be a man," Max said.

"Probably. He was tall and big. In a devil's costume with a mask, it would be difficult to say for sure."

"It occurred to me," Jake said, "the original intention was to frame Max. Then you conveniently appeared."

"It makes sense," Max added. "I was the only one in a devil's costume."

Alyssa didn't look convinced. "I don't know. The second baby being taken, then I was threatened. I think it's a deliberate attempt to frame me."

Jake decided to voice an idea that had been hovering in the back of his mind. "It could be two separate agendas we're dealing with. Phoebe could have been responsible for the baby being taken and Alyssa being threatened. But she certainly didn't plot her own murder."

Alyssa said, "The two have to be connected."

"Not necessarily." Jake's sixth sense had kicked in big-time. He needed to talk to Wyatt LeCroix.

CHAPTER 33

Clay stood at the back of Charbonnet's Funeral Home and said nothing as Hattie took over, the way she always did. Gordon, of course, had been "tied up." So far she'd ordered a mother-of-pearl coffin lined with pink silk and one hundred and fifty lavender roses, Phoebe's favorite, for the church where the service would be held. Now, she was working on the music.

Clay didn't know what the rush was. There had to be a full autopsy, which wouldn't be completed until the end of the week. He didn't want to appear callous, so he'd accompanied Hattie. He leaned against the wall, thinking.

Max had given him back his company without a cent changing hands. What was that all about? Max was a crusty old fox. Clay wondered if he was up to something, then decided Max had been crazy about Phoebe. This could be his convoluted way of honoring her memory—give back the family business. On the other hand, Max could be up to something. As soon as this messy funeral was over, Clay was going to Max to find out what was happening.

"Clay, the choir from St. Anthony's is available. That would be perfect, don't you think?" Hattie asked.

"Absolutely. Phoebe would love it." This was a total lie. Phoebe hated church choirs, loathed spiritual music, and rarely attended services. Naturally, Hattie tried to impress her own wishes on her daughter in death as she'd done in life.

If Clay could put his finger on the one single reason the LeCroix family was so screwed up, it would be Hattie. A doyen of social power, obsessed by her own reign as the Orion krewe's Mardi Gras queen, she'd been determined to relive her moment of glory through her daughter. The discovery of Alyssa, the skeleton in the closet, had thrown Hattie completely.

His cell phone rang, and he headed toward the door opening into the hallway before answering it. His secretary, Ami Sue, the big-boobed, blond bimbo was hysterical.

"They're moving us out. What am I going to do?"

"Moving? Who?"

"They say Mr. Williams sent them. We have to be, like, out of the building by five o'clock."

Jake must have ordered this, not Max. The old man had been nuts about Phoebe. She'd died Saturday night; Max had returned Duvall Imports the following day. It was now Tuesday, just days after what Max had to see as a tragic death. He wouldn't boot out Clay's company, but Jake would.

Jake had been jealous of Clay from the moment they'd been introduced. Clay could understand it. Jake came from humble beginnings. Nothing short of his father's phenomenal success could have elevated poor white trash from Mobile's docks to New Orleans' society. It was only natural that Jake was insecure and vengeful.

"Call Wyatt LeCroix and tell him that we're moving into his offices until I can arrange for new office space."

Ami Sue asked a few more totally stupid questions. Couldn't she have more initiative? It wasn't going to happen when you selected a secretary based on her bra size instead of her brain. He reminded himself to fuck her then fire her. He'd been saving her for a rainy day, and this was it.

What made this situation with his company dangerous was Dante. Somehow he'd taken charge. Heroin had been loaded on one of Clay's ships. He had no doubt this was just the beginning. Clay wasn't stupid enough to think Dante was in this alone. He had the backing of Venezio and the mob—no question about it. If Clay tried to weasel out of their deal, no telling what would happen.

Continuing to sleep with Maree was only encouraging her to think he would marry her. With Maree came Dante. They might as well be joined at the hip. He would demand Clay continue to smuggle in heroin. There had to be a way out of this—a way back to Alyssa.

Short of killing Dante and Maree, Clay didn't see a way out. It was something to consider.

"She's better," Alyssa told Jake, referring to her aunt. "But this has been hard on her."

"Right, but she's a trooper." He leaned back on the sofa, his arm around Alyssa. Max had left hours ago, after apologizing to Alyssa yet again. Shawn had brought Thee down for an early dinner, then taken her upstairs to rest.

"I didn't want to say it in front of Max, but I think Phoebe may have hired the man with the knife. He might be the same man who paid the nurse to move the baby into the closet near Thee's room."

"Why didn't you want to talk about it when your father was here?"

Jake wasn't sure exactly how he felt about his father, but his feelings had changed considerably since Max went to the authorities at tremendous consequences to his own life. *I have no intention of losing you again.* His father's words came to him, the way they had many times already. In his own way, Max cared about Jake, and he was sorry he hadn't been a better father.

"My father had a blind spot where Phoebe was concerned."

"He *chose* to believe anything she said."

Derision underscored every syllable she uttered. He couldn't blame Alyssa. Max had been responsible for the trouble she'd had over Patrick's disappearance. She was again facing prison. She had a right to be angry.

"I'm not proud of what my father did, but I am grateful that he went to the police and told them everything as soon as I found out he had fathered Phoebe's child."

"What if you hadn't discovered the truth?"

"Max would have gone to the authorities the minute he learned about Phoebe's murder."

Alyssa stared across the living room. It had been hastily put back together after the search, and things weren't quite in their proper place. He thought she was silently condemning him for sticking up for his father.

Jake tried again. "He's told the police everything he knows. The things that matter most to him like a political career, being Mardi Gras king, and having a place in society will be impossible now."

"He did it for you, didn't he?" she asked.

He silently applauded her intuitiveness. "Yes. I told Max that I love you, and I don't want you to suffer any longer for something you didn't do."

She gazed at him for a minute as if she hadn't heard what he'd said. "You're in love with me?" she whispered incredulously.

Shaking his head in mixed tenderness and exasperation, he pulled her closer until their lips were a few inches apart. "I'm crazy about you. There's nothing I wouldn't do to get you out of trouble."

"Thank you," she whispered, but she didn't say she loved him.

"I want to marry you and have a big family. That's how much I love you."

She stared at him for a long moment, and for the life of him, Jake couldn't tell what she was thinking. He had so much to give her, endless abounding love, but would she accept his gift? When she still didn't respond, acute disappointment replaced anticipation.

"Jake, I can't think about my personal life until this is over."

She spoke in a soft, low voice, but each word was far sharper than a slap. Love and doubt collided, then twisted into a tight knot deep in his gut.

"I understand," he replied even though he didn't, at least not completely. He'd wanted her to give him a sign, no matter how small, that she loved him, wanted to share her life with him.

Brizt, brizt. His cell phone chirped from where it was clipped to his belt. He pulled it out and flipped it open. Sanchez was on the line.

"I just spoke with my contact at the police station," the detective told Jake. "Your father's information has made quite an impression. The fact that Phoebe lied about her baby's disappearance puts a whole new light on the case."

Jake watched Alyssa cross the room and go up the stairs. No doubt she was going to check on her aunt. He waited until she was too far away to hear him. Max was a sore point between them, and he didn't want to make the situation any worse.

"Do you think they'll charge my father?"

"Nah. I don't think so. They've checked out everything Max told them and it's been true."

"Good." Jake thought being ostracized socially was punishment enough.

"Did you know Gordon LeCroix came to the police this afternoon?" Sanchez asked.

"I had no idea." He looked up and saw Alyssa coming down the stairs.

"He told them he's Alyssa's father. That threw them.

LeCroix also said he'd persuaded Alyssa to go into the study and speak with Phoebe."

"Does he have an alibi?"

Sanchez laughed, but Jake was not amused. Alyssa had sat down, looking pensive, but she hadn't sat beside him. Instead she was in the chair directly across from him, the coffee table with a stunning orchid plant separating them. So much for true love.

"Gordon's hard to track. He admits he was downstairs during the party, but he insists he went upstairs after talking to Alyssa. With so many vampires around, in masks and all dressed alike, it's hard to prove or disprove the whereabouts of a lot of people. Of course, a nun and a priest and a devil stuck out as did the woman in the feathered vampire number."

"Have they questioned Wyatt LeCroix?" Jake wanted to know.

He intended to see Wyatt himself, but he didn't mention this to Sanchez. Jake didn't want Sanchez to think he was second-guessing him. The private eye had done a damn fine job—faster and better than the police— but Wyatt knew more about his sister than anyone.

"The detective in charge of Phoebe's case went to Wyatt's office this morning, but I don't think he seriously interrogated him. Phoebe and her brother were known to be close. Why would he want her dead?"

"Money. Isn't that what the FBI says? Right after crimes of passion, killing for financial gain ranks next as the cause of murder."

"According to the last will they found, which is five years old, Phoebe's money would go to her parents. Wyatt claims there's a new will on file with an attorney in Baton Rouge. Wouldn't you know, Wyatt didn't remember the lawyer's name. The police are trying to track him down."

"Baton Rouge. Why not here?" Then it hit him. "Daddy's an attorney. Word gets around. She didn't want her parents or Clay to find out she'd changed her will."

"Who knew what went on in her mind?"

"Got that right."

"Wyatt and Clay say they know nothing about it. Clay, I believe, but as I told you, Wyatt seems to know more than he's telling."

"Yeah," Jake said. He was hardly listening now. Alyssa was watching him, her expression vacant, devoid of emotion. A burning sensation feathered through his stomach.

"There is some good news." Sanchez sounded upbeat.

"That's great. Alyssa will be glad to hear it." He tried to catch her eye, but she was staring up at the ceiling now.

"They are going to give Clay Duvall a lie detector test tomorrow afternoon. I didn't have to push for it. This was their idea after some people at the party said they thought he went downstairs. Of course, with all those vampires, it's hard to be positive."

"It won't hurt to run the test."

"I won't be surprised to find out Clay offed her. He's a scumbag. I have a tail on him. He was at the LeCroix home receiving condolence callers until a little while ago. He claimed he had a migraine from all the stress and said he was going home to get some sleep. Where do you think he went?"

Jake didn't hesitate. "Clay's spending the night with Maree Winston, the woman in the feathered vampire getup."

"Right. It looks like another night of kinky sex. The Bahamian psychic is there, too. I'm pulling the tail off Clay and have him do an in-depth on Troy Chevalier. We haven't taken a good enough look-see at him yet."

"Great work," he said, and he meant it. "There's a bonus in this for all—"

"Oh, one other thing. The ballistics test is being done at the FBI lab."

"Really? Why?"

"They want an accurate report from a state-of-the-art lab. It'll take at least two more days to get it."

"Is there any chance the FBI won't be able to match the bullet to the gun?" Jake asked as he tried to catch Alyssa's eye and reassure her with a smile.

"Abso-fucking-lutely! A .22 is notorious for twisting and getting whacked out of shape. I guess the murderer didn't realize that."

"Or maybe he did." It would be another circumstantial trap for Alyssa like last time. "This gives us some valuable time to find the killer."

Jake hung up and explained all he'd learned to Alyssa. She was attentive, but didn't comment until he'd finished.

"Clay knows more than he's telling," she said. "Maybe he didn't actually kill Phoebe, but he's hiding something. That's why he left the LeCroixs'. Guilt. Sanchez should keep his man on it."

"It's fairly late. I think Clay's in for the night. Considering all he's uncovered, I think we should trust Sanchez's judgment."

"I suppose you're right."

"Let's see what they learn from the lie detector test."

The way she talked, her eyes never quite meeting his, told Jake all he needed to know. There was nothing more to say. The ensuing silence stretched over light-years of time even though it was only a few minutes. Jake told her to get some sleep, then left.

CHAPTER 34

Alyssa sat in the living room of her aunt's town house, unable to move, barely able to think. Something inside her had seized up the moment Vincent Crowe said they would arrest her again if the ballistics on the bullet matched the gun. She'd told herself to be brave, but now she thought it might take a great deal more fortitude than she possessed.

Jake was undoubtedly right—if the killer had taken the time to plant the gun, then it must be the murder weapon. The bullet had to match the gun, and no doubt, the top-notch technicians at the FBI would prove it. She'd be sent to jail for a crime she did not commit.

"Jake loves me," Alyssa whispered to encourage herself.

She closed her eyes and saw his expression as he'd told her he wanted to marry her and have a family. She pictured his wide-shouldered, long-waisted body, the concern lingering in his dark eyes even when he tried to hide it.

Despite his tendency to toss out humorous one-liners, Jake was earnest and steadfast and absolutely true. If you were facing the worst crisis of your life, he would be the one to have at your side.

She loved him, she honestly did. She hadn't been able to look him in the eye for fear he would see the truth and know how much she loved him. She had no right to drag him down with her. This could go on for years and years. He'd be an old man when she was released—if they released her. Without question, she knew he'd wait if he believed she loved him.

Alyssa opened her eyes, whispering, "If you love someone with all your heart, you know when to let them go."

That's what she'd done. She'd seen the disappointment lurking in his eyes when she hadn't responded by telling him how much she loved him. It had been the hardest thing she'd ever done, but she would do it all over again.

He'd walked out the door, saying he needed to talk to Wyatt, but she knew he wanted to get away from her to hide the humiliation he must feel. He was an insular man, close to almost no one. She'd managed to penetrate the invisible shield he kept between himself and others. She'd rewarded him in the most unforgivable way.

If only she could step out from under the dark cloud of the past and into the sunlight of a new beginning with Jake. If only. The words swirled through her brain like a mantra. If only, if only, if only.

"What are you doing?" she muttered under her breath. "You're sitting here like a victim just waiting."

Jake was doing everything he could to help her. Why wasn't she trying to help herself? Sanchez said the FBI lab would take up to three days to analyze the bullet.

Two days in jail had seemed like an eternity. Three days on the outside, doing her best to clear herself, would pass in a heartbeat. But if she had a prayer of having a life with Jake, it was all the time she'd been given.

Where should she start?

The instant she asked the question, something in her brain clicked. Clay. He had the key to this nightmare.

She didn't know how she knew this, but she did. An embryo of a plan formed in her mind, and she glanced down at her watch.

It wasn't yet ten o'clock. Jake had advised her to get some rest because he knew how little sleep she'd gotten in jail, but she didn't want to waste a single second. Clay was at Maree Winston's home on Julia Street.

She looked down at her rumpled dress and knew how terrible her hair must look as well. She'd taken a shower in jail but the harsh soap and shampoo were nothing like the gentle, fragrant brands she preferred. Rushing up the stairs, she concentrated on her plan and even managed to smile to herself.

Jake sat in his car down the block from the LeCroixs' mansion. Cars lined both sides of the narrow street. Wyatt's black Lexus was parked out front, and Jake had no doubt Wyatt would be there most of the evening.

Clay could be a creep and duck out, claiming a migraine, but Wyatt would stay to the end. Jake settled back, leaning his head against the headrest. Immediately, he thought about Alyssa.

I love you.

He'd never considered saying those words to any of the women who'd waltzed through his life, and yet he'd never meant any words more. He only knew he'd never felt happier, more alive than when he was with her. She brought the type of companionship he'd always craved even though he hadn't realized it.

"Face it, partner. She doesn't love you."

He'd said the words out loud, and they had a hollow, aching echo inside the car. It was stuffy, and he rolled down the window rather than attract attention to a lone man sitting in a car by turning on the engine to use the air conditioning. A thin mist of warm, moist air redolent with the scent of gardenias and soil still wet from the recent rains swept into the car.

It was hotter, more uncomfortable now than it had been. For a moment, it blocked Alyssa from his mind. Then his image of her returned with startling clarity. The look on her beautiful face when he said he loved her had told him that he'd just drawn the joker, not a winning ace.

Something had splintered inside him into a million sharp pieces that pierced him every time he thought about Alyssa. He'd trade everything he had or ever hoped to have if she would love him. Holding raw emotion in check, he realized it was hopeless. You can't make deals with the universe.

Maybe things would change if they could find the killer and get Alyssa out of this mess. Maybe and maybe not. Why delude himself with false hope? It wasn't his style.

Get over it!

Okay, she didn't love him. They'd had fun—not to mention great sex—but she hadn't fallen for him. A tragedy, sure, but . . . "Stop trying to make a joke out of everything," he told himself.

No matter had she felt, Jake still loved Alyssa. He wasn't going to turn his back on her now. She was innocent, and he intended to prove it.

He forced himself to concentrate on the crime, and he narrowed his lists of suspects. Wyatt was a definite possibility. Troy was a good candidate—if Phoebe had intended to back out. Clay ranked right up there. Even Max couldn't be eliminated.

Motive and opportunity, he reminded himself, the lifeblood of every crime. All four men had their reasons to want Phoebe dead. Who else might be out there?

The Bahamian psychic who was involved in some sort of kinky sex intrigue with Clay and Maree might have his own reasons—God only knew what—for wanting Phoebe dead. Maree might . . . his thoughts drifted away, remembering the stunning brunette in the feathered vampire outfit. *Playboy*'s idea of a female vampire.

Nah! Maree couldn't be guilty. The odds were against it. More men committed murder than women by far.

A trickle of sweat dribbled down his temple followed by another. He'd hoped to catch Wyatt as he left, but if he stayed here much longer, his clothes would be saturated. Why not make a condolence call and see if he could have a private conversation with him?

Inside the brightly lighted mansion, floral tributes by the dozens lined the foyer. Clusters of them stood in the corners of the rooms Jake could see from the entrance. After waiting outside, the cool blast of air chilled the fine sheen of perspiration covering his body.

He recognized a few people, but he didn't see Wyatt or his parents. Making his way through the living room, where still more flowers stood on every surface from the mantel to the sofa tables to the sideboard, Jake said hello to those he knew, but kept moving, his eye out for Wyatt.

"Jackson, dear, isn't it awful?" gushed a woman just behind him.

Jackson? No one called him by his full name unless they didn't know him. He turned and found Marie-Claire Duvall. He'd met Clay's mother a few times at social occasions and when Max had forced him to have dinner with the family right after TriTech had acquired Duvall Imports.

"Yes, Mrs. Duvall. It's a tragedy."

"Poor Clay. He's so broken up."

Yeah, sure. Right now he was probably humping Maree. "Where's the family?"

"I'll show you." She took his arm in the old-fashioned way as if she couldn't make it across the room on her own. She was a silver blonde with a natural air of sophistication. Jake could see where Clay got his looks. "They're on the sunporch looking at pictures of Phoebe when she was Mardi Gras queen."

God forbid.

Even more flowers were banked on the perimeter of

the sunporch where Hattie and Gordon were sitting with a handful of friends, going through photo albums. Off to one side stood Wyatt. Bingo.

"Look who's here," announced Clay's mother in her honeyed drawl.

The group turned to him. Heat gathered under his collar, and he cursed himself for being so inconsiderate. These people had lost someone very special to them. He'd come just to corner Wyatt.

"Mr. and Mrs. LeCroix, I'm sorry for your loss." Damn! What do you say at times like this that doesn't sound trite? "Phoebe was so young. Her whole life was before her."

"Thank you. We appreciate you coming," Gordon said with quiet dignity.

Hattie glared at him with burning reproachful eyes.

"Where's Clay?" he asked, all innocence. "I'd like to tell him—"

"He was devastated, completely devastated," Hattie said. "Poor boy had to go home. Dr. Martin gave him a prescription for sleeping pills."

"He's brokenhearted," added a woman he didn't know.

Jake orchestrated a concerned nod. This was proof positive you could fool some of the people all of the time.

"I understand the police have released the killer," Hattie said, venom infusing every word.

He had no doubt she knew how close he was to Alyssa. He was damn tempted to tell her off, but he heard a little voice in his ear. His mother. She was reminding him to be more sensitive. No matter what he thought of Hattie and the way she'd treated Alyssa, the woman had lost her daughter in a brutal murder that would haunt her until the day she died.

Gordon spoke up. "They don't have enough evidence to charge anyone yet. The police are still investigating."

Jake tried to catch Wyatt's eye, but he was studying

the top of his mother's head. Jake opened his mouth to express his sympathy to Wyatt and get his attention, when a woman swanned into the room, a blur in his peripheral vision.

"I hate to be the bearer of bad tidings."

Ravelle. Oh, shit. Tidings? Hadn't they gone out with hoop skirts? All eyes were on the television gossip.

The skinny old crone with the blue-black hair bent and kissed the air near Hattie's cheek. "I grieve for you, my dear, dear friend. Tragic, so tragic. Your loss is my loss."

Ravelle turned, smiling with exaggerated sadness at the small group. Had she spent too much time in front of a camera, or what?

"That's why I want to tell you in person what my secret sources at the police station tell me about dear Phoebe's murder. It'll be on the eleven o'clock news, but I wanted you to hear it from me first."

Uhh—ooh. Gordon didn't look too thrilled either. Jake wondered if he'd told Hattie about his trip to the station. If Ravelle were a true friend, she'd take Hattie aside to tell her. Of course, Ravelle was a media maven who lived for as much attention as she could get.

"The police know what happened to your grandson."

Hattie gasped. "Baby Patrick?"

Ravelle glanced meaningfully at Jake. "Max Williams had him."

"You, bastard, you." Hattie catapulted off the sofa and slammed into Jake. "I'll kill you. He was my grandson." She pummeled Jake's chest with her fists. "My only grandchild."

The unexpected outburst caught Jake off-guard. He stumbled backward, barely managing to stay upright as she rammed into him. An instant later, Gordon had grabbed her from behind and pulled her away.

"Your father's nothing but a redneck. Imagine him mincing around my town, trying to be somebody, when he had my little Patrick."

Jake lost it. "Max was the baby's father. He loved him. That's why he took him."

Silence dark as a closed coffin settled over the room. Jake could see even Ravelle had been taken by surprise. Her informant wasn't all that good. He had unearthed only a portion of the story.

"You liar, you," shrieked Hattie. "My darling Phoebe would never allow white trash to touch her."

Once again, Jake's mother called to him from the grave, and he didn't tell Hattie about the other creeps Phoebe had seduced. Don't lower yourself to her level.

"Lordy, lordy, save me from these animals." Hattie collapsed against her husband.

"Oh my, she's swooned," cried Marie-Claire. "Call Dr. Martin."

Swooned? He had to be a redneck. No woman he'd known swooned. Not his mother. Certainly not Alyssa.

"My crew's just outside," Ravelle informed Jake. "New Orleans wants to hear the whole story."

"Drop dead, bitch."

Once again the room plunged into shocked silence. His father might have withered under the accusing stares, but Jake didn't give a damn what these people thought of him.

"Wyatt, come on. I need to talk to you."

Phoebe's brother's head jerked up with a 'who me?' look. He reluctantly followed Jake out the side door into the garden.

Jake yanked off his tie and shoved it into the pocket of his sports coat. He was still overheated. Shrugging out of his jacket, he said, "Let's cut the shit. I know all about the Port Authority scam."

A sheepish expression crossed Wyatt's face. "I knew you'd figure it out sooner or later."

Jake inhaled a stabilizing breath, knowing his next few words might mean the world to Alyssa. "Get this straight. I'm willing to let it go, pretend I know nothing about it, or I can call the IRS right now unless you tell me what I want to know. You'll lose your CPA license. Your name will be worthless. You'll bring even more sorrow on your family."

Jake looked into Wyatt's eyes, and he saw the man was thinking it over. His sixth sense kicked in. A lot more must be at stake than he'd realized. Wyatt should be jumping at an opportunity like this.

He grabbed Wyatt by his designer tie. "Want me to beat the crap out of you, then call the authorities?"

"Okay, okay. I—I'll tell you whatever you want to know."

CHAPTER 35

Jake and Wyatt stood in the backyard where a lagoon-style pool took up most of the yard. Beyond it was a small pool house with changing rooms. Jake had been here once for a summer barbecue right after they'd acquired Clay's importing business.

"O-okay, okay. What do you want to know?" Wyatt sounded leery.

"Start by telling me about Gracie Harper. Do you know who killed her?"

"Give me your word you won't tell anyone about the Port Authority scam."

"You have my word."

Wyatt let out a long, audible breath. "My sister did it."

"Why am I not surprised? Did Phoebe pull the trigger or did she have someone do it for her?"

"It was an accident. The nurse was going to talk to some detective, and Phoebe was afraid the truth would come out. She went to see the nurse, hoping to persuade her to keep quiet, but something went wrong."

No kidding.

"From day one, Gracie Harper was a bleeding heart. She got plenty of money to hand over the baby to your father, but for Gracie, it didn't end there. She kept calling to check on the kid for years. When he died, you'd have thought Gracie was responsible, the way she carried on."

Jake's instincts had been correct. Wyatt was a class A prick. He cautioned himself not to allow his true feelings to show. Too much was at stake.

"When the detective started to ask questions, the woman freaked. She called Phoebe and said it was time to tell the truth. That's why Phoebe went to see her."

"I take it you were in on the kidnapping from the very beginning."

"Yes. Phoebe came to me in a panic when she discovered she was pregnant. She knew Mother would have a hissy fit. Imagine, a pregnant, unwed Mardi Gras queen."

Stranger things have happened.

"Phoebe had always had a thing for Clay, but she also liked older men. I think she expected to play around, then marry Clay when she was ready to settle down. Clay took up with Alyssa, and well, Phoebe nearly came unglued. My sister wasn't the most stable person in the world, you know."

Go on, you can't mean it.

"Phoebe decided if she married Clay, Mother would accept her pregnancy because she was set on having her daughter marry into the Duvall family. Tricking Clay turned out to be easier than we thought."

"Lucky Clay."

Wyatt chuckled. "Clay was fried when he discovered what had happened. He was crazy about Alyssa, but he couldn't deny the baby might be his. He didn't have any choice but to marry Phoebe or have his parents disown him."

"He suspected the baby might not be his, right?"

"Absolutely. He told Phoebe that he'd have tests run. That's why she persuaded your father to take the baby."

Jake was again amazed at how unaffected Wyatt was,

considering his part in all this. Like his sister and mother, Wyatt was self-centered to the point of almost being delusional. They seemed to think they had a god-given right to do whatever they wanted.

They lacked a moral compass as his mother would say. He might be the redneck Hattie claimed, but his values weren't screwy. He was better than this family, and so was Alyssa.

"What about the second baby who was taken when Alyssa's aunt was in the hospital?"

"Phoebe arranged for some goon she knew to pay a nurse to move the baby, never intending to actually kidnap it. She wanted to frighten Alyssa into leaving town. She was afraid Alyssa would find out what happened to Patrick and tell everyone. When it backfired and the nurse confessed, Phoebe had the same guy threaten to kill Alyssa."

"That didn't work either."

"Right. Alyssa's a lot tougher than people realize. I know. I lived under the same roof and saw how my mother treated Alyssa. She survived and went on to be successful."

Jake nodded, then commented, "All this seems a bit extreme just to keep Clay from finding out the baby wasn't his."

"In the beginning, Phoebe cared what Clay thought, but their marriage was never a happy one. She would have divorced him sooner, but she liked her place in society. She would be—would have been—the first to admit it."

"She sure made it sound as if she still loved Clay when she kept accusing Alyssa of trying to steal him."

"My sister was clever. It was a big act. She didn't want anyone to know—especially my mother—that she was divorcing Clay and moving to Paris. Mother would have nagged the life out of her to stay. To her divorce is unthinkable—especially divorcing the son of the Duvalls."

"Unthinkable," Jake agreed.

"After she met Troy Chevalier, she visited Paris and met his parents. She went nuts for their life there."

"I've been to Troy's home in Paris. I can see how Phoebe would have been intoxicated by their lifestyle. It's about as close to royalty as she could get," Jake said. "A quantum leap from New Orleans."

"Then you understand why she was terrified that the Chevaliers might find out about the baby and refuse to let their son marry her."

For a second Jake was speechless, then he said, "What? Are you telling me that Phoebe did all this to keep Troy's parents from learning the truth?"

"Well, yes, and Troy, too. She never told him the whole story about the baby. My sister was a little screwy at times."

No shit.

"Phoebe was genuinely sorry about blaming Alyssa for taking the baby. In her own way, Phoebe was proud of all Alyssa had accomplished and a touch envious. Then Alyssa discovered they were sisters and wanted to be friends, Phoebe felt even more guilty."

"So she accused Alyssa of trying to steal her husband in front of a bunch of women including Ravelle, who turned it into a death threat."

Wyatt raked his fingers through his hair, saying, "I'm not excusing what she did, but Phoebe needed to keep my mother from finding out she was leaving New Orleans to live in Paris until the last minute, when it would be too late to do anything about it. Phoebe told me she was going to talk to Alyssa and apologize."

"She did talk to Alyssa, then Phoebe was killed probably within minutes afterward. Do you have any idea who killed her?"

Two deep lines of worry appeared between Wyatt's eyes. "No, I have no idea, but I don't for one second think it was Alyssa. I want the killer caught."

"If you had to take a wild guess, who would you say did it?"

"I've asked myself this question more than once. The way I see it, there are two possibilities. Clay didn't want the divorce, but Phoebe wasn't fooled. She knew he didn't love her. She'd been having him tailed for over a year. He was having an affair with Maree Winston. Phoebe knew Clay wanted to dodge an expensive divorce settlement."

Clay. It figured. He might have had his Bahamian buddy do the actually killing. Jake doubted Clay had the balls to do it himself, but who knew?

"Phoebe wanted out, and she needed her money. She'd given Clay everything in her trust fund to rescue Duvall Imports. It was still shaky. That's why we ran the scam at the docks."

Jake silently congratulated himself. From the very first, he'd sensed the company was in trouble.

"We were afraid you'd discover what was going on and cut off the company, so Phoebe persuaded Troy to alter the report. She wanted to buy time and force Clay to come up with the settlement money so she could start over. When Clay saw she was serious, he killed her."

"Sounds logical. Most murders are crimes of passion or greed." Jake waited a moment, but Wyatt didn't continue. He prompted him. "The second possibility?"

"You're not going to like this."

"Max?"

Wyatt nodded slowly. "He's loved Phoebe for years. He was always around, willing to help her, willing to do anything, even buy Duvall Imports. Phoebe told Max about the divorce the day before the Vampire Ball. Wow! He was furious."

Son of a bitch! Max had never mention this. Why not? Something inside Jake snapped. He didn't like admitting it, having kept Max at a distance all these years, but he'd come to care for the man who was his father. He didn't want him to be a cold-blooded killer, but he had to concede that it was possible.

Alyssa knocked on the door of Maree Winston's apartment. From inside she heard reggae music and voices.

The door opened a crack, but it was enough for Alyssa to recognize Maree's beautiful face. "Alyssa!"

Maree pulled the door open and Alyssa stepped inside. "I'm sorry for coming over so late, but I need to talk to Clay."

Maree's dark eyes narrowed almost imperceptibly but Alyssa noticed. The woman was crazy about Clay. Great, she was welcome to him.

"I'm right here," Clay called from the sofa.

She walked into the small room and saw a huge man with blue-black skin sitting next to Clay. The man smiled at her but the glint in his eyes was positively chilling.

"Hey, babe, have a drink." Clay held up a tumbler full of an amber liquid. The slight slur in his speech and dilated pupils told her Clay was half-drunk.

"Merlot, please."

"Does this look like a bar?" snapped Maree.

Clay jumped up and put his arm around Alyssa. "Hey, cool it," he told Maree.

"There's white wine, mon. A tasty chardonnay."

"That would be nice." The last thing she wanted was a drink, but she needed to appear relaxed and ready to celebrate.

"Aren't you going to ask her how she knew where to find you?" Maree said to Clay.

"At the party, Phoebe told me she was having you followed," Alyssa volunteered. "She said you were having an affair with the woman in the feathered dress. I'd met Maree at Max's party and remembered her name. When you weren't at home, I thought you might be here."

Clay nodded, accepting the lie. Alyssa had fabricated this story rather than say Sanchez had been tailing him.

"Come on, babe. Sit down." Clay led her to the sofa and pulled her down beside him so she was wedged between Clay and the big man with Clay's arm still around her. "This is Dante, a friend of mine."

Alyssa smiled—or attempted to—but it was difficult. Dante smiled back, exposing teeth that were large and strikingly white in his dark face. Despite the smile, her instincts told her not to trust him.

"Maree, the wine, remember?" Clay asked.

The woman flounced out of the room in a swirl of black silk. Even though she'd changed into a flattering lavender dress, Alyssa felt positively dumpy compared to Maree. She supposed it didn't matter. Her mission was to plant a few seeds of doubt in Clay's mind and see what happened.

"How did you get out of jail?" Dante asked as Maree returned with a glass of wine and plunked it down on the coffee table in front of her.

She gazed up at Clay, trying for a look of adoration. "You know I didn't kill Phoebe, don't you?"

Clay smiled down at her, and for a moment, she was reminded of the old days when she'd believed she loved him.

"I'm so sorry about Phoebe. I truly am. We didn't always get along, but what happened was horrible."

Clay nodded with the suggestion of a smile creeping across his lips. He didn't seem upset at all. Well, what did she expect? He was here—not with family or home grieving.

Maree had taken a seat in the chair across from them. "Are you out on bail?"

Alyssa shook her head, her eyes never leaving Clay's. "No. I was never charged. You see, the killer made this teeny-weeny mistake." She pulled her eyes away from Clay's acting as if this was difficult but she felt the need to be polite.

"Mistake, mon. What mistake?"

Alyssa steeled herself and gazed at Dante. He appeared friendlier now. Maybe it had been her imagination spurred on because she was preparing to lie. "Well, Phoebe was killed with a .22. Those bullets twist when fired into a body. That makes it difficult to run a ballistics test. They tried but couldn't match the bullet that killed her to the gun."

"They let you go for lack of evidence?" Clay asked.

Alyssa attempted a gloating smile. "They let me go because they know I'm innocent."

She noticed the tight frown on Maree's face and the half-dazed expression on Clay's. He was drunker than she'd first thought.

"There's evidence that can clear me," she continued, injecting as much sincerity as possible into every word.

"What evidence?" Dante asked.

"I'm not certain," she hedged. "Forensic evidence. Who knows? A drop of blood. A fiber. I'm thinking hair since they took a hair sample from me. They work miracles with DNA, you know."

"That'z great, babe." Clay planted a wet kiss on her lips.

She threw her arms around him, telling herself to play this to the hilt. "I'm no longer a suspect. You have no idea how happy that makes me." She took a swig of wine. "Let's celebrate."

"Celebrate," Clay agreed, and he raised his glass.

She knew if the killer who so desperately wanted her out of town or in jail thought she was out of the woods, he would try again. This time he might try to kill her, but she didn't care. The long two nights she'd spent in jail had given her plenty of time to think. She valued her freedom, her aunt . . . and Jake above all else. She had to risk her own life in order to save it.

* * *

The telephone woke Jake the next morning. He fumbled for it on the nightstand beside his bed. Benson's head popped up as the dog surged onto all fours from the bench at the foot of the bed.

"It's me."

Jake mumbled something back to Sanchez.

"I know it's early, but I thought you'd want to know."

Uhh-ooh. Jake sat up and braced himself. "Okay, shoot."

"Last night at eleven-thirteen, Alyssa went to Maree Winston's apartment. According to my operative, Dante Benoit and Clay Duvall were there. Alyssa didn't leave until shortly after one."

Alyssa went to see Clay right after Jake had said good night. Why? His head suddenly seemed dull, heavy. He managed to say, "Didn't you tell me you were going to pull off the tail on Clay and concentrate on Troy?"

"Yes, but another operative became free at the last minute. I have him working on Chevalier."

"I see," Jake muttered but he didn't understand a damn thing. He clearly recalled telling Alyssa that Sanchez would be shifting his manpower away from Clay to Troy. No doubt, she'd gone there thinking she wouldn't be observed. He said good-bye, then dropped the receiver into its cradle.

Benson leaped up, placing two paws on either side of Jake's chest, his tail wagging furiously. The retriever kissed his face in long warm slurps of his tongue. Usually, this made Jake smile, but not today.

No doubt Alyssa had sought out Clay because she was looking for answers. But instead of clearing herself, she might end up dead.

CHAPTER 36

The following day, Alyssa awoke to soft light slanting through the shutters on her bedroom windows. She lay in bed, staring up at the coffered ceiling, recalling her conversation with Clay last night.

He seemed to think it was perfectly natural for her to come to see him. No doubt, he believed she still adored him. Maree obviously thought so, too. She kept glaring at Alyssa while Dante added little to the conversation.

The man gave her the willies. Dante claimed to be a psychic, but her intuition told her that he was a con artist or worse. What was Clay thinking? He was a snob and a closet racist. Why would he hang out with Dante?

She wasn't sure what she had expected to accomplish. Her vague feeling Clay was the key to finding Phoebe's murderer might be way off. It was apparent Clay was not mourning the loss of his wife, but did that mean he killed her?

Clay could have had her killed. Dante. He instantly popped into her mind, and she tried to remember the size of the man dressed in the devil's costume who had gone into the study with Phoebe. She'd assumed it was Max because he'd been wearing the same costume, but it might have been Dante, who was also a tall, big man. Under normal circumstances, Dante would have been spotted, but with a mask and costume, no one would have noticed him.

"Criminy," she said out loud as she got out of bed. "You're no closer to the truth than you were."

She dressed, trying to keep up her spirits, telling herself she had two more days. She couldn't just sit around and wait to see if Sanchez could solve this. If she stirred the pot, no telling what might happen.

Someone wanted her out of the way. She'd been threatened with death. Would the person make a move now? She was offering herself as bait and banking on someone trying to get her.

She needed a bit of luck. The police wouldn't release any information that would compromise their investigation. If they didn't make a statement about her release—and her attorney assured her that they wouldn't—then she could pretend she wasn't expecting to be arrested again and get away with it.

This might make her enough of a threat for the killer to come after her. She would need to be very cautious. She didn't have a gun, but a small canister of pepper spray would be helpful. She'd been too busy to pick up the one she'd ordered. She'd better get it today. Buying another cell phone was important, too, but it wasn't as urgent as having a way to defend herself.

"Hi, there," Shawn said when she came downstairs to the kitchen.

"Good morning." Alyssa bent over and kissed Aunt Thee on the cheek. "How are you feeling?"

"As good as new." The *Times-Picayune* was spread out in front of Aunt Thee, who was reading it and nibbling on a wedge of whole wheat toast. "Oh, my. You're not going to believe this," Aunt Thee said. "You've had your fifteen minutes of fame. Now it's Max Williams's turn. There's no mention of you anywhere in the paper.''

Alyssa read the headline in a font reserved for bombings and serial killers. WILLIAMS ABDUCTED BABY. Zane Welsh had written the article. Alyssa remembered Jake telling her about the obnoxious reporter's visit to his office. Offensive or not, the man was accurate, she decided as she scanned the article.

"Did you know all this?" Aunt Thee asked.

"Yes. Jake told me."

"You two missed the evening news," Shawn told them. "Ravelle had part of the story. She claimed Max took the baby—period. No mention of him being the father. Now the old bat has egg on her face."

Alyssa tried for a laugh, but it was hard. The media might be hot for another story, but she was dead certain the police were still trying to pin Phoebe's murder on her. She had to do something, but what?

She poured herself a glass of orange juice and decided to go to see her father. He'd seemed sincere about wanting to help her, and she assumed he'd gone to the police. She knew he lunched every day at the Mayfair Club. Would he freak if she walked in to see him? It would certainly send a very public message that the killer would be certain to receive: She wasn't afraid to go anywhere, even to the ultraexclusive Mayfair Club.

"Alyssa Rossi is on line two," Spencer told Jake.

"Alyssa, did you get a decent night's sleep?" he asked the moment Spencer transferred the call.

"After the Gray Bar Hilton, anything is an improvement."

"Gray Bar Hilton?"

"That's what the prisoners call jail."

"Gotcha." He wished she would tell him that she'd gone to Maree Winston's apartment. He didn't want to have to ask.

"Jake . . . I need to tell you something."

He gripped the receiver hard and waited.

"I want to thank you for all you've done for me. I-I know I seemed . . . callous or something last night." There was a distinct quaver in her voice now. "If the worst happens, I want you to know I appreciate you more than I can possibly say."

Appreciate? Gimme a break. People appreciated fine wine and art. Either she loved him or she didn't. He didn't know how to respond without making a bad situation worse.

"I hope someday I'll be in a position to have a life," she said.

"You will, Alyssa." He wanted to share with her the information he'd forced out of Wyatt LeCroix. Before he could say a word, Spencer came into the office and shoved a note in front of Jake.

Your father is outside. He's really upset.

"Look, I've got to run," he said as he motioned for Spencer to show Max into the office. "I'm going to be tied up here until about eight. Then I'll come over. Okay?"

He hung up and Max walked through the door. His father stopped in front of his desk, his dark eyes troubled. He clenched and unclenched his right hand. Jake came around the desk and stood beside him.

"What's the matter?" Jake asked.

"You've seen the papers, the television." The bitter edge of cynicism colored each word. "This is when you find out who your friends are."

Jake wondered if his father had many real friends. He'd spent his life pursuing success, then his aspirations became political. It didn't leave much time for friendship.

"How can I help?" Jake asked.

"Go to lunch with me at the Mayfair Club."

"Sure," Jake responded although he dreaded going into the snooty club under the best of circumstances.

He could tell, though, how important this was to his father. He checked his watch. It was eleven-thirty, too early for the cadre of businessmen who convened in the Mayfair's dining room around one o'clock.

"There are a couple of reports I'd like you to look over," Jake said. "Then we'll go to lunch."

"There's something else . . ." Suddenly, Max's voice became thick, unsteady.

Uhh-ooh. Jake braced himself. This could get interesting.

The door to the office swung open, and Spencer sailed in, frowning. "Duncan Thomas is outside. He says it's an emergency."

Just when he thought things could not get any worse. "Send him in."

He ventured a sideways glance at his father. Max's left eyebrow lifted a fraction of an inch, the way it did when he was concentrating.

Duncan Thomas, a thirty-something man with a beard already grizzled with gray, was head of overseas operations for TriTech. He stalked into the office and greeted them, his brow furrowed in a tight frown.

"One of Duvall Imports' ships has been seized in Singapore. Heroin was found in its container cargo," Thomas announced in a breathless rush.

"Yes! Yes!" Jake gave his father a high five, and they both started to laugh.

Thomas stared at them, slack-jawed. Normally, having any ship seized was a royal pain in the butt—not to mention expensive. But having the Singapore government seize your ship was the worst news imaginable. The government had gained worldwide notoriety for publicly spanking teens for graffiti. When it came to serious crimes like drugs, Singapore had zero tolerance.

Jake told him, "We're laughing because TriTech no longer owns Duvall Imports. Singapore will probably keep the ship."

"It's Clay Duvall's problem," Max added.

"I see," Thomas responded but it was clear he didn't.

"We found out Duvall Imports was pulling a scam at the docks here," Jake explained. "We cut them loose this weekend. We have no legal ties to the company."

"That fast? How?"

"It's like a quit claim," Max told him. "Essentially we gave Duvall back the company. I had him moved out of the building on Monday right after my attorney filed the necessary documents with the court."

"I guess this is good news," muttered Thomas.

Not if you're Clay Duvall.

"Someting went wrong, mon."

"Wrong?" Clay couldn't believe Dante's cavalier attitude. "I'll never get the ship back. It'll cost me a fortune to bail the crew out of prison. You assured me this was a foolproof plan."

They were sitting in the small makeshift office that Wyatt had given them when Jake kicked Clay's business out of the TriTech building. His agent was looking for a suitable suite of offices, but it would take time.

Dante smiled, a flash of white-white teeth in his dark face. "You blame de captain. We try again."

Now was the time to dump Dante and Maree. He was sick of them both. Alyssa had come back to him. It was clear that he could have her now, and he didn't want to risk getting dragged into a drug scandal.

"I've made de arrangements, mon."

"No!" The word exploded out before Clay could temper it with an excuse.

Dante surged to his feet and hauled Clay out of his chair. "Don't you be tellin' me no. I own you."

Clay tried to wrench out of Dante's grip, but he was too strong—physically. Intellectually, Clay knew he was superior. He'd had all he was going to take.

"Dante, it's over. No more smuggling on my ships."

The Bahamian threw back his head and roared, his

arms vibrating and shaking Clay. When he stopped chor-
tling, the fury in Dante's black eyes sent a bolt of primal
fear through Clay.

"I do own you, mon." He grabbed Clay's crotch, his
big hand engulfing his penis. A knowing smile creased
Dante's lips, then vanished as he squeezed. "All of you."

Dante laughed again, a low, mean snicker. "De TV
in Maree's bedroom. D'ere's a camera inside it."

Shit! A hidden camera. Clay's bowels cramped, and
for a moment he thought he was going to lose it.

"I have tapes. How you say? Insurance." He squeezed
again, harder this time. "You dump me. I dump on
you."

"You're bluffing, " Clay responded to keep up a good
front.

"Try me, mon. Try me."

Dante released him, and Clay dropped back into his
chair. Without another word, the psychic walked out
the door. Clay slumped in his seat.

He could imagine what would happen if anyone
found out. It had been a ménage à trois, that's all. Who
wouldn't experiment if they had the chance? But if
anyone saw those tapes, they would misinterpret them
and think he and Dante had a thing for each other.

What was he going to do now?

He leaned back and studied the ceiling, thinking. He
refused to let Dante hold his business, his life, hostage.
If he did, this would just be the beginning. No telling
were it would go next.

Cheating the IRS was a national pastime, but dealing
drugs was something else. He had a name, an image to
protect. He'd made a critical mistake, but he could
rectify it now.

He had no choice but to get rid of Dante. If the
psychic was killed, Clay would have to deal with Maree.
Maybe he could arrange for it to look like an accident,
then Maree wouldn't be suspicious.

He stood up and started to walk down the long hall to

Wyatt's office. He stopped before he left the cubbyhole where he'd shoehorned in his computer and files. He wasn't sure he wanted to discuss this with Wyatt.

Clay wasn't sure how he'd explain his relationship with Dante to his brother-in-law. He might have to take care of Dante himself. A wave of apprehension swept through him as he imagined coming face to face with Dante. No way. He'd have to shoot Dante when he wasn't looking.

"You're a crack shot," Clay whispered to himself. He silently blessed his father for all the times Nelson Duvall had insisted they go hunting. It was a Southern tradition Clay had dreaded. Now his experience with guns was going to pay off.

Thinking of his father reminded Clay that he'd promised to meet him for lunch. Afterward they were going over to help Hattie LeCroix finalize funeral arrangements. Clay couldn't imagine what was left to discuss, but his father was a Southern gentleman to the core. Ladies *always* needed help.

Alyssa walked into the Mayfair Club's dining room and looked around the room filled with businessmen. She didn't see Gordon. Of course, he was home with Hattie. With the funeral two days away, it stood to reason he wouldn't be out in public.

She spotted Clay in a corner booth with his father. He didn't see her, and she turned to leave before he noticed her and she had to deal with him. She rushed out of the building into the stifling, moist heat of a spring day that felt more like summer.

"Alyssa, Alyssa," a man called.

She stopped, shading her eyes with her hand. Gordon LeCroix walked toward her. He was dressed in a gray business suit and crisp white shirt. He appeared to be oblivious to the heat, but lines of worry etched his brow.

"I heard the police released you," he said, his voice pitched lower than usual. "Are you all right?"

For a moment, she was tempted to tell him the truth, but resisted the impulse. She was positive her father hadn't murdered Phoebe, but the killer might be someone he knew. She didn't want that person to think she was still under investigation.

"I'm fine, really. They don't have any evidence against me, so I'm free."

"Never a doubt," he replied, but he didn't sound upbeat. "Are you meeting someone?"

"No. Actually, I was looking for you."

"You've heard."

What now? She swallowed with difficulty, then found her voice. "Heard what?"

"Ravelle has managed to find out what I told the police. She called Hattie a little while ago to warn her. On the five o'clock news, she'll announce you're my daughter."

She couldn't ignore the urge to put her arm around him. "Hattie was devastated. She took it out on you, didn't she?"

"She tried, but I walked out. I've had it." His lips thinned with irritation. "Do you have time to have lunch and talk?"

Feeling awkward, she casually dropped her arm, saying, "Sure."

Inside, they were told they'd have to wait a few minutes. There were no free tables. Clay and Nelson Duvall saw them, and Clay walked over, beaming.

"Would you like to join us?"

Inwardly, Alyssa groaned and tried to come up with an excuse. Everyone in the room was watching them.

"Thanks, but we need a little private time together," her father said.

"Oh, a-a-ah, sure. Dad and I are coming over to the house later," Clay said to her father, but his eyes were on her. He returned to the corner booth, smiling and greeting men he knew.

"I've never liked him. It was Hattie who wanted Phoebe to marry into the Duvall family."

"Do you think it's possible"—Alyssa lowered her voice—"Clay killed Phoebe?"

"Maybe. Stay away from him, you hear?"

"Yes, sir." She laughed but couldn't help asking herself where this man had been when she was growing up. Despite the past, she liked him, really liked him.

The waiter showed them to a table that had been vacated and reset. Alyssa was aware of the people tracking them with their eyes, but her father seemed oblivious.

"I'm getting a divorce as soon as the funeral is over," he said when they were seated. "I should have done it years ago. Hattie is unstable and getting worse. She sees a psychiatrist, but it doesn't seem to be helping. I can't take much more."

"There's nothing like finding someone who loves you," she said, a catch in her voice. "You're still young. You could be very happy."

"Does Jake Williams make you happy?"

She saw no reason not to be honest with him about this. "I love him." She shook her head, disgusted with herself. "You know, I have no idea what I saw in Clay."

CHAPTER 37

Jake walked into the Mayfair Club beside his father. Whatever had been troubling Max seemed not to have been important. Since discovering Duvall Imports had a ship involved in trafficking heroin, Max had been in better spirits. So was Jake. It confirmed his suspicions. Clay Duvall was worse than a major sleaze. He was a crook, a drug trafficker.

Jake stopped in the lobby and turned to his father. The low buzz from the dining room drifted out into the empty lobby.

"You made a huge sacrifice for me," Jake said. "I won't forget it. I know it has caused you a lot of grief."

Max shrugged it off. "I deserved it. I was a foolish old man in love with the wrong woman. I had taken the baby. I should never have allowed Phoebe to persuade me to keep quiet. I hope your Alyssa will forgive me."

Your Alyssa. He wished.

"There is one other thing I need to tell you," Max added.

Uuh-ooh. That hinky feeling again. Jake couldn't imagine what Max was going to say, but judging from his taut lips and clenched right fist, it was something Jake did *not* want to hear.

"I did go into the study the night Phoebe was killed. It was me Alyssa saw."

Anger mushroomed inside Jake. So many lies. A lifetime of lies. He hardly knew how to deal with Max, this man who was his father.

"Why did you lie?" Jake wondered if he'd lied about anything else. Shit. How much worse could this get?

"I didn't exactly lie to you. I dodged the question or didn't answer it. I was too embarrassed to admit Phoebe had dumped Clay—" his voice broke with huskiness— "but wasn't going to marry me. She'd told me the day before, and I was trying again to talk her out of it."

"So you let Alyssa take the fall." He told himself to calm down. They probably could hear his voice inside the dining room.

"No. I told the police." Max drew in a sharp breath. "I just couldn't make myself tell you. I did everything Phoebe ever asked. I pushed you to buy Duvall Imports even though I didn't think it was worth a damn. Then she repays me by . . ."

Jake knew what it was like to be obsessed by a woman who didn't love you. It sucked. He understood Max— he thought—but he couldn't quite bring himself to forgive his father.

"S'okay. The police know the truth. That's what counts."

"I want to have a solid relationship with you," Max said. "I don't want anything between us. Not the past. Not a woman. Nothing."

Jake nodded his agreement. Talking about his feelings always made him uncomfortable. Knowing all his father had done made it hard to forgive or forget. He started walking toward the dining room.

The beeper on his belt vibrated. "Just a minute," he said to Max, knowing cell phones weren't allowed inside the dining room. The message on the beeper said to call Sanchez. "I have to take this." He pulled his cell phone from his pocket and hit the speed dial.

"I have some info on the psychic, Dante Benoit," said Sanchez the minute he recognized Jake's voice. "Dante poses as a psychic, but he makes his money smuggling drugs into the country. He's a bigger player than you might think. He's connected to Venezio and the mob."

He moved across the lobby to the window overlooking the street, so no one could overhear him tell Sanchez about the seizure of the ship in Singapore. "Put a tail on Dante," Jake said, and Sanchez agreed. "One other thing. You can stop looking for a second man dressed as the devil. It was my father."

For a long moment there was nothing but silence. "Do you think Max could have . . ."

Jake had wondered the same thing. He thought about it for a moment, then said, "No, I don't believe he killed Phoebe. He's guilty of a lot of things, but not murder."

"Something a little odd happened."

"What in blue blazes could be odder than this mess?"

Sanchez chuckled. "Troy Chevalier went to pay a condolence call on the family. Hattie LeCroix lit into him and called him a French faggot who'd lured her daughter away."

"Okay, so? Anyone who knows Troy realizes he isn't gay."

"That's not the strange part. When I interviewed Chevalier, he was surprised Hattie knew about them. Phoebe wasn't going to tell her family until Clay agreed to some type of a settlement and she was far away in Paris."

Jake thought a moment. "Clay told Hattie. Considering the trouble Duvall Imports has, Clay enlisted his mother-in-law's support to avoid a divorce. You've still got Clay under surveillance?"

"You bet."

"Keep close tabs on him."

Jake said good-bye with Sanchez promising to get back to him with any new information immediately. He caught up with his father and went into the dining room. The maitre d' looked at Max as if he were a dog turd on a stick and informed them there was no table available.

Jake scanned the room and noticed Clay with his father. No help there. At least half a dozen men who knew Max well were having lunch, but they all were pretending to be absorbed in conversation or eating. No one made eye contact with them.

Max's quick, darting glance around the room betrayed his concern. His father had anticipated this snubbing, expected it. Still, he was here facing everyone. Jake grudgingly admitted he was proud of his father. He'd told the truth and was bravely dealing with the consequences.

On the far side of the room, he spotted Alyssa with Gordon. Considering Max's confession about the baby, Jake could hardly suggest joining them. Gordon looked up, saw them, and rose. He crossed the room in long strides, headed in their direction.

Why me? Jake braced himself for the inevitable scene. A fight at the Mayfair Club was not his idea of a power lunch. Conversation had stopped just as if someone had flipped a switch.

"Max, Jake, you're here." Gordon's smile appeared genuine. "We're saving places for you."

He led them to the table, talking the whole time about the unseasonable heat. Was this guy for real? He seemed to be oblivious to the tension in the room. His peers expected him to ostracize Max, but Gordon wasn't going along with the program.

Jake let his father sit next to Alyssa, and he took the chair next to Gordon, who hadn't stopped smiling relentlessly like someone in a toothpaste commercial. The other diners returned to their meals and their conversation.

Whew! At least his father hadn't been totally humiliated. Actually, having Gordon accept them with open arms told everyone that he didn't blame Max for taking the baby. It was more impressive than having one of Max's so-called friends invite them to their table.

Gordon leaned over and whispered to Jake, "Alyssa tells me she's in love with you. I can see why. You're just like your father. You have guts."

Jake mustered a smile, his eyes on Alyssa. She was stunning in a bright blue dress and a strand of her own beads. In love with him, huh? Why would she tell her father, a man she wasn't close to, but not tell him?

Duh! He got it. No wonder he loved her. Jake couldn't keep a shit-eating grin off his face.

Clay watched Alyssa with the three men. Why were they so happy? Alyssa had come to him last night, not Jake. Clay told himself not to doubt her love, but the cocky expression on Jake's face made it difficult.

"What do you suppose Gordon LeCroix is thinking?" Clay's father asked. "He claimed he wanted to have a private conversation with that—that—woman. Then Gordon saves a seat for the man who kidnapped his grandson. Outrageous."

"Max was the father." Clay couldn't resist saying, "If you remember, when Phoebe announced she was pregnant, I told you I didn't think the child was mine."

"Yes, well . . ." His father gave an anxious little cough. "I suppose we should go over and see Hattie. She'll be very upset when she hears about this."

Clay realized his father didn't know Alyssa was Gordon's daughter. He'd known for years, because he'd been close to Wyatt and Phoebe. Hattie had kept the truth from all her friends, including his parents.

He watched his father sign the check and write down his membership number. He could tell him about Alyssa, but he didn't bother. Instead, he concentrated on developing a plan to get rid of Dante.

Tonight, the night before Phoebe's funeral, would be perfect. Everyone would expect him to be home grieving. Cousins of Phoebe's would be spending the night at the house. He could pretend to go to bed then slip out.

He would make up some excuse to have Dante meet him at one of those seedy jazz clubs the Bahamian frequented. Parking being what it was along Frenchman Street, Dante would have to park on some dark side street. Clay would be following, and he would shoot him from inside his own car.

Wait! Not his Masarati. It was too memorable of a car should someone witness the drive-by shooting. Maree had a forgettable black Toyota. He'd come up with some excuse and borrow it.

"Aren't you coming?" his father asked.

Clay hadn't noticed his father stand up. As they left the dining room, Nelson Duvall made it a point to say hello to several friends, but not to go over to Gordon's table.

This group could turn on you quicker than a snake, Clay decided. It was something he'd always known, of course, but it had never occurred to him that he could be banished. His rightful place as a Duvall, a golden boy with looks, and a family lineage, could be taken away from him, after all.

It had just been a simple ménage à trois that had gotten out of hand. That's all. But Clay couldn't imagine these people understanding. He'd be dirt, worse off than Max Williams.

On the way to the LeCroixs' house, Clay's father rattled on about his golf game, their second home in Sarasota, and their plans for a trip to Tuscany. Clay could have told his father about the problems at Duvall Imports, but he didn't. The father had screwed up the business after generations of success. His advice was worthless.

* * *

"Oh, Nelson, what am I going to do?" Hattie flung herself at his father the second they walked into the house.

It was midafternoon now and hotter than Hades, but at least it was cool inside. Clay told himself to let his father handle this woman while he concentrated on working out his plan.

"Now, now, Hattie," Nelson Duvall said. "I'm here to help. Tell me what's happening."

Hattie had been crying. Her eyes were bloodshot, but they still had what Clay thought of as his mother-in-law's feral glint. She got that look when someone crossed her.

"Ravelle's going to be on the evening news, telling everyone Alyssa is Gordon's daughter," wailed Hattie. "It's dreadful. So embarrassing."

His father led Hattie to the sofa, his arm around her, and they sat down. Clay took a chair nearby. From the agonized expression on his father's face, Clay knew the man had no idea what to say.

"We just saw Gordon at the Mayfair Club. He was having lunch with Alyssa and Max and Jake Williams," volunteered Clay.

"The Mayfair Club?" Hattie screeched. "He's with her in front of everyone who counts?"

Clay nodded solemnly, stifling a smile. He had always despised his mother-in-law, the social climber. Sticking the knife in and twisting it gave him more pleasure than he'd had in all the years Phoebe had forced him to spend time here.

"Is she Gordon's . . .ah . . . daughter?" his father finally asked.

"Y-yes," Hattie replied between dramatic sniffles. "Imagine, I took care of her the way I did my own daughter. All those years and I never knew."

Clay almost said: That's a bald-faced lie. He knew why Hattie had done it. She always bent over backward to impress his parents. The woman had known from the start about Alyssa, but she'd kept it a secret.

"Have you called a doctor?" his father asked. "He would prescribe something to . . . to make you feel better, and help you get through this ordeal."

"I have medication, but I hate to take it. I want to be brave, yet it's so, so hard. My poor, beautiful Phoebe is gone, and Gordon is spending his time with her killer. Why don't they throw that woman in jail?"

"Good question," his father replied. He rolled his eyes at Clay, the message clear: Do something, say something.

"Is anyone staying with you?" Clay asked.

Hattie shook her head. "People have been here, but I'm too distraught about Phoebe and now this—this news. The maid is sending away visitors, and I'm not taking calls."

What she meant was she was too embarrassed to face her friends. Clay sat there, his mind wandering while his father convinced Hattie to take a sleeping pill and get some rest. Clay couldn't get out of there fast enough. He had a plan to put into action.

"I need my car," Maree protested. "Why can't you take Phoebe's Jag?"

"Her cousins from Biloxi are using it."

It was nearly six o'clock, and he was standing in the tacky living room of Maree's carriage house. Air conditioning had been an afterthought in the ancient building, and a swamp cooler wheezed out moist air that was only marginally cooler than it was outside.

"Oh, all right. I can never say no to you, darling."

Her voice was sweet, flirty. He knew what was coming

next. He endured a kiss and what was intended to be a seductive brush of her body against his. When she'd finished, Maree pulled back, her lips parted and moist.

"Can I come with you?"

He automatically corrected her. "May I come with you?"

"Whatever."

Her pouty look was supposed to be sexy, but he wanted his life back. He wanted to be rid of this woman as well as Dante. She'd tricked him into engaging in a threesome and filmed it. He'd never forgive her. She probably was in cahoots with Dante. It was all he could do not to put both hands around her soft neck and choke the life out of her.

"No, honey," he forced a caress into his voice. "You can't come with me. This is business."

"Am I going to see you tonight?"

"Maree, I've got a house full of Phoebe's relatives. Tomorrow's the funeral. It'll look suspicious if I'm not at home."

She ran her tongue across her lower lip, a petulant gesture that he found more annoying than usual. First things first, he told himself. Once Dante was out of the way, he'd decide how to handle Maree.

Dante was far too cunning to have left the tapes here. They must be hidden at his apartment. With luck, he'd be able to get rid of the troublemaker, then search his apartment.

"What about tomorrow night?"

He tried for a placating tone. "I'll still have a house full of people, but I may be able to get away. It'll be really late, though."

That satisfied her, and Maree smiled the slightly aloof smile that once had reminded him of Alyssa. "I'll be waiting."

"Don't be disappointed if I don't come over," he

said, preparing her for what was going to happen. "One of her relatives might want to stay up late talking about Phoebe."

"When are you bringing back my car?"

Good question, he thought. "In a few hours," he said, although he didn't have any idea how long this might take.

"Put the key in an envelope in my mail slot with a note about where to find my Toyota. I'm going to be out with Dante at Funky Butts."

Hot damn, Clay thought. Now he knew where Dante was going to be. He wouldn't have to call the psychic and come up with some story. Now all he needed was a time.

"You'll probably still be here when I'm done," he said as casually as possible. "Funky Butts doesn't get going until eleven or so."

"We're meeting in the bar at eight."

Interesting, Clay decided. Funky Butts was one of the liveliest clubs around. The ground floor was a classic dive bar, but upstairs a variety of jazz acts were featured. None of them started playing until after nine at the earliest. Dante must be meeting someone in the bar. It didn't matter to Clay. He had the information he needed.

Another, more pleasing, thought crossed his mind. He could kill them both at the same time. Then he wouldn't have to deal with Maree later and risk her blabbing about the tapes to the police.

"Thanks, babe." He made himself kiss her good-bye. On the way to her Toyota, he revised his plan. He'd go right home and tell the relatives he was taking a nap, and to wake him at nine for dinner at the Mayfair Club. He'd slip out, kill them both, and return home. He'd have an iron-clad alibi.

The note Dante had sent him popped into his mind.

Ashes to ashes,
dust to dust.
If God won't have you,
the devil must.

He laughed out loud. In no time Dante—and Maree—would be dust. Served the fuckers right.

CHAPTER 38

"What do you mean? You've got my number?" Alyssa asked Jake. "Of course you do. You're calling me, aren't you?"

"Wiseass." The smile in his voice came over the telephone.

"You love me. Admit it. Your father told me so."

She tried for a joking tone, cursing herself for not telling her father to keep it a secret. "That blabbermouth."

"I know what you're trying to do. You want everyone to think you've gotten off scot-free. You're trying to flush out the killer."

Sheesh! She thought she could fool Jake, but he was far too perceptive. "Something like that," she conceded. "But it's not working. I haven't even gotten a threatening phone call."

"It's a dangerous game. I don't like it."

"Jake, what choice do I have? They'll arrest me again. I have to do something."

"Let's talk about it. I called to tell you I'm going to be late. Sanchez needs to see me."

"Does he have new information?"

"I don't know what he wants. So far, it's been details

that don't add up to much. I'll fill you in when I see you. I should be there in about an hour. I know it's late—''

"It might be all the time we have."

Two beats of silence, then he asked, "Did your see the evening news?"

"Yes. Ravelle was in all her glory when she told New Orleans I was Gordon LeCroix's love child."

"Love child. Is that what she said?"

"Her words exactly. I wonder what Gordon thinks?"

"Don't worry about it, Alyssa. Gordon was cool at lunch. My father and I both appreciated what he did."

"So did I," Alyssa admitted, although she wondered if he might have some ulterior motive. "The truth is out in the open—about the past anyway. Now if only we can find the killer."

"We're closing in. I can feel it. I have a lot to tell you about the case. Details, no big breakthrough. I'll explain when I see you."

She hung up and went to check on Aunt Thee. Shawn was in the upstairs sitting area outside her aunt's bedroom, reading a magazine.

"I'll just say good night," Alyssa told him. The nurse was a stickler for maintaining a schedule and not tiring his patient. She knocked softly on the door.

"Come in," called Aunt Thee.

"I want to say good night. Jake's been delayed, but by the time he arrives, you'll be asleep."

Aunt Thee nodded. She was already in bed, the lightweight comforter spread over her. She patted a spot beside her, and Alyssa sat down.

"I've been thinking," her aunt said. "Shawn is such a dear, and he plans to study for his real estate license. He wants a career change. I've offered to let him stay here, if he'll look after me. That way you can get a place of your own without worrying about me. It'll give you and Jake some privacy."

As she had so many times over the years, Aunt Thee

had considered Alyssa before herself. Alyssa knew she would rather have her live here than Shawn, but she believed she was hampering Alyssa's love life. She bent over and kissed her aunt on the temple.

"I think that's an excellent idea, but not because of my love life. You know it's only a matter of time before I'm arrested again. If Shawn's here, I'll feel better about you."

A sheen of moisture glistened in Aunt Thee's eyes. "Don't say that. You'll find the killer. I know it."

Alyssa tried to give her a confident smile, but it was difficult. She wished she could be so sure, but she wasn't. There was one thing that she did know and should share with her aunt while she still had the opportunity. She'd confessed to her father how she felt about Jake, but not her aunt.

"I think I might be in love with Jake."

Her aunt's face broke into a wide, open smile. "I knew it the moment I saw you two together. You're perfect for each other." She patted Alyssa's hand. "As I told you before, I can hardly wait to be a grandmother."

Alyssa rolled her eyes. "You're getting way ahead of things. I might spend time in prison. I have to settle this before I can think of having a life. I—"

The telephone on the nightstand rang and interrupted her train of thought. She almost reached for it, but it stopped mid-ring. The low murmur of Shawn's voice came from the other room.

"If you're arrested again, I'll do everything in my power to help you. I'm very secure financially. We can mount the best defense possible, but I don't think it'll come to that."

She wished she shared her aunt's optimism, but she didn't dare. She thought it was better to prepare for the worst. "Thank you for all you've done. Everything—"

"Alyssa," called Shawn from the doorway, "telephone."

"Just a minute." She leaned over and gave her aunt another kiss. "Good night. I'll see you at breakfast."

"Tell Jake hello," her aunt replied as Alyssa rose. "And give him a kiss for me."

Alyssa walked out of the room and shut the door quietly behind her. Shawn had left the sitting area, but the telephone's receiver was on the sofa table. She picked it up, expecting Jake and hoping he wasn't delayed again.

"Alyssa." It was Gordon LeCroix. "I need to talk to you."

There was a disturbing note in his voice, and with a pang of concern, she realized she'd come to care about him. He'd been so understanding with Max at the Mayfair Club. Everyone else was primed to snub him, but her father, without a word from her, had done the right thing.

"I'm alone. I can talk."

"Not on the telephone. I—I need to see you now. Can you come over here?"

She couldn't imagine walking into a house filled with Hattie's friends, all of them blaming her for the killing. But if her father needed her, Alyssa couldn't refuse him. He was reaching out; she had to meet him halfway.

"No, no," he said. "We don't need any food. We have more casseroles than we know what to do with."

What was he talking about? she wondered. She hadn't volunteered to bring any food.

"Flowers? No. We have too many already." His voice sounded a little hoarse and he was rattling on, which wasn't his style. He was clearly upset about something. Phoebe. He'd lost a daughter, a child he'd loved in his own way.

"I'll come right over." She glanced at her watch and saw it was quarter to nine. Jake wasn't due here for another half hour.

She heard a muffled sound as if Gordon had put his

hand over the receiver. "Alyssa, don't mention this to anyone."

Hattie, she thought. He doesn't want her to know. With Phoebe's funeral tomorrow, Hattie was probably hysterical. "Do you want me to come in through the back door?"

After a long pause, he said, "No. Don't bother. I don't need anything."

She hung up, rushed into her room, and grabbed her purse, thinking of Gordon—her father sounded strange. She met Shawn going down the stairs. "I have to go out. If Jake gets here, ask him to wait. I should be back within the hour."

He agreed, and she raced out of the house, thinking the faster she got over to the place she'd once called home, the sooner she'd be back here to see Jake. What could her father want to talk about? Possibly he had something to say about Jake or Max. She'd had to leave them at the Mayfair Club without getting another chance to speak to Gordon in private because she'd promised Aunt Thee she would take her to the doctor for a checkup.

That must be it, she decided as she trotted into the passageway leading to their parking garage. Both lights were on but they were dimmer and cloaked the narrow passageway in dark shadows. She stopped in her tracks and reached into her purse for the tiny canister of pepper spray she'd purchased that morning.

Maybe it was just her imagination, but suddenly a blinding awareness that something was lying in wait made her fingers tremble. She found the pepper spray and clutched it in her hand. Squinting at the shadows, she walked down the corridor. It was hot and dank with the smell of mold growing after the latest rainfall, but she didn't see anything.

She took another step forward . . . then another, her hand raised, ready to trigger the debilitating pepper spray.

* * *

The telephone rang and Jake snatched up the receiver. It was ten after nine. Sanchez was half an hour late, which wasn't his style. "Jake Williams."

"Sorry, I'm late. I'm within a few blocks of TriTech. Stay right there. I've got good news."

Sanchez hung up before Jake could press him. Good news. It was about time. Things were looking up, he decided. Gordon LeCroix's acceptance of his daughter and his apparent forgiveness of Max would make it hard for others to condemn them.

He picked up the telephone to call Alyssa and tell her that he was going to be even later than he'd thought. Shawn answered and said Alyssa had gone out.

"Where?"

"She didn't say. A man called and asked for her, then she left."

"Who was it?"

"I have no idea."

Jake hung up. His fingers had turned to ice. He drummed them on the top of his desk. Why would she go out when she was expecting him? He didn't like it one damn bit. If only she'd bought a new cell phone.

She was probably chasing down some lead, the way she had last night when she'd visited Clay. He cursed himself for not making her promise to stay home.

Sanchez burst through the door, all smiles. "You are not going to believe this."

"Try me. These days, I'm prepared for anything."

"Clay Duvall is under arrest for murder."

Jake slapped the top of his desk with the palm of his hand. "I knew he'd killed Phoebe. I knew it!"

"No. Not Phoebe. He shot that drug dealer, Dante a block away from Funky Butts', and he wounded Maree Winston. Since I had tails on both Dante and Clay, my boys were able to nab him before he got away. Plus, they'll make excellent witnesses. Both are former FBI agents."

Jake didn't get it. "A love triangle gone bad? Or does this have something to do with Phoebe's murder?"

"I wish I knew. The woman is in critical condition, but before the police arrived, she told one of my operatives there is a video tape in Dante's apartment."

"This can't be coincidence. It has to have something to do with the murder."

Sanchez flopped into the chair beside Jake's desk, clearly exhausted. "We'll know soon enough. My guy passed on the info to the police. They're searching the apartment. I'll juice my man inside the station to tell us what's on the tape."

"Great," Jake replied, and he meant it. His sixth sense could feel this case cracking open. At last.

Sanchez checked his watch. "They arrested Duvall at a little after eight just over an hour ago. I was already on my way to see you when I got the call. I wanted to tell you in person what I was able to find out from the FBI about the .22 bullet. I didn't want to chance talking about it over a cell phone. My buddy at the FBI lab could lose his job, if they knew he'd leaked information."

Jake nodded. Even he was careful with cell phones during business negotiations. They were not as secure as land lines, and anyone with the right equipment could listen.

"The official FBI report to the NOPD will say the bullet is too damaged to match it to the .22 found at Alyssa's."

"Way to go!"

"Don't start celebrating yet. The unofficial word will be that they believe the bullet came from that .22, but there's enough doubt that an expert witness from the defense could refute their claim. What they're telling the prosecutor—indirectly—is more evidence will be needed to prove their case."

"We're right back where we started."

"No. My source at NOPD says there isn't any new evidence."

"Alyssa will be convicted in the court of public opinion—again—unless something in Dante's tape clears her." Jake stood up. "I'm going over to see if she's home. I just called there, and she'd gone out even though she was expecting me."

"Gone out? Why?"

"I don't know. It's probably nothing. A man had called her. Maybe she went to the pharmacy or someplace to pick up something her aunt needed."

Sanchez followed him out the door. "I'm going home to get some sleep, but if you need me, call."

There were few cars on the street and the lamp in the living room was the only light visible from the front as Alyssa parked near the home where she'd grown up. Not even the porch light was on. Evidently, all the condolence callers had come during the last two days when Phoebe's funeral had been delayed by the autopsy.

"No, that's not it," she whispered to herself. "Hattie's too humiliated to have callers."

Alyssa looked around cautiously before she unlocked the car and got out. Something in the passageway had spooked her. Undoubtedly, it was her own imagination, but she'd slipped the pepper spray into the pocket of the linen blazer she was wearing—just in case.

She checked the bushes on either side of the walkway as she made her way up to the unlit entrance. A passing car's lights swept the porch and assured her no one was lying in wait.

She rapped the antique fox head knocker on the front door and waited. The door opened a crack, and Alyssa expected to see the maid. She recognized Hattie's eyes even in the diffused light coming from the streetlight. The hateful woman didn't turn on the porch light or ask what she wanted. Instead the door swung open and Alyssa stepped into the hall dimly illuminated by lamplight spilling out from the living room.

"Gordon wanted to see me."

"Of course he does."

Her voice was a gritty rasp, and Alyssa knew she'd been crying. About Phoebe? Or was she more upset over Ravelle's shocking report? Knowing Hattie, what her friends thought was probably more important. Alyssa told herself to put the past in the past and not be unkind. In her own way, Hattie had loved her daughter.

"Is he in his study?"

"Where else?"

Alyssa walked down the hall to the study, where she'd spoken with Phoebe just a few short days ago. She heard Hattie shuffling along behind her. Was she going to be part of this conversation?

She stopped outside the closed door to the study. Light seeped out from under the door, the way it always had when she'd lived here and passed by. She raised her hand to knock.

"Don't bother. He's expecting you," Hattie said from behind her.

With a sudden sense of foreboding, Alyssa opened the door and stepped inside. She stopped. A scream rose in her throat and stalled there as she took in the room.

Gordon was in the chair at his desk, tied in place by miles of silver duct tape. A handkerchief had been stuffed in his mouth. His eyes were wide with fright.

In the heartbeat it took for her to analyze the situation, Alyssa spun around. With a demented smile plastered to her face, Hattie leveled a gun at Alyssa's heart.

CHAPTER 39

"Wake her up," Jake told Shawn when the nurse couldn't shed any light on the man who'd called Alyssa. She wasn't back, and it was almost ten o'clock. A snake of fear slithered across the back of his neck, threatening to choke the air out of him.

"I don't think it's a good idea. She—"

"I don't give a shit what you think." Jake grabbed the man's arm, and Shawn gasped. "Alyssa is in danger. Since you don't know where she went, Thee may."

Shawn jerked away from him, but took him up the stairs to the second floor where the bedrooms were located. Shawn cracked Thee's door, then gently eased it open. He flicked on the bedside lamp from the switch by the entrance.

Thee's head was propped up by two pillows and her eyes were wide open. "It's Alyssa, isn't it?" she cried the moment they came through the door. "Something's happened."

"We don't know," Jake responded.

Thee struggled to sit up, and Shawn dashed over and helped her into an upright position.

"She received a telephone call from a man, then left. Do you know who called her? Did she go to meet him?"

"I don't know. Shawn said she had a call. Alyssa kissed me good night. She never came back to tell me she was leaving."

"Then why do you think something has happened?" asked Shawn before Jake could.

Thee shook a helmet of pewter gray pin curls. "I couldn't sleep even though I'd taken a mild sleeping tablet. I kept thinking about Alyssa, and the more I thought, the more something ... well, something tugged at me. Then you two came in here, and my first reaction was that you had bad news about Alyssa."

Jake spoke to reassure her even though alarm bells were ringing in his own head. "Don't be upset." He put his hand on Thee's shoulder. "It's probably nothing."

"I can't imagine what would make Alyssa leave before you arrived."

"She could have called me, but she didn't."

"Alyssa was in a hurry," Shawn volunteered. "She told me to give you the message."

Jake attempted to figure this out in a rational way. He honestly felt the case was cracking, but something was eluding him. A missing link. One small piece of the puzzle. He should be able to zero in on it, but right now, he couldn't.

"Troy Chevalier is a possibility," he said, thinking out loud. "So is Wyatt LeCroix or her father, Gordon LeCroix."

"What about Clay?" Thee asked.

"She couldn't have received a call from him. Clay was arrested earlier this evening. He shot a man, killing him and nearly killing a woman Clay had been having an affair with."

"Oh, my stars!" exclaimed Aunt Thee. "I can't believe it. Clay Duvall? What happened?"

"I don't have time to go into details now. Finding Alyssa is more important."

"You're right."

"Perhaps there is someone else you aren't aware of,"

suggested Shawn, a helpful note in his voice. "Someone from Italy."

Aunt Thee shook her head. "Alyssa had been busy with her career in the months before we moved. She wasn't seeing anyone. She has professional contacts in Italy, but they wouldn't call this late."

Jake thought out loud. "What would make her run out at this hour?"

A spark of something in his brain triggered an unexpected insight. He replayed what Sanchez had told him about Troy Chevalier's run-in with Hattie LeCroix.

"She's at the LeCroixs'," he told them as he sprinted out of the room.

Alyssa watched, every nerve tense as Hattie kept the gun trained on her while she ambled over to Gordon and yanked the handkerchief out of his mouth. "Say something to your—daughter."

"She's crazy, Alyssa. She's always been crazy." Hattie backhanded him, and Gordon's head snapped. He grimaced in pain, a guttural moan escaping his lips. "I tried to warn you. She had a gun to my head. I—I had to be careful."

"Is that what all the casserole and flowers stuff meant?"

"Yes, I—"

Hattie whacked him again. "You sneaky—"

"Run the first chance you get, don't worry about me," Gordon told Alyssa. "I'm getting what I deserve."

"Deserve?" Hattie cried, sweeping the gun back and forth to keep both of them in line. "I deserve better than this. I gave you everything. My youth, my beauty, my—"

"Your ego, your ambition. Don't tell me I was the love of your life," Gordon said. "I was a step on the ladder of social success. From the very beginning, you didn't love me, and on some level I must have known it. That's why I fell for Pamela Ardmore."

Hearing her mother's name, something wrenched at Alyssa's heart. Despite the horrific situation, she imagined the love that once had bound her parents. Considering the gun aimed at her, Alyssa wondered if she would ever have a chance at true love. The future shimmered like a mirage, out of focus, out of reach.

JAKE!

Her mind cried out for him, but her brain knew she was here all alone, the only one to save herself—and her father. A bizarre mix of fear and utter calmness came over her.

"Are you saying you never loved me?" Hattie asked.

"Yes. That's exactly what I meant." Her father strained against the restricting duct tape binding him to the chair. "Earlier this evening, when I told you I was going to divorce you, I meant to say—politely—I had never loved you."

"You bastard!" Hattie shrieked. "You've made a fool out of me."

Alyssa stifled a groan. This was the heart of the conflict. Hattie and her pretensions. Gordon may have sequestered himself in his room, ignoring his children, but Hattie had been far worse. She'd belittled them, forcing Wyatt to attend a military academy while Phoebe had been given no choice but to become a Mardi Gras queen like her mother.

"Don't move," Hattie warned, although Alyssa or Gordon had not made any attempt to come toward her. "I'll shoot."

"What do you want?" Alyssa asked as calmly as possible. She lowered her hand to be able to reach into her pocket for her only hope, the pepper spray.

"I want, I want." Hattie's arm flailed, arcing across the room dangerously. "I want my life back. I want to have a Mardi Gras queen who will give me a granddaughter destined to become another Mardi Gras queen. I don't want all this—this sordid, ugly stuff. A love child. A baby fathered by white trash.''

Alyssa tried for a placating smile. ''I understand, I—''

''Shut your mouth! I've been on to you from the moment you moved in.''

''I was seven years old—''

''True, but your mother put you up to it.''

In that instant, what Alyssa had already known kicked in with force. Hattie *had* gone over the edge. The woman had been unbalanced for years, but the stress of Phoebe's death and the resulting revelations had tipped the scales.

''Yes, you're right,'' Alyssa said, trying for a sincere tone. ''My mother was jealous of you. She managed to get pregnant, but Gordon refused to marry her. She blamed you. Mother always said if I had the chance, I should—''

Brring-brring. The telephone on Gordon's desk silenced her. The three of them stared at it. Out of the corner of her eye, Alyssa saw Hattie's gun was still aimed directly at her father's head. She couldn't pull out the pepper spray and fire it without risking his life.

''I haven't answered the phone all day,'' Hattie informed them. ''It's just a friend calling to sympathize. I—''

''Hattie, you poor dear,'' a disembodied voice came over the line. ''It's Ravelle. Are you there, pick up if you are.'' A pause ensued, then Ravelle continued, ''Clay Duvall has been arrested for murder.''

At the word ''murder'' Hattie swung her arm so the gun was now trained on Alyssa.

''Murder?'' The word escaped Gordon's lips like a gasp.

''Murder?'' echoed Alyssa. She couldn't believe it. Clay Duvall wasn't the type, not at all.

''Clay killed a man and wounded a woman. The police think Maree Winston was his mistress. Do you know anything about it?" Another long pause as if the television reporter expected Hattie to pick up the telephone. "I want to come over there with my crew and do an interview with you. Call me."

The line went dead and the machine clicked off. A moment of stunned silence followed. Alyssa struggled to interpret the news. Clay was under arrest. Could this have something to do with Phoebe's death? Dare she hope to be cleared?

"It's your fault!" yelled Hattie. "Clay was himself until you came back here."

She knew it was futile to remind Hattie that Clay had brought her home to New Orleans. The woman could not be reasoned with. She would have to be overpowered. The only chance Alyssa had was in her pocket. All she needed was an opportunity to fire the canister of pepper spray.

"What are you planning to do?" she asked.

"I'm going to shoot you both so it will look like a murder-suicide," Hattie replied in a self-satisfied tone that told Alyssa this had been well-planned.

"There won't be any powder burns," Alyssa said. "The police will never buy it. Even if they do, the tape you have around Gordon will leave telltale marks. They'll catch you."

Hattie lunged toward Alyssa, the gun pointing right at her. "You think I'm stupid, don't you? Well, I know how to conceal the crime. I'm going to burn the house down afterward. That way no one will be able to tell if you fired the gun or not."

Alyssa blinked several times, speechless. Hattie adored this house. It was the symbol of her ascent to the pinnacle of the social pyramid in New Orleans. Burning it certainly meant she'd gone over the edge into some deep mental abyss Alyssa knew nothing about.

"You've worked so hard on your home. Where will you live?" Alyssa asked.

Hattie advanced toward Alyssa. "Do you seriously

think I could stay in New Orleans after all that's happened?''

"Where will you go?" Alyssa asked. "This has always been your home."

"When I get the insurance money, I'm going to relocate in Palm Beach."

"Impossible!" Gordon said emphatically. "The insurance on this house couldn't buy you what you'd need in a ritzy place like Palm Beach. It's underinsured."

"You'd get a lot more money if you sold it," Alyssa added.

"The insurance policy is in the file cabinet right over there," Gordon said. "Check it for yourself."

"Don't try to put one over on me." For the first time, Hattie seemed unsure of herself. She thought a moment, then smiled. "We'll go out to the pool house. It'll be easier to burn down anyway."

"Hattie, let's forget about all this," Gordon said gently. "You need help. You're my wife. I'll stick by you until—"

"No!" The word exploded out of Hattie like a shot from the gun. "You can't trick me. Even if you meant it, I can't stay here and face everyone."

Something inside Alyssa twisted into a cold knot, and she finally accepted that they would never talk Hattie out of this. The anxiety she'd kept at bay swept through her. When it receded seconds later, something crystallized in her mind.

"Why did you kill Phoebe?"

Gordon shook his head a little, silently denying it. Alyssa braced herself, convinced she'd blurted out the ugly truth. Murder was one thing, but killing your own child became a whole new level of insanity.

Hattie's gaze never wavered; she kept the gun trained on Alyssa. "It's your fault."

Everything is my fault, Alyssa told herself, and it had been since she had moved into this house. It didn't matter if she could deal with it, but she tried to imagine what poor Phoebe must have felt when her own mother aimed the gun at her. On some level Phoebe must have known how sick Hattie was. That's why she'd taken elaborate precautions, pretending she still cared about Clay and accusing Alyssa of trying to lure him away.

"Hattie, tell me it isn't true," Gordon said with a low moan.

"She was leaving—the ungrateful little bitch. She was divorcing Clay and moving to Paris." Hattie's tone was matter-of-fact as if this explained everything. "Phoebe wasn't going to tell me. I overheard her talking to that faggy Frenchman."

"She and Clay were never happy," Gordon said.

"Of course, they were happy." Hattie wiggled the gun at Alyssa. "Then she came home and started chasing him. Phoebe didn't want to be humiliated, so she decided to divorce Clay."

"I can't believe you shot our daughter." Tears flashed in Gordon's eyes.

"I wasn't going to let her leave," she replied without a hint of remorse. "I took one of your guns, the small .22, and—"

"My gun. Oh, God, no."

"You planted it at my aunt's house, didn't you?"

"Yes. It wasn't hard to get in." She smiled, obviously proud of herself. "I came through the main gate behind a boy delivering flowers. When the nurse took the vase upstairs, I walked right in, planted the gun, and left."

"You missed your calling," Alyssa said, thinking how demented this woman was. They would have to be clever—and lucky—or she *would* kill them. "You should have been a cat burglar."

"Shut up! I'm tired of talking. We're going out to the pool house. On the way, we'll stop by the garage."

"Why the garage?" Alyssa asked although she had a good idea, but she wanted to buy time.

"Do I look stupid? I have cans of gas in there. You can tote them out to the pool house."

It was a wild thought, but going to the garage was a welcome idea. Anything to take up time. With luck, Jake would come to Thee's house, discover she was missing, and know something was wrong.

Don't rely on anyone but yourself, cautioned an inner voice. Look for an opportunity to use the pepper spray.

"Peel the tape off dear, dear Gordon," Hattie said.

Alyssa hesitated, looking around as if she didn't quite understand. Her only weapon was time, and she had to use it in any way she could.

"Now!" Hattie screeched.

Alyssa took her time walking over to the chair where her father was bound by miles of silver duct tape, her eyes on the gun as if she feared walking too fast and being shot.

The look in her father's eyes beseeched her to do something, anything. Hattie hovered close, making it impossible for Alyssa to pull the pepper spray out of her pocket without endangering their lives. She inspected Gordon's body, trying to find the end of the tape.

"By his elbow," Hattie said.

Alyssa found the frayed end of the duct tape and pulled on it. The tape barely moved, so she yanked harder, deliberately overworking to use up time. Slowly the tape separated from the layer below. Alyssa laughed to herself. She couldn't imagine what had gone on when Hattie had tied Gordon to this chair, but she had overdone the tape. It was going to take a long time to unwind it.

"Where are the scissors?" Hattie asked after a few long minutes of Alyssa tugging at the tape.

Gordon hesitated, then replied, "Second drawer in the desk. Maybe the third drawer down."

Hattie kept the gun leveled at Alyssa's temple. "Cut off the tape. Make it quick."

Alyssa searched the second drawer. A stapler, paper clips, pens, pencils, and erasers, but no scissors. "It must be in the third drawer."

"Hurry up." Hattie waved the gun in front of Gordon's face. He flinched, but didn't utter a word.

Alyssa opened the next drawer and fumbled through file folders, Post-it pads, and envelopes. She found the scissors, but kept rummaging through the stuff.

"Come on, Come on," urged Hattie in a high-pitched voice.

"Just a minute." Alyssa stalled. "I don't think they're in here."

Hattie slammed the butt of the gun against the top of the desk. "Don't fool with me."

CHAPTER 40

Jake pulled up the street and spotted Alyssa's rental car near the LeCroixs' house. Where were the mourners who always made condolence calls? True, there had been two days to pay their respects, but some of them should be here tonight.

This was *not* a wild goose chase, he decided. His sixth sense had kicked in big-time. Alyssa wouldn't come over to see her father and not call to tell Jake where she was or that she would be late.

Hattie.

He should have guessed she was the killer the minute Sanchez told him how shocked Troy had been to discover Hattie knew their secret. But who would have thought a mother would murder her own child?

The woman wouldn't hesitate to kill Alyssa. He attempted to steady his erratic pulse. What if he was already too late to save her?

He hadn't had the chance to tell her about his conversation with Troy Chevalier or his subsequent discussion with Sanchez when he'd learned how Hattie had treated Troy. If he had, Alyssa might have figured this out. After all, she'd lived for years with Hattie. He blamed himself for letting her walk into danger without having a clue.

Jake shucked his jacket and tie, tossing them onto the backseat before opening the car door to the suffocating, moist heat. He raced up the walk to the dark porch. He rapped the fox head knocker and waited. He tried again. Nothing. He peered into the living room window. A single lamp was burning, but he didn't see anyone.

"Aw, crap," Jake muttered to himself. Had they gone somewhere else? Not necessarily. Just because no one answered the door didn't mean they weren't here.

He circled the house, thinking. If they weren't here, his next move was to call Sanchez. The detective could roust as much manpower as money could buy, then turn the Big Easy upside down until he found Alyssa. Son of a bitch! His cell phone was in his jacket pocket back in the car.

The backyard was eerily silent. The pool lights glowed in the lagoon-like pool. He craned his neck and looked upward to see if there were lights on upstairs. The second floor was as dark as a tomb.

He was turning to leave and call Sanchez when a flicker of light across the yard captured his attention. Then it vanished. Now there was nothing but the dense darkness of the backyard beyond the pool. He waited a moment. There it was again, the strobe of a flashlight coming out of the backdoor of the garage.

He edged forward, a step at a time. Who was out there? He inched closer, concealed by the azalea bushes, then came to an abrupt stop, his heart lurching in his chest. He recognized Alyssa and Gordon. Each of them was carrying a can or jug of something. Behind them, a gun trained on Alyssa, walked Hattie.

Relief surged through him, threatening to make his knees buckle. Alyssa was still alive. If he could come up with a plan, he could help her.

His relief was short-lived. The trio disappeared into the pool house. He had to act fast. He could run back to the car and call the police, but Alyssa might be dead by the time they arrived.

He raced over to the small pool house where the lights had gone on and peered through the window. It was a single room furnished with white wicker chairs and a matching love seat. Off to one side was a small bar with glass shelves. Two saloon-style doors opened off the main area into changing rooms.

"Gasoline," he whispered to himself when he saw what Alyssa and Gordon had been carrying. It didn't take a rocket scientist to see what Hattie had in mind.

She waved the gun at them, saying something he couldn't hear. Alyssa and Gordon unscrewed the caps on their cans of gasoline and began to pour it around the perimeter of the room. Hattie stayed right behind Alyssa, the gun aimed at her head.

Jake's first thought was to throw a rock through the window, but that might frighten Hattie into shooting. How could he distract the maniac without spooking her? With his next breath, he had the answer.

He walked over and knocked on the door, a light knock intended to get Hattie's attention without alarming her. No one answered. The door was solid wood, and from where he was standing, a bush blocked his view into the window. He knocked again, then opened the door.

He stepped into the pool house. "I hope I'm not interrupting anything."

Hattie glared at him, madness, stark and vivid, glittering in her eyes. She'd herded Gordon and Alyssa together. The gun was trained on Alyssa's head.

"Jake," Alyssa said.

It was just a single word—his name—but in it Jake heard relief and love. If he lost her, he had no idea what he would do.

"You must want to die with them," Hattie said.

"You're going to kill them? What a brilliant idea. I never would have thought of it."

His bizarre reply confused Hattie for a moment, but the gun never moved.

"Are we having fun yet?" Jake asked her.

"I always hated you," Hattie said. "You're such a wise apple."

"Wise apple? That's a first." He tried for a laugh. "I thought you might like to know the police are on the way."

"You're bluffing."

He gave her a shit-for-brains grin. "Why would I walk in here unarmed, if I hadn't called the police?"

Her expression told him he'd just rolled snake eyes. "It doesn't matter. Alyssa will be dead by the time they get here."

Jake took a step forward. "Gordon or I will get you. It's impossible to shoot all three of us at once."

"That's right." Gordon spoke for the first time in a firm voice.

"It doesn't matter," she responded, a sickening note of triumph in her voice. "Alyssa's brains will be splattered all over this room."

"If the police aren't here in time, I'll kill you." Jake meant every word.

"No, Jake," Alyssa spoke up. "Promise me you won't kill Hattie. Being brought to trial and found guilty in front of all her friends would be worse than death for her."

"You're right. I'll hand her over to the police." He took another step forward.

"Don't move!" yelled Hattie.

He stopped, judging he was about five feet away from them. "Gordon, be prepared to grab Hattie."

A noise from out in the yard took them all by surprise. Hattie cocked the gun. A white-hot burst of fury and adrenaline surged through him. The room narrowed, focused into one small target. Jake lunged forward, tackling Alyssa to get her out of the way just as Hattie fired.

Enraged, Hattie shrieked, "You're dead! You're dead!"

He landed on top of Alyssa, quickly rolling off her

toward Hattie. In a lightning movement, he grabbed her legs and yanked hard. Jake had a momentary impression of a face contorted by deranged fury.

Hattie collapsed backward, but she managed to squeeze the trigger. The bullet zinged by his head in Alyssa's direction. Gordon threw himself over his wife's body. With a surge of insane strength, Hattie bucked and threw Gordon to the side. Jake grappled for the gun, unable to stop her from firing again.

He yelled at Alyssa to stay down, or thought he did. With the blood pounding in his brain and the noise from the gun reverberating in his ears, it was hard to tell. Suddenly, the room was deathly quiet, and Jake realized he had the gun.

"Are you okay?" he called to Alyssa through a red mist in his eyes.

"Yes," she responded, tears in her voice. "Gordon's been shot."

Jake raised his head, dimly realizing the gun was empty and Hattie had stopped struggling.

"Oh, my God! Jake!" Alyssa cried. "You've been shot, too."

The red haze obscuring his vision was blood. He reached up and touched his head. Blood was gushing from his scalp. Alyssa scrambled over to him, all the color leaching from her face.

"It's not serious. A bullet grazed me. That's all." He swiped at his forehead with the back of his sleeve. "What about Gordon?"

"H-he's unconscious."

The door to the pool house flew open. In waltzed Ravelle and her television crew, cameras rolling. Hattie hadn't moved since emptying the gun, but now she huddled against the wall, her face covered.

"We're here with the LeCroix family where so much tragedy—"

Jake vaulted to his feet, then staggered to the side,

light-headed. "You stupid bitch! Did you call nine-one-one?"

"No," answered the man with the camera.

"Get on it! A man's dying here!"

He dropped to his knees beside Gordon. His shirt was soaked with blood. Alyssa was attempting to stop it with her hands.

"Father, hang in there. Don't die on me."

In those softly spoken words, Jake heard an echo of what was in his own heart. No matter what had gone on in the past, this man was her father. If he died, Alyssa would never have the chance to really know him.

Alyssa sat in the hospital waiting room, Jake's arm around her. She permitted herself to revel in the safety of his body, to savor the bone-deep ache of love she felt for him. She was still shaking inside from the ordeal even though it was nearly three in the morning.

"Gordon's going to make it," Max assured her for the hundredth time since they'd wheeled Gordon into surgery. Max had joined them at the hospital the minute he'd seen the late-night newscast.

She prayed he was right. Jake's wound had been superficial; a bullet had nicked his scalp. It had been taken care of in the emergency room. The bullet hadn't struck her father's heart but he had lost a tremendous amount of blood.

"I can't believe Ravelle didn't call the police when she heard the first shot," Alyssa said. "A few minutes could have made the difference."

"Getting a scoop was more important." Jake's voice was thick with disgust.

"If my father dies because she failed to act, I'm going to strangle that woman. There won't be a jury in the country who'll find me guilty."

"Don't talk like that. Gordon will pull through."

"I'm going to call the District Attorney in the morning," Max said. "I'm sure Ravelle broke a law by not calling the police when she realized a crime was in progress."

"Good idea," Jake said, "but I don't believe what she did is considered a crime. It won't hurt to make a stink, though, and let everyone know what a scumbag she is."

After a moment of silence, Max asked, "Do you suppose they'll find Hattie competent to stand trial?"

"That's hard to say," answered Jake.

"Let's hope so," Alyssa said. "A public trial would be Hattie's worst nightmare."

"Did anyone contact Wyatt?" Max asked.

"I'm sure the police did. He's probably arranging for an attorney for his mother."

"You'd think he'd be here," Alyssa said.

The door to the surgical unit swung open, and Dr. Robinson walked out. He was the same surgeon who had operated on Aunt Thee. He recognized her.

"Hello, again." He smiled. "I've got good news. Your father came through the surgery in fine shape."

Alyssa barely heard the doctor's explanation of how the bullet had struck Gordon's collarbone, shattering it and causing tremendous loss of blood. He wasn't going to die, thank God.

She hadn't realized how fond she'd become of her father until she knew Hattie planned to kill him. Gordon LeCroix had his faults, but she couldn't help loving him. When he was out of the hospital, she intended to spend more time getting to know him.

"Go home, and come back in the morning. By then your father will be out of the recovery room and in ICU. He'll be allowed to see family members only."

They thanked him and left the hospital. Even though it was very late at night, the air was hot, sultry. Alyssa didn't mind. It felt good just to be alive, to know those she loved the most were alive as well.

"I need a nurse," Jake said, touching the bandage on his head. "You'd better come home with me."

Max drove them over to Jake's loft, then said good night. Alyssa could tell by the way he'd behaved when he arrived at the emergency room to see Jake that he truly loved his son. She found it hard to understand what he'd done with the baby, but it was easy to forgive him. He'd lost both the child and the woman he'd loved. How sad it would be to spend so much of your life loving someone who didn't love you.

"Yo, Benson," Jake called when he opened the door to the loft, flicked on the light, and found the retriever waiting for them, his tail whipping through the air.

"Good boy," Alyssa crooned, and the dog licked her extended hand.

Jake shut the door, then pulled her into his arms. He kissed her cheek, her jaw, the curve of her neck.

"I have to call Aunt Thee."

"At this hour?" He kissed her lightly on the lips.

"I know she's still up. When I called her from the hospital to tell her what happened, I promised—"

"Okay, okay." He led her across the room to the telephone beside the sofa. "I'll call her for you."

He dialed the number, and she almost protested, but couldn't. Half his head was bandaged, a reminder of how close he'd been to losing his life. For her. She could still feel the rush of warmth, of hope that had invaded every fiber of her being when he'd brazenly sauntered into the pool house and asked if he was interrupting anything.

She loved him more than words could say. When she'd been faced with certain death, her only thought was she wouldn't ever know what true love could be like. She'd been given a second chance, and she was going to make the best of it.

"Thee, it's Jake." She listened to him talking to her aunt. "Gordon is going to recover . . . . Yes, that's right. We're at my place." He gave her the thumbs-up sign. "Of course, I'm going to marry her."

Alyssa groaned. Was Aunt Thee that old-fashioned?

Of course. She'd loved one man and suffered with him when he'd been stricken with Parkinson's. She wanted nothing but the love of a lifetime for Alyssa.

When he hung up, she asked, "You're going to marry me? Why? Are you pregnant?"

"Very funny." He grabbed her and towed her into the screened-off bedroom area. Benson was right at their heels, evidently thinking this was some game.

The room was darker, diffused light coming up and over the screens to illuminate the ceiling while leaving the wide bed in shadows. He yanked back the coverlet to expose crisp, white sheets. With a sigh, he flopped backward onto the bed.

"My wound. It's like, like killin' me. You'll have to take my clothes off."

She began unbuttoning his blood-splattered shirt. "What am I going to do with you?"

He threw a hand over his face like a wilting violet in an old-time movie. He sounded suspiciously like he was suppressing a laugh. "Have your way with me."

"You're on!"

She had stripped off his clothes, no easy feat considering his size, in just a few minutes. She flung each item over her shoulder. Benson gathered them up and made a pile on the bench at the end of the bed.

"You're wounded. Do you think you should be—"

"Take off your clothes, Alyssa. Cut the BS." He settled back against the pillow to watch. "It'll make my head feel better."

"Yeah, right." She tossed her linen blazer aside easily enough, then kicked off her shoes. Benson dove off the bench to retrieve them. "I'm taking pity on you."

She slowly unbuttoned her blouse, then flung it aside. With a twist of her hand, she released the button on her skirt and stepped out of it. Peeling down her pantyhose took longer. Inch by inch they freed her body, exposing it to the cool air in the loft.

"What about your bra?" he asked.

So much for the striptease, she thought. Here she was standing in front of him naked except for her bra. She unhooked it and tossed it to Benson.

Jake reached out and grabbed her with both hands. He pulled her onto the bed, then rolled on top of her, his weight pinning her to the mattress. He was smiling, a totally satisfied, all-male grin. His erection nudged between her thighs.

He kneed her legs apart. "I love you, Alyssa. I want to marry you, have children, and be happy."

She inhaled deeply and thrust her face into the curve of his throat. The heat and male scent of his body made her lift her hips to encourage him. "You were right all along. I do love you."

"It must be my bedroom eyes."

EPILOGUE

One Year Later

"You're a stunning bride," Aunt Thee assured Alyssa. "I knew you would be."

"Then why am I so nervous?" Alyssa asked.

Aunt Thee adjusted the train on Alyssa's crystal-white wedding dress. "All brides are nervous. You're even more anxious because of all that's gone on this year. You've been in the spotlight."

"True." Alyssa gazed at her reflection. She had to admit the strapless silk wedding dress she'd designed was gorgeous. From the front it looked like a sheath, clinging to every curve, but from the back of her waist, pleats fanned out into a train.

Around her neck was a sweep of microbeads of lavender jade interspersed between the antique emerald beads she'd found in the flea market in Italy. Completing the set was a matching bracelet and earrings. She knew this jewelry was the most innovative of her designs. She'd already been offered a fortune for the set, but she'd never part with jewelry she'd designed for her own wedding.

"I want to be a jewelry designer, a wife, and a mother.

It's hard when you can't walk down the street without everyone recognizing you."

"You'll have a private life again. Don't worry."

She wasn't worried exactly, but she was concerned. The stress of the last year had changed them all. Clay's sensational trial for murder and attempted murder had been followed by Hattie's even more dramatic trial for killing her daughter. Alyssa and Jake's fathers had been at the center of both trials.

Without the tourists, New Orleans wasn't a terribly large city. Everywhere she went people asked her about the murders with a curiosity she found morbid. Two families had been shattered. For them life would never be the same—especially her father.

Having his obviously unbalanced wife judged competent to stand trial meant Gordon LeCroix had been forced to spend weeks sitting in a courtroom and listening to lawyers rehash his daughter's brutal murder and the subsequent attempt on his own life. He'd gone through it with dignity and courage. He'd seen to it that Hattie was represented by Mitchell Petersen, the same lawyer who had helped Alyssa.

Gordon blamed himself for not realizing how unstable Hattie had become, and he was frantic every time he thought about Alyssa almost being killed. If the ordeal hadn't been hard enough on her father, just after Hattie was sentenced, the IRS clobbered Wyatt with tax evasion. He'd managed to get off with a hefty fine, suspension of his accounting license, and six months in a minimum security federal prison.

It was nothing compared to the death sentences Hattie and Clay had received. Alyssa told herself not to feel sorry for either of them, but some part of her couldn't help wondering if the dual tragedy couldn't have been prevented.

Alyssa and Jake had decided to wait until the trials were over before getting married. It was too hard to concentrate—and enjoy—planning a wedding when so much of their time was focused on events in court. They did share a few laughs with Gordon and Max when Ravelle was fired for not immediately calling the police.

"Alyssa, it's time." Her aunt touched her hand. "Your father is waiting to walk you down the aisle."

The "aisle" was the red carpet put down across Aunt Thee's courtyard where a small number of guests had been invited to see her marry Jake. Many were friends from Italy, but other were friends she and Jake had made during the turbulent year after Hattie had tried to kill them.

The string quartet began to play. "A kiss for luck and everlasting happiness," Aunt Thee said as she kissed Alyssa on the cheek.

Aunt Thee, her matron of honor, slipped out the door of the downstairs powder room where they had been making last-minute adjustments. Alyssa gathered her skirt and stepped into the hall where her father was waiting.

"You look lovely," he said, staring at her, a mist in his eyes. "You're the image of your mother."

Tears stung Alyssa's eyes and she held them open as wide as she could to keep from crying. "I wish Mother was here. I'd like her to see how happy I am with Jake."

"She's in heaven, darling. She knows."

"I'm sure she does, and I'm sure she'd want to thank Aunt Thee for being such a wonderful stand-in."

"I'm sorry I wasn't much of a father," he said. "Forgive me?"

"Of course, I forgive you."

They heard their musical cue, and her father said, "Time to hand you over to the lucky devil." He helped her lower her veil.

On her father's arm, Alyssa stepped out into the courtyard. Twilight shadows and flickering candles created romantic wavering patterns of dark and light. The world looked gauzy through the veil. At least she hoped it was the veil, not tears.

The small group was seated in a semicircle broken in the center by the red carpet sprinkled with white rose petals. Ahead stood Jake and his best man, Max, dressed in tuxedos. Nearby was Aunt Thee, her only attendant in a pearl-gray suit. Off to the side, tail wagging, sat Benson. He had been groomed until his fur gleamed like freshly minted gold, and he was wearing a tuxedo collar.

They moved up the aisle slowly and Alyssa tried to smile at her friends, but she couldn't stop looking at Jake. His expression conveyed all his love.

"Why are you crying?" Jake whispered when she stood beside him.

"I'm so happy."

She didn't remember another thing until the judge said, "You may kiss the bride."

Jake lifted her veil carefully. He kissed her, just a brush of the lips at first, then he pulled her close and gave her one of his trademark kisses. When he finished, everyone was clapping. Benson bounded up, barking, tail wagging.

"There's more where that came from," he whispered. "I love you."

She didn't have to tell him she loved him. It had to be written all over her face.

Romantic Suspense from

Lisa Jackson

__Treasure
0-8217-6345-8 $5.99US/$7.99CAN

__Twice Kissed
0-8217-6308-6 $5.99US/$7.50CAN

__Whispers
0-8217-6377-6 $5.99US/$7.99CAN

__Wishes
0-8217-6309-1 $5.99US/$7.50CAN
